DISCOVERY

Wrapped in Thorne's embrace, Emlyn returned his kiss. Her heart set up a rapid beat, and an inner coil turned slowly in her body, a strange, hot, melting blend of fear and joy, as he kissed her cheek, her ear, her throat, burning his warm lips lower, teasing at the neck of her gown. Drawing loose the ribbons of her chemise, he slipped his fingers inside and slowly pulled the silk, sending her heartbeat into a deeper, stronger rhythm. His finger and thumb found and explored the soft, delicate, supple weight of her breasts. His tongue coaxed out lightning shivers and sent them streaming through her body. She gasped, arching toward him, and ran her hands through his hair as his hands skimmed the layers of silk up her bare legs. And now it was she who was parting his clothing until his flesh pressed hot against her cool skin. . . .

The Black Thorne's Rose

ANNOUNCING THE

TOPAZ FREQUENT READERS CLUB
COMMEMORATING TOPAZ'S
1 YEAR ANNIVERSARY!

THE MORE YOU BUY, THE MORE YOU GET

Redeem coupons found here and in the back of all new Topaz titles for FREE Topaz gifts:

Send in:

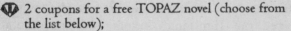 2 coupons for a free TOPAZ novel (choose from the list below);

☐ **THE KISSING BANDIT,** Margaret Brownley
☐ **BY LOVE UNVEILED,** Deborah Martin
☐ **TOUCH THE DAWN,** Chelley Kitzmiller
☐ **WILD EMBRACE,** Cassie Edwards

4 coupons for an "I Love the Topaz Man" on-board sign

6 coupons for a TOPAZ compact mirror

8 coupons for a Topaz Man T-shirt

Just fill out this certificate and send with original sales receipts to:

TOPAZ FREQUENT READERS CLUB-1ST ANNIVERSARY
Penguin USA • Mass Market Promotion; Dept. H.U.G.
375 Hudson St., NY, NY 10014

Name_____

Address_____

City_____State_____Zip_____
Offer expires 1/31 1995

This certificate must accompany your request. No duplicates accepted. Void where prohibited, taxed or restricted. Allow 4-6 weeks for receipt of merchandise. Offer good only in U.S., its territories, and Canada.

THE
BLACK
THORNE'S
ROSE

by

Susan King

A TOPAZ BOOK

TOPAZ
Published by the Penguin Group
Penguin Books USA Inc., 375 Hudson Street,
New York, New York 10014, U.S.A.
Penguin Books Ltd, 27 Wrights Lane,
London W8 5TZ, England
Penguin Books Australia Ltd, Ringwood,
Victoria, Australia
Penguin Books Canada Ltd, 10 Alcorn Avenue,
Toronto, Ontario, Canada M4V 3B2
Penguin Books (N.Z.) Ltd, 182–190 Wairau Road,
Auckland 10, New Zealand

Penguin Books Ltd, Registered Offices:
Harmondsworth, Middlesex, England

First published by Topaz, an imprint of Dutton Signet,
a division of Penguin Books USA Inc.

First Printing, September, 1994
10 9 8 7 6 5 4 3 2 1

Topaz is a trademark of New American Library,
a division of Penguin Books USA Inc.

Printed in the United States of America

This is for David, with love

Prologue

Five horsemen rode relentlessly over the moonlit surface of the earthen road, their cloaks billowing like black wings on the wind, their sword hilts and mail armor glimmering. As the riders reached the cavernous mouth of the forest, the fierce pounding rhythm of their approach penetrated the dark silence.

A young man in a leather hauberk, his long dark hair pluming out behind him, rode at the center of the group. Carried along by the brutal pace, he leaned forward, pulling against the ropes that anchored him to the saddle and bound his hands behind him.

The riders plunged into the sudden gloom of the forest, hardly slowing at each curve in the road. A canopy of dense foliage obscured the moonlight, hiding the swift forward progress of the others who ran through the trees ahead of the horsemen, unseen and unheard. A man and two children slipped between the oaks that edged the path, pausing to watch as the riders galloped closer. One of them reached out a hand and gestured to the white dog who ran with them.

Reacting to a whispered command, the dog leaped forward and ran down a wooded slope, an eldritch blur in the milky light. Landing on the path in front of the approaching horses, it growled viciously.

The leader's horse shied violently and knocked sidelong into the others. Panicked, the guards strove to restrain their mounts. The prisoner twisted to look around, fighting to keep his precarious seat. Large as a wolf, the white dog continued to prowl the width of the path ahead of them.

"Destroy that animal," the leader snapped. Three swords were scraped from their scabbards. The fourth guard aimed a loaded crossbow at the pacing dog. A shrill whistle

sounded then from beyond the path, and the dog bounded
into a thick hedge just as the quarrel slammed into the earth.

Unseen behind the jostling cluster of horses, a man hun-
kered down on foot and moved swiftly toward the prisoner.
The keen edge of a dagger glinted in his hand, and with a
few quick, precise slashes, he severed the captive's constraining thongs. Feeling the release, the prisoner spun
around, but saw only the quivering of a nearby thicket.

As the leader of the guards motioned the group forward,
the horses moved unevenly along the path, lacking their
earlier momentum. With his freed hands still clasped behind
him, the prisoner kicked sharply at his horse's sides. The
mount sidestepped nervously, falling behind the others.

The road narrowed to pass between the jutting roots of
two huge oak trees whose branches intertwined overhead. As
the men rode beneath the natural arch, the prisoner reached
up to grip a low tree limb. Placing his feet on the saddle, he
launched upward and disappeared into the dark foliage. Unaware, his guards rode ahead, until one glanced back, yelled,
and wheeled, followed by the others. Above their heads, the
fugitive slipped still higher into his aerie.

"That were a hound from the hill, a demon fairy's beast
that appeared to us back there," one man said as the group
slowed to pass again beneath the overhanging oak branches.

"Aye, or an enchanted wolf," another agreed. "I vow, this
Black Thorne must be in league with forest spirits."

"Spirits or no, Lord Whitehawke will have our heads if
we lose the Thorne again," another guard grumbled.

"Aye, 'tis Whitehawke's prize," the captain said, turning
in his saddle. "We must find him. Etienne, Richard—search
that way." He gestured into the forest. "Use the crossbows,
and shoot high. He's likely in the trees."

Richard snorted. " 'Tis madness to pursue the Black
Thorne into this wood at night. We are far south of our own
territory."

"Other demons might wait in such a place," Etienne
added.

"Whining piss-ants," the captain snapped. "He is here
somewhere. Find him." He cantered away.

Transparent fingers of moonlight penetrated the deep forest tangle to create eerie shapes. Peering into the shadows

from the safety of the path, the guards moved stealthily in different directions, swords and crossbows held ready. Each man made a quick sign of the cross on helmet or hauberk. Soon they rejoined near the forest entrance, circling their horses and arguing.

High up in the oak tree, Black Thorne began to descend, dropping silently to the forest floor. The base of the oak edged a glade, and Thorne froze his movement there. Across the moonlit circle, the white hound watched him intently, a low growl humming in its powerful throat.

For an instant he believed that the guards were right after all: this was no common animal, but rather a hound from the hill, one of the white dogs said to accompany fairies. He considered this because an actual fairy—tiny, perfect, formed of golden and silver cobwebs—stood next to the hound.

She moved forward, across the circle. In a pale cloud around her shoulders, delicate strands of hair glistened and silvered in streams of moonlight. She walked with a slight bounce.

He blinked, and breathed again. No magical creature, but a child, a young girl. Small for her age, perhaps twelve or thirteen, she was dressed in a long loose tunic and soft wrapped boots. Padding beside her, the dog was as high as her waist.

Thorne stood slowly, a lean shadow blended with the curve of the old tree. The girl paused and tilted her face to look up at him with frank curiosity, her eyes large and luminous. The white hound growled again, and she rested a hand on its head. "Hold, Cadgil," she said. " 'Tis a friend."

The dog quieted for a moment, then looked to one side, tensed, and bared its teeth again.

From beyond the glade, Thorne heard a faint shushing sound. Reaching out, he grasped the girl's thin shoulder.

"Into the tree!" he whispered urgently, lifting her onto a lower branch. Light and quick as an elf, she scampered higher. He leaped up after her to crouch on a thick branch.

The dog continued to pace beneath the tree, and the child leaned down. "Cadgil! Go—find Wat!" she whispered.

The whistle and thunk of arrows filled the clearing. A branch above Thorne trembled as an arrow burst through the leaves. As the girl cried out softly, he caught hold of her small, outstretched hand and pulled her down beside him to share the wide, stable branch.

Another barrage of arrows whizzed and exploded through the trees. Thorne covered the top of the girl's head with one arm; wanting to shield the child from harm, he also needed to hide the pale, bright head from view. Though her small shoulders quivered, she made no sound. A bolt whined through the thick foliage directly over their heads, chunking into wood, spitting leaves onto their heads. They ducked, curled together like a roosting hen with a chick beneath her wing.

Silence filled the glade. When no new shots came, Thorne raised his head to eye each irregular shadow in the glade.

Below the tree, through the screen of leaves, he saw the shadowy figures of two mounted guards on the forest path. As he held the child tightly, a prayer he had not recited since childhood echoed in his mind. He watched while the guards spoke, then turned their mounts and rode out of the forest.

Sighing, he tilted his head against the tree trunk in relief, only to straighten when new voices drifted up from the glade.

"Wat!" the girl called, smiling. She scrambled out of the tree so fast that Thorne, in his mid-twenties, felt like an old man as he clambered down after her. As he reached the ground, he saw the white dog jumping eagerly at the girl. Two other people crossed the glade toward them: a tall blond youth, perhaps fifteen, so like the child that they had to be siblings, and a burly man in a mail vest.

"Mother of God, ye're safe!" the man said in hushed tones, touching the girl's shoulder. Her brother laid a hand on her head and smoothed her hair with silent concern.

Turning, the man said softly, "We are in your debt."

"Nay, I am in yours," Thorne said. "I would be a prisoner still, but for the hound. Are you the one who cut my bonds?"

"Aye. My name is Walter of Lyddell. If you be the one they call the Black Thorne, I have a message for you."

The outlaw inclined his head in alert anticipation. His dark hair, glossy as ebony in moonlight and worn long in the Saxon style, swung against his bearded cheek. "I am he."

Walter nodded, his dark eyes sharp and the set of his wide

jaw grim. "Listen now, for your escort may yet return. The Baron de Ashbourne bids me urge you to return north and continue your efforts as before," he said. "Speak not of this encounter, but know that others are with you against Lord Whitehawke's cruelty." He blew out a gusty breath, and looked hard at Thorne. "The guards were likely taking you to the king's dungeon at Windsor, lad. 'Tis a foul pit where madmen are made."

"So I thought as we traveled south. My thanks, then, Walter. Tell the baron that I will honor his trust in me." He glanced at the girl and her brother. "These children—yours?"

"Nay, sir. They tagged after me, though I knew it not till too late. I trow they would let no other command their pup."

Thorne nodded. "My thanks for what you have done this night," he said quietly. "I shall not forget it. Before God, I pledge my life to each one of you in payment."

Walter placed a hand briefly on Thorne's shoulder. "We must go. Beyond the glade, sir, that way"—he pointed—"is a horse, saddled and tied to a hazel tree. You will find a bow and quiver there as well."

"God keep you, sir," the girl said. Thorne glanced down at her small, delicate face. Moonlight washed the color of her eyes to silver as she gazed at him with a subtle blend of childish curiosity and mature concern.

The still air was split by the click of a crossbow quarrel sliding into place. Walter caught the girl's arm and pulled her away. They dove into the bracken, followed closely by the boy and the dog. Thorne spun quickly to head toward the waiting horse. The shot, when it came, burst into an empty glade.

Thorne ran, his long muscular frame moving with fluid control. Shouts penetrated the thicket behind him as the guards crashed through the undergrowth. The air was soon thick with the high whine of sailing arrows, cracking into wood and earth and leafy boughs. He raced on untouched, ducking branches and leaping over bracken to reach the horse.

Yanking the tethered reins loose, he threw himself into the saddle and guided the horse toward a narrow track that sloped down to the path. A bow and a full quiver hung from the saddle, but he did not take time to use them.

Arrows whipped past, a stinging, vicious hail. One grazed his jaw, nicking it. Another struck hard, penetrating his leather hauberk below the shoulder blade. Reaching behind, he pulled at the shaft as he rode, his teeth clenched in agony, and tore the bolt loose with a brutal yank.

Hoofbeats thundered behind him, but the destrier was fast and steel-nerved, and Thorne was an excellent rider, unencumbered by the weight of armor. Soon he was well ahead of the guards, heading north along the ancient road. By dawn he had lost his pursuers in a white mist, and took a drover's track over the mountains.

Although the arrow had pierced deep into his back, he pressed on for two days, increasingly weak, until he reached the familiar northern moors. There, in the midst of a cluster of standing stones, he fell from his horse and collapsed at the base of an ancient monolith as if it were his headstone.

Chapter One

A trick of the wind took her last arrow. Released from the bowstring and caught on a breeze, the shaft traced a high arc and flew past its target. As it disappeared into a stand of leafy trees near the forest path, Emlyn de Ashbourne sighed and shouldered her bow. Drawing her green cloak close against the chill, she pulled her hood up to cover her flaxen braids and set off toward the path.

Several of her practice shots had gone awry today, more from inexperience than tricky breezes. Of the dozen gray-feathered arrows she had taken with her, there were only four left in the leather quiver suspended from her belt. This one would have to be retrieved if she wanted to continue shooting.

Emlyn moved quickly beneath the thick forest canopy, surrounded by the noisy rustle of leaves in the crisp spring air and dappled sunshine. She was glad that she had taken the risk, slipping away to the greenwood after months of stale confinement.

In a forest like this one, late last autumn, her brother Guy, baron of Ashbourne, had been arrested by King John's men. Cautioned by the castle seneschal who feared for their safety, Emlyn and her three young siblings had not gone beyond the walls of Ashbourne Castle all winter. Even now, no one knew where Guy was kept, or whether he remained alive.

Archery, which her brother Guy had begun to teach her before his capture, had been forgotten until this afternoon. Emlyn had not fared well, her stance and pull stiff, her fingers like wood on the waxed hempen string. Today, with no intention to hunt, she had come here hoping to practice again.

Not accurate enough with the short lady's bow to bring down small swift animals or birds—though God knew any game was needed at Ashbourne these days—she nevertheless had been intrigued since childhood by the weapon's graceful speed and the challenging skill it demanded. Target shooting in the bailey always drew Emlyn to loudly cheer the men as they aimed at bales of hay, and at straw effigies dressed to resemble French soldiers or, lately, King John.

Glancing around for her lost arrow as she walked, Emlyn neared the forest path, where the dense tree cover began to thin. Startled by a sudden metallic jingling sound, she quickly hid behind a broad oak, her heart pounding.

"By God's feet and bones!" The angry oath, spoken in a male voice, carried in the clear air. Emlyn set down her bow and cautiously peered out.

A few yards away on the path, a man in full chain mail armor sat upon a large black war-horse, angled away from her. The graceful curves of the man's voluminous blue cloak covered the animal's hindquarters. From the high saddle cantle hung a white shield with a painted design.

While the green and white device of a hawk and a branch was unfamiliar to her, Emlyn knew that such a shield, together with the fine horse trappings, could only belong to a knight of rank. He might be a king's man, she realized. Wat had warned her of just such a danger in the forest. She ducked back out of sight.

The horse stepped slowly, circling on the path. Emlyn wondered why the knight seemed wary, his sword drawn and held ready. The forest silence was punctuated by the soft footfalls of the horse, the faint jingling of armor, and an occasional burst of curses.

Alarmed, thinking there might be others nearby, she was anxious to retreat into deeper cover, and took a step back. Underfoot a dry branch snapped loudly.

Immediately, the knight turned his head and saw her between the trees. He spun the great black stallion and launched forward. "You there! Hold!" he roared.

Emlyn stopped. He reined in the huge horse a few paces in front of her. She looked up at the destrier's great dark head, then across the expanse of its powerful chest and shoulders, to the long mail-encased leg of the knight.

And saw her missing arrow protruding from his thigh.

She stared at the quivering shaft as it stuck out at an awkward angle from his upper leg. Sticky blood had painted a circle of deep carmine around the imbedded point. Her eyes rose in slow agony to the knight's face.

Beneath dark, straight brows, his eyes blazed with the same steely glint of his armor. "Come out of the wood," he ordered, his deep voice reverberating in the crisp air.

Emlyn hesitated, her eyes fixed to the arrow. In a panicked haze, she began to consider the enormity of what she had done. Drawing a trembling breath, she stepped toward the horse, her heart racing. The knight towered above her as she stood still.

He stared at her for a moment, then shoved his sword back into its scabbard. "Maiden, I must remove this bolt from my leg," he said. "I require your aid."

Emlyn looked up in surprise. Closely framed by his chain mail hood, his features were finely shaped, though grim and hard beneath dark stubble. He lifted a brow expectantly.

She frowned at the arrow. "Sire," she said in a small, tight voice, "I do not think I can reach it."

"My armor is heavy," he said, his words clipped. "If I dismount I will not easily get up again with an injured leg. Remove the weapon you shall, maiden, and now." He pointed to a wide tree stump. "Stand over there."

Emlyn obeyed silently, wondering as she went if everyone did this man's bidding with a meekness equal to hers. But then, 'twas true she had just shot him. She stood on the stump and waited as he positioned the animal alongside.

"Take hold of the arrow," he directed, and she curled her fingers around the shaft. Removing his gauntlet, he slid his hand beneath hers to press down on his leg. His touch was cool against her skin. "When I say, you shall pull fast and hard."

"Sire, I—" she faltered, biting her lip.

"I would do it myself, were you not here."

Nodding, she tightened her grip and took a long breath. The knight inhaled deeply at the same instant. She glanced up to find him watching her, a keen sharp light in his gray eyes.

"Pull!" he commanded. She did so, mightily. His long exhalation vibrated with the undertone of a suppressed cry as the arrowhead ripped backward through the fleshy hole it had made. Warm blood spurted over their hands.

Emlyn saw then that the wide point would not come through the chain mail and the legging cloth as easily as it had gone in. She carefully worked the barb free from the net of metal rings, aware of the knight's grim silence.

Finally she drew the arrow completely out and pressed the heel of her hand against fresh bleeding. When she withdrew a linen square from her sleeve, the knight took it and began to staunch the flow himself. She glanced up to see him frown as he applied the cloth, his lowered eyelashes sooty crescents above his unshaven cheeks, his lips tight with pain.

In her left hand, Emlyn held the bloodied arrow uncertainly. She could not very well wipe the point clean and drop it into the quiver concealed beneath her cloak.

Reaching down, the knight lifted the arrow from her grasp to examine the shaft. "There are no marks of ownership here. This is a hunting arrow, with a wide barb for small game." He looked sharply at Emlyn. "Tell me what you know of this attack, maid. Where is the knave who bowshot me?"

"Attack?" She bit nervously at her bottom lip.

"There was no follow to the bowshot, no brigands that I saw, nor poachers either." He leaned forward, his gray eyes hard and cool as frost over stone. With his free hand, he closed his long fingers firmly around her shoulder. "Why are you in this greenwood, maiden?"

Although her first impulse was to break free of his grasp and flee into the forest, reason, and years in a nunnery, advised her to confess. But when she opened her mouth, only a dry, airy sound came out, as if a mouse had squeaked. She was terrified of his reaction to the truth. Ruthless knights such as this one had seized Guy. This man might harm her, even kill her for the offense she had just committed.

Balancing the shaft lightly between two fingers, the knight held the reins loosely in the same hand. With the other hand he still grasped Emlyn's shoulder. "Speak! Did you come with your father or brother to shoot the king's deer?"

"Nay, sire. This is a timber wood belonging to Ashbourne Castle—a hedge and ditch keep the deer out."

He glanced to where she gestured with her free hand. Just visible through the trees, a thick hedge rounded the outer part of the forest, oddly flattened. When properly cared for, such a barrier discouraged larger animals, especially deer, from entering the wood to eat tree sprouts and strip bark from trees grown for lumber.

"Because the king recently ordered all hedges lowered," she said, "the hedge has just been trimmed. The rest has collapsed from winter storms. The deer will roam freely here soon, with naught to keep them out of the timber wood, thanks to King John. This path is an old one, hardly used, that leads to the castle."

"A timber wood," he said dryly. "And no other here but you."

Emlyn took a deep breath and decided to speak the truth. Her heart beat wildly as she rushed out her confession. " 'Twas neither an outlaw nor poacher who shot you, my lord. 'Twas my own arrow from my own hand." She tensed, ready to flee, but his grip on her shoulder was strong enough to rent the joint apart should she pull away.

A moment of silence, then a powerful laugh split the air above her head. "What quarrel have you with me? Black Thorne the outlaw is long dead, they say, and no other would dare attack my family!" He lurched forward to shout at her. "Protect not your family, your heart's-beau, or your husband! Where is the knave who bowshot me!" His voice lowered dangerously. "Play not with me, maid. I am short of temper with pain and my need to be elsewhere!"

Emlyn cringed and raised a trembling hand to her face as a hint of the full force of his anger was bared to her. Her movement opened her cloak, and the leather quiver suspended from her belt bounced against her hip. Four identical arrows rattled within.

He stared at the quiver, then looked at her. " 'Tis true."

"Aye, my lord," she said in a small, timid voice.

"Why would you attack me?" His tone was near a growl.

"I intended no injury to you, sir knight," she said earnestly, " 'twas an accident. I was practicing the bow." He watched her in silence. "A wind came and took my arrow. I aimed at the bole of a beech tree," she added lamely.

Still he said nothing, but the uncomfortable pressure around her shoulder eased. "In sooth, my lord, I am no goodly archer."

"Aye," he grunted. "That you are not."

She nodded miserably. "Alas, by Our Lady, I crave your pardon. 'Tis not meet to injure a man so."

"Not meet indeed." He let go of her suddenly, and she reached up a hand to massage the ache. The knight blew out a long breath as he watched her for a moment, his dark brows pinched in a frown. "Well," he said. "I must give you my pardon, since I cannot have you spitted and roasted. Though not for lack of urge, I assure you." He held the arrow out to her. "Begone from here, and quickly."

Accepting the offending shaft reluctantly, Emlyn stepped off the tree stump and glanced back up at the knight. Above dark stubble, his cheeks were splashed with pink, and his eyes glowed like steel in the sun. Even the harsh lines of pain and anger did not mar his elegantly sculpted face. Remembering that he was bleeding and in pain, Emlyn wondered if he had far to ride.

"One thing else, maid," he called. "I would know the name of my assassin."

Before she could reply, a shout rent the quiet forest.

The knight turned in his saddle to call an answer. Hoof-beats thundered softly on a hidden part of the forest path. Emlyn grew agitated, eager to flee; she should never have strayed, alone and unprotected, so far from the castle.

"Go, then," the knight said, seeming to sense her urgency. "But leave the shooting to able men from now on." Turning his mount, he rode toward the approaching horseman.

Emlyn had been suffering remorse and deep sympathy for the injured knight. Now, suddenly, his parting words filled her with anger. Stomping into the dense cover of the timber wood to pick up her small bow, muttering a few unkind phrases that went better unheard by anyone, she turned to-

ward Ashbourne. Once inside the enclosure, she would be
safe from the threat of bowshot young knights. She would
not, however, be safe from her nurse Tibbie's wrath until she
was well occupied within the keep.

Arriving breathlessly in the foyer adjacent to the great
hall, Emlyn pulled aside the red curtain that covered the hall
entrance and peered inside. By the rood, she thought, I have
missed supper and am surely caught.

Near one long wall, a few servants worked together to
push back the few planked tables and narrow benches that
had been used for the late afternoon meal. A girl swept at
the rushes, while another stacked used bread trenchers to
take them away for distribution in the village tomorrow. A
long table of heavy oak, its polished surface empty, stood
adjacent to the huge stone hearth in the far wall.

"Lady Emlyn! There ye be!" A voice, husky and warm,
boomed with little effort across the length of the great hall.
Emlyn winced. She had not noticed Tibbie in her hasty sur-
veillance.

The short, squat, powerful woman crossed the room like
a rolling thundercloud, her layered skirts boiling around her
legs. Emlyn, resigned, held the curtain open wider. "Aye,
Tibbie?"

"Let me take yer cloak, m'lady—" Tibbie burst through
the curtain, one arm out to pull Emlyn's cloak off. Backing
into the foyer, Emlyn fumbled with the bronze pin that secured her mantle.

Tugging at the heavy wool, Tibbie gasped in anguish.
"Emlyn de Ashbourne, 'tis soaked this cape is! Give it
here!"

Emlyn squirmed out of the garment. " 'Tis barely damp."

"Damp, aye, and muddy as well. Here's bits of leaves and
suchlike." Tibbie drew the material through her plump fingers, picking out snagged twigs and leaves. She fixed a bale-
ful eye on Emlyn in the gloomy torchlit foyer. "Ye've been
outside the walls, with no guard, nor even a dog to protect
ye, I wot."

"Aye, so," Emlyn sighed, knowing from long experience
that no secret survived long around Tibbie.

Throwing the cloak over her arm, Tibbie folded her hands

over her plump stomach and waited, eye to eye with Emlyn. Neither woman was tall, and while Emlyn was as delicate as if she were formed of gold and ivory, Tibbie, twice as wide, could have been made of brass and oak.

" 'Tis still as a tomb here, some days," Emlyn said. "And so I escaped. Wat would not have given me permission to go, nor would you. 'Twas only to the timber wood."

"Sir Walter is no old fool, and ye should harken to him. What would happen if ye'd met the king's men in the forest? Wat says they're always about now, and no telling when they'll come for ye, or all of us, God save us." Tibbie sketched a hasty cross over her wide bosom, and placed her round fist on her hip.

A shiver of dread whispered through Emlyn as she thought of the knight in the forest. She recalled the look in his eyes when she had put her hand around the arrow embedded in his thigh. Now the fear that she had felt in those moments came rushing back.

Tibbie and Wat, the castle seneschal, had become fiercely protective of her, and of the younger de Ashbourne children, ever since Guy's arrest while out on a hunting party. The long winter had been fraught with tension, which had increased when the king demanded an exorbitant fee; a fine, his messenger had said.

Left as chatelaine, Emlyn had done her best to care for the children and the household. She had managed to send some silver marks to the king, though that had drained the coffers; but coin was the only hope of seeing Guy safe again. Throughout the long winter, Emlyn had tried earnestly to keep her thoughts on God and to turn her anger to forgiveness. But she had found this to be exceedingly difficult.

Though her parents and older siblings were gone now, either by God's will or another's, the three younger ones were safe and well in her care. After Guy's capture, Emlyn had made a vow to the Holy Virgin never to leave the children, wanting their lives to be free from the losses that she had known. That, at least, she felt able to pledge in good faith, as their sister and sole guardian.

Tibbie surged on. "And what," she asked pointedly, "was ye doing in the forest alone? Why did ye not bring Cadgil?"

"Practicing," Emlyn said. "And Cadgil is getting too old."

"Tish-tosh! Never the bow and arrow?" Tibbie glowered at her. "Since ye was a child, ye've been taken by the things. 'Twas that outlaw Black Thorne ye had the misfortune to meet. Otherwise yer a biddable maid."

"Oh, Tib," Emlyn said, sighing. "Guy saw no harm in the archery. He first showed me. And many ladies hunt with bows."

"Pah! Those fine ladies that traipse about in the forest with hunting parties are after bigger game than rabbits, mark ye! Few of them care an oat for the niceties of the arrow sport, but for the young lords that may be on a hunt! Had ye not spent these past years in the convent, ye'd know that."

Tibbie took a quick breath and rushed on. "Would ye sneak away from those who would protect ye from the maws of that wicked king—God forgive me, but he's a one and we do know it—to go out shooting at wee birdies? Ye should be at yer prayers for poor Baron Guy, God save him." Another fingered cross hit the air. Tibbie sighed and shook her head, her crisp white wimple swinging. "Truly, I cannot hold it against ye."

Emlyn blinked. "Tib?"

"Aye, I cannot blame ye for fleeing this tomb, as ye say, on such a fine day as this. Didst catch any game with that arrow thing, as would help out in the kitchens?"

In over twenty years of living under Tibbie's constant chattering and expostulating, Emlyn was accustomed to the nurse's sudden changes of mood and direction of thought. Tibbie's thoughts blew like quick breezes, her words following hither and yon like dry leaves. No one could be more loving or protective, but those under her care sometimes suffered from the constant flow of lively, opinionated, and incessantly loud chatter.

"Emlyn, love, didst get us a rabbit?" Tibbie repeated.

"N-nay, Tibbie, not a rabbit, not exactly a rabbit. I am not a very good archer." Hardly, she thought to herself, cringing at the memory of the blue-cloaked knight. Sooty lashes, dusky eyes, warm hands and sharp words flashed through her mind.

"Wellaway, though the Lord knows we could use extra fare

for the table these days, with few enough men to hunt for us all," Tibbie said. "The king's fines have taken nearly all we have. We must send out a hunting party soon, for the barrels of salted meat are near empty."

Emlyn sighed at the bare truth of Tibbie's observation. Despite the normal bustle of a castle household, with servants and craftsmen at work in the keep, kitchens, brewhouse, stable, and smithy, supplies were dwindling. And the reassuring presence of Ashbourne's castle garrison was conspicuously absent.

Only a few armed men strolled the parapet now. When Guy had been taken, all but a few of their paid men-at-arms had gone elsewhere, many ordered out by the king's messengers. With few men available for hunting, any contribution was valuable. The lack of soldiers also meant that Ashbourne could not withstand, for long, an attack from outside.

"We have survived thus far," Emlyn told Tibbie. "Somehow, I will pay the rest of Guy's inheritance fee. The flocks this year are abundant. The wool will fetch a good price."

"Pray 'twill bring enough for that grasping king," Tibbie grumbled.

"Certes, he will accept another payment in part."

"Hmmph," Tibbie commented sourly, sniffing. Emlyn smiled, knowing well that the nurse's admonitions could be laced with as much honey as vinegar.

Emlyn also relied on the wisdom and experience of Walter de Lyddell, who had been her father's seneschal and had remained when Guy became head of the household. With such guidance, Emlyn had been able to keep the castle in a semblance of normalcy, much to her satisfaction. She wanted to protect her younger siblings, wherever possible, from the current predicament, for she considered the children her most significant responsibility. Her father had entrusted them to her and Guy when he had died.

"The twins must be well and truly occupied, for all seems peaceful here," she said to Tibbie.

Tibbie blinked, her short fuzzy brows raised high over summer blue eyes, and one round cheek dimpled suddenly. "Quiet is well occupied? For a child? My lady girl, quiet children are sometimes the wickedest of creatures! Ye and yer brother Guy, bless him, the king's a bastard, forgive me,

Lord," she muttered under her breath, her index finger flying, "such a pair to keep up with, and yer sister Agnes and brother Richard before ye—God bless that young man's departed soul, and watch over Lady Agnes in her convent!" She drew a breath and hurried on. "I was younger then, and kept after the brood of ye, just as I do now with the twins and that precious babe, sweet Harry."

Emlyn smiled. "Christien and Isobel are likely at a good game of draughts in the solar."

Laughing at this unlikely image, Tibbie crossed the little foyer and reached up to hang Emlyn's cloak on a wooden peg beside other cloaks. "I sent those twins to the kitchens a while ago—they were still hungry after supper, and the cook promised them a sweetmeat each. Little Harry is already sleeping, bless his soul." As she spoke, a child's sudden screams reverberated from somewhere inside the keep, well above their heads.

"Saints and angels, the Saracens are come again," Tibbie muttered, nodding her head wisely.

"I will tend to it." Turning, Emlyn ran lightly up the curving steps that led to the bedchambers above the great hall. As she went, her soft leather soles beat against the uneven stone surface in odd rhythm with the echoing, shrill cries.

Chapter Two

Steadying his black destrier on the crest of the hill, Baron Nicholas de Hawkwood studied Ashbourne Castle with a keen analytical eye. Cold spring air had sharpened objects to a jewel-like precision, and the castle gleamed like a gilded reliquary on a mound of green silk. High limestone walls glowed dull gold in the late afternoon sun, surrounded by acres of soft meadows and verdant, lacy forests.

Impervious to the castle's sparkling charm, the baron crossed his gauntleted hands over his saddle bow and swore loudly. Every shift of the horse's shoulders seemed to jar the tender wound in his thigh. He had been waiting here for over an hour, yet Lord Whitehawke apparently was content to let him sit. Sighing in exasperation, he rubbed his aching, stiffening leg. This mission was hardly as uncomplicated as the king had promised.

Scanning the austere, square castle again, Nicholas judged Ashbourne to be Norman-built, old but solidly made. The simple design of keep, curtain wall, and four mural towers was meant to outlast centuries. But he knew the castle was ripe for plucking.

Inside were servants, a few men-at-arms, and a handful of children: no barrier to his task. The castle would fall quickly and silently, not to the sword, but to the pen. King John's writ was tucked inside the lining of Nicholas's blue cloak. The crisp black lettering and official royal seal transferred Ashbourne, along with its environs and properties, to the possession of his father, Whitehawke.

He curled his lip in distaste, wanting no part of it.

At the rhythmic sound of hoofbeats, he glanced over his shoulder. A knight in a green cloak rode toward him and casually reined in his pale dappled horse beside the baron's black steed.

"Where is Whitehawke?" the baron snapped impatiently.

The young knight looked at him and shrugged. "Not along the southern road, my lord, though I rode back a few miles. Your guards are headed this way, and may know something of him."

Muttering a low curse, Nicholas pushed back his mesh hood and turned his head, his long dark hair whipping in the chill breeze as he searched the landscape. " 'Twould be like Whitehawke and the king to alter this course at the last."

His companion rubbed his red-gold mustache and then snorted in surly agreement. "Aye, my lord, as 'tis like you and Lord Whitehawke to be at odds once again."

"Leave it, Perkin, will you," he snapped. "I have no desire to do this, yet I must follow the king's orders." As he shifted in his saddle, a sharp pain flashed through his thigh.

"Becalm yourself, my lord. You are even more irritable than when I left you here. How does your injury?"

" 'Tis minor, as I told you."

"We should search for the hunter whose arrow caught you."

"Nay. 'Tis a scratch, a foolish accident." He looked away, his mouth grim. Never, he thought, would he admit that a girl had accidentally shot him as he rode unaware through the greenwood. He and Peter de Blackpoole—Perkin was a boyhood nickname—had fostered together and were as close as brothers, yet Peter's hungry wit was always eager for fodder; Nicholas was aware he would feast on this if he knew.

Peter scratched his unshaven chin, his beard glistening gilt and coppery, as he looked across at Ashbourne Castle. "Think you the chit in that keep is old enough to wed?"

"The chit is old enough," Nicholas said curtly. "The four youngest issue of Rogier de Ashbourne still reside in the castle. The chit is the eldest of those. I assume they are adolescents."

He assumed more, but kept the knowledge to himself. Years before, he had offered for the eldest girl's hand in marriage, owing her father a debt of honor. But Rogier de Ashbourne had died unexpectedly before the agreement was made. And Nicholas had just learned that King John had given the girl to his father, Whitehawke.

"Well, motherless babes would be naught for Lord Whitehawke to conquer," Peter said cynically. "He gains a young bride with a fine castle. You, my lord, did not fare as well."

"Hardly," Nicholas muttered. The king had assigned him custody of the three younger de Ashbournes. He nearly groaned aloud at the thought: nursemaid by the king's decree.

"Where the devil is he?" he growled, scanning the road behind them. " 'Tis late afternoon already."

"Perhaps an enemy waylaid him in the greenwood," Peter mused, his eyes, blue as the cloudless sky, twinkling merrily.

"Cease your jesting, Perkin, I have not the mood for it," Nicholas said. "You know that my father will not set foot in a forest if there is a way around. He is perpetually late because of his silly superstitions. The warrior is becoming an old woman." He stirred on his horse. "I vow, if Whitehawke does not arrive soon, I will leave this deed happily undone."

"You grow impatient with age, my lord. Neither are you known for ease of temper," Peter chided him. Turning his head, he suddenly narrowed his eyes. "Ho! There, along the old roman road, comes your illustrious elder."

The ancient road lay like a pale undulating ribbon across the open sweep of the downs. A group of riders cantered along its length. In the lead, on a huge white destrier, rode a tall man dressed in black armor, his long white hair flying out like a silk banner.

"At last," Nicholas said.

"Who is with him? A garrison of thirty—nay, forty. At least you had the grace to bring only eight. And—be damned—"

"Hugh de Chavant at the front."

"That frog-eyed bastard," Peter snorted. "Why is he here?"

"Would you speak so of my cousin? He is captain of my father's guard now."

Peter shot him a disgusted glance. "So he has won the trust of Whitehawke."

"He always had that. Whitehawke has lately given him a

small barony on the Welsh border, though there is scarcely a living in it. He is still forced to earn his keep as a garrison commander."

"Well, I must have sympathy for him there. Being your garrison commander has not made my fortune, my lord," Peter mused. "A landless younger son, left to seek my way in the world." He rolled his eyes skyward with dramatic flourish.

"You could become a monk." Nicholas cocked an eyebrow.

Peter laughed. "My sword is too happy by my side. And I yearn for land of my own. The tourneys have yielded me but two small manor estates. I must work harder if I am to rest in luxury."

"I would gladly give you my position as Whitehawke's heir," Nicholas said. "He disinherited me again before Yuletide. But last month, when we were forced to smile and be kin for the king's benefit at court, he informed me that I was his heir for good and all. Until he sees some other evil in me, I trow."

Peter shot him a serious look. "Let us hope he does not discover the true evil in you, sire."

"Aye." Nicholas' expression was grim as he urged his horse forward. "Pray God it does not come to that."

The piercing shrieks emanated from within a small chamber, and were now joined by a higher, much angrier cry. Emlyn paused at the top of the stairs, then shoved open an arched wooden door. Although Isobel's screams burst from a deep window embrasure, Emlyn noted immediately that the child was not in danger. The second set of keening wails came from within the curtained bed. Emlyn lifted Harry out and balanced him on her hip, clucking a soothing sound, then turned toward the other two.

"Christien! Isobel! Stop this!" she said in a loud and firm voice. Harry hiccuped in her arms and locked his warm, chubby legs around her waist.

Christien, brandishing a wooden sword, had backed away when his older sister had entered the room. Now he sheepishly lowered the point of his sword. Emlyn stepped past him.

Isobel lay curled in a deep niche, shrieking with six-year-

old gusto, her back pressed against the cruciform opening
meant to be used by crossbowmen and archers in defense of
the castle. The aperture was large enough to let in air and
sunshine, but too small for a child to put out more than an
arm or shoulder. Years earlier their father had ordered an
iron bar placed across the arrowloop, for the room was the
children's sleeping chamber, which they shared with Tibbie.

"Here, Isobel, come out," Emlyn said, helping the snif-
fling girl out of the deep ledge.

Isobel turned to stare accusingly at Christien. Legs spread
apart stubbornly, he folded his arms, his build sturdier than
his twin sister's fragile frame, his honey-brown hair lighter
than her glossy dark locks, though both shared eyes the deep
color of bluebells. Harry, calmer now, peered curiously from
one sibling to another, his soft pale curls bobbing with his
hiccups.

"She is my prisoner," Christien said, appealing to Emlyn.
"She is a Saracen warrior!"

Isobel, recovered quickly from her disturbance, stamped
one little pointed felt shoe. "I am a Saracen princess!
Knights may not ever wave their swords at ladies, nor push
them from windows!"

"I did not push you! You cried because I bested you! And
you are not a noddy-head princess!"

"You are King Richard and I am to be your queen!" Isobel
shouted.

"I'll have no queen!" Christien retorted.

Emlyn stepped between them. "Enough, both of you. This
chamber is no place for playacting. Harry was asleep. And
you know full well the danger of any window. Christien,
your sister is your charge. You are the elder by minutes, and
will be a knight one day. No knight ever treats a lady with
such disrespect. Even a Saracen lady."

"Warrior," muttered Christien.

Emlyn sighed, looking at her brother. "You dearly need
some boys to play with, I trow. Well, apologize to your sister, and best remember this in your prayers at bedtime." She
brushed soft waves of hair from his brow. "And ask Saint
George to show you greater courtesy."

"Aye, Emlyn," he answered grumpily, and mumbled an
apology.

As he spoke, Tibbie burst through the door, her wide bosom heaving. "By the horns of Moses! What have ye two been doing up here? Not Saracens and Christians again, is it, and waking our Harry as well. And where is the little serv-ingmaid I put on yer tails when ye went to the bakehouse?"

Isobel and Christien looked guiltily at each other and stood shoulder to shoulder. "We left her there, eating honeycakes."

"I shall take them to my chamber, if you would coax the babe back to sleep," Emlyn said, and handed Harry to Tibbie. Sucking his thumb, he rested his head on Tibbie's shoulder.

Emlyn led the twins out and down the short corridor to her own room. "If you are quiet, you may watch me work."

The children burst enthusiastically into her bedchamber, a small room shaped from the thickness of the castle wall, and bounced on a cushioned window seat while she changed into a dry gown of soft blue wool. Setting a belt of embroidered silk low on her hips, she knelt to search under the bed for her felt shoes.

Tibbie disliked the disorder in Emlyn's chamber, but a lit-tle cheerful chaos had always been natural to Emlyn. Even her years in the convent had not ended her tendency to gen-tle clutter. She had never conformed completely to the rigor-ous discipline of the convent, and had been told often that she was impatient and should pray for serenity. While the cloistered atmosphere had fostered her strong need for peace and quiet, it had not had much effect on her sense of orga-nization.

When she had changed, she sat on the window seat and undid her thick braids to brush out the tangles. Rippled from tight plaiting, the silky length of her hair gleamed in varie-gated colors: pale flax mixed with golden-wheat blond and scattered strands of walnut, the color of her straight, serious brows. Brushed out, her fragrant hair fell to her hips, full as a cloud. She did not take the time to rebraid it, but set a white veil on her head of exotic, gauzy cotton, secured by a silk cord. Tibbie, she thought, will likely grumble about the loose hair.

Afternoon sun spilled into the room through the pillared, arched window, falling in golden bars across the red brocade cushion on the window seat. A wayward breeze dipped through the unshuttered window, bringing a faint waft of sweet orchards.

Emlyn inhaled the cool air and leaned her head against the window post, looking beyond the castle walls to the green crown of the forests and gently swelling downs. Out there, she thought, lay an unfettered, joyful, wild freedom, such as few men, and fewer women, truly had. Certain that she would never know such an existence, she sometimes wondered what life would be like without walls, or guards, or the strictures of duties and obligations.

"You missed supper," Isobel observed.

"Aye, I went out into the greenwood to practice at the bow."

"In the forest alone? A lady must never go out unescorted!"

" 'Tis spring, so the Green Man's about," Christien said. "Look out, he'll have your head with his axe." Crossing his eyes, he hung his tongue out of his mouth. Isobel squeaked nervously.

Emlyn sighed. "I shall tell you something less eerie than the tale of the Green Knight next time. Perhaps I shall recite Bevis of Hampton. He fought a dragon," she said. Christien's eyes popped wide, and he nodded eagerly. "But never fear the forest, dearlings, 'tis a beautiful, peaceful place," she added.

Most of the time, she corrected herself silently, though she resolved to go there again to hone her archery skill, what little talent it might be. Bowshot knights be damned.

"Will you work now?" Christien asked. Emlyn nodded, rose, and went to a slant-top desk, on which lay one loose parchment sheet, weighted at the corners with small rocks. Above that, a wall shelf held small clay jars of ground pigments, clamshells for mixing paints, assorted brushes, a horn of ink, and quill feathers. Emlyn reached up for a jar and two brushes, set these on the desk, then sat on a three-legged stool.

The flat parchment was partially covered with carefully made black and red letters. The words were not by her own hand, but she could read them, and write as well, thanks to the lady abbess in her convent, who maintained that noblewomen should have well-occupied minds as well as hands. Emlyn and the other girls had been taught reading, writing, a little mathematics, philosophy, and theology, in addition to the usual handicrafts.

The convent had a small scriptorium where the nuns copied and decorated a few precious books for their own use. Once the nuns discovered that Emlyn had a facile hand, she had spent many hours in the scriptorium, painstakingly copying letters until they swam before her tired eyes. Just the thought of such work set her right hand to rhythmic flexing, as if her fingers had a cramp. But she had always loved any chance to paint images.

Her father had approved of her training. His youngest brother, her uncle Godwin, was a monk in a York monastery, an established painter whose work graced the plastered walls of several churches and castles in the northern regions. Godwin was a scholar as well as an artist; she knew that he was currently writing a chronology of the kings of Britain, illuminating its pages himself.

When Emlyn was a child, Godwin had visited one Yule and had playfully showed her how to handle a brush and paints. She had loved the magic of the fluid, bright colors across the thick parchment surface, and had painted ever since.

A breeze lifted a curling lock of hair from her shoulder as she began to work. Propping the heel of one hand against the white cloth, she rotated the tip of a loaded brush to fill in the armor of a knight with *grisaille,* a gray wash. Painting the miniscule rows of chain mail for a scene of knights in battle was tedious, and she was eager to finish. But she was satisfied with the firm drawing and pleased with the slanted composition that conveyed the furor of battle.

Christien and Isobel stood behind her, breathing softly, uncharacteristically quiet as they watched her work. As she twirled the tiny hairs of the brush, she told them that this picture, along with others stacked on a shelf, illustrated the heroic French poem of Sir Gui de Warwyck. She read a little of the French text aloud from the parchment sheet. The children had heard part of the adventure story before, for Emlyn often read or recited tales to them at bedtime, or in dreary weather.

"I like the part about Sir Gui's fight with the dragon," Christien said.

"You only like dragons, and swords, and war-horses," Isobel said disdainfully.

"See, now that I have done the last of the armor, I can start on the caparisons," Emlyn said. "There are two blues here. Help me choose." She removed the beeswax plugs from two small clay jars, and the children leaned over to see the rich hues.

The ultramarine blue, saturated and bright, was made from ground lapis lazuli, imported from the Holy Land and therefore precious and very expensive. Emlyn had only a tiny bit, which she used sparingly. The other was a darker indigo, made from a common woad plant. Both dry pigments had been mixed with whipped egg whites. For other colors, especially reds and greens, Emlyn had been taught to add a variety of ingredients to the mixture: yolks, honey, wine, beer. Her uncle Godwin's painters, she knew, even added earwax to certain reds to produce luminosity.

They chose the woad and she filled in a cloak and a horse's caparison while Christien and Isobel hung over her shoulder.

"Guy will treasure this manuscript," Isobel said.

"He had better," Emlyn said, laughing. "I have been working on this gift for him for nigh half a year." She had continued to paint the manuscript despite her brother's capture, feeling that to abandon it was to abandon hope for Guy.

Several months ago, she had purchased through her uncle Godwin an unfinished manuscript, which she had intended to complete as a New Year's gift for Guy. Godwin had sent a packet of loose parchment pages, a copy of the story of Gui de Warwyck, made by a scribe in the monastery workshop. Several pages contained blank rectangles where she had added the painted illuminations. The finished manuscript would be sent back to Godwin to be bound, and covered in leather and wood and a little gold leaf, if she could afford it.

Finishing the blue cloak, Emlyn placed the brush in a small pot of water and picked up a clean rabbit's-hair brush. She chose a jar of vermilion made from iron salts, allowed

Isobel to pry loose the little plug, and asked Christien to fetch a clamshell to hold a dab of the new color.

A knock at the door preceded, just barely, Tibbie's head. "Oh, my lady," she said, her face lined with concern.

"What is it, Tibbie?" Emlyn asked.

"Sir Wat wished to meet with ye in the great hall. He is on the parapet now, and ye may catch him there if ye hurry. There are riders coming this way!" she blurted.

Emlyn was seized by panic as she thought of the blue-cloaked knight in the forest, and fairly flew down the curving steps to the foyer. There, she opened a door and ran across a connecting platform, rather like a covered wooden bridge, which linked the keep to the broad curtain wall. She hurried along the wide wall walk toward Wat, stopping to glance over the parapet.

Moving up the road that led toward Ashbourne, a gyrating mass of color and sparkle resolved, in the late golden-pink afternoon, into a garrison of armored soldiers.

"Sweet Mother Mary in Heaven!" She drew in her breath sharply. Leaning forward, her fingertips pressing into rough stone, she had the curiously detached sense that she was watching an illuminated miniature come to life.

Forty or more helmets glistened and bobbed rhythmically in the sunlight. Two men rode in the lead, banners flapping behind them. One, on a pale horse, was dressed all in black, his brilliant white hair unprotected by helm or hood. Beside him, riding a black destrier, was a knight cloaked in blue, with steel mesh armor glinting beneath.

Her stomach clenched violently when she saw him.

Gaining the broad meadow that sloped up to the castle gate, the group cantered across the grass, the horses' hooves sending up clods of earth and flowers as they came steadfastly toward Ashbourne. Pennants fluttered from a wooden pole attached to the bannerman's saddle: the topmost flag showed the royal crest, while the other, displayed by a sudden gust of wind, carried a design of a green hawk on a white background.

Emlyn turned away from the edge of the parapet to lean against the hard stone. A low groan whispered through her lips, and she felt slightly sick.

She had shot an arrow into a messenger of the king.

Chapter Three

"The man in black? Aye, him I know. The other, in blue, I cannot say for certain," Walter de Lyddell answered Emlyn as they stood together on the wallwalk and gazed down on the horsemen. The bannerman had requested entry in the name of the king, and now awaited an answer from the porter, who in turn awaited word from Lady Emlyn or the seneschal.

"Bertran de Hawkwood, Earl of Graymere, called Whitehawke, after that white head of his," Wat continued. "A powerful lord, and a cruel man as well, I have heard. He has more small barons in his pocket than you can name, and King John's favor as well. A pair, those two, a couple of slimy toads."

Emlyn laid a hand on Wat's arm, the old, tarnished steel mesh cold and heavy beneath her touch. Tall and broad, his eyes dark as walnuts in his grizzled and seamed face, he wore the dark red cloak that identified him as a man of the Baron de Ashbourne. Wat had been her father's closest friend and castle seneschal for twenty years. Now he glanced down at Emlyn with paternal tolerance as she peeked furtively over the crenellated wall.

"What might Lord Whitehawke want here, Wat?" she asked.

"It seems he bears a message from the king, my lady."

"What do you suggest?" She felt capable of nothing beyond a fervent wish that the blue-cloaked one would go away.

He sucked in his breath sharply, his jowled face creased in thought. "They do not challenge us, but ask only for entry. I suggest we admit only the earl and the one who rides beside him. They will leave their weapons at the gate, and their men can camp in the field until the king's message has been delivered."

Emlyn nodded, her head jerking stiffly with the movement. "I shall not greet them in the bailey, though 'tis my duty. But—I cannot. I leave that to you," she said.

Wat nodded and called out the order to the gatemen. The pulleys squealed as thick ropes slowly drew up the first iron portcullis. Emlyn gathered her skirts and fled back to the keep.

Tibbie and the twins stood before the windows in the great hall, the children perched on a bench beneath a row of tall triple-arched windows that were set with stained glass above and wooden shutters below. Christien complained loudly that Isobel had the best space in front of the one open casement.

"The colored glass is not much good for seeing out, but it does make pretty colors on the floors, just there," Tibbie said, gesturing at pools of amber and red on the rushes. "Now, Isobel, shove over, before I move ye m'self." Tibbie turned as Emlyn approached. "Ye will receive them, my lady?"

"Aye," Emlyn said, and went to the hearth end of the long room, the hem of her blue skirt whispering sibilantly on the rushes. The hound Cadgil, resting his yellowed head on his paws, lay on the warm hearthstone and whined softly as she came near. Emlyn bent to scratch his head, and then sat in a high-backed carved chair, determined to greet the messengers graciously.

Tibbie came near, her round face drawn and lined with apprehension, her eyes rimmed pink. "Let us hope they bring good news, and pray the king does not want ye prisoner as well."

"King John has no quarrel with me, Tibbie. I have naught of value—only some property left to me by my mother. Any dowry I had is gone to the king." Emlyn sighed. "You know I will end in a convent like my sister Agnes."

Tibbie shook her head. "The king is a sly one, my lady girl. Ye've learned that lesson well, for Lord Guy is not here."

Emlyn pinched her lips silently, knowing that Tibbie was right. The king could not be gainsaid or trusted. She shivered inwardly. If these messengers brought news of Guy's death, then Christien was the next baron.

She stifled a quick urge to grab the twins, fetch sleeping Harry, and run away, anywhere. So much already lost, so much more to lose. Her eldest brother Richard, when a knight of twenty, had been killed in Poitou years earlier, while fighting alongside English knights for King John. Almost two years ago, her mother, past the age for easy bearing, had died shortly after Harry's birth. Late last summer, her father had caught a fatal ague. And then, in the autumn, Guy had been taken.

The shock and pain of each loss had piled on her like lead weights on a fragile golden scale. There were times when she could hardly breathe, could hardly think rationally, under the crushing burden. And she had discovered, to her dismay, that women had little power to sway or change what men determined. Soon she would hear the king's next order, and be expected, even forced, to obey. Gripping the carved armrests, she felt slightly dizzy, her heart beating rapidly.

"Emlyn!" Isobel called from her perch by the window. The children jumped excitedly on the bench. "They come!"

Iron-trimmed boots thudded on the outer staircase. Emlyn summoned a calm into her voice that she did not feel. "Tibbie, take the children to their chamber, and stay there with them." Tibbie nodded and shooed the children down from the bench, sending them before her like geese. They disappeared noisily up the backstairs that wound behind the hearth chimney.

The ornate chair carvings were cool and hard beneath her trembling fingers. A profound silence, dense as mist and smoke, filled the great hall. The curtain at the far end of the room split open and two men entered with Wat, crossing the floor with heavy, purposeful steps.

Rising slowly from the chair, Emlyn folded her trembling hands demurely before her. The blue-cloaked knight was tall, and walked with an easy swing in his stride, showing no trace of a limp. Perhaps the wound was minor after all, she thought with relief, in spite of the blood she had seen.

The knight's eyes, stone cold and severe, bored into her skull as he approached. She knew the instant he recognized her as the girl in the forest. Mustering a semblance of the cool control expected of a noblewoman, she stepped forward smoothly.

"My lords, God give you greeting," she said. "I am Lady Emlyn de Ashbourne, sister to the baron. You are welcome here." Wat stood beside her, his sturdy presence like a benediction.

Whitehawke was only a bit taller than his companion, though heavier and large-boned. He towered over Emlyn and bowed, his deepset and hooded eyes pale blue, pricked by tiny black pupils. Ivory brows matched the glossy, creamy white hair that hung to his shoulders. He took her hand in sausagey fingers.

"I am the Earl of Graymere, Bertran de Hawkwood, my lady," he said. "Whitehawke." His voice was a deep bass rumble. He inclined his head toward the younger man who stood beside him. "My son, Nicholas de Hawkwood."

The introduction hit her like a physical punch. Dear saints. She had not only loosed an arrow into a messenger of the king, but into the son of an earl. If these men had any influence, Guy's fate was in sure jeopardy.

The knight's angry expression upon entering the room had softened to a more pensive look. He gingerly bent his left injured leg to shift his weight to the right, the gray gleam in his eyes piercing as good steel. "My lady, greetings," he said. "I am the Baron of Hawksmoor. We bring a message from King John. But first we would ask of you some refreshment."

Emlyn realized that Whitehawke had not introduced his son properly, omitting rank and title. Holy Virgin. A baron in his own right. Her head trembled like a heavy flower on a stalk.

"My lord," she squeaked out, her throat tight. Crossing to a small cupboard, she took out a glazed jug and two silver cups, engraved and chased with gold, their pedestal bases shaped to comfortably fit a man's large hand. She placed the cups on the long oak table by the hearth and poured good French wine, red as rubies, handing over the goblets with a softly murmured blessing.

As the earl and his son drank, Emlyn squeezed her fingers together anxiously. Nicholas de Hawkwood pushed back his mesh hood, his dark hair unruly beneath, and rubbed his slate-shadowed jaw, watching her in cool, silent assessment. Another fierce blush crept up her neck, and she turned away.

The earl stood by the open window, conversing quietly with Wat. The setting sun cast a pink glaze over White-hawke's hair, and his blackened armor gleamed dully beneath his black cloak. Powerfully built, his body heavily muscled, his features leonine, he was handsome still, though harsh. He looked like some aged, mythical king, a ferocious mix of elven and human.

Emlyn approached Whitehawke timidly. "My lord, though I would hear your message, I will have a repast brought. We ate earlier, not expecting guests." Her stomach churned with nervousness, and she had not eaten since morn. "The meal will be simple, but filling and hot. Food shall be sent to your men, as well." She was grateful for the ritual formula of a castle greeting to distract and direct her: food and drink and cordialities before business, except in emergencies.

"Our thanks, lady," the earl said gruffly, then looked away to ask Wat about the horse stock in the stable.

"Lady Emlyn," Nicholas de Hawkwood said, beckoning to her. Emlyn turned to see him perched against the table, fondling Cadgil's ears. Frowning with resentment, she wondered why the dog, who never left the comfort of the fire for anyone but the family, had gone to the baron. She went to him as well, dreading the encounter. Though he had been silent about his injury, she assumed he wished to have his wound tended.

The baron leaned toward her until his head was close to hers. When he spoke, his voice was so quiet, dark velvet on a breath, that she, too, leaned forward, straining to hear. Mixed odors of wood smoke, metal and leather, and a tired, sweaty smell lingered about him. To her confusion, she found it warm and masculine and quite pleasant, and though she knew she should step away from him, should be repulsed, something held her there.

"Do you order food for us now, my lady," he said quietly, "you should know that Lord Whitehawke eats no meat."

"But Easter is past, Lent is done," she said, confused.

"No Lenten penance, this. He never eats animal flesh."

"None? How does a man live without meat?" Unable to

conceal her surprise, she glanced over her shoulder. Whitehawke hardly looked deprived.

"Fish is his only flesh food," de Hawkwood answered.

"Why is that?" She placed her fingertips over her lips, about to apologize for so personal a question.

The baron seemed not to mind her impertinence. " 'Tis a penance," he answered, shrugging.

What a sin the earl must have committed, to vow so, she thought. "A priest set such a penance?"

"He set it himself, long ago." As he turned his head a beam of late sunlight touched his face, filling his eyes with a sudden gray-green transparency. Long black lashes lowered over the brief gleam. His cheeks, peppered with short dark hairs, were suffused with a rosy blush above a firm jaw and a pleasantly shaped mouth. "A well-deserved penance," he murmured.

Sensing that she could ask no more, though she burned with curiosity, Emlyn pressed her lips tight. The baron leaned against the table, resting his injured leg, long fingers idly scratching the dog's head. Cadgil wore an expression of silly contentment. "Shall I send for someone to tend you, sire?"

He turned his gaze on her. "Pardon?"

"Will you have someone—ah—tend to your needs, my lord?"

"I will accept a hot bath later this even, my lady."

She nodded. "A servant will prepare your bath in the solar."

He leaned close. "I would prefer that you attend me, my lady." His low voice seemed to hum in her chest.

She gaped at him, and he lifted one eyebrow slightly. "My lord," she said crisply, "I will be glad to offer you the customary bathing of the feet, and can divest you of your armor. If you require assistance, the squire Jenkin can help you. I will fetch a skilled healer—"

His quiet words cut across hers. "In this matter, my lady, 'tis best if you attend me alone. Only one other knows of my—er, disability. Since I cannot call a knight out of the field to tend my bath, and you can be present by custom, you will do so."

Emlyn nodded, feeling a rush of her earlier guilt. Beckoning to Jenkin, who waited at one end of the room, she ordered the bath for later, and gave instructions to be relayed to the cook concerning the meal, taking care to request that a fish or egg dish be added for the earl. With a small swell of pride, she knew that the food would come quickly and would be of the best quality, even if supplies were low.

Jenkin took off at a lanky half run, scattering rushes as he went, and tore down the stairs, calling for the steward.

"Your servant seems ill-trained," observed Whitehawke.

Emlyn whipped her head around, startled. "He is not a servant, sire, but a squire. He fosters here, first with my father, and then with my brother Guy. He is young, and full of the eagerness of youth."

"He should be whipped for leaving a hall in such an unseemly manner," Whitehawke returned.

"I have never had any servant or squire beaten, nor did my father or mother before me," Emlyn replied curtly.

"My lord Whitehawke, if I may interrupt," Wat said mildly, "the lad is bare twelve, a good lad, the son of a cousin of Lord Percy. While Lady Emlyn will not allow any servant to be beaten, they accord her the finest loyalty."

"They must have been trained by charm, sire," drawled the baron. "I vow 'tis not the strict discipline that your lordship would demand. And yet there are castles where discipline and beatings are lax, and the servants still perform satisfactorily."

"I would not tolerate such in a castle of mine," Whitehawke growled. "A lord rules best with a hard fist."

"Aye, 'tis the philosophy of your house, sire," his son replied. "Ah, behold. Here are the servants come to set our table, and behind them, the first part of the feast arrives." He gestured toward the doorway, where Jenkin and three servants entered, carrying platters and dishes. Nodding to Emlyn, he sketched a little bow. "Beauty and grace triumph over the whip."

Uncertain of his mocking tone, Emlyn decided the better course for her was to address the task at hand. She began to supervise the setting of the table and the arrangement of several platters, which were brought in and set on a small side table.

A serving woman spread a bleached linen cloth over the

oak table and laid down a silver saltcellar with an elaborate cover shaped like a dove, and two silver spoons with engraved handles. Square bread trenchers, thick and pale, were placed beside covered dishes, and wooden platters of apples and cheese were set down as well.

Jenkin stepped forward to serve the meal, and the other servants left the room, bowing awkwardly toward Whitehawke, obviously unused to demonstrating homage. As the guests sat and rinsed their hands in rosewater, Wat excused himself, saying he would ensure that Whitehawke's garrison was provided for before dark. Emlyn declined to sit with them, waiting nearby.

"Is the fish fresh?" Whitehawke asked.

"Of course, my lord, caught from our own garden pond," she answered. Whitehawke nodded and accepted a portion of a trout pie, while his son was served a savory meat and vegetable stew. When Jenkin offered roasted onions and baked apples, Whitehawke, chewing vigorously, gestured toward the onions.

" 'Twas with grief that I heard of your father's death, Lady Emlyn," Whitehawke said, salting his food heavily with his fingers as he spoke. He picked onions and carrots and bread sops out of his trencher with his knife, ignoring the spoon. "His death, and the imprisonment of your brother, has placed Ashbourne in a precarious state. The push of one greedy baron or another would do you in without the king's generous protection."

"King John has afforded us no protection, my lord," she said, puzzled.

"But he has been most interested in Ashbourne." Whitehawke locked a brief glance with his son.

Nicholas de Hawkwood signaled that he was finished, though he had eaten little, and Jenkin quickly removed the trencher.

"My father and I have been at court for several weeks," the baron said. " 'Twas there that we heard of your father's death and the arrest of your brother Guy. Many wondered who might take over this parcel."

"Take over the parcel!" Emlyn straightened indignantly. "My brother is baron of Ashbourne by right. He paid the succession dues, but the king arrested him because the relief fee was higher, suddenly, than what had been paid. Ashbourne's revenues have been exhausted by taxes and dues and fines, and the king even claims the profits to come from this spring's lambings and wool. But when the last of what is owed is sent to the king, my brother will be released. 'Tis a hateful fee, a ransom in truth, but 'twill be paid. No one will take this land, my lord."

"But your brother is young," Whitehawke said. "And a young baron is often no baron at all. As well, the king suspects your brother of treason."

"Treason!" she exclaimed. "I have heard no charge of this."

"He has been sympathetic with those rebellious barons who, since last autumn, have demanded a charter of liberties," Whitehawke said smoothly. "He is known to have met with other barons at Bury St. Edmunds concerning the old charter of King Henry, on which some think to base a new charter. Your brother has not paid his relief, and refused the scutage fee last year when he and many other barons refused to fight for King John in France," he said as he shot a venomous look at his son. "It rests with the king to decide what shall be done with your brother's inheritance, since the property of a criminal becomes that of the crown." Cutting into a pulpy baked apple with his eating knife, he slipped a wedge into his mouth.

"I wish to know the contents of the king's message," Emlyn said through gritted teeth. "Is my brother safe and well?"

"For now, Lady Emlyn," Whitehawke said, demolishing the rest of the soft brown apple, "I thank you for a fine meal." He dabbled his fingers in the rosewater and wiped them on linen. "Soon you will know the contents of the king's writ. Excuse me. I would consult with my men." He stood and nodded, then crossed the room, his heavy boots beating a forceful rhythm.

Emlyn expected the baron to rise as well, but he stayed, thoughtfully watching his father's exit. Golden firelight played across the lean planes of his stubbled jaw and slender nose. He looked, she thought, like a painted sculpture of a brooding, armored Saint Michael, colored with deep tones, beautiful and severe. The only softening of the image was in the mahogany mass of his hair, which feathered and waved against his cheek and the firmly muscled column of his neck.

He turned his head to look at her. Beneath dark brows, his eyes shone like smoke reflected in a silver cup. "By your leave, lady," he said softly, rising. With a whispered unevenness in his gait, he crossed the room and disappeared through the curtained doorway. By the hearth, Cadgil raised his head briefly to pant after the baron, then rested again.

"Ungrateful wretch," she murmured affectionately to the dog as she passed by in pursuit of the baron.

The small foyer was lit by glowing resinous torches set in iron sconces high on the wall. As she glided through the curtain, the baron turned around and nearly collided with her. "This message is more than another demand for money," she insisted. "Tell me. I would hear it now."

"Nay," he said. He did not step away, and neither did she.

"What of my brother? Tell me, my lord."

"I think not." He lifted his chin to gaze slowly around the foyer, hands on hips, the torchlight edging his profile. "This mural stair is a fine space for decoration, my lady."

The foyer and staircase, called the mural stair because it was claimed from the thickness of the massive outer wall, or mural, of the keep, was a simple broad platform with stone steps leading down to the wide, arched outer door. Another flight of curving steps led upward to the bedchambers.

The walls of the mural stair were covered with images. Flowing, sinuous figures and decorative borders were painted on plaster coated over the stone, and gleamed with deep rich color in the amber light. Flanking the entrance to the great hall, two armored knights faced each other on red-caparisoned horses. Angled down the side stairwell, white-robed archangels floated over diamond-patterned backgrounds of red and blue.

"These paintings are skillfully made," he said. "Are they the work of some local artist?" He glanced down at her.

Hesitating, Emlyn groped for an appropriate response, distracted by the matter of the king's writ. The baron indicated the paintings and asked his question again. She pursed her lips and frowned. The paintings were partly her own work, done over a year ago with her uncle Godwin, shortly after

her return from the convent. Bad winter weather had extended one of Godwin's rare visits to his brother's family,
and he had begun the wall friezes then, the knights as a gift
to Emlyn's father, the angels in memoriam to her mother.

Proud of her uncle's ability, Emlyn was entirely uncertain
of the value of her own contribution, which consisted of the
decorative borders, and the hands and feet and flowing drap-
eries of the archangels. More accustomed to painting tiny
manuscript images, she had learned a good deal that winter
about creating large-scale wall imagery.

"My uncle, Godwin of Wistonbury Abbey, did them," she
answered finally. She would far rather discuss the king's
document. "He is a monk in York, and trained as a painter.
He does murals for parish churches, sometimes castles. The
income is a benefit to his order, so he has dispensation to
leave the abbey occasionally. At Wistonbury, he heads a fine
scriptorium."

"He has a strong command of color and line. I know the abbey. 'Tis not far from Hawksmoor Castle, my home," he said.
"Perhaps I shall acquire a manuscript from there." He turned to
study the painted section of the two jousting knights in the faint
flickering light, his chain mail creaking quietly as he moved. "I
should like to examine these more carefully in the morning before we depart," he said.

Emlyn was seized with a sudden chill, not of flesh but
spirit, an apprehension, as if he referred to her leaving with
him. She blinked away the thought. Certes, he spoke of his
departure in the morn with his father and the garrison.

He looked down at her, improperly close in the small
space. The faint fragrance of wine and cinnamon wafted as
his warm breath gently stirred her hair. When she shifted
away, he went with her, and his arm pressed close to her
shoulder as they stood side by side looking at the frieze.
"Perhaps I will even request that your uncle come to
Hawksmoor," he mused.

She glanced up. The lean planes of his face, the dark gloss
of his hair and the deep glints in his eyes reflected the warm
light, lending him such a striking beauty that, for an instant,
Emlyn found it difficult to concentrate on the conversation.
His broody intensity existed in more than dark elegance,
steely eyes, and a reserved manner. Every word, every action,

seemed to have an undercurrent, like a river, silent, secretive, powerful.

She did not know what to expect from him. Because he had seemed utterly somber and without humor, she had thought to be berated soundly, and publicly, for her deed in the forest. Yet he had barely acknowledged that she had shot a hole into his leg hours earlier. His discretion confused her enormously.

She wondered if his silence honored some inner chivalric code, or if, instead, he plotted some hideous revenge. Like the dangling sword in the ancient story, a threat swung over her own head as long as the de Hawkwoods were at Ashbourne. Let them deliver the king's message, she prayed, and depart in the morn.

". . . of a sanctified nature?" She stared up at him, her eyes widening slowly. What had he said? She frowned and scrambled to put the lost echo of his words together. He had spoken further about his castle Hawksmoor, but she had not been listening.

He leaned closer, the low, mellifluous vibratto of his voice entering her skull. "You are pale, and seem distracted, my lady. I will say it again." He enunciated precisely, as if she were deaf. "There is a new chapel at Hawksmoor. Might your uncle agree to paint images there, of a sanctified nature?"

"You must ask his superior, the abbot," she answered primly, embarrassed at her inattentiveness. She hoped his leg pained him, she thought sourly, standing so long beside her.

"Then I shall do so."

"Tell me what the king's document says," she said. "Tell me what you know of my brother Guy."

"Nay," he answered.

"Why have you brought so many men here?" she asked. "Do you need an armed garrison against a girl and three babes?"

"Three babes?" he asked, looking perplexed.

"I have two small brothers and a sister," she replied. "One of whom is little more than an infant. We will give you no trouble, sirrah, should you choose to take our home by force."

"No one mentioned an infant." He frowned, distracted.

"And force is not our mission here." Placing both arms on either side of her head, he trapped her against the wall. The light glinted off the mesh that covered his arms, and his breath was spicy with onion and cinnamon as he stood over her.

"I have had some little trouble from you already today, demoiselle," he reminded her softly. "I do not anticipate more. Cease your questions, and accept what comes."

She felt pinned by his eyes, thoroughly aware of his strength and masculinity. For a wild moment she thought he was going to lower his head and kiss her. She pressed the back of her head against the wall and pinched her mouth shut, staring at his lower lip, full and soft, and the even white teeth behind it.

"The king's document is not my doing," he said. "God knows, if I had been consulted, it would read differently than it does."

"Tell me some word of my brother, sirrah," she said.

He looked at her for a long moment. "Your brother is alive and fares well, from what little I have heard of him," he finally said. Dropping his arms, he stood back. "Now direct me to the solar, my lady. I would rest until my father returns."

"That little door in the far corner leads up some steps to the gallery, where you will find the solar," she answered. De Hawkwood nodded curtly and spun on his heel.

Emlyn, shivering in the cool air, grabbed her green cloak from the row of wall pegs by the stairs, whipped it around her shoulders, and returned to the deserted hall. She went to the hearth and knelt beside Cadgil, who nuzzled at her hand and rested his head on her knee until she rubbed under his jaw, staring into the flames.

Chapter Four

Whitehawke's voice was deep, tinged with arrogance and capable of thunder. Listening to the formal opening phrases of the king's document, Emlyn sat in a chair angled toward the fireplace, her hands and feet cold, her throat dry as straw.

Nearby, within the wide pool of light emanating from the huge fireplace, Nicholas de Hawkwood leaned against the oak table. Wat stood beside her, a fierce guardian, his jaw set like iron.

"Let it be known and carried out with expedience," Whitehawke read, "That all properties belonging to the barony of Ashbourne are forfeited to the crown. Guy de Ashbourne shall remain in our custody due to the debt of five thousand marks owed the crown."

"Five thousand!" Emlyn exclaimed indignantly. " 'Twas two thousand marks just past Yuletide!"

Whitehawke slid her a sharp look and read on. "The youngest issue of Rogier de Ashbourne are given into the care of Nicholas de Hawkwood until the debt is paid in full to the crown."

Emlyn gasped. The king would have the children. She had not anticipated this. She dug her fingernails into her palm and looked at the baron, whose face was shadowed and unreadable. He seemed cold and military, hardly someone to entrust with children. Her brothers and sister were very young, Christien not even old enough to foster in a knight's household, Isobel timid as a rabbit, Harry barely even walking. Holy Mother Mary, she prayed, help me to endure.

She knew that the king had taken other children, ostensibly as wards, but actually as hostages. Some had never been heard from again. A few years earlier, several little boys,

Welsh princes, had been made political hostages. They had been hung. Uncurling her fingers and breathing deeply, she forced herself to concentrate. "Continue, my lord," she said.

Whitehawke bowed his head and handed the document to his son. Nicholas de Hawkwood explained, summarily, that Ashbourne Castle had been bestowed upon Whitehawke for the good of the estate. "In addition, there is to be an exchange from Ashbourne to the crown of thirty oxen or twenty men, in good faith."

Emlyn listened with a growing numbness. She doubted there were even fifteen guards in total at Ashbourne now, and the oxen were all in use by her villeins.

"Lady Emlyn," the baron said, "the king declares your betrothal in marriage to Lord Whitehawke."

Her downcast eyes flashed open to meet Nicholas de Hawkwood's steady gaze. In the firelight, gossamer strands of hair glistened and curled around her face, and she felt the flush drain from her cheeks.

Inwardly, she fought against pricking tears. Her throat constricted and her breath came quickly. Think, she admonished herself, 'tis not a moment for weeping, but for a clear head. Even had she anticipated such an action, what power did she have against it?

King John could strike with cruel efficiency when he wanted to render a baron helpless. Using the parchment writ, he had torn apart her family as surely as a beast tears its prey. Guy would remain in prison, perhaps die there, his home and lands granted to another; the children might never return to her care; and she had been promised in marriage, without her consent, to an old man with a cruel reputation.

The enormity of the king's animosity threatened, like a violent storm, to overwhelm the remaining structure of her life. She swayed briefly, and through a haze, felt Wat place a steadying hand on her shoulder.

Closing her eyes and breathing slowly, she felt as if a cool, numbing fog filled her. Another breath, and another, and she was able to raise her head with a measure of dignity, and look at de Hawkwood. His steely gaze did not waver from hers.

"Can the king do this?" she asked him in a hollow tone. He nodded slowly. Emlyn fought to separate her gaze from his. She turned to Wat. "In truth, this is a minor dispute. I do not understand the king's actions. What then of Guy?"

Wat snorted in disgust. "King John does what he pleases, my lady. 'Tis apparent he sees no minor dispute here, and has set a mighty sum upon it. His pouches must be empty again, and his ire has been raised by the rebellious actions of so many barons asking him for a charter of liberties of late. I'll wager others are feeling a similar sting from him."

"If your brother is accused of treason, the king has a right to punish him and his. There is no merit in argument, my lady," Whitehawke said. Emlyn could not bring herself to look into Whitehawke's pale, icy stare.

"Surely King John knows that women, babes, and sticks of furniture will give him no resistance," Wat responded bitterly.

A low bench beside her chair held a chess game, its progress interrupted. Emlyn reached out a slim finger to touch an alabaster playing piece, her brow furrowed. "Women are as pawns in the game that men play all over England," she murmured. "Not even queens, only pawns to be shoved here and there and bits of land taken with them."

She raised her head. Irresistibly and inexplicably, she was drawn again to the intent, calm gaze of the young baron.

"You cannot refuse a marriage ordered by the king, Lady Emlyn," he said evenly. "Nor may you keep the children with you once they are officially removed from your custody." Emlyn, hearing his low, soothing tone, wondered fleetingly if he had some sympathy for her predicament after all.

"My consent will be needed for the marriage," she answered.

"Consent is not necessary," he answered bluntly. Whatever she had imagined in his tone had shuttered. Feeling very much alone, despite Wat's presence, and gripped by a strong, sudden fatigue, she slumped a little in the chair.

"Best prepare your belongings, my lady, and those of the children," Whitehawke said gruffly. "We depart on the morrow." To Nicholas he added, "I will check into the arrangements for the garrison before I retire. Should you sleep this night within the castle, see that you do not cuckold me with my bride." With a brisk turn, he strode rapidly from the room.

Through the mist of her tumultuous feelings, Emlyn heard the bitter distrust in Whitehawke's words to his son. Though she looked up at the insult, Nicholas de Hawkwood remained silent.

Emlyn picked up a stone chess piece and rolled it in her palm. The alabaster was smooth and cool, quite unlike the fire beginning to blaze within her. Inwardly, she churned with fury at the king's raw injustices. And Whitehawke's vicious directive to his son had felt like a direct, physical blow to her gut.

Her upbringing urged her to accept this as her woman's lot. But years of strict religious discipline, meant to subdue undesirable attributes in the female character, suddenly collided with the early years of freedom under her parents' gentle care. The natural spark, the resolute spiritedness that had fueled her childhood, long discouraged and cooled, now caught flame as she sat and idly twirled the little stone chess piece in her hand.

With a sudden ferocity, she knew that she could not acquiesce easily to the king's demands. Uncertain what she might do in particular, she had, at least for the moment, a direction: unaccustomed, impulsive, and necessary resistance. However futile it was to object to a royal order, objections rose inside of her and demanded expression.

She stood, and her cloak slipped from her shoulders to pool, forgotten, on the rushes. Her slender form was silhouetted against the firelight, and her hair fell freely to her hips in a dazzling halo. Squaring back her shoulders, her spine straight as an arrow, she raised her chin and looked directly at Nicholas de Hawkwood.

"Obeisance to our king is expected of all his subjects," she said. "But this betrothal is made without my consent. Such marriages are not legal in the sight of God and the Church."

"The Church continues to debate that. However, the matter does not give my father much concern," he replied, his eyes locked with hers.

"And you, sirrah, become the children's guardian against my will as their natural, God-given guardian." She drew a breath against the anger that fought for release. "If there is a way to stop this assault to my family, rest certain I will find it."

The alabaster chess piece was clenched tightly in her fist. On angry impulse, she flung the stone at the wall, not thinking where she aimed it. Flashing narrowly past Nicholas's head, it cracked against the fireplace hood and fell to the floor. Emlyn spun on her heel and exited the hall as quickly as she could.

Nicholas retrieved the stone pawn and weighted it in his hand. Then he flipped it over to Wat, who caught it deftly.

"It seems even a little pawn could crack a man's skull," Nicholas said wryly. Eyes wide, Wat nodded in agreement.

De Hawkwood turned to pour a fresh cup of wine. "In sooth, Sir Walter," he said, "Lady Emlyn is assuredly a fine beauty. In that, my father has done well." He downed some of the wine and pursed his lips a moment. "But she has a sharp temperament. At first, I admit, I thought her a woodenhead. 'Twould be better if she was, for a thinking wife is often a dangerous thing." He sipped again. "Or so my father would believe," he added softly.

The heavy oak door slammed against the stone jamb with enough force to wake the dead. Emlyn cursed long and loudly as she marched the length of her small bedchamber, setting two fat candles to flickering as she passed by. She paced anxiously, stopping to punctuate a breathless tirade with an occasional kick to the bedstead, the door, and on a particularly aggravated turn at the corner, to the stone wall.

Hearing a soft knock, Emlyn yanked the door open, nearly spilling Tibbie into the room. "Sir Walter himself came as I was putting the wee ones to bed," Tibbie said.

"He told you of the king's message?"

"Aye, he did that." Tibbie went to a wooden chest and knelt with a heavy sigh, settling her skirts around her wide body. She opened the lid and began to sift through its tumbled contents.

"Yer things are ever in a tangle," she said, "and ye shall need fine things for yer marriage day." She pulled out a gown of mauve sendal, its shimmering folds creased. "This will do, with a hang by the fire."

"I shall not dress to please this king's demon," Emlyn snapped, stomping over to sit sullenly on the bed.

"Aye, my lady girl, 'tis no great matter what you wear," Tibbie conceded, speaking gently. "But these men mean to take you away on the morrow. I shall pack as much as I can for the journey." She watched Emlyn's downcast face for a moment. "Ah, by the sweet Virgin, it angers my heart to know that a stranger can do this to ye, with naught to be done in yer defense. But such is life. We must make of it what we can."

Emlyn said nothing. Tibbie chattered on, not much caring for silence except in church. "I vow, those years spent in the convent did naught for yer sense of how to keep yer things in good order." She glanced up quickly. "Still, ye'll be a fine countess, as fine a lady as yer lady mother and yer sister Agnes, who is a capable prioress at Roseberry Abbey."

Emlyn ran her fingers wearily through her hair, sweeping it away from her face. "I once thanked the Blessed Virgin that Agnes's choice freed me from the convent walls. Would that I had stayed there," she added darkly.

"Wellaway, yer father knew ye were not made for the contemplative life, and he brought ye out of there."

Emlyn nodded glumly. "While I could sit at a desk for long hours working at my pictures, I could not kneel so long in prayer, as do Agnes and her nuns."

"Lord Rogier also called ye back for the sake of the little ones, and to take yer lady mother's place here." Tibbie leaned back on her heels and regarded Emlyn with her bright gaze. "And a more loving mam they could not have had. 'Tis cruel to take them from yer care. Mayhap when yer wed, they can be sent to yer new home, though yon Whitehawke seems a sour old goat. Yer father would have seen ye married well and proper. Not like this."

Lifting and folding as she spoke, smoothing each garment, Tibbie made neat piles of wool and silk: long, tight-sleeved gowns, soft loose chemises, and neatly shaped hosen. Plunging her ample arm back into the chest, she drew out a silk veil.

"I shall be up the night, packing yer chests with all ye own. These men are fools. How can this be done in one night? Ye must have bed linens, and furniture, and Lord

knows how many things will be needed for the children—"
Tibbie quickly stifled a sob behind her hand.

Emlyn raised her hand to her forehead wearily. Her hair
streamed around her, glistening in the candlelight. "Oh,
Tibbie. By all the saints, what has happened takes my very
breath. Guy, the castle, the children—all gone"—she sucked
in sharply, fighting a sob—"and I am to marry an old man."

Tibbie shook her head slowly. " 'Twas for coin this was
done. Our lord king is no better than a cutpurse with a black
heart, God forgive me," she said, rolling her eyes upward.
"But harken. Many a girl has wed an older man quite happily," she said, so brightly that Emlyn glanced at her with
suspicion. " 'Tis said that William the Marshal and his wife
joy in their marriage."

"Whitehawke is so cold, with his white hair and pale skin.
He has the eyes of a dead man," Emlyn muttered.

"Never say such a thing!" Tibbie gasped, crossing her
bosom. "Ye know not—" she stopped abruptly, her eyes
wide.

"What is it?" Emlyn demanded. Tibbie shook her head
rapidly. "Say me what you know!"

"Oh, my lady. They say Lord Whitehawke did an evil
thing long ago, and now must make amends, or his soul is
condemned to hellfire forever."

"What evil thing?" Emlyn asked. "Who says?"

"The steward told me, and Wat mentioned, that the earl
eats no fleshmeat as penance—"

"This I know. Buy why?"

"And he founded a convent to pray for her soul—"

"Whose soul!" Emlyn exclaimed, leaning forward.

"They say the earl murdered his first wife. The baron's
mother." Tibbie looked at her with wide, anxious blue eyes.

"Ah, God." Emlyn bowed her head. "I feel in my bones
there is some truth to this. The earl and his son bear each
other a deep, bitter hatred. I want no part of such a vile family, Tibbie. How can I break this betrothal? And the children
need me, Tibbie, they cannot go with that—baron—" Emlyn
stood suddenly, and began to pace the room, not agitated,
but pensive.

"The king commands, my lady, and ye must obey. 'Twill

serve yer brothers and sister better if ye do. With all his pen-
ances and prayers, the earl's soul is likely redeemed."

"None can offer me aid in this but myself," Emlyn said
thoughtfully. "There has to be some way to end the betrothal."

"Emlyn, harken now. Obey church and king. 'Tis yer
woman's lot, though ye've been dealt a sad portion of late,"
Tibbie said gently. "Yer sweetness may be just what
Whitehawke needs. What he did was long ago. And I expect
ye'll be apart from the little ones only a short while."

Emlyn scowled, her skirt a swirling shadow as she traced
the perimeters of the little chamber. Then she stopped, and
slanted a look at Tibbie. "There must be some way to gain
the children back into my custody, if I have to steal them
myself."

"Go with care, or ye may regret it," Tibbie murmured.

"I care not what Whitehawke desires of a wife. If I can
find no way out of this marriage, then I will paint or draw
or practice archery as I have always done, and he can like or
dislike, 'tis no matter to me. Perhaps he will have done with
me if I displease, and let me go to a nunnery."

"Well, 'tis not a fine way to begin a marriage, but 'tis better than ye were," Tibbie sighed, rolling her eyes.

A knock at the door, sharp and quick, interrupted them.
Tibbie pulled the door open to admit a young servant girl.
"What is it, Jehanne?" Emlyn asked.

"The young baron, my lady. He sent me to fetch you to
tend his bath."

"What!" Tibbie said. "Tell his lordship that Lady Emlyn
has retired for the even. Have the lady tend to his bath, by
all the holy virgin saints, I—"

"Jehanne." Emlyn cut across Tibbie's tirade. "Tell the
baron that I will come." The servant stood still, her mouth
slightly open in surprise. "Go, Jehanne, before your tongue
dries out."

When the door was shut, Tibbie thrust her face toward
Emlyn, her hands fisted on her hips. "What do ye do? No
chatelaine need tend to a knight's bath, 'tis an old custom
and none abide by it now. If ye mean to wipe his feet, that's
done by some, but ye should stay here and send yer regrets!"

"I must go, Tibbie. And I would ask you to fetch clean

bandaging cloth, with a poultice of comfrey, or something for a muscle wound, and join us there. Be ever quiet about what you bring, hide it beneath a towel. Pray, Tibbie, do this for me."

Tibbie gawked at her. "Sir Walter did say ye winged a chessman at the young lord, but I did not know ye'd left him bleeding by the fireside."

"Just be there, Tib." Emlyn opened the door and left.

The chamber her parents had shared, and where Emlyn and her siblings had slept as small children, was airy and pleasant, even at night. A tall triple-arched window, shuttered now, dominated the room. Fragrant green rushes mixed with herbs made a thick carpet, and flames crackled brightly in the hearth. At the center of the room was a large wooden tub filled with hot water, steam rising in misty whorls. Jehanne stood in the shadows by the wide bed, folding linen towels.

Nicholas de Hawkwood, standing near the hearth, turned as Emlyn entered. He flicked a glance at the maid. "That will be all," he said. "Leave us."

Emlyn sighed. "Thank you, Jehanne. You may go." When the girl had gone, the baron shrugged off his blue surcoat. It fell to the floor in a heap.

"Help me with my armor, my lady," he said. She came close and stretched to untie the leather thongs that connected the hood to the neckpiece, and that to the hauberk. He stood motionless, his breath on her cheeks and hair. The back of her hand scratched against his stubbled jaw, and he lifted his chin away, barking directions at her all the while.

She helped him ease off the mesh short-sleeved hauberk, so heavy that she stumbled a little with the weight of it. He reached out a hand and together they lifted it to a bench. Next he told her to remove the quilted vest beneath his hauberk, then his stiff leather boots, which she did.

"Cease with your orders, my lord," she finally said. "I am full aware how to divest you of your armor. I have an older brother and until last summer a father, both of whom accepted my help from time to time with this."

Sitting without comment on the edge of the bed, he untied the groin fasteners, and removed the armor from his right leg. When he bent to pull the mail legging off the wounded leg, she knelt to help him. Clad only in a long white linen shirt and quilted leg pieces, he began to tug next at the bulky trews.

"Give me a hand, 'tis crusted onto my flesh," he said. She hesitated and stepped away. "Come here, what in heaven are you shy about? 'Tis because of you I need this damned bath, now help me get out of these."

Emlyn knelt down before him and began to peel away the quilted leggings, first the right, which came away easily, then the left. His bare leg was long and tautly muscled, dusted with fine dark hairs, and he smelled of steel and leather and sweat.

As she pulled down the left trew, the blood-soaked cloth that had been stuffed inside popped up, stuck to his skin. She turned away to soak a cloth in the warm tub water, then softened the crusted bandage, gently prying it away.

When she saw the wound, Emlyn gasped. It was an ugly puncture, as large and deep as a man's thumbnail, gaping open and inflamed around the edges. "Oh! This looks very painful, my lord," she blurted, her hand resting gingerly on his thigh.

"Aye," he said. " 'Twill need a few stitches to close it."

Emlyn bit her lip as she wiped at the wound again. Without careful ministration, the muscle would not heal properly, and an infection could poison his entire body. A strong garlic and onion poultice would be necessary in the bandage overnight. She wondered in awe at his strength and endurance, for he had hardly limped, and had given no notice of his discomfort.

Brought up to manage a household, Emlyn knew something of healing arts. She had tended many a minor injury, and fevers and agues among her family and the servants; she had been present at birthings and maintained steady vigils at her parents' sickbeds, but she had never sewn living flesh together.

He winced as she pressed the wet cloth. After she finished, he began to unlace his bleached linen shirt. "I know 'twould be easier for my own man to help me with my bath, and for you to cleanse my feet only. But," he said, his voice muffled as he pulled his shirt over his head, "I have come here directly from the king's court with no valet. No one else need know of this injury. And since you inflicted it, you can help me now."

So saying, he stood, quickly unlaced his white woolen braies, banded like a loincloth around his hips, and lightly dropped them down. Emlyn gasped and turned away in confusion. She had a clear, if rapid, view of a long, sleekly muscled torso, dark hair swirling across his chest and down over his stomach. Below that, clustered black curls framed his thick, relaxed nether parts.

Emlyn blushed furiously. She had never seen a completely nude man, though she knew it was common for many women, even unmarried, to administer to male guests and relatives at the bath or for medical reasons. Modesty was not a great concern among men, she had heard. Here was certain proof of that.

She heard a splash and thunk behind her as he stepped into the tub and sank down into the steaming water with an audible groan that sounded like a mixture of pain and relief.

Embarrassed and uncertain of the propriety, and quite unwilling to stay alone with him for long, Emlyn fervently prayed that Tibbie would arrive soon with the necessary bandages and herbal ointments. Secrecy or not, Emlyn did not think it wrong to keep the injury from Tibbie, who was skilled with medicines. And who could stitch flesh.

Emlyn gathered a towel and a chunk of oil and herb soap from the table beside the tub, then handed him the soap, striving to keep her eyes averted. She felt the brush of his fingers as he took it from her, and then heard a series of splashes as he dunked his head into the tub to wash his hair.

Leaning back, he drew his knees up and rested his arms along the top of the deep, roomy wooden tub. She glanced at him. Firelight threw an amber web across his face and tautly muscled shoulders. His eyes were like silver stones, and his glossy wet hair curled around his high forehead. He had his father's smooth, clear complexion. Her searching gaze drifted to his mouth, the lower lip full and soft, the clean line of his jaw disrupted by a small crescent scar on the left side of his chin, showing pink and shiny through the shadow of the stubble. His chest above the water was covered with dark, wet hair.

For a tall man with a large frame, he was lean as a willow, his shoulders wide, square and powerful, his muscles smooth and tight. She knew that even the bulk of armor and cloak could not disguise the strength and grace of his long, lean build.

Suddenly Emlyn felt foolish, staring at him as if he were a feast for her starving eyes. How weak, how lustful, to succumb even for a moment to the visual temptation of his face and form. He was no welcoming feast for any eye, she reminded herself; his beauty was classic but hard-edged, and he had a disagreeable temperament.

Had he possessed a pleasing manner with his handsomeness, he would have been a fine man indeed. But such men—considerate of women's sensibilities, fair and kind—were rare. Most, but for her father, lived only in the epic stories that she loved to hear and read by the firelight. This man's harsh manner, his very presence in her home, irritated her beyond measure.

She sighed and picked up a towel. Still, she reminded herself, she was responsible for his injury. He had not disgraced her in the hall. His request for a bath was pallid compared to what he might have said in front of his father.

He was looking at her from under half-lowered lids, and she blushed again. "Shall I send for someone to shave you, my lord?"

He shook his head as he soaped his hair. "Nay, not tonight. And though 'twould likely be pleasant, I'll not ask you to scrub my back," he said. Squeezing a soapy cloth over his head, he shut his eyes as the foamy water ran down into his face. "But you may rinse my hair." He gestured blindly toward a bucket of clean water. Emlyn fetched it and lifted it over his head. The quicker this ordeal of the bath was done and over, the better.

She dumped the contents of the bucket, and the water coursed over his head and shoulders in smoking streams. He yelled and sat upright.

"God's blessed arse!" he bellowed, sputtering, "could you not make certain if 'twas hot or cold? You nearly scalded the skin off my bones!" Shaking his head, he rubbed the water from his eyes, and fixed her with a vicious glare.

"Oh, my lord, I am sorry," she said anxiously, patting the towel over his head and shoulders with genuine regret.

Snatching the cloth away, he held it to his face, then began to dry his hair with it. "God's eyes, woman, are you bent on murdering me this day? I've been arrowshot, near clubbed by a pawn, and now boiled like an eel. Are you serving poison in the wine this even as well? Shall I be on guard through the whole of the night, or shall I leave now to preserve my life?"

Emlyn had turned to fetch another dry cloth, and spun back to whip the towel into his face. It fell against his chest and sank into the water. "Certes, my lord, feel free to leave now. I shall haul open the gate for you myself!" She stepped away, intent on leaving him to his bath. He shot out his hand and grabbed her arm as she passed the tub.

"Hold, lady. I shall stay until my duty to the king has been properly discharged. And have you forgotten your duty to me?"

She looked down at him, her chest heaving. Heat rose in her cheeks, pink from the steaming she had given him. Her hair frilled wildly around her face and clung in damp curls to her neck. She knew she looked more like a serving wench than a noblewoman, and she hardly cared. If she did not squelch her anger soon, she would look like a hound from hell.

"Your wound will be tended, my lord," she said through her teeth. "Other than that, I have no duty to you."

His grip on her arm was wet and warm, and he tightened it. "None, lady? A pity," he murmured. "You fulfill your obligations so sweetly." His tone oozed sarcasm.

She tried to wrench away, but succeeded only in splashing her fingers in the hot soapy water. "Would you cuckold your own father, then?" she asked.

His fingers pressed deep. "You have the tongue of an adder."

"You have the heart of one. A man who would steal babes"—she pulled against his grip, her sleeve sopping.

He sat toward her, water cascading down his chest, lapping warm over her fingers. "This writ was not my doing, lady. We both are its victims." Slowly, while he spoke, he ran a thumb along the line of her wrist to her palm. Shivers spiraled through her arm, into her breasts, and sank into her belly.

With a wordless exclamation, she tore away from him, and he let her go. "If you are done with your bath, there is a chamber robe on the bed," she said haughtily, gesturing toward a garment of soft, pale wool that Jehanne had folded across the bed.

A loud rap on the door barely preceded Tibbie, who burst in before the sound had faded. "My lady," she said breathlessly, "I have brought bandages and ointment."

The baron gaped at Tibbie from his bath, and she scurried over to him. "Now, my lord, let me see yer head."

"My what?" he asked, dumbfounded.

"Yer noggin, where my lady bashed ye." She bent forward. Scooting the soaked towel carefully over his groin, he pointed with one finger toward the thigh wound, just visible below the surface of the water.

Tibbie gasped. "My lord! Lady Emlyn did that with a chess piece?"

"Nay, Tibbie," Emlyn said. "With an arrow." De Hawkwood cast her a quick frown, and she grimaced at him. "I will leave you two to deal with this. My part of the bargain is done, my lord. Your wound will be tended. Tibbie is a careful surgeon. Surely you would not want my hand upon you again this even."

"Surely I would not," he growled as Emlyn slammed the door behind her.

Chapter Five

"Demoiselle, you have directed your servants to over-load these carts." As Nicholas de Hawkwood walked briskly across the bailey toward Emlyn, his deep voice carried to her in the cold morning air. Raising one hand, he gestured toward two wagons piled high with iron-bound chests, rolled bedding and tapestries, and several large bundles wrapped in cloth. Servants brought yet more items to the vans.

There was no trace of a limp as the baron approached her. Although the dark circles below his eyes and the tension in his mouth and dark-whiskered jaw hinted at fatigue, he was once again the imposing knight she had met in the forest. A long surcoat of azure blue, belted low and patterned with embroidered golden hawks, covered his armor, and his cloak draped back from his wide shoulders. Freed of the mesh hood, his long dark hair whipped softly in the breeze.

De Hawkwood stood over her. "There are furnishings aplenty at Hawksmoor and at my father's castle at Graymere," he said. "I will order the second van unloaded."

Emlyn struggled to mask her growing rancor beneath serene features. "My lord baron," she replied, "the children are being forced to leave their home. I will not have them separated from all that is familiar. Those are necessary items."

De Hawkwood was silent as he watched the bustle surrounding the two wagons. One of his own men-at-arms, clad in the dark green surcoat worn by his garrison, emerged from the stables carrying a child's brightly painted wooden saddle and slung it onto the growing pile in the second wagon.

He shook his head in dismay. "Infants may require some

coddling. But you would fain send the entire keep, piece-meal."

"You have many soldiers equal to the task."

"Soldiers disdain to do the work of servants, though I see my own men are eager enough to do your bidding. But not a one will drive nor ride a cart. Lord Whitehawke and I will take one wagon only. By your leave, lady." Nodding curtly, he turned to go.

"Nay, sirrah, hold!' she said. Pausing at her haughty tone, de Hawkwood looked over his shoulder imperiously.

Anger flashing in her eyes, Emlyn moved toward him, then hastily cast her eyes properly downward and unfisted her hands. She would not relish being called an adder again.

"I also prepare to depart, my lord," she said. "Since my clothing chests and bed frame must be packed, and the windows need to be removed as well, prithee say to your father that we cannot travel until afternoon, or even the morrow.'

"By God's body, windows!" he exclaimed, turning full around.

Emlyn tilted her chin defiantly, unable to play demure any longer. "We have good glass windows at Ashbourne. I would have them packed and moved to my new chambers. If they remain here they will likely be broken by your father's soldiers."

"My lady," he said, his words clipped. "We are not leaving because the season has changed, or because the game has run out. We are not moving the household because you are bored and the minstrels have gone south. We are following royal orders to vacate immediately."

"By all that's holy, you ask three children to ride out like soldiers, with naught but the cloaks on their backs," she replied hotly, glaring up at him.

He glared back. "What drags down the axle of that van over there is hardly naught, my lady. One wagon will be loaded only. God knows it will slow us greatly."

Her trembling fingers, clutching the neck of her cloak, betrayed the inner tumult that she struggled to conceal. "Your father bid me ready the children and myself this day. 'Tis hardly past dawn, yet you seek to depart."

A muscle jumped rapidly in his cheek. "Strive no more to keep us here, lady. Whitehawke is impatient to be gone." His customary control appeared to waver dangerously, and he drew a long breath. "Aught else? I would hear it sooner than later."

Emlyn scowled up at him. "Walter de Lyddell should continue to steward Ashbourne in my absence. He knows the land, and our people here."

"I have already suggested as much to Whitehawke. Sir Walter is very capable, and Ashbourne will profit under his care."

"My mother's cousin, Mistress Isabelle—Tibbie—should accompany the children to Hawksmoor."

"My lady aunt will tend to their needs at Hawksmoor."

"Tibbie cares for them as if they were of her own womb, as she has looked after all the children of this family." Tears unexpectedly sprang and pooled in her eyes as she looked up at him. The slight lift of her head sent one drop in a tiny rivulet down her cheek.

De Hawkwood looked away quickly, then nodded his head with a resigned sigh. "Aye, then, your Tibbie may come with us."

Emlyn blinked, surprised at his compliance. His cheeks burned with a deep rosy tint that spread out of his unshaven jaw and sparked his gray eyes to blue-green, like an instant of sun in a cold sky. She stared at the transformation. No blush of emotion could warm this stone man, she thought; only cold air could redden his cheeks. His father's skin had the same tendency to color easily, she had noticed. But she was convinced that there were no tender hearts among the de Hawkwoods.

"Delay us no more, my lady," he said curtly, then turned away and crossed the bailey in long strides to join Whitehawke. Pensively she watched him walk away. De Hawkwood had rightly perceived her attempt to delay the children's departure. She desperately wanted more time with her siblings, and certain matters needed her attention before the castle and its affairs came under Whitehawke's control. She simply could not leave now.

At least a full day, probably longer, would be necessary to spread word to the tenants advising them of the change in ownership. She sighed. Whitehawke would not likely show

the same concern and generosity extended by the de
Ashbourne family.

Since childhood, Emlyn and her brothers and sisters had
known many of the families in the nearby villages and
farms. The land had been seised to the family by the Conqueror, and generations of Ashbourne barons had demon-
strated fairness and leniency as lords of the demesne.
Willing help had always come from the villeins at planting,
harvest, and market time, even now, when King John's taxes
and fines had begun to drain Ashbourne's full coffers.

The lord and his family had always given back to the people, in land, goods, coin or charity. When the monasteries
had closed during the interdict that had cast England out of
the church in penance for the king's actions, Rogier de
Ashbourne had taken responsibility for the charity cases
usually attended by the monks. This last winter, Emlyn had
made certain that the poorest families and the eldest villeins
were provided for.

She knew that King John's writ would change the very nature of the relationship between these people and their lord.
If Wat continued as castle seneschal, the lord's traditional
duty to the villeins would be met, as long as Whitehawke
did not interfere. She wondered how far the earl's cruelty
extended. Perhaps he reserved his hatred for members of his
own family.

Walking through the bailey yard, she approached the stable where Whitehawke stood with several others, including
his son. Tall and broad, the earl was conspicuous in his polished black armor and black cloak, his white hair flowing
over his folded hood. Nicholas de Hawkwood gestured toward the wagons, and his father barked out some comment.

Whitehawke turned abruptly as Emlyn neared, and glowered, his white eyebrows pushed low over his eyes. "I am
told there is much to be done before you are free to depart,
my lady."

"Aye, my lord," Emlyn stammered under his heavy, icy
stare. "There are certain matters that require my attention."

"There is no longer any matter at Ashbourne that need involve you. Only see to your packing." He glared at her, his
jowls trembling. "And we bring no windows with us, by the
bones of the saints!"

Emlyn inhaled sharply, throwing back her shoulders. These men obviously had moved few households, or they would know the value in removing good leaded glass windows to install elsewhere. The frames were transportable. The more Whitehawke and his son resisted, the more determined Emlyn became to bring the windows with her. Besides, hours would be required to remove and wrap them for the journey, hours that she needed.

"I shall not begin my wedded life with only a few garments hastily thrown in a sack. I must have linens, furniture, and my mother's windows. And the children need their own possessions."

"There'll be no colored church windows in my keep!" he roared. Two or three of his soldiers edged away.

The strain of the past evening and this morning had tested her mightily. Emlyn could hold her temper no further. "If you must have me to wife, sir, you shall have windows and more!" she said loudly.

Nicholas de Hawkwood turned away to smother a smile. Emlyn flicked a glance in his direction, then flashed her eyes back to Whitehawke, towering over her. His narrowed blue eyes were icy points in his broad, reddening face. True rage seemed to gather in his cold gaze, and Emlyn resisted an urge to step away.

The earl's voice had a low, dangerous hum. "Do as you please, lady, until you reach my castle and my bed. Then shall we learn who master and mistress be."

Emlyn paled at the implication. Whitehawke spoke to Nicholas. "We will wait no longer upon a bratling bride. I shall accompany your retinue part of the way. We depart within the half hour." Nicholas nodded briskly.

The earl turned back to Emlyn. "Stay you here at Ashbourne and fill wagons at your leisure, but quit this castle within the week. Hugh de Chavant, captain of my guard, will remain to escort you to my castle at Graymere."

Emlyn stared up at him, shocked into silence. Her efforts to delay the time of departure had gone terribly awry. The children would leave with Nicholas de Hawkwood's escort, with Whitehawke, but without her. In declaring that she was not ready, she had given Whitehawke an opportunity to outwit her.

"One week, my lady. Time enough to tear the privies from the towers if you wish them packed as well." Whitehawke turned his back abruptly and strode across the bailey.

Panic squeezed her chest and throat. She launched forward in pursuit, but de Hawkwood stepped quickly in front of her. As she careened into his mail-covered chest, he grabbed her shoulders to steady her.

Gulping in air, she twisted against his grip. "Dear God, you would truly take these children from me," she breathed hoarsely. "Let me go. I must speak to him."

"Hold, my lady. You are hardly the one to wrestle such a dragon as Whitehawke. Listen well. Be wary of Whitehawke, and provoke him not. Learn now that what he orders, you must obey."

A sob escaped her, and she pressed her lips shut. She refused to cry here, before servants and strangers. She would not dissolve into a helpless puddle in this man's arms. Anger, for the moment, formed the structure that held her together.

"God curse your father," she said between her teeth. She jerked away from his grip. "And you, my lord, should have greater honor than to take babes hostage. 'Tis a coward's way to siege a castle."

"My lady, I but obey the king," he replied tersely. "The children are surpassing young. I would rather not be burdened."

"Tell your king that I refuse both this betrothal and your guardianship." Her eyes flashed a cerulean flame. "I promise you, by God's will, I will have these children back from you."

"Brave words for a spit of a girl," growled de Hawkwood. "Do you have spiteful thoughts, my lady, learn to hold your tongue." He lowered his voice. "Some have been imprisoned for less."

"Prison, my lord, could have tortures no worse than what my family has endured of late!" As Emlyn whirled away, one golden braid whipped out with the force of her spin to brush his arm. Several delicate strands tangled in the steel mesh. Fuming, she gave the braid an angry yank, pulled loose, and stormed away.

"Damned daft knights, to follow such cupshotten royal orders," Tibbie muttered.

Emlyn reached over and lifted Harry's warm, solid weight from Tibbie's arms, nestling him against her hip. Isobel stood beside her, and Emlyn put out her free hand to stroke the child's glossy dark curls. "Go, Tibbie," she sighed, having explained the arrangements, "and pack your satchel."

Tibbie nodded, her eyes misted pink, and turned to walk forcefully through the bailey, not missing an opportunity to elbow one of Whitehawke's soldiers out of her path. Skirts flapping furiously, she mounted the outer stone steps of the keep, loudly voicing her opinions as she climbed.

Christien, just arrived from the stables, pulled at Emlyn's cloak, his brown locks unruly in the cool breeze, his eyes blue as sapphires and dancing with energy. Harry reached out a fat hand to tug at his brother's hair.

"Emlyn," Christien said, ducking Harry. "Can I ride with Sir Peter on his war-horse? Sir Peter said I might. I do not want to ride in the van with women and babes." He wrinkled his nose.

"Most of the way, you will be in the van. But if Sir Peter says aye, then you may ride some." She smiled at his simple, innocent excitement, in contrast to timid Isobel, who had clung close to Tibbie or Emlyn all morn.

Harry pulled at her cloak hood, obscuring her face, and Emlyn twisted away. Isobel and Christien laughed as she pried the cloth out of Harry's fat, stubborn fingers. The sweet childish trills swelled Emlyn's heart with love.

"Must we go with that wretched old white-haired man?" Isobel was petulant, a result of an early rising and the day's confusing events "He was mean to Cadgil in the hall at breakfast."

"Are we prisoners? Do we go to a dungeon?" Christien asked.

Emlyn kept her voice light to hide her apprehension. "Hush, dearlings. None of us are prisoners. Lord Whitehawke will go on to his own castle, called Graymere. You shall stay at Hawksmoor for a little while with Baron Nicholas." Uncertain how to tell them of her betrothal, she had not yet mentioned it. The children had been presented with enough changes for now.

"The baron I like well enough," Christien said. "He is fine and strong, and looks like a king. His black war-horse is called Sylvanus. Syl-van-us." Christien tried the name nimbly.

"Why do you not ride with us?" Isobel asked.

"There are matters I must tend to here first," Emlyn said gently. "You will be safe and happy at Hawksmoor, sweetings, until I come along later and fetch you."

Harry struggled to get down. Holding him firmly, she bent to squeeze the three children together into a lumpy, fierce hug, inhaling their combined odor, redolent of milk, wool, apple pasties, and warm young skin.

"Be brave," she said softly. "Christien, remember, a true knight protects those who need him. You and Isobel watch after Harry, and see that he always has someone near him." They nodded solemnly. "Be true friends all." She kissed each soft cheek. "I will come to you as soon as I can." No one, not even a king, she thought, can take you from me forever.

"Come, chickens, we shall make a cozy nest," Tibbie called on her way to the wagon, and the twins dashed off to join her.

The wagon was ready, the load strapped tightly, the horses harnessed, the canopy top set up to provide protection for those who rode within. As Emlyn carried Harry to the van, she saw that the vehicle swayed slightly, and was hardly surprised to discover Christien and Isobel bouncing wildly inside.

Wat leaned over the side of the wagon, and Christien and Isobel spilled out like puppies from a basket to climb into his arms. He held them both, then lifted them back inside and briefly touched Harry's head. His brown eyes crinkled with strain as he nodded to Emlyn and then to Tibbie before turning away abruptly.

When Tibbie was settled on a wooden crossbench, Emlyn kissed Harry again and lifted him into Tibbie's lap. Her eyes swam with distorting moisture. As if she moved through a dream, she kissed the twins, ruffled their silken heads, adjusted their cloaks, and reminded them to behave, to listen, to pray, to eat their meat and vegetables, to wash. Lastly, she embraced Tibbie.

The wagon lurched into motion, cushioned between ranks of horsemen riding in widely spaced pairs. Whitehawke rode in the lead. Nicholas de Hawkwood, with Peter de Blackpoole, passed her after the wagon lumbered away. The baron nodded briefly to her, his gaze piercing before he turned away.

Slowly the escort crossed the bailey, watched by the solemn servants who filled the yard. Wheels creaking, wooden body swaying rhythmically, the van rolled beneath the immense portcullis arch, followed by the last of the guards.

As Christien and Isobel lifted their hands to wave at Emlyn, their small pale faces were touched by a sudden bewilderment.

Four days later, by the time the escort skirted the ridge of the long dale that stretched out below Hawksmoor, Nicholas was exhausted. The cumbersome wagon had slowed them down, and the surprising number of necessary stops for the children had been an exasperating delay. The journey had taken much longer than he had planned.

Traveling north to the York shire by the old Roman roads had added the most time. Whitehawke had insisted on following roads that trailed over downs and past farms and nestled villages. Nicholas had ground his teeth in frustration whenever they circuited clusters of forest, forgoing those straight, quick paths. But the weather had been mild, and the children had proved remarkably hardy travelers despite a penchant for asking repeatedly if that manor house or this castle was Hawksmoor.

Now, at last, Hawksmoor was visible in the distance, three of its six curved towers glinting pale gray in the afternoon light. Seen from the south, the vast protective curtain wall rose as if cut from sheer rock, built on a promontory that jutted out over a river. The rock base sloped steeply away at the back to meet wide moors and forested land.

They would cross the river at a shallow place and travel around the perimeter of the impenetrable shell wall to the western barbican gate to be admitted. At the river, Whitehawke and his men would veer east for Graymere.

Nicholas breathed a sigh of relief in anticipation of that

splitting of ways. He turned to look at his father, who rode beside him, apparently caught up in his own thoughts.

"God's very bones. The Ashbourne chit is fierce as a cat," Whitehawke commented. "Mark me, she will soon comply like a proper wife. Once I have bedded her, she will learn to show quick respect." He smirked at Nicholas. "All a sharptongued woman needs is a taste of a proper man," he added slyly.

Nicholas pressed his lips together in silence, his cheeks reddening in fury, while his father laughed breathily.

"Better she were wed to me than to such as you," Whitehawke continued. "I fair doubt you could handle her will. But I'll not tolerate such arguing from any female."

"I vow we saw Lady Emlyn's temper because we took her home and her siblings away from her, my lord," Nicholas replied evenly, his fingers tight on the reins.

Whitehawke rode beside him for a while longer, then spoke again. "The wedding shall take place one month hence, time enough for all to arrive at Graymere, including the bride." The earl glanced over at his son. "Do not bring the brats when you come, I want no hearts rendered at my wedding feast. The girl will likely ask me to take them in."

"They are her family. No doubt she expects their wardship to be given over to her husband."

"King John has set the nursery chore upon your shoulders, not mine. Keep them at Hawksmoor until the king decides their fate. If he remembers them."

Nicholas sighed wearily at the thought of having permanent wardship. "I must decline your invitation, my lord."

"You will not." Whitehawke glared at his son.

"I leave for London soon."

"You ride with the barons who plan to roust the king!"

"Nay, my lord, though I go there to speak with them."

"Nay, say you? I know you support those rebels, the barons who are bent on destroying the very king who has enabled me to fatten the inheritance that may one day be yours!" The pinkish tint under the earl's skin deepened. "By God, I will get me another son and have done with you. The girl looks healthy enough to produce any number of worthy sons."

Nicholas did not flinch at his father's words. For years he

had heard that Graymere might be his, and might not. Far better, he had often thought, to have no inheritance than to have this one held over his head and snatched away regularly according to his father's mood. He had developed his own holding, Hawksmoor, inherited through his mother, into a thriving demesne. Graymere Keep, as far as he cared, could go to the dogs or to the monks when Whitehawke died.

He summoned patience. "The barons gather near London, not to overthrow the king, but to support the forming of the charter that we demand. Those few barons who actually threaten the king's life and property are rough dissidents, my lord." He had explained all this to his father before. "There are many who lend reason and logic to the rebellion."

"A dissident you were once. Surely you are as passionate in your objections to the king as Eustace de Vesci and his group." Whitehawke snorted contemptuously. "Overthrow the king, they mean to do. 'Tis a sad crossing we have come to. My generation understands loyalty to a king as yours does not."

"Many wish reform for English law, my lord, though you be not among them."

"Aye, and my company is strong. William the Marshal himself is against this action of the barons, as are many others."

"I have great respect for the marshal. There is no finer man in England. I believe he resists the charter out of loyalty and concern for King John. In any course, we are fortunate to have his sense and intelligence near the throne."

Whitehawke bristled. "Yet you disagree with a man whose experience and judgment far exceed your own?"

"I would see a better system for the baroncies, sire. We all must look to the future of our holdings. King John cannot be trusted. Who among us knows his property is safe, should the king have a fit of temper or greed? The fate of the de Ashbourne family could be my fate, or yours, one day."

"He is our king!"

"He is small-minded, and though he has a keen mind, he is full of poisonous bile. His taste for vengeance is too strong for us to suffer without check."

"Eustace de Vesci and Robert FitzWalter have vengeance on their minds as well," Whitehawke countered.

"That is true. Both of them have been directly insulted or harmed by the king's mean bent, and their resentments drive them on. They are good, strong leaders, but they have the rebellious faction under them. Other, calmer minds are involved in the movement. Many barons would have a set of guidelines, my lord. The king can fight a handful of barons and bring them to their knees, but he cannot stop the united power of nearly all the English barons." He shifted his reins, tightening them to halt his destrier, and looked directly at his father, who stopped beside him.

"The time has come for new laws in England," Nicholas said. "John is not the king that his father was. He is brilliant, aye, but he has no heart. The country slides into chaos beneath his heavy hand. We must protect our lands and our families from such abusive power. England has always had laws to protect its people. We cannot countenance a king who ignores laws."

Whitehawke was visibly perturbed, working his chest like a bellows, his face flushed, the color spreading into the roots of his white hair. "For me, I have had no trouble with John. He is generous and fair with those who support the good of England."

Nicholas huffed disdainfully. "The good of John, you mean."

Whitehawke glared at him for a moment, his eyes blue ice beneath furred white brows. Nicholas could hear the man breathe, loud and wheezing. "If these young barons had offered true obeisance to the king—as you each pledged to do when the sword was laid upon your shoulderbone—then we would not have this sorry state. You will be beaten down, every one of you. Why do you persist in supporting this bedeviled charter of liberties? God gives liberty to man through church and king. Men do not declare such for themselves."

"Mayhap 'tis time men tried, sire," Nicholas answered.

"I have misjudged you. I had hoped that you would lose the wildness in your heart. Your mother's blood taints you. Still, mayhap age will becalm you and bring you some sense."

A muscle bunched along Nicholas's jaw as he kept silent. He had given up long ago attempting to reason with his father, having tried both logic and rebellion. Whitehawke seemed to glory, at times, in his crystalline hard judgments: the world was as he declared it to be. No alternative point of view existed in Whitehawke's microcosm, and he dictated the shape of the larger macrocosm from within the center of his little sphere. Not even the tragic death of Nicholas's mother had showed him the faulty crack in the haughty structure of his world.

Eventually, Nicholas had accepted the futility of his efforts to explain his views to Whitehawke. Instead, he had learned to give away little of himself, keeping his distance unless forced into Whitehawke's company by king or by region, since Hawksmoor and Graymere were only eleven miles apart.

"Mayhap age is all I need," Nicholas replied dryly.

"Age has a settling effect," Whitehawke agreed affably. "And I look to this marriage to settle me further." He grinned suddenly, reminding Nicholas of a great large-toothed wolf. "But I vow I am young enough still to relish my fair bride."

The unwarranted image of his father behind bed curtains with Emlyn de Ashbourne, his meaty hands exploring her delicate body, made Nicholas's blood simmer with anger; he suppressed it with an effort. "I would speak with you concerning a particular matter, my lord," he said curtly.

"Eh? What is that?"

"I have lately had word from my seneschal that you have directed workmen to begin building in the northern end of Arnedale," he said. "That site is partly on land that belongs to me. I must ask that you order your workmen to cease."

Whitehawke slanted a look at his son. "'Tis not your land."

Nicholas sighed. "Let us not step into that mire. None of the land in the dale is yours, yet you persist in claiming it, and now building on it. My seneschal assures me that your latest project does indeed extend onto Hawksmoor land. Whether the rest of the dale belongs to you or to the abbeys of Wistonbury and Bolton is not part of this question. Simply instruct your masons to choose another place to build, and take up further argument with the abbots if you wish."

"I am tired to the bone of arguing with the abbots and with you over this matter. That dale is mine, from your mother's dowry, and I will prove it in time," Whitehawke growled.

"Do not build on my property, my lord," Nicholas said in a flat voice. "I will be forced to stop you if you continue."

"Hawksmoor is disputedly mine as well, do not forget," Whitehawke said. "However, since I have need of a keep in that area, the Arnedale site is best."

"I warn you, my lord. Cease this plan of yours."

"Would Hawksmoor not benefit from a well-fortified neighbor? There have been troubles enough in that area. Consider it well." Whitehawke nodded, then whipped his horse's flank and rode away.

Nicholas clenched his jaw and turned in the saddle, his eyes hooded and expressionless, to see the van pitching and rolling toward him. The children waved, and Nicholas lifted a hand, feeling a raw tug at his heart. He sighed gustily, releasing some of the tension left from speaking with his father, as he watched the wagon approach.

Taken from the familiar safety of their home, the children tumbled and cavorted now in the wagon, resilient, untroubled. But then, they had one another, and Mistress Tibbie, and a sister who had sworn to gain them back.

He remembered her slender hands reaching up to adjust the little girl's hood, to touch the boy's forehead. The loyalty and the love that existed so easily there was enviable. He might give whatever he had, he thought, to see such a love shine, even briefly, in his own life.

Only his mother, who had died when he was seven, had offered him such a pure love. Her memory lingered like a sweet refrain played on silver bells: a warm embrace, a gentle voice, shining dark hair scented with roses. Years later, he had learned what his father had done to her, and he had come to realize how much contempt his father held for him. Returning the sentiment had hardened his own heart.

Watching the van rumble along, he lifted the reins and allowed Sylvanus to walk slowly onward. He felt a sympathetic bond with the de Ashbourne children, for he, too, had been sent from his home at the age of six, to foster with his uncle, the Earl John de Gantrou, who was married to his mother's sister. But Lady Julian had reared him gently, and her husband had been a good man with a hearty laugh and a strong sense of duty. Peter and his own cousin Chavant had fostered there, too.

The strong, loving influence of his aunt and uncle had been a blessed counter to his father's opinion of him as he reached manhood. Whitehawke had made it quite clear that he considered Nicholas less than acceptable as a son or as a knight. Any weakness he had was pointed out, any strength he had was ignored.

He had developed a tolerance for much of his father's meanness, and felt that the resistant, reserved facet of his character was, perhaps, his mother's legacy. Lady Blanche had gracefully endured Whitehawke's cruelty and jealousy for years before it had killed her. That death, above all else, Nicholas found unforgivable.

But he sometimes sensed a human, vulnerable side to his father. He hesitated to judge Whitehawke as evil, knowing that his own life and deeds could measure ill, were he himself judged.

The children called out, asking him to wait, and he halted his horse. Rubbing the animal's sleek, smooth neck, he continued to muse as he watched the van draw nearer.

Surely there was no honor in taking these children from their home. At times he felt tainted with dishonor, like the sour undertaste of bad wine. As long as he stayed at odds with his father, honor would elude him. And as long as he continued secret defiances against Whitehawke, no matter that he acted on behalf of others who were harmed by his father's harshness, he would not know the full flavor of chivalry.

Emlyn de Ashbourne was right: taking children was a coward's ploy, unworthy of any baron who opposed King John. Her barb had stung as much as her arrow in his thigh. But she did not know that he had accepted the chore to keep the children from Whitehawke's custody. That, at least, he could do, though he owed Rogier de Ashbourne's family more, much more, than that.

Four years ago, wanting to repay a debt owed to her fa-

ther, Nicholas had made a discreet offer for Emlyn's hand.
He had been accepted by her parents, but the girl had been
young and still in a nunnery, and Rogier's death had pre-
cluded a final arrangement.

He was certain that no one knew of this offer. Now, with
the girl given to Whitehawke by royal writ, Nicholas could
only accept the guardianship of the children. But there had
to be a way to fulfill his debt to the family, and he would
find it.

Now that he had seen Emlyn de Ashbourne, he regretted
that his offer of marriage had never been finalized. Kindness
was laced through her like a vein of gold, despite all that anger she had voiced. She had courage, wit, and temper
enough to spark his quick temper. Yet she was guileless even
so, and possessed a gentle, alluring beauty. Such a woman
was a rare gift. Whitehawke, he feared, would only sully and
damage her.

As the wagon rumbled alongside his horse, the little boy
called out at the sight of the great destrier, stretching out a
hand to touch the black's sleek muzzle. Nicholas walked the
horse closer, and both children reached out, the girl timidly
extending her small hand, her brother massaging the horse's
broad neck with fearless enthusiasm.

Nicholas smiled and answered their questions about
Sylvanus. Glancing up, he saw Peter riding back toward the
wagon.

The knight pulled up his dappled horse beside Sylvanus,
sending Christien into loud ecstasies. Behind him, Tibbie
yanked at the boy's tunic when he nearly overbalanced in his
enthusiasm, and threatened that he would not pat another
horse the rest of the journey if he did not settle down.

"My lord," Isobel said. Nicholas raised an eyebrow toward her. "Are we at Hawksmoor yet? We've been riding a
long time."

Nicholas smiled and pointed. "There, past that wide strip
of forest, do you see the towers against the sky?"

The children clambered over each other to look, and
Tibbie breathed a huge sigh. "At last, my lord. They've
asked nigh a thousand times since we left." She turned away
to pick up Harry, who had awoken from a nap, his eyes
blinking wide.

Peter slid back his mesh hood, shaking loose his coppery curls. "That stretch of forest ahead has no easy way around, as you know, my lord. Whitehawke has decided to enter."

"Swords at the ready, bows drawn among the archers," Nicholas repeated the familiar litany of defense. "How long has it been, Perkin?"

"Since Whitehawke was accosted in a forest? Eight years."

"Yet he does not forget."

"Have you ever known him to forget any slight? Especially such as happened then, to his men and his goods?"

"'Twas a thorough rousting, those years ago."

"Aye, 'twas that indeed, and more. Did he not lose gold and plate, and shipments of grain and goods that went to his castle through the forest? And several men as well?"

"Aye, the men. Well, I vow, loss of men is always to be regretted."

"For two years Whitehawke suffered the revenge of a forest outlaw." Peter looked directly at Nicholas, his blue eyes gleaming. "Think you he will ever slacken his defense? Nay, he will enter a forest fully armed for the rest of his life."

"Particularly since the Green Man has begun to harass his convoys," Nicholas commented.

"Aye so. Pray we do not meet that hellwretch today. The little ones would have the nightmare after them for months."

"Oh, Jesu," Nicholas groaned. "Not in my hall."

"Sir Peter, I want to ride with you," Christien called. "You promised me."

"Certes, lad," called Peter, grinning. Nicholas wondered at Peter's easy humor. His own mood felt heavy as a lead coffin. "Later, though," Peter continued. "Now we must advance with caution, for we approach a dangerous forest." Christien's eyes grew large as dishes, and Isobel squeaked nervously.

"Have a care, Perkin," Nicholas muttered, "else you'll have them awail for the rest of the journey." Peter's eyes sparkled mischievously.

"Are there outlaws, sir? We have no outlaws near Ashbourne, my lord. There's no dangerous forest, only a timber wood, where my sister shoots her bow," Christien said.

"What?" Peter asked. Nicholas scowled and would have interrupted, but Peter pursued it. "Your sister? Not this charming lady here?" He winked at Isobel, who giggled.

"Nay. Isobel only likes to be a silly princess." Isobel pushed him, but he ignored her. "My sister Emlyn uses a little bow and arrow betimes. She's not very good. Guy tried to show her how, and was teaching me, too."

Peter raised his eyebrows at Nicholas. "Lady Emlyn is an archer, my lord. Did you know?"

Nicholas felt his cheeks burn. Peter smirked happily and leaned forward. "She caught some big game the other day, I vow."

Christien blinked. "How did you know she was out then?"

Peter laughed out loud, a delighted hoot, and grinned.

"Ride on, simpleton, and remind the men to arm when they enter the forest," Nicholas snapped.

"I will, but they need not beware such an enemy as haunts the timber wood at Ashbourne." Still grinning, Peter wheeled his horse and cantered toward the guards who rode behind the wagon.

Nicholas shifted his reins, took leave of Tibbie and the children with a brisk nod of his head, and rode ahead. For all his friend's triumphant crowing, Nicholas knew Peter would be discreet, though wisekin remarks would fly fast for a while.

He rubbed his thigh with the palm of his hand. The injured muscle, irritated by days of riding, had been aching fiercely, though with Tibbie's stitches and ointments it would heal well. He would rest when he reached Hawksmoor, but only for a day or two. In mulling over what he owed the de Ashbourne family, a plan had begun to form in his mind. To pursue it, he would have to leave Hawksmoor fairly soon.

The escort entered the forest, passing along a wide, tree-arched path shaded with cool green light. Nicholas could feel his body relaxing gradually as the forest began to work its usual magic on him. As always, the soothing sounds of birdsong and rustling leaves, the fragrant air and bright, warm sun shafts deftly kneaded the tense knots from his muscles and his mood. This was where he truly felt most at ease, though he had performed some dangerous deeds within forests.

He would come back to the greenwood as soon as he could, once the children were settled at Hawksmoor, and once he had gained some rest and determined how long before he would have to ride to London.

Smiling to himself, Nicholas allowed that, just perhaps, his father was wise to beware the forest. At least for a little while longer.

Chapter Six

In the end, the windows remained at Ashbourne. Impatient to join their fellows at Graymere Keep, Whitehawke's guards did not wait for a carpenter to be summoned from the village, and quickly bungled the task of removing the pins that secured the wooden frames. After one of the arched glass panels cracked, Emlyn hotly declared to Hugh de Chavant that leaving the windows at Ashbourne was preferable to losing them altogether.

Chavant, whose wall-eyed, lopsided glare made her distinctly uncomfortable, had been charged with ensuring the safe arrival at Graymere of Whitehawke's new bride. But when the weather produced solid sheets of rain that turned the roads to muddy strips, the trip north became a treacherous and soggy prospect. They were forced to postpone travel for almost a week.

Emlyn was satisfied with the extra time, for Ashbourne's planting season had begun. She spent many hours in consultation with Wat, discussing crops, tallying the counts of newborn lambs on the surrounding farms, and assisting in decisions for each tenant farm regarding how many sheep were to be sold at market or kept for another season of growing. With so much debt at Ashbourne, the income from raw wool was especially important now.

Even as she resisted the idea of becoming Whitehawke's wife, Emlyn nevertheless dutifully prepared for her unwelcome wedding. Gowns of bright silks and embroidered samite, old-fashioned in cut and once made for her taller mother, were brought out of storage. Skilled needlewomen fitted Emlyn and remade the gowns in a newer style, close to the torso and snug at the wrists.

Emlyn and the maidservant Jehanne sorted and packed,

filling a few wooden chests with garments rolled in dried rose petals. Her embroidery frame was dismantled and packed in a wooden casket with cloth and yarns. New sheets were hastily sewn from bolts of white linen found in one of the storerooms as a concession to Jehanne, who grumbled that if the earl had been years without a wife, there was no telling the state of his bedchamber.

The thought of sharing a bed with the earl had sent cold dread through Emlyn.

Carefully rolling the leaves of Guy's manuscript in silk, she stacked them in a chest to be kept at Ashbourne and sent for later, once she was settled. Wrapping some brushes and pigment pots in chamois leather and old parchments, she put them into a leather satchel to bring with her. As an afterthought she added spare garments in the roomy bag: a thick blue cloak and a gray wool gown, a chemise, woolen hose, and a linen headdress.

In bright, cold sunshine, twelve days after her siblings had left, Emlyn bid Wat farewell and rode beneath the portcullis, her green cloak fanned over her horse's withers. Dry-eyed, her expression stony, she left Ashbourne, followed by three loaded carts and over a dozen guards.

Riding through a dismal gray mist on the third day, Emlyn pulled her cloak tighter and snuggled deep into the thick warmth of her hood. Her gauzy headdress brushed against her jaw and throat, and she tucked her chin down, welcoming the cocoon of veil and cloak and hood, feeling as much lonely as chilled. Each footfall on this journey had increased the dread that sat like a great, cold stone in her heart. She rode to Graymere more prisoner than bride.

Jehanne sat in the wagon that rumbled alongside Emlyn's horse, with the cart-driver, a young servantman from Ashbourne. While Hugh de Chavant cantered in the lead, the guards rode in solemn pairs, wearing the russet cloaks of Whitehawke's garrison.

The caravan moved steadily through the fine, blurring drizzle. To one side, Emlyn saw a steep grassy slope, cluttered with stones. The incline fell away toward a valley floor, which was covered by wet clinging mists.

The quiet, but for the rhythmic footfalls of horses and the

creaking and jingling of wooden wheels and metal armor, suited her present mood well: Emlyn was thinking. Riding her horse over the surging heathery ground, she had turned her thoughts inward, examining her situation as if it were a cut gem, each aspect a facet with a possible flaw.

If there had been enough gold to buy Guy's freedom, none of this might have happened. She desperately wanted to be with the children, and every intuition she had warned against this marriage. Whitehawke, she sensed, would never allow the children to live with her, nor would he produce the coin to free Guy.

She gave her head a tiny hopeless shake. Women rarely, she knew, resisted marriage plans made by male relatives and overlords. Occasionally a woman who was very unhappy with a betrothal entered a convent for life, or even wed another man before the day. Both solutions were liable to bring down the wrath of the rejected party on the woman's family.

Emlyn almost laughed out loud. Certes, no man existed who could marry her in Whitehawke's stead. Her only choice was to claim a call to God and retire to a convent, though she already knew how unsuited she was to monastic life. For years, she had expected marriage, and had wanted a bond of friendship and respect such as her parents had known, a haven of peace suited to creating and loving.

Clearly, Whitehawke offered no haven. Though babes might come, there would be no peace, no love, no warmth of spirit with him. She would far rather find happiness in a farmer's croft.

Stiff and uncomfortable after hours in the leather-covered wooden saddle, she shifted and sighed. Whitehawke's disagreeable reputation was not the worst, she thought; at least he seemed penitent about his sins. He was wealthy and handsome, though much older. Emlyn could see where the son had inherited his height and build, and his tendency to blushing skin. She pushed the thought away.

But Whitehawke's brutish and unyielding nature alarmed her most. Wat and Tibbie had both named him a cruel man. Even his son Nicholas had been cryptic but definite about his father's sinfulness. How had the first wife died, she wondered, that the blame was fixed on Whitehawke? And why his peculiar penance?

Emlyn knew there was bitterness, laced with hate, between the father and son. Better she never married than wed into such a mean-spirited clan. But any defiance of the king's orders was as risky as sailing full against an icy northern gale.

'Tis too late, she thought morosely; naught can interrupt the course of these wedding plans. Surrounded by the earl's own guards, she rode straight to his keep.

Brooding unhappily, she listened trancelike to the rattle and chirp of the cart wheels. Suddenly a new thought burst in her mind like a hot spark. She straightened her spine with the shock of its clarity, and Nicholas de Hawkwood's words in the mural stair came back to her.

She smiled a little. Perhaps there was a way to be with the children and be free of the betrothal. The idea was more foolish than dangerous, she realized, but no better solution had occurred to her. How ironic that Nicholas de Hawkwood had provided her the chance to thwart the king's plans.

"My lady." Jehanne's voice interrupted her concentration.

"Aye?" Emlyn turned and smiled at Jehanne, who had offered to accompany her on the journey, sensibly pointing out the impropriety of one woman traveling with several soldiers for several days. Emlyn had been grateful for her company.

"My lady, the mist grows thick as soup, and we approach a forest," Jehanne said. "Think you we will stop, rather than go on in such weather?" Her eyes were wide, and Emlyn was puzzled by the girl's quavering tone.

Absorbed in her thoughts, Emlyn had not noticed that wet whorls of fog had begun to obscure the surrounding countryside. A forest loomed out of the mist, deep green, dark with rain.

"I know not, Jehanne," she answered, and saw Jehanne frown. "What is wrong? Are you ill?"

"Oh, my lady, I do fear a journey in these white mists. Here in the northern places, the woods and moors be haunted."

Emlyn sighed impatiently. "Jehanne, those are stories."

"Aye, such as you have told yourself, 'round the great hearth come a snowy or rainy even. But where might such stories come from, my lady? Thomas has heard that the haunts are real." Jehanne tapped the cart-driver on one shoulder. "Thom, tell Lady Emlyn what we spoke of," she urged.

The young man, a servant from Ashbourne close in age to Emlyn and Jehanne, looked somberly at Emlyn and tipped his forelock. "My lady, me ma and uncles are from these moors, and I have heard the local tales of forest spirits and demons of the old evil. Sightings, there have been, even recently, of demons."

Emlyn frowned. "The old evil, Thomas?"

"Aye, the old pagan evil, still practiced by some."

Sensing the young man's distinct uneasiness, Emlyn felt a frisson of apprehension, though she was convinced that such evil did not truly exist. Emlyn and her siblings had been taught acceptance, rather than fear, for the older ways. Their maternal grandmother had been of Celtic descent and had practiced old rituals and healing arts, combing them with a fervent Christian piety. The old pagan "evil" was simply a religion based on appreciating the goodness and giving nature of the earth, and could be easily and joyfully combined with Christian beliefs.

Thomas spoke again. "Do you know of the demon of the forest, Jack o' the Green?"

Emlyn turned in surprise. "The Green Man? Every little child knows of him, Thomas, he is a legend, a silly figure in the mummer's plays. A man in the village near Ashbourne, each May, hangs a wreath on his head and dances about, covered in flowers and leaves. 'Tis a common thing."

Thomas nodded grimly. "My lady, here the Green Man is real. Many have seen him. He steals children, and sheep and pigs for his demonic purposes."

Jehanne looked up, her brown eyes wide. "My lady, will aught happen to us out here?"

Emlyn shook her head and laughed softly. "We will surely be safe enough, for we are not children, nor do we have sheep or pigs. Besides, what sensible creature of any sort would venture out on such a wet day as this! You two are as full of fears as a dying man who imagines the devil sits on his bedstead!"

"Think you then, the Green Man is not real?" Jehanne asked.

Emlyn smiled, her eyes dancing. "The only Green Man I know is old Tye from the village. Remember the sweetmeats he would give us, and the juggling tricks he knew?"

"Chavant comes this way," Jehanne said suddenly.

Emlyn looked up as Hugh de Chavant rode back along the escort line toward them. Although he was said to be among Whitehawke's most trusted and able men, Emlyn had found him to be dull, with little humor and sly mannerisms.

Chavant drew up beside her and nodded briefly. "Lady Emlyn." His independent eye wandered, sluggish and yellowed, away from the dark brown eye that gleamed at her now. "If you are fatigued, we will rest now. The forest should offer us some protection from the rain."

Emlyn felt a vague unease whenever Chavant looked at her, even if both eyes were on her at once. "I can continue, my lord." Secretly spinning the web of her new plan, she made a suggestion. "But we may stop at an abbey for shelter and hot food. I have an uncle at Wistonbury Abbey, not far from here."

Chavant frowned, drawing his thick black brows together. "Wistonbury is to the south. Such a detour is not convenient, since we move northeast. Lord Whitehawke's garrison would not find much welcome at that abbey. The weather worsens, and I fear 'twill turn to heavy rain later. I will offer you rest now, just under those trees, else we push ahead as quick as we can."

Emlyn sighed. She had had enough of rain, mud, and the endless chilly miles the escort had covered. And if she could not stop at the abbey, her plan would not progress so easily as she had hoped. "I wish to stop at the abbey," she insisted.

"We cannot do that. We can reach Graymere by nightfall if we travel quickly." Chavant scowled. Emlyn found the effect on his eye interesting. "Were it not for the carts, my lady, we would have been there sooner. There will be no other stops."

"As you wish, my lord." She sighed, deciding to forgo the matter for now. Some instinct whispered that she should not force a request with Chavant.

He leaned forward confidentially. "We enter a forest, my lady, and I must tell you that it may abound with thieves."

Emlyn looked up quickly. In truth, she thought, a band of forest thieves would be not unwelcome, were it not so far-fetched a possibility. Such a dilemma might afford her a chance to flee altogether. She bit anxiously at her lip.

Chavant smiled. "We will protect you, my lady. Lord Whitehawke has always demanded extra precautions in the forest. The men are well experienced in encounters with dangerous fiends." He pulled himself up to his full height, which was not considerable. In his russet cloak, with his un-tidy dark hair sticking out around the edge of his mail hood, and his yellow-toned skin, he looked like a short, square rooster.

"Outlaws, my lord?" Forest outlaws had always piqued her interest. While she found such tales fascinating in gen-eral, she yearned to hear mention of one particular man. "A frightening prospect. Are there brigands in this area?"

His eye slid briefly away. "You need have no fears on this journey, Lady Emlyn. We can protect you." With a gleam in his wobbly glance, he leaned toward her. "Only one outlaw dared to challenge Lord Whitehawke, but he was vanquished years ago."

"Oh? I wonder if we at Ashbourne have heard of him."

"He was called the Black Thorne, a surly young Saxon wolf-pup. He attacked every escort and supply wagon that came to and from Graymere Keep. We pursued him relent-lessly, when I was first with the garrison. But Black Thorne disappeared about eight years ago, after he escaped Whitehawke's guards. He has not been seen since that night."

Emlyn's heart thudded rapidly. At Ashbourne, years ago, they had heard a rumor of Thorne's death. "Disappeared, my lord?"

"Long dead and gone, my lady, though we never found a body. The local villeins reported his death. He was like a wild dog on the earl, was the Thorne, and would not have suddenly let go without reason. Dead, aye, long ago."

The girl who had adored the memory of a kind, handsome Saxon still existed deep within Emlyn. But now she was grown, and pledged to marry the bitter, angry old man who had caused Thorne's death. Emlyn felt a tight knot form in her stomach.

"Why would he have attacked Lord Whitehawke so, my lord?"

Chavant shot her a wobbly look. His lazy eye had been, when she had first met him, disconcerting to watch. Now, from the peculiar slide of his glance, she knew he was displeased with her question. "As to why he stole numerous shipments, gold and fine things among them, we never knew, though Whitehawke supposed it had to do with the land dispute." Chavant scratched at his scruffy chin stubble with blunt, grimy fingers.

"Land dispute?" She looked up curiously.

"Aye, between Whitehawke and the monks of two abbeys hereabouts, over sheep ranges and building rights in that dale below us. Arnedale, 'tis called, and lies just south of Hawksmoor and west of Graymere. These are matters that barons and clergy do often argue about, my lady. The Black Thorne was likely the son of a shepherd, or even a relative of an abbot or monk, who thought, like some, that Whitehawke was diminishing churchland."

"Whose land is it? Has the dispute been settled?"

" 'Tis Whitehawke's legally, through his wife's dowry. He awaits final word from the royal courts regarding his claim. 'Tis a formality only, after all these years."

"With the Thorne gone, my lord, surely this area is safe."

"Most of Thorne's attacks took place in the forest, which is why Lord Whitehawke remains cautious and will only travel the main roads. He thus has protected himself from outlaws." He paused and gave her an exceedingly odd glance. "Still, my lady, there are certain—fiends—about in the area."

"I will surely look to you for my protection, as I have since we left Ashbourne," Emlyn said demurely. Chavant bowed with a stiff smile and rode to join the guards at the lead.

Jehanne turned to Emlyn. "You do treat my Lord Chavant with more politeness than I could, I vow, my lady." She shivered.

Emlyn leaned toward Jehanne and whispered, "He does treat us with better consideration if I am sweet to him, have you not noticed? He is an odd man, I vow, and disagreeable in his way, but he does not rankle my anger the way Lord Whitehawke does, or his son." Her cheeks suddenly flushed at the thought of the son, and she lifted her chin defiantly.

At the mention of Nicholas de Hawkwood, Jehanne dimpled prettily. "Ah, the young baron is a fine man," she breathed, "a beautiful man, like a dark angel."

Emlyn blushed brighter as she remembered, suddenly, the baron seated in the steaming tub, his muscled torso glowing wet and sleek in the firelight, his hair in dripping dark tendrils around his deceptively angelic face.

Then she imagined his hair peaked with horns: there, that was better. "The de Hawkwoods, father and son, do not deserve our admiration, Jehanne," Emlyn said primly. Though Jehanne nodded, her eyes still sparkled.

After uttering her righteous words, Emlyn retreated into the folds of her thick cloak, feeling somewhat humbled by the undeniably lustful images of Nicholas de Hawkwood that played across her mind.

"I like it not, my lady," said Chavant in a low voice.

Riding slowly beside him, Emlyn murmured in agreement. The thick layers of moisture had quickly increased in the hour or so since they had entered the forest. Now they traveled through a fog so dense and white that they could scarcely see one another. Mist filled the arms of the trees and sat upon the ground like the ghosts of giants, curling and rolling and rising up in monstrous shapes, swallowing each horse and man ahead of Emlyn, as if they disappeared into an enchantment.

Chavant cantered ahead of her, his russet cloak and the gray rump of his horse fading and vanishing. Trusting her horse's instincts and relying on her keen hearing to guide her, Emlyn followed. The lead horsemen carried lighted torches, but from her position in the line, she could not see the glow.

As the escort continued its creeping progress, the slightest sounds—the creek of leather horse trappings, the jingle of chain mail, the rhythmic squeak of wooden wheels—took on a round, hollow echo, straining Emlyn's taut nerves.

Stretching the stiff muscles of her neck and shoulders, she

looked around at the bright spectral wall of mist. A drizzle
began again, dampening her cheeks and hands, coloring a
few clinging, exposed curls at her cheeks and brow to honey
gold.

Ahead, she heard the low drift of excited conversation.
Straining to listen, she was unable to determine the words.
Moments later, she heard another exclamation.

"What is it?" she called out. "Chavant! What is wrong?"

"Hush!" Chavant replied, emerging from the mist ahead.
He held up a hand for silence, and swept an arc with his
head as he listened, squinting into the fog.

"What is it?" she whispered loudly.

" 'Tis naught. Ride on," he hissed.

"Perhaps we should stop after all, my lord," she said.
"The fog is so thick—"

"Never would I stop here! We must be out of this forest
by dark. If we follow the path carefully, we will come to the
edge of the wood soon enough. The moors will be in heavy
fog as well, but the way will be far easier."

Another excited murmur drifted back to them. "My lord
Chavant," Emlyn persisted. "What is happening?"

Chavant sighed, a deep blast of frustration. "The men say
that we are being watched, perhaps followed."

Emlyn's slender brows shot up in surprise. Who would
dare to accost the escort of Lord Whitehawke's betrothed? If
she had any personal enemies, she certainly was with them
now. No brigands would be about in such foul weather. Anyone with a scrap of sense was in front of a cozy fire.

"But who would follow us?" she asked Chavant. He rode
close enough to fix her with his uneven, fierce glance.

"None of this earth." His eye drifted to one side and
stayed there. "We ride on. My lady, you would be more
comfortable and safer in the wagon."

Emlyn regarded him steadily. She had refused the same
suggestion twice already today. "Nay, my lord," she said, a
trace of stubborn pride making her words brittle.

"As you will, then. Follow the path, and look for the
lights. I will send Gerard back to carry a torch in front of
you. My lady." He bowed, a brief snap of his head, and was
soon enveloped in the smothering mist.

Emlyn kicked at her horse and moved ahead, bending

down to search the ground beneath her horse's hooves for the flat, grassy surface of the path. Satisfied that she was still on it, she straightened and rode toward the creaking sounds up ahead.

"There!" A voice cracked through the moist air. Emlyn jumped as if she had been struck.

As she turned her head, a swirl of mist between some ghostly trees moved and thinned to reveal, a short distance away, a horseman. He sat quite still, a large, vague shape.

The mist seemed to withdraw and form an amorphous halo around the man and horse. Emlyn saw him clearly for an instant before the fog rolled and spilled over him once more. He was not one of the guards, for he wore no russet cloak or mailed hood. Emlyn was unsure for a moment what manner of clothing he wore. Tall and very broad on the pale horse, his massive body was draped in textured green. His hair flew in wild shapes around the huge oval of his head, and his eyes were deep pits.

She gasped. This was no man, but a huge and fearsome creature, a giant formed of intertwined branches and leaves, as if he were a tree come to life. The huge body sat on an equally massive mount, its coat a pale green color.

One thick arm, more like a sturdy branch sprouting leaves, lifted. Something glittered, an axe or sword, in its leafy fingers. The creature turned and seemed to point directly at her with its long arm.

Someone shouted again, behind her, and a horse neighed.

"Ride on!" bellowed one of the guards. "Ride on!" Three or four soldiers tore past her, jostling her horse and spinning it around. One guard reached out to grab her reins and bring her ahead with them, but he dove too late and missed. "Follow, lady!" he called, galloping past.

Panicked, she kicked at her horse, but the animal spun crazily around, twisting against the jerk of the reins. A wall of deep, white mist quickly surrounded her. Cold wet air sat heavily on her hands and cheeks, entering her lungs with each rapid breath. She was disoriented, dizzy from the spins of the horse and the bright, damp cloud that obscured all steadying landmarks. Finally the horse stopped circling in response to her tugs on the reins, and stood still, its sides bellowing heavily, sensing her hesitation and unsure itself where to proceed.

Muffled shouts came from somewhere to her left. Pressing her feet in the stirrups, she urged her mount in that direction.

Her heart thumped uncomfortably. She wanted to spur and ride ahead, but she was afraid to go any faster, worried that the horse would stumble or fall, frightened that each uncertain step took her closer to the forest beast.

She had seen the creature. The apparition had been no trick of the mist. Wiping the back of her hand across her eyes as if to clear her vision, she halted the horse. She could see nothing now, either before or behind her, but swirling, pale, thick fog.

"Chavant!" she cried out. "Gerard! I am here!" Her voice picked up a shrill, eerie echo.

"Lady Emlyn!" someone called. "Lady! Stay where you are!" He sounded very far away.

"Here! I am here!" she cried.

Ahead of her a tiny light glowed suddenly, like a golden star in a white sky. Here, then, must be the guard sent to bring her a torch. Sighing with relief, she urged her horse forward, riding slowly toward the light.

From out of the mist, a large dark shape appeared in front of her horse, off to one side. "Thanks be to God," she murmured.

Her horse's bit was lifted and pulled slightly. She let the reins go slack, willing to be led to safety, and leaned back in her saddle with relief. Then she jerked forward suddenly.

A huge green claw closed around the bridle. Emlyn screamed. The lead horse had pale green hindquarters and a yellowish tail.

She screamed again, heard the shouts of the guards, and tried to turn her horse. Confused, her mount reared back on its hind legs. Emlyn slid out of the saddle, and one hip hit the hard ground with a painful whack.

She tried to sit up. Her horse kicked out and an iron shoe grazed the side of her head. Knocked sideways, she shook her head groggily and rose up on her knees, scuttling away to avoid another kick. As she went, she stumbled over her satchel, grabbed blindly at it, and crawled into the bracken.

She could hear the creature coming behind her, riding as

if the mist were no deterrent to his unearthly vision. He forged through the forest, hard and rapid, plunging toward her. Emlyn ran, breathless and disoriented, blinded by swirling fog, her head spinning and aching from the horse's blow. Her only thought was purely instinctive, without reason: an urge to get away, and fast, from the creature. She ran, noisy and directionless.

After a while, she realized that the only sounds were her own heavy breathing, and the crash of her own feet through the undergrowth. She stopped and listened. Silence filled the heavy air. She heard no sounds of pursuit. No creature. No guards.

She ran shaking fingers through the tangled curls that fell into her eyes, pushing them back. No one was near. Then a new thought, the first logic that she had allowed herself for several minutes, emerged.

She was free of the escort.

Moving quickly, she had been running through the forest, in spite of the mists, for several minutes. Soon she heard a faint drumming sound, deeper than the beat of the fine, constant rain: the thunder of horses.

Frantically she plunged into the dripping gorse, sliding on wet leaves and flattening her body along the roots of a wild hedge. She had hardly pulled in a few heaving lungfuls of air before a group of horsemen careened past. Peering through a gap in the thicket, she glimpsed, through wisps of fog, four of Chavant's guards halted close by.

"Ho!" called one guard loudly. "Lady Emlyn!"

She pressed her brow against cold leaf muck, inhaling the moldy odor with shallow breaths, staying still as a rock.

"Where the devil did she get to?" one of them muttered. The horses pranced and snorted. Her heart a soft riot in her chest, Emlyn curled into a quivering ball beneath the dripping thicket.

Search and call as they might, she had made up her mind to hide. She would go to her uncle's monastery. Godwin would help her. He could send a formal protest to the Pope, and she hoped he would take her to Hawksmoor Castle to fetch the children.

When the little ones were settled with relatives in Scotland, Emlyn would commit her life to God, and enter a convent in grateful thanks for her family's safety.

But she could go no further until the fog cleared. Her greatest concern was meeting that horrible creature again. Though she feared getting lost, questioning Chavant earlier in the day about the countryside had yielded useful information. An eastern path through the woods, he had said, would lead down to the dale. Across the dale lay the river, where she could hire a boat to take her south to Wistonbury Abbey.

"We must search further," she heard one of the men say. "If the demon took her, she's in the wood. And if he let her go, we'll find her."

Another guard muttered a low curse. Emlyn heard a leathery creak and the chime of chain mail, and saw iron-trimmed boots touch the ground as two men dismounted. They walked a stone's throw from where she lay, slashing with their sword blades through tangled, wet branches.

Shivering equally with chill and fear, grateful that her green cloak blended with the leaves, she lay still. Moisture seeped through her saturated garments. She had a tickling urge to cough, and covered her mouth and nose.

After a while she heard footsteps, murmurings, and the sound of horses cantering away. Sliding backward to inch out from beneath the dripping thicket, she grabbed up her fallen satchel. As she launched forward to run, shouts exploded behind her.

She burst ahead, dodging grizzled brambles and shrubbery, leaping fallen tree limbs, plunging into the deep misty greenwood. Faint shouts sounded behind her. She crashed onward.

Exhausted finally, she stopped behind a wide oak, slumping to her knees among wet ferns. Whooping breaths burned her throat. Her soaked hood slid down, baring her bright hair to the mist, as she listened for her pursuers.

Distantly, then louder, came the heavy noises of armored men crashing through the undergrowth. Emlyn muffled a fearful sob in the base of her throat and climbed as quickly as she could into the sheltering oak. From somewhere came the high cutting whoosh of an arrow, followed by the breathy grunt of its victim. She peered cautiously through the branches.

In a stand of slender birches, the bright rusty splash of a guard's cloak swirled in the fog as he fell. An arrow protruded from his neck. The second guard bent to his companion, then stood slowly. With a horrified expression, he backed away, and spun to make a noisy exit, calling for the other guards.

Alarmed, Emlyn looked about for the hidden marksman.

Had the mist not swirled slightly away from him, she would not have seen him among the shrouded, blurred trees, for his green clothing and greenish skin were barely distinguishable from the surrounding foliage. He was taller than any man she had ever seen. The Green Man paused for a moment, and then moved away, shouldering a longbow and shaking his shaggy, leafy head.

If Emlyn had never believed in the reality of demons before, she had just changed her mind.

How long she huddled in the oak tree, shivering with cold and shock, she did not know for certain. She must have slept a little, though she felt drained rather than rested. The dismal afternoon light had been replaced by a dense, spongy blackness.

Dimly she recalled an icy drizzle that had set a wet sparkle to the wool of her cloak. Hours must have passed while she crouched in the tree, at first too frightened to come down, later deadened by exhaustion and bone-chilling cold.

In the oppressive darkness, sleety rain pattered the leaves that sloped tentlike overhead. Leaning back, stretching her stiff arms and legs, she noticed that her head, where the horse's hoof had grazed her, ached painfully, and felt bruised and blood-crusted. Her stomach was queasy.

Wetness permeated her clothing, hair, and skin. She needed shelter desperately, but knew that if she left the tree now, she would only trudge deeper into the forest and lose any sense of direction.

Sighing, she reached into the satchel for the spare cloak, managing to pull its dry folds around her. What little warmth she gained was agonizingly slow in gathering, and she thought yearningly of soup, and furs piled high, and a blazing fire.

Coughing, she wiped her face with a corner of the cloak,

feeling a little more comfortable curled in the thick wool. Sleep began to surround and fill her like a dark mist.

A sudden foggy awareness slammed into her like a fist in the belly, and she sat upright. Her head knocked against a lower bough, sending it softly swinging. Groggy, she listened for whatever had awoken her.

Some animal, pray God not a wolf, prowled around the base of the oak. Hearing the faint stealthy rhythm of careful steps, she drew her stiffened legs slowly up.

When the walking ceased, Emlyn ceased breathing, wondering frantically if she could scramble farther up into the tree.

Then the deep velvety darkness of her aerie was pierced by a blast of cold air and a shaft of moonlight. The mist had cleared. She saw a tall forest creature on two long legs reaching out toward her. Emlyn gasped and pressed against the trunk, her heart slamming against her ribs.

"Dear God. There you are." The voice was as soft and deep as the night shadows. "Come here." Emlyn whimpered, too weak and frightened to scream. She beat clumsy, meaningless blows at the solid, strong arms that surrounded her.

"Nay," she rasped, her voice hoarse. "Who are you?"

" 'Tis Thorne," he said gently. She pushed at him. "Dearling, 'tis Black Thorne." She stopped in amazement. He spoke again. "You are safe now. Come with me." He gathered her, suddenly unresisting, to him and lifted her in his arms.

Thorne. This must be a dream. But she felt the warm, solid play of bone and muscle as he carried her away from the tree. Warm breath blew over her cheek as she tucked her head against his shoulder, and prickly wool and slick leather pressed beneath her cheek. She smelled wet leather and a spicy, earthy odor. No dream this, she thought groggily.

Without the strength to question the strangeness of it, she burrowed into the warmth of his arms and gave in to an irresistible lethargy. His bearded cheek brushed softly against her brow as he carried her into the forest.

Chapter Seven

"My lady. My lady." The voice droned on, and had been droning for a while, like a small fly buzzing persistently at her ear. She swatted at it.

"Lady Emlyn. Are you awake?" She turned her back as a barrier to the voice, and the fur coverlet slipped. Cool dry air caressed her bare shoulder. Through eyes blurred with fatigue, she saw a dark stone wall mere inches from her face, its rough surface glazed with firelight. Turning her head, she saw the sloped walls and low ceiling of a small, oddly shaped chamber, dark but for a small central fire.

"Lady Emlyn." This time she let the voice lead her to a face and a form. "My lady. Yer awake." A woman stepped forward.

Sturdy and round, she seemed tall, even given Emlyn's point of view from a pallet of furs on the floor. The woman crossed the small space to kneel beside her. Broad shoulders and an ample bosom were clothed in a thick homespun wool of warm onion yellow. The face above the simple neckline was round and pleasant, with pink cheeks and blue eyes, and brown tendrils escaping from a plain linen headwrapping. She seemed young, only a few years older than Emlyn.

"I am Maisry, Lady Emlyn. These are my sons." She gestured to two little boys who stood on the other side of the low central hearth. The taller of the two had smooth shining hair, bright as carrots in the firelight. The smaller one sucked his thumb solemnly, golden-red curls rioting around his head.

"The eldest is Dirk, and the little 'un is Elvi," Maisry said. The boys came near, and Maisry reached out an arm to draw them close. They snuggled beside their mother and gawked at Emlyn with huge eyes. She smiled, and the little one blinked, sucking faster, his plump cheeks flushed. Both boys wore tunics of brown wool with dark leggings and soft leather boots. The older one was no more than four or five, the younger one a little older than Harry, probably only just out of breechcloths.

Emlyn glanced back at their mother. Remembering who had brought her here, she felt a flutter of disappointment. Thorne had rescued her last night—he was not dead, but her befuddled mind could not question that as yet—and so these must be his wife and sons.

She felt a little lost to think him settled, a married villein. But then, several years had passed. He would not have waited for a little girl, no matter how often she had thought of him.

She began to sit up, and the fur slipped with the movement. Gasping at her emerging nakedness, she snatched at the wayward fur covering. "Where are my clothes?" she squeaked.

"There. They should be dry by now." Emlyn noticed her two cloaks, blue and green, draped over a bench with her blue silk gown and white chemise, her woolen hose and shoes arranged on a low stool beside the fire. "Ye must have taken an awful chill in those wet garments. Soaked and near frozen, I hear ye were."

"I do not remember much of last night when your husband rescued me," Emlyn replied.

Maisry stared at her for a moment. "My lady," 'twas not my husband who found ye. Thorne did, and tended to ye himself until this morn, when he came to our farm and asked me to come up here. We have been here since midday. Ye've slept the day near round. 'Tis after dusk."

Emlyn blinked, trying to absorb all of this. Pungent smoke from the fire stung her eyes, then cleared as a draft of chill air wafted from a far corner of the room. She wiped at her bleary vision, dimly aware of a pounding headache.

"Are you not Thorne's wife, then?" she asked, puzzled, too tired to sort it out. Somehow she had slept through a full day. Thorne must have taken care of her last night, and must have removed her clothing. She blushed, remembering naught beyond his warm, strong arms and his low, comforting voice in her ear.

"Oh, nay. My husband is Aelric of Shepherdsgate. We live just beyond Kernham—that's the nearest village in the dale. Aelric is a sheep farmer," Maisry added, stroking Dirk's red hair. The woman's hands were smooth, slim-fingered, and graceful. She looked quizzically at Emlyn. "Poor dearling, ye've the headache, I know. Let me fetch ye a drink." Maisry went over to a shelf, a natural niche in the stone wall. Choosing a cup from among the few wooden dishes on the shelf, she bent to scoop water from a wooden bucket.

Emlyn glanced around the room. In the middle of the hard-packed dirt floor, the fire blazed and crackled in a confining circle of round stones. The walls were dark and shiny, without windows, the ceiling low and curved. A bench, a chest, and a few wooden stools were placed about the room. The doorway was beyond a crude-cut corner, where she saw the fluttering edge of a dark curtain. Emlyn realized that the chamber was actually a cave.

Returning to where Emlyn lay on the fur-covered pallet, Maisry knelt and offered her the water, which was cool and tasted slightly of the old bucket. Emlyn swallowed and winced at the pain that jumped in her temple.

" 'Tis a deep bruise, my lady. Now that yer awake, I shall tend it with an ointment, but first, surely ye'd like to dress." She turned to her sons. "Dirk, you may share an apple with Elvi. Mind he does not eat the seeds nor skin, and play yonder." The children settled down in a corner with a small pile of wooden men, with which they proceeded to stage a noisy battle. Maisry fetched Emlyn's chemise and hose and silken gown, water-streaked and rumpled, but dry and warm. Emlyn dressed, then sank weakly down on the soft furs.

"If you have any mint, or chamomile, I could prepare an infusion for this headache," Emlyn said.

"I have brought some herbs with me. First let me fold up the fur, so," Maisry said, reaching over to roll a coverlet into a fat cushion. "Rest here, my lady, and when I have seen to supper, I will see to ye."

Emlyn leaned back, the fur warm and yielding at her back. Maisry moved efficiently around the cave, feeding the flames until they burned brightly, setting water to boil in a small iron pot, and stirring the contents of a larger kettle that had been simmering, suspended on an iron rod, over the hearth. Then she disappeared through a low passageway at the back of the main chamber, and returned with a large jug and a small wineskin. Setting them on the low bench, she arranged loaves of dark bread and a wheel of pale cheese and covered those with a cloth.

When all was ready for supper, Maisry set a round basket on the floor beside Emlyn and sat down again, removing an assortment of small cloth bags and a fat clay jar from the basket.

"How did ye hurt yer head, my lady?"

"I fell from my horse and he kicked at me," she said.

Maisry nodded and pressed against Emlyn's bruised, swollen temple with gentle fingers, then probed her skull with both hands. "Thorne asked me to come up here, as I know some healing. He was mickle worried about ye, my lady. Even a little frantic, he were, insisting that I come soon, for he could not wake ye. But 'twas a natural, exhausted sleep ye were in, poor chick."

Emlyn listened drowsily, relaxing almost immediately under Maisry's soothing touch, light as an angel's caress. Though the bruise smarted, a subtle heat from the woman's hands seemed to ease the pain and draw it away.

Maisry sat back on her heels and sifted among the little bags, plucked a few and set them aside. "Ye've a goose egg, my lady, that must pain ye dearly. I will make a soothing hot infusion to drink, which will relieve the ache and reduce the swelling. But first, a little greeny ointment."

Maisry opened the clay jar and scooped two fingers into the contents. "I make it from elder leaves mostly, and a little walnut and almond oil. 'Tis messy, but helpful for such bruises. I have an herbal shampoo for ye to use, but ye must not wash yer head for a few days." She smeared the slick, bright green stuff on the side of Emlyn's temple.

Dirk laughed at the sight from his perch by the fire, Elvi laughed because his brother did, and Emlyn grinned at both. "You are a knowledgeable healer, Maisry," she said.

" 'Tis a gift the Lord has given me, I suppose. Many come to me, though they bring their animals as often as their families." She laughed lightly. "Whatever the Lord wants me to heal, I try my best. My granddam taught me much of the old ways, herbs and plants and such, and I have learned some on my own." She finished applying the ointment and wiped her hands on a cloth.

Sorting through the little cloth bundles, Maisry sprinkled a few dried herbs into a square of cloth, and dropped the bundle into water boiling in a second, smaller kettle.

"Do you know Thorne well?" Emlyn asked.

"Aye, though he keeps much to himself and is gone for long stretches of time. He's a forest-reeve here, and reports to the monks who own this land."

"Have you known him long?"

Maisry nodded. "Oh aye." Stirring the infusion, she poured the hot brew into a cup and handed it to Emlyn.

Sipping carefully, Emlyn discovered a pleasant minty taste with a hint of chamomile and other herbs she could not identify. She leaned back, holding the hot wooden cup.

Maisry sat near Emlyn. "Eight years ago, Aelric found Thorne out on the moors, near dead with an arrow that had pierced his lung. He was badly then, badly." She shook her head at the memory. "For weeks we knew not if he would live or die, though I did my best, and prayed night and day for him. He stayed with us a long time, recovering from his weakness, and hiding."

"You know who he was, then?" Emlyn asked carefully.

Maisry narrowed her eyes. "Aye," she said slowly. "Do ye, my lady?"

"My father had given him aid that night. At first we thought him safe away, but then my father heard the rumor that he had died that night." Emlyn glanced at Maisry.

Maisry nodded. "So yer the one," she said softly. "He did say, this morn, that he owed ye a debt. We helped to put about the rumor of his death—he asked us to do that for him. He stayed with us till he was stronger, and we told folks he was a cousin of mine. When he left, we heard little from him for years, though he has come and gone frequently in the past two years. But in all that time, we have never wanted for anything." She laughed. "He has given us coin and stores and shown us countless kindnesses. We've been repaid many times over. He's a good man, is Thorne, with an honorable heart. He takes a debt seriously. If he owes ye aught, he will make it good, my lady."

"He saved me last night. 'Tis enough."

"Likely not enough in his eyes," Maisry said. "He does not forget. But better old debts than old grudges, as they say."

She went over to stir the contents of the steaming black pot, and in a few minutes, Emlyn was served a bowl of hot savory soup, thick slices of bread and cheese, and a small cup of mead from the wineskin. She ate hungrily, dipping chunks of bread to scoop up vegetables and broth. The cheese was mild and moist, and the mead burned sweetly in her throat.

Maisry gave the children their dinner, and then ate a little herself. When they were finished, she cleaned up the few dishes by wiping them with a damp cloth, and sat by the fireside to croon a soft song to the boys. Lulled by the song, Emlyn relaxed against the deep, soft furs and soon dozed.

"Aelric!" Maisry's exclamation startled Emlyn awake, and she struggled to sit up. The man who had entered the cave was very tall and heavyset, dressed in cloak, tunic, and braies in shades of brown. A startlingly red and wiry mass of hair stood out from his head and a matching beard covered most of his face.

Maisry hastened to his side, and Dirk bounced nearby until Aelric bent to swing him up in the crook of his arm. When Maisry introduced her husband to Emlyn, he nodded shyly at her across the bright hearth. She smiled, but her attention was caught by the other man who entered the cave just then.

Thorne smiled warmly at Maisry and Dirk, murmuring a greeting in the casual manner of those who are well-acquainted. Though he glanced over at Emlyn almost as soon as he came in, he leaned toward Maisry, softly questioning her and listening intently to her answers.

Emlyn watched him, fascinated. Her vague childhood memory agreed well enough with his appearance. He was tall, though not nearly as tall and broad as Aelric. His long, slender legs were encased in dark wool braies, and leather boots wrapped with thongs to the knee. His torso was long, narrow at the hips, his shoulders wide and square. He was clothed in a leather jerkin studded with metal rings, worn over a brown tunic, the hem of which swung just above his

knees. A green hooded cowl, pushed back, framed his shadowed face, with its short, thick beard. Dark hair waved past
his shoulders.

Nodding to Maisry, he walked toward Emlyn with a
graceful swinging stride. Her heart beat a rapid patter as she
nervously craned her head up to look at him. Firelight illumined his face and chest in red and gold as he looked down
at her, revealing an aquiline nose and dark brows slashed
straight over his eyes.

"Greetings, my lady," he said, and squatted down beside
her.

As he tipped up the corner of his lip in a half smile, she
saw that his heavily lashed eyes were of some medium
color, but whether green or blue or gray, she could not be
sure in the firelight. He was handsome, almost beautiful in
a wild, dark, tangled way. Emlyn was aware that each movement, each expression, seemed to emanate strong masculine
power, with an underlying reserved gentleness.

After all these years, she thought, here was Thorne, with
her. Realizing that she stared at him with her mouth open,
she snapped it shut.

"I see that Maisry has treated your injury," he commented.
Emlyn raised her hand to her head, suddenly self-conscious
of the unattractive green slime that coated one side of her
face.

Reaching over, he pushed her hand down, his fingers dry
and cool. "Nay, my lady, let it be." Long fingers grazing her
skin, he slowly lifted the heavy mass of her loosened braid
away from the side of her face. A few golden strands clung
to her cheek, and he combed them back. Tiny shivers traveled along her throat and into her belly at his light touch.
Some image or feeling, like a vague memory, flashed in her
mind and was quickly gone.

"Keep your hair out of the way, or 'twill be bright green,
especially as pale and fine as 'tis. We've all had a coating of
Maisry's greeny ointment at one time or another." He smiled
again, a curious tilt of one side of his mouth, half obscured
by the black mustache and beard. His voice was deep and
gentle.

Sitting, he leaned back against the wall, one leg drawn up,
his arm casually draped over the raised knee. Maisry handed

him a bowl and a hunk of bread, and then a moment later returned with a cup brimming with ale. He thanked her and ate. Emlyn watched him, and when he caught her glance, she flicked her eyes away, embarrassed. Aelric ate also, seated on the floor opposite the fire, with Maisry and Dirk beside him. Elvi snored softly, curled on a pile of furs nearby.

Thorne swallowed a long draught of ale and dangled the wooden cup between finger and thumb, swirling it for a moment.

"What do you recall of last night?" he asked, looking directly at Emlyn, his black-fringed eyes piercing. Elongated light and shadow played across his face.

Emlyn squinted at him. Her head had begun to ache again, and her thoughts were as vague and smoky as the little fire. "I remember little," she answered. "I am lacking in my wits right now, so I ask your pardon."

" 'Tis no wonder, my lady," he murmured. "You were near frozen and sick with a head wound when I found you."

Swallowing a little more of Maisry's lukewarm infusion, she was not at all certain that her fragmented thoughts and nervousness were caused by the blow to her head. Thorne's presence beside her made her feel breathless and dizzy, as if she had been spinning wildly. Blushing furiously at the hazy memory of being gathered cozily into his arms, she sat up. "I saw—or dreamt I saw—the Green Man. My horse bucked in fright, I fell, and ran from the creature. Then you found me. I remember hearing your name. After that—" she shrugged.

"You passed out on my shoulder soon enough," he said. "And the Green Man is a legend, my lady," he added, sounding amused. "I heard some perplexing noises and went looking, expecting some trapped or injured animal. Instead I discovered a wet and cold girl clinging to a tree."

She opened her mouth to affirm that she had indeed seen some forest creature, but he reached out a hand to tip her chin up and tilted her head gently toward the firelight. "Tell me, Lady Emlyn, why you were in the forest last night." There was a subtle tension in his voice.

"Tell me, sir, how you know my name," she said.

He stroked her cheek lightly with his thumb and she shivered inside, waiting to hear his answer. "We met, years ago, you and I," he said softly.

"Aye," she whispered, her heart beating fast, "I know."

After a moment, he withdrew the warm comfort of his hand and stretched out one leg, his toes nearly touching the firestones, and raised the other knee, resting his hand there. "Now, my lady," he said, "we must talk. We can openly speak of your situation here. Aelric and Maisry are my trusted friends."

Maisry leaned forward and spoke quietly to Dirk. He nodded and went to lay down beside Elvi. Aelric waited until the boy had closed his eyes, then spoke, his voice a low rumble. "There were soldiers near Kernham today. They were asking after Lady Emlyn." He glanced briefly at Thorne. "When they stopped at the field where I was plowing, I told them nay, I had seen no one. They warned me to speak no lies."

"What did they look like?" Emlyn asked.

"Four of them, armored, in the rust-colored cloaks of Whitehawke's men."

"You recognize Whitehawke's men?" Emlyn asked.

"The earl is well known in this dale, my lady," Aelric said. "We are not far from Hawksmoor where his son is baron. Besides, Whitehawke covets this land."

"This is the dale that he claims?" She remembered her earlier conversation with Chavant concerning the land dispute that had set Thorne against the earl.

"Lord Whitehawke has argued for years with Wistonbury Abbey and with Bolton Abbey over the rights to the dale," Thorne told her. "Though the monasteries are both south along the river, the monks own much land here, thousands of acres, good land. They have tenanted farms and vast herds of sheep. Lord Whitehawke claims that the whole area originally belonged to his wife and is now his, including the farms, the herds, and all the profits as well. Lately he has sent workers to begin the foundation of a castle at the upper end of the dale."

"Aelric and I farm a parcel of the land for Wistonbury, and we raise sheep in agreement with the abbot," Maisry added. "Our living comes from what extra we produce on the farm, and a portion of the sheep. The monks, being our overlord, take produce from the farms and make a very good income from the wool each year. 'Tis most of their income, the wool, y'see."

"Has Whitehawke brought his claim before the king?"

"Aye," Thorne answered her. "Whitehawke has hounded the king about the matter for years, but so far the court has reached no decision. The verdict must involve the Pope because part of the land is church property. The case has been delayed because King John and the Pope cannot agree well on any matter."

"What of his son, the Baron of Hawksmoor? Does he support his father's claim?"

"The baron has so far done naught," Aelric said.

"But his lands are nearest the dale," Emlyn commented.

Aelric shifted his large, muscular body and thoughtfully sipped his ale. "Aye, Hawksmoor is a few miles north of here, but 'tis across a river, and well away from the center of the dale, where most of the sheep roam. So far, the baron does naught for or against the claim, though 'twill be his dispute should his father die before 'tis settled."

"So, aye, my lady, we do recognize the livery of Whitehawke here," Thorne said.

Maisry leaned forward. "Why were you alone and lost in the wood, my lady, and why do you hide from Whitehawke's men?"

Emlyn looked around at them, her eyes huge in her pale face. Aelric and Maisry waited patiently for an answer, their faces, reflecting the golden firelight, open and honest. There was a sense of acceptance, of quiet friendship offered her within the firelit circle. Shyly, she glanced at Thorne. He watched her steadily. Such calm strength radiated from his gaze that she felt oddly safe and protected near him. Closing her eyes for a moment, she sent a quick prayer heavenward. Wanting very much to trust these people, she also greatly needed aid.

"I think," she said carefully, "that you do not care much for Whitehawke, and so I trust that you would not give me away to him." She shifted and sat upright, and explained to them the circumstances of her betrothal, and then told of the escort's calamitous encounter in the fog. "When the Green

Man appeared beside our path, I ran, and got lost. The man who sends guards after me is Baron Hugh de Chavant."

"Why did you run, my lady?" Maisry asked.

"Such betrothals are decreed wrong and sinful by the Church, though men persist in forcing marriages. Whitehawke is said to be very cruel, and I cannot in good conscience marry him. So my only choice is to flee." Emlyn looked from one intent face to the next. "I have decided to give myself to God."

"You will go to a nunnery?" Maisry asked in amazement.

"Aye, but there is more." She told them about her siblings. "My little brothers and sister are now, I presume, prisoners at Hawksmoor Castle." She twisted her fingers in her lap.

Looking up, she met Thorne's eyes. Shadowed in the flickering light, he nodded slowly for her to continue.

"Lord Whitehawke frightens me," she said softly. "Entering a convent would serve as penance, since I dishonor the betrothal. I can accept that. But I fear that the little ones would suffer for my actions—" She drew a shaky breath, and then another. Tears welled in her eyes and trembled on her lashes. "I must know them safe and happy, if the king will not allow me to raise them myself. When I have seen to their well-being, then I would retire to a convent willingly."

"What would ye have done with the little 'uns? Ye cannot gain back custody," Aelric said. " 'Tis a king's order."

Emlyn sniffed, wiping her cheek on her wrist. "I would have them removed somehow from Hawksmoor Castle. We have cousins in Scotland, and they can be sent there for the nonce."

Maisry gaped at her. "Remove them from Hawksmoor?"

Emlyn shrugged. "My uncle is one of the monks at Wistonbury, and my eldest sister is a prioress at another abbey. Perhaps they can aid me—"

"How could a monk help you?" Thorne interrupted, an impatient edge in his voice. "No use to ask the king for mercy regarding children. He has no soft mother's heart."

"My uncle can request guardianship as the senior of our family now. As a religious, he may catch the king's ear. Nicholas de Hawkwood could be told to give the children over to my uncle. And Godwin is a scholarly man, with knowledge of the law. He will likely send a petition to the pope as well, asking that the king rescind the order."

"He could do so." Thorne tossed a small stone from the floor into the fire. "But likely naught would come of his efforts. The children would stay where they are." He glanced at her. "Do you consider that they may be well and safe at Hawksmoor? The baron of Hawksmoor is no ogre, lady."

"I have met the baron, and he seems a cold and heartless man to me," Emlyn said. "I will not have my brothers and sister in a strange place. Children must have a loving home to grow in."

He tossed another stone into the fire, and another. Tiny sparks flared up from the flames. She watched his profile, obscured by waves of dark, glossy hair, tangled, unruly.

"What you will, my lady," he said at last, so softly she barely heard. Then he raised his head and looked at her. "What then of you? If you go into a nunnery, Lord Whitehawke can retrieve you. You are still his betrothed. If he wishes, he can use any method to force you to wed."

She had not thought of this. "I must take the chance. My uncle can send me to my sister Agnes at Roseberry Abbey. Whitehawke may consider me too much trouble. He has Ashbourne already, with or without me to wife."

Thorne nodded as he stared into the fire. "Roseberry is far north of here."

"Aye," Emlyn said. "Agnes entered Roseberry out of grief for her husband's death. Soon after, my father brought me out of the convent where I had been schooled. He said he was arranging a good marriage for me. He did not live to see it through." She shrugged. "Whitehawke would never have been my father's choice."

Maisry had been listening with great interest, stirring in her seat, opening and closing her mouth, growing more impatient with every exchange. Now she leaned forward, her round face shining in the firelight. "My lady, if ye were already betrothed, the king's orders would be null. Ye say yer father made arrangements for ye to be wed?"

"No agreement was reached. I never learned the man's name." Emlyn passed a trembling hand over her forehead, as if to rub away the persistent dull ache that lingered there.

"If Lady Emlyn were betrothed," Maisry said, "or if she were to marry another before Whitehawke found her, he would have no claim on her."

They all looked at Maisry. Sparks flew up from the crackling hearth as they stared in thoughtful silence.

Finally Emlyn smiled ruefully. "Who would wed me now? Naught will undo this betrothal, and I must commit my life to God. Whitehawke, if he is a pious man, will honor my choice."

"How may we aid ye, then, my lady?" Aelric asked.

"You have already helped me greatly, for which I thank you. But I would leave on the morrow to see my uncle. If you could supply me a pony, I will see that you are repaid."

Maisry shook her head, framed in the linen wimple. "Nay, my lady. Ye must rest three or four days at least, or ye will suffer much dizziness and headache. The bone in yer head may be cracked, with so much bruising."

Emlyn sighed, knowing Maisry was right. Her head pained her still, and she felt a creeping weakness throughout her limbs. She had ignored waves of dizziness each time she turned her head. "Perhaps a short stay here would be best," she said.

" 'Twould give Chavant time to leave the area as well," Thorne said, "if you are wholly certain that you do not wish to rejoin his escort."

Emlyn frowned at his slightly cynical tone. "I will stay only a day or two," she insisted, leaning back against the fur cushion. "I must go to Wistonbury." A cozy exhaustion began to swirl through her. She wondered hazily if Maisry's headache remedy had a sleeping herb added to it.

"Aye, lady, see him you surely will," Thorne said softly, and leaned over to draw a fur coverlet across her legs. "Rest now. There will be time enough to talk."

"Will I see you again?" she asked him sleepily.

His face was close to hers, and his breath blew soft on her brow. She could feel the warmth of his body, an odd, deeply comforting sensation. "I will be here, should you need me. Rest now," he murmured.

She nodded, grazing her eyelashes down to relieve her tired eyes, but she found that she could hardly lift them again.

* * *

Her throat was very dry when she woke, and though the dull headache persisted, her mind felt clearer. Stretching her arms over her head, she yawned, then looked around the cave. She was alone. The faint light at the cave mouth, edging the dark curtain in pink and gold, hinted at dawn.

Pushing back the furs, she stood up, her legs a little wobbly as she crossed the cave. She scooped water out of the wooden bucket with a cup and drank thirstily, then sat by the banked fire and nibbled on an apple. In spite of the morning light, the cave interior was still dim. Drawing her knees up under her chin, she stared into the warm glow of the hearth.

Her heart beat a soft, rapid patter in her chest. Black Thorne had come back into her life just when she needed him most. She had no doubt that the bearded, quiet forester was indeed the old enemy of Whitehawke. When he had entered the cave last night and looked at her, she felt that she knew him well, as if the distance between now and a moonlit summer night eight years ago had never existed. He had looked at her with the same sense of familiarity, she was certain of it. Of anyone, she thought, she could trust this man. And he owed her family a debt.

She whispered a prayer of thanks. The saints had sent her a brave knight, or near enough to one. She had found a warrior to reclaim her brothers and sister, a hero like Bevis, or Roland, or Gui de Warwyck, who would champion her. She had only to convince him. Smiling, she hugged her knees to her chest.

As he slipped in through the curtained doorway, she was deep in thought, unaware of his presence until he stood near her. She sat by the low hearth as if in a trance, her arms curled round her knees, her flaxen hair glorious with a glowing light of its own, flowing over her back to froth and spill onto the floor

Her quiet beauty, surrounded by that ethereal halo of hair, had nearly taken his breath away when he entered the cave. Finely carved features, slender limbs, delicately shaped hands; he had already had opportunity, when he had peeled off her icy garments and wrapped her in warm blankets, to assess her firm, taut body, her rounded breasts, flat stomach, and smallish hips. She was not a large woman nor ever would be, though she carried herself with a proud grace that made her seem taller. Now, sitting here at his feet, she looked as fragile as glass.

"Lady Emlyn?" he questioned softly. She raised her head and stared up at him as if she had never seen him before.

By the rood, he thought, the head wound has turned to the worse. "Lady?"

She fixed him with a look that was ferocious and elfen all at once. The delicate line of her nose and throat contrasted the stubborn squarishness of her jaw. Straight dark brows gave her expression further seriousness, above lake-blue eyes flecked with tiny circlets of gold around each pupil.

Her small face was an intriguing blend of willfulness and vulnerability. Thorne felt an urge to protect her, a response, in part, to the subtle blend of child and woman he sensed in her. He felt, too, a strong current of desire flow through him, a burning glow in the core of his body when he looked at her. The warm cream of her skin nearly drove him to reach out a hand to touch that silkiness. He flexed his fingers closed.

"Black Thorne. We heard that you were dead," she murmured.

Sighing, he knelt near her. "In a sense 'tis true." Tossing kindling into the hearth, he used a stick to coax the fire to greater strength.

"Though I was a child, I never forgot you," she said.

"I remembered you as well," he replied softly, "and your brother, and Wat. I heard that your father had died, and that his family was in difficulty. I was greatly concerned."

"You already knew who I was when you found me," she said.

He smiled. "Of course, my lady. Did you think I recognized the skinny child in this beautiful woman?" Reaching out then, unable to stop himself longer, he touched the tip of her chin gently. She lowered her eyes and blushed a clear pink.

He lowered his hand and jabbed again at the hot embers with the stick. "Your father was a fine and generous man, a great loss. When I heard of your brother's capture, I knew that you might soon need a friend. I have, as much as possible, followed news of your family, in case I could be of aid to you."

She looked surprised. "How have you had news of us?"

He shrugged. "A reeve has many sources throughout the shire, my lady. When word came of your betrothal to Whitehawke, well, to be honest, the man is vile. I would not soon see the daughter of a friend wed to him. And I remember my debts."

"How did you know that I was lost?"

"I knew the escort would be bringing you through the dale, and so Aelric and I kept a watch, difficult enough in the mists. We soon found out that the escort had some trouble. At first we could not find you in the mists, though we heard you right enough, noisy as a wounded pig."

He grinned at her, and she smiled back. His heart felt lightened by her smile. Sweet rood, how dazzling her hair and eyes were in the firelight. He inhaled, feeling a wash of desire as they laughed together, aware that his body responded to her quickly. He had not yet decided what course to take, and this turn in his feelings was alarming.

Her brows drew together, charcoal slashes above her clear eyes, a direct and sharply curious gaze, and his heart thumped. Squatting on his haunches, facing the fire, he fed the flames with deliberate movement, thinking all the while as fast as a whirligig. What to say to her, and how much. I dare not tell her now, he reminded himself. But he knew that he had already begun to trust her, though he never trusted quickly.

"You look very familiar to me, as if I knew you well. But I have not seen your face for years," she said, tilting her head and narrowing her eyes. "Have I?"

His smile faded like a dream, replaced by a stony coolness. Trust, sometimes, was a selective thing. " 'Tis my father that you see in me, I trow," he said quietly. Shifting his weight, he sat down beside her.

"Your father?"

"Lord Whitehawke."

She sat upright, dropping her arms from round her knees, staring at him in disbelief. "You are—brother to the baron of Hawksmoor?"

He shrugged, and opened his hands, palm up, in silence.

"Glory God," she breathed, and leaned toward him. "You harangued your own father, those years ago?"

He nodded. "A long tale, my lady."

She blew out a soft breath and peered at him. "Aye so. There is a strong resemblance to the baron, though I cannot see your face so clear beneath the beard. And your eyes are quite green." She frowned, touching her teeth to her lower lip, then burst out, "Thorne, you are my friend, I trust."

He glanced away. "Aye, I am that."

"And you owe my family a debt."

"Aye," he said, wary of her direction. "And I think when I deliver you safe to your uncle I will have met that debt."

"You could help us more than that." Her eyes were bright with eager thoughts. He dreaded to hear them.

"Gain my brothers and sister back from the baron," she said.

He drew a hand slowly across his jaw, scratching through his thick, short beard. "Abduct them, you mean to say?" He raised an eyebrow at her.

She fairly sparkled in the firelight, her eyes shining, the soft ripples of her hair glinting, her even teeth white against rosy lips. She nodded. "Aye, you could do so. 'Twould not be hard for such as you."

He sighed, knowing that a cold deluge would be best here. "Lady, those children are in no danger. Hold off your fancies, and think with cool wit instead. I have no men to attack a castle. And where in heaven would you keep the children?"

"As I told you, with relatives in Scotland."

"And how do you mean to get them there? If you commit yourself to a convent, what then for the children? Think carefully, my lady. They are soundly kept where they are now. What if those in Scotland will not take them? Will they reside in religious houses with your uncle, or with you?"

"They need their family around them. They are so young, and I promised my father—" She stopped abruptly and jumped to her feet in a dash of blue silk. Whirling, she paced and turned before she spoke again. When she did, the fierceness in her tone brought him to his feet in surprise.

"I promised my father I would keep them safe by me always!" She pressed her clenched fist to her mouth. A sob

burst out of her slim frame, and she spread her
fingers over her face.

He watched her crumple, feeling a dismal helplessness.
Something whorled in his gut, as if he had suddenly absorbed her anguish. Reaching out, he took her by the arms
to support her, and she wilted against him, crying. Gently, he
gathered her close, stroking the soft, fragrant mass of hair,
patting her shoulders in a soothing rhythm until the storm
began to subside.

"Hush," he said, his cheek on her head. "Hush. You have
done no wrong."

She sniffled and laid the palms of her hands against his
chest. "We promised our father, Guy and I," she said. She
swallowed another sob. "But now Guy is gone, too. The
promise has come to me, and I must keep it."

"A promise is a sacred thing," he said into the gossamer
crown of her hair. "Well I know that. And a father lost is
never regained elsewhere in your life. But you have no fault
in what has parted you from the children."

"I must honor his wishes." Her voice was thick and trem-
ulous. " 'Twas the last thing he spoke of, their welfare. Oh,
God," she cried. "I cannot bear to be away from them.
Should some harm come to them—" her voice broke.

He held her in the secure fold of his arms and rubbed his
thumb in circles on her back. Suppressed sobs shook her in
tiny quakes, and he slid his hand against her neck, thin and
as vulnerable as a child's beneath his fingers. He inhaled the
smoky, herb-scented silk of her hair, felt the slight, warm
burden of her in his arms, and felt a measure of her pain.

" 'Twas wrong for them to be taken from me," she
sobbed.

"I see," he said. He closed his eyes. "I see, now."

Chapter Eight

"Oh, ow, ease up, Maisry!" Emlyn said, wincing. "I am not one of your sheep, to be scrubbed raw!"

Maisry lifted her fingers from Emlyn's soapy head. "Hold yer head over the bucket, and I shall rinse ye," she directed. Emlyn, kneeling, squeezed her eyes shut as a warm deluge cascaded over her head and into a large wooden bucket. Maisry lathered her hair with a rosemary decoction followed by another plunging rinse, then wrapped linen toweling around Emlyn's head.

"My head is still quite tender," Emlyn pouted.

"Well, aye, 'tis only the second day since ye cracked yer nod. But ye shall feel all new again, with clean hair."

"Could I not have a bath?" Emlyn looked at the two buckets, one for clean warm water, and one to catch the soaped rinsings.

"Thorne has no tub here, my lady. He bathes in a pond, cold as ice 'tis, too. When yer strong enough for the walk, ye shall come to our farm and use our tub, big enough even for Aelric. For now, if ye wish, we'll heat more water for a quick washing with a cloth."

Emlyn nodded, then toweled her head gently. "I must leave here as soon as I can, Maisry. Tomorrow, or the next day."

"Not yet, my lady. Thorne said he will take ye to Wistonbury when I feel yer ready for the journey."

"Ah," Emlyn said as she set the towel about her shoulders and took the wide-toothed ivory comb that Maisry handed her. "Then you and Thorne will say when I may leave, and not I?"

"Well, my lady, if I said my thoughts, 'twould be a long while before I declared ye ready to leave." Maisry picked up the bucket and walked to the entrance to toss the soapy contents out the door. She peered into the sunshine, looking for Elvi and Dirk, who played nearby. Satisfied that they were safe, she came back into the cave.

"What do you mean?" Emlyn asked.

Maisry knelt next to Emlyn and took the comb to work the tangles out of Emlyn's hair, her fingers as gentle for combing as they were for healing. "I mean, my lady, that no woman should have to shut herself in a convent to avoid a marriage. I would keep ye here, if I could, to save ye from that."

Emlyn sighed. "I made the decision, however ill or blessed, to resist the marriage. There is nowhere else I can go. A woman alone ends with relatives or in a nunnery. And you know that Whitehawke will find me, sooner or later. I must give my life to God in order to save it, I think."

"It saddens me to think of ye like an old apple, shut away in that holy barrel. Ye should have a husband and many babes; I have seen yer loving ways with my own Elvi and Dirk. Prithee, my lady, do not hasten to this end." Abandoning her gentle strokes, she tugged at a knot of hair impatiently.

"Do you think I want this?" Emlyn said impatiently. "I have no other choice! My home is gone, I have no land, no wealth, no sure family. No man would wed such a poor prospect. So, the convent."

"My lady, there is one who would wed ye."

Emlyn laughed. "No soul on earth would take on Whitehawke for the sake of a penniless, landless woman."

"My lady, forgive me, but Thorne would have ye, I trow."

Emlyn turned to stare at Maisry, wet locks hanging unheeded in her eyes. "Thorne?"

Maisry nodded and began to comb again. "Aelric and Thorne would shake my bones to hear it. But aye, Thorne would have ye to wife, and in faith, I trow ye'd be well suited to each other."

"Thorne would have me to wife?" Emlyn repeated, dumbfounded. In spite of her incredulity, something quickened inside her, as if her heart kept pace with a running step.

"Would ye not have him, a good man, and handsome? My lady, as ye said, ye've no landed family, no coin or title, and who knows what fate brings for any of yer blood. But if ye married another man, the betrothal would be annulled by virtue of the greater vow, and ye'd have no need to retire to a convent."

"Perhaps you are right, Maisry, but Thorne would not—"

"I believe he would, and gladly. Let not this cave worry ye. He has a bit of land, though I know not where. Aelric knows, I think. Thorne often goes away from here, traveling to that place." Maisry put the comb down, and drew out the full length of Emlyn's hair, shaking it gently. "Sit closer to the fire, my lady, and yer hair will dry, fluffed as a cloud."

Emlyn shifted over and turned her back to the fire, facing Maisry, who sat with her long sturdy legs curled beneath her skirts. "Has he spoken of this to you?" Emlyn asked.

Maisry shook her head. "He has said naught. Yet I have seen him look at ye as if ye were a candle flame, and he a man in the dark." At Emlyn's stunned glance, Maisry held up a palm. "Aye. 'Tis yearning, and something else, as if ye trouble him. Mayhap his debt to ye weighs on his mind. He is a secretive man, and has ever kept to himself as long as I have known him. But he has need of a wife, I say." Maisry nodded wisely to herself.

"If he is so secretive, mayhap he is married already."

"Nay. Aelric knows more of him than I, and has never mentioned such to me." Maisry leaned forward. "This is only what I think, and mayhap ye must forgive my foolish words, my lady. Likely Thorne and my husband would happily hang me for saying such." She smiled. "Wait here a bit, and I will fill the buckets and heat the water for yer washing." She got up as she spoke, and went out the doorway.

Emlyn skimmed her fingers thoughtfully through her hair. Maisry's suggestion was not unwelcome, she had to admit. Blessed saints, she thought fervently, I would rather spend my days with a kind husband who owned naught but a pallet in a cave, than in a castle with Whitehawke, or shut fast in a convent.

She recalled the gentle way Thorne had held her while she cried. He had treated her more like a frightened little girl than a woman. She had needed that then, but she had wished, later, that he had shown his heart to her. He obvi-

ously had no such feelings for her as had quickened in her
for him.

Besides, a man who must live freely would not fix himself
to a wife. She shook her head and shoved the hair from her
eyes. Maisry should create love poetry in a noble court, with
such imagination.

Thorne possessed the qualities of a hero out of a roman de
chevalerie, she thought, like Gui de Warwyck, or Bevis of
Hampton or Havelok the Dane. Like them, he had beauty,
strength, and courage. He had been gentle and chaste with
her. And he had a strong, righteous sense of honor.

But such men, she reminded herself coldly, existed only in
stories, not in the hard, true world. She had been unable, after all, to convince him to play the bold knight and rescue
her siblings from Hawksmoor. His logic had been like water
on her fire. And then he had held her as if she were a babe.

She sensed an intriguing depth within him, but a distance
as well, as if his true self were protected behind a screen.
Even if she could see behind that screen, mayhap his inner
character would be dark. He was, after all, a bastard son of
Whitehawke. Blood often ran true.

Shifting about in front of the fire to dry the other side of
her hair, she ran her fingers through the rippling strands,
drying to the color of sunlight on gold. This much she knew:
Thorne would never marry her, despite what Maisry thought.
He would see her to the abbey and then disappear from her
life. His debt to her was not that great, after all.

Yet she felt as if he had tied silken strings to her heart,
and each time she saw him, heard his voice, the strings
pulled. Her heart thumped when he came near. She must
have been a little in love with him since she was thirteen.
Now that she had met him again, he was surely no disappointment to her. Surely she had yearning in her own eyes
when she looked at Thorne.

Sighing, she rested her arms on her upraised knees. 'Twas
all a silly, fanciful dream. Best that she leave and go on to
the abbey to meet whatever fate God had planned for her.
She could not hide in this cave forever. If she stayed here
longer, saw more of him, she feared her heart would hurt too
much.

* * *

"By the saints. 'Tis longer than ye are tall." Maisry laughed delightedly as Emlyn hoisted the longbow. "Well, tilt it, then. Mayhap if ye pull it up, ye'd clear the end of it out of the grass."

Tight-lipped with concentration, Emlyn lifted the bow and drew the string back until her arm ached and trembled. Aligning the arrow again when it slipped from the nock, Emlyn sighted the slender trunk of a birch tree, then released the arrow. It flew, rapid and sure, far past the target to sink, trembling, in a gorse bush. Emlyn chose another tree, a wide oak. Certes, she could hit this one. She nocked another arrow and lifted, fighting the wobble of a bow that was too long for her.

"Oh! That squirrel will live to tell the tale, I trow," Maisry said. "Look how it runs."

"That squirrel was in the way," Emlyn said defensively. "It was hiding up there and got nicked." Leaning against the bow, she rested a moment, and tossed her long, thick plaits back over her shoulders. She stood in a glowing shaft of sunlight that sparkled and poured through the leafy canopy. The surrounding forest floor was speckled with buttercups and bluebells and primroses, scattered among green ferns and grasses. She inhaled the spring fragrances, gloriously invigorated after more than a week shut in the cave, with its hazy fire and damp walls.

Emlyn had cajoled and finally begged until Maisry had agreed that she could go out. Thorne's cave was high above the dale, tucked in a fold at the base of a rocky cliff; she and Maisry, with the boys, had ventured down the wooded hillside that sloped away from the cave toward the bowl of the dale. They had stopped in this forested area near the valley.

Adjusting the too-large leather glove that protected her hand, Emlyn lifted the heavy bow, nocked an arrow and drew the string taut. "See that oak limb, where two branches curl together? I shall aim at the trunk just below."

"Stay behind Lady Emlyn, boys," Maisry cautioned. "Best we are not in front of her." The boys scrambled well away.

"Maisry," Emlyn warned. "Hush." She pulled and released.

"Oh my! Ye nearly struck the thing."

"It was very close," Emlyn agreed. "I think I am getting the feel of this hand-bow."

"Ye say ye've done this before?" Maisry asked doubtfully.

"Aye, with a ladies' bow at home," Emlyn said. "Certes, I need more practice, and I've never tried a longbow. There were a few bows in Thorne's storage room, but some were wrapped. This one was nearest the door, so I took it, with some arrows." She nocked a third arrow, lifted, and shot. A slender leafy branch, high up, fluttered to the earth.

"Well," Maisry said wryly. "Ye did catch the tree then."

"Ho!" a voice called. Emlyn and Maisry turned to see Thorne and Aelric moving down the wooded slope behind them, bathed in cool green light.

"What is this?" Thorne asked, lifting an eyebrow at Emlyn.

Though she tried to smother it, she could not seem to stop the smile from bursting out as he came near. His eyes, as green as new oak leaves, twinkled at her. Then he lowered his eyebrows sternly. "Well? What do you outside, in plain sunlight? And with my longbow?" She thought a smile played at his lips, too.

"I borrowed it, with some arrows, and a glove for my hand," Emlyn said. "I pray you do not mind. Today I feel strong, and wanted to come out. Maisry and Dirk and little Elvi have been very encouraging," she said, casting a look at Maisry.

"Oh, aye, Lady Emlyn needed the air, surely. And if ye wait a bit, there'll be something for the cooking pot," Maisry said, smiling up at Thorne.

"I saw. Acorn soup," he said. Aelric and Dirk laughed, and Emlyn scowled a bit, blushing.

Thorne pursed his lips, scratched his bearded chin idly, and then sighed. "Well, you would pursue this, so let us get it right, at least." He turned to Aelric and murmured a few words. With a quick nod, Aelric spun and climbed back up the hill.

Thorne took Dirk with him, stepping over soft tangles of undergrowth, to fetch the arrows already loosed. Emlyn and Maisry watched Elvi struggle to lift the big bow, laughing at his bravado, though they swooped together to stop him when he grabbed a handful of steel-barbed arrows from the quiver.

In a few moments, Thorne and Dirk came back up the hill, and Aelric returned with another bow. He handed it to Emlyn.

"Now, my lady," Thorne said, "if you want to shoot, try a bow more your size. This one is a smaller hunting bow. I have not used it since I was a boy. I have been planning to give it to Dirk when he is a bit older." Emlyn lifted the shorter bow, which was nearly as tall as she but easier to balance, and nocked the goose-feathered arrow he handed her. She lifted and aimed, all the while listening to his voice as he stood behind her.

"Tilt it a bit—aye. Now draw back just to your chin. Well," he said, touching the tip of her chin with the lightest fingertip caress, "the arrow is really too long for your short arm. Draw to here." His fingertip brushed the corner of her jaw, just below her ear, and a shiver spiraled through her. As he took his finger away, she blushed again, feeling the heat in her cheeks and throat, and looked straight ahead.

"Now pull—steadily, girl, don't let it wobble away from you. Keep your bow arm straight. And lift your other elbow. Higher."

"She leans into the belly of the bow," Aelric observed.

"Aye, so," Thorne agreed. "Turn your shoulders as if you were flat to a wall. Don't lean into the space between the bow and the string." She felt his fingers again, pulling back on her shoulders, kneading them a little. He ran his fingers lightly down her spine, lingering at her waist for a moment. "When you draw, keep your body straight but relaxed. And breathe," he added. "Breathe in as you draw, and out as you release."

At his touch, such utterly pleasant shivers spread throughout her body that she had to make an effort to concentrate on his words. Then, trying to put his instructions to good use, Emlyn shot four arrows, one after the other, toward the same spot she had aimed at earlier. The fourth shaft grazed just past the trunk of the oak, closer than she had done yet.

Applause greeted this effort. Emlyn, serious, nocked and lifted the bow, endeavoring to remember Thorne's instructions.

He stepped up behind her as she steadied her stance. "My lady," he said at her ear, "this little bow shoots very sweetly.

Just let your fingers slip off the string. Gentle as a breath. If you pluck too hard, the arrow will fly to one side or the other. Let it go smoothly, girl," he murmured. "Sweetly."

She felt his warm fingers press her shoulder through the silken fabric of her gown. His breath feathered the hair at her brow for an instant, like a caress. She flicked a nervous glance at him. "Breathe with the shot," he whispered, and stepped back.

She breathed, and released the string as if it were a thread on the wind. The arrow chunked into the wood, very near her target, and stuck.

She turned, pleased, to look at Thorne, and he nodded at her, smiling with a tiny lift of his lip. "An archer yet, she'll be," he said to Aelric. "There'll be game meat for supper after all."

"Not this even, sirrah," she retorted. "I can only hit a still target. A large, still target."

He grinned. "Sweetly, my girl, sweetly will do it," he said.

Maisry stepped up to Emlyn, Elvi held snug against one hip. "Sweet as honey, and the bee stuck fast," she whispered. Emlyn's eye popped open wide, and Maisry laughed, a delicate happy trill. "We must be going, my lady," she said, "with all the preparations for the morrow to be done yet."

"The morrow?" Emlyn asked.

" 'Tis the first of May!" Dirk crowed. He had been lifted high onto his father's shoulders. "We shall have games in the village, and lots of food, and girls will dance around the may tree. Not me," he added, "only girls."

He grabbed two fistfuls of Aelric's hair, and clucked as if his father were a great red-maned horse. Emlyn smiled and waved as they left. She turned to see Thorne standing with leggy ease, his longbow propped in one hand like a walking stick. He watched her evenly, his thoughts sheltered behind green eyes.

"Well," she said, "do you say a bow will shoot sweetly, then show me how 'tis done."

"I will, my lady. But first put on your cloak and hood."

"Why? 'Tis a warm, lovely day."

"Aye, but your hair is bright as a beacon fire. Better you

were not out here at all. Lovely the greenwood may be, but
'tis dangerous for you." He bent as he spoke, and chose an
arrow from the quiver on the ground, hefting the shaft
lightly in the palm of his hand. "That is, if you still desire
to hide, and then go on to the abbey," he added softly.

Emlyn put her green cloak over her blue silk gown, fastened the brooch to close it snug, and pulled her hood up.
From a distance, better she looked like a pillar of moss than
glinting gold. And though a part of her wanted to stay in the
forest with Thorne, she lifted her chin with a decisiveness
she did not truly feel, and answered him. "Certes, I wish to
go on to the abbey."

"Then I shall take you there tomorrow," he said, his back
to her. "Do you like primroses?"

He straightened suddenly, nocking the arrow and drawing
the string, one fluid and graceful motion, quick as the lift of
a hawk's wing. Emlyn barely marked the aim and draw before she saw the bolt arc high, skim through the trees, and
sail down.

"Where did it go?" she asked.

"Where I meant it," he said. "There." He pointed. Between two birch trees, over two hundred feet away, gray
goose feathers trembled deep in the center of a cluster of
yellow primroses that cascaded over a fallen tree.

Emlyn laughed, shouldered her bow, and picked up her
skirts to run down the slight incline toward the landed arrow.
She heard Thorne running behind her, and she laughed
breathlessly, the first to halt at the fallen tree.

Reaching for the arrow at the same moment, their hands
touched around the slender shaft, deep in the soft blossoms.
Thorne drew the arrow out, and small yellow petals scattered
at Emlyn's feet. She lifted her eyes to his, and slowly
slipped her fingers from the arrow shaft, giving it up to him.

His eyes were as green as the cloak she wore, his hair and
beard as dark, in this shaded part of the wood, as raven
feathers. A memory flashed through her mind, of pulling the
bloody shaft from Nicholas de Hawkwood's thigh, his hand
together with hers.

In spite of Thorne's eerie resemblance to the baron, she
quickly dismissed the thought. This warm, gentle man was
completely different from his hard-edged half-brother. The

look he gave her, piercing yet apprehensive, stopped her heart, and an odd tingle began in the core of her belly. Her breathlessness was not from running, now. She leaned in toward him.

Thorne plucked a primrose, sun-bright and fragrant, and touched it to her cheek. She put up a hand to take its damp softness into her fingers, still looking up at him.

Suddenly he raised his head and looked to the side. Then he grabbed her shoulders and dragged her to her knees, going down with her. She gave out a little huff of surprise as he threw her onto the ground beside the fallen log and landed heavily on top of her. What little air she had left went out of her like a squashed wine bladder.

"Sirrah—" She panted, pushing at him, shocked by his aggressiveness, "I am a modest woman—"

He clapped a hand over her mouth and pressed the length of his torso, solid and hard, over hers, one knee between her legs. "Your virtue is safe," he muttered in her ear. "Hush." His short beard tickled her cheek, and the leather of his hauberk pressed against her neck. They waited, silent, breathing in tandem after a few moments, their bodies accepting and adjusting to the contour and swell of hips and legs and torsos.

Emlyn, curled beneath him, heard the faint pounding of hoofbeats in the greenwood. Thorne lifted his head to look, and she struggled to see as well, but he held her down. Silently, his eyes warned her to freeze her movements.

The creaking and thumping noises of several horsemen came alarmingly close and seemed to last a long time. Thorne's hand covered her mouth and jaw firmly, and his breath was gentle beside her ear. She smelled wood smoke and leather, and the sweet trace of crushed primroses on his fingers. Watching the subtle pulse in his throat, she sensed the vital rhythm of his heart.

Her own beat a fierce rhythm as if in response. The weight and contour of his body fitted well to hers. She placed her hand on his back; he tightened his fingers over her mouth.

As he turned his head warily, watching and listening, his inky black lashes swept over irises of striated greens and grays, like moss growing over stone. Emlyn was close

enough to count the black hairs of his eyebrows, to notice
the copper and brown hairs threading his thick black beard.
His cheeks were flushed a high, clear pink, warming the
cool colors in his eyes.

After a time, Thorne removed his hand slowly from her
mouth, frowning and touching a finger to his lips for silence.
He shifted and stretched out beside her on the verdant forest
floor, beneath the shadow of the log and its trailing, glowing
mantle of primroses. Ferns tickled the side of her face and
crowded over her shoulders, and a cluster of pale yellow
flowers fell onto her cheek. He reached over to push the
blossoms away from her face and rested his hand on her
shoulder. Propping his head on his other hand, he looked at
her.

"Damn," he said softly.

She frowned up at him. "Chavant's men?"

"Aye." He exhaled sharply. Emlyn waited for him to
speak again, but he lay quietly, rubbing his thumb absently
over her shoulder. Her heart thumped, hard and strong, with
each circling touch. Peering up at the treetops far above, he
looked as if he were thinking.

"Thorne."

"Hmmm?"

A curious melting feeling had begun in her arms and
chest. She wanted to move closer, to feel more of the
warmth and strength that emanated from him, wanted to
spread the glow further through her body. Yet she was afraid
to move; he might stop rubbing her shoulder and get up.
"Will they come back?"

"Likely not. They will ride on, having found no one in
this part of the wood." He squeezed her shoulder gently,
then took in a deep breath and sat up. Emlyn could not quell
her flutter of disappointment. "Come, girl," he said, holding
out a hand, "you must be gone from this part of the wood."

Ignoring his hand, she stood and smoothed out her skirts.
When she looked up, he was offering her a handful of primroses.

"Here," he murmured, " 'tis what we came down the hill
to get." He lifted an eyebrow and she smiled faintly, accepting the flowers. With one finger, he tilted her chin to look
into her eyes. "Are you fearful, then? The men are gone."

Mutely she shook her head, and turned away, sniffing the primroses shyly. She could hardly tell him that what subdued her was a shocking, lustful urge to lay in his arms, on the forest floor or anywhere, until Judgment Day.

"My lady—" he said, his voice a bare whisper. She looked around hopefully. He took a step closer and raised a hand to touch her face, his fingers brushing down her cheek to her throat. As he leaned toward her, a feeling began within her lower body, heavy and glowing. Her knees trembled oddly as she moved forward and lifted her chin.

The feel of his lips on hers was soft, warm, a little dry; a simple kiss, brief and gentle. When it ended, Emlyn gazed into his eyes silently, and glided closer, a little hesitant, sensing that she wanted more but not knowing what to ask of him. She placed her hand on his chest, feeling cool leather and the soft thump of his heart beneath her fingertips.

Thorne grazed his fingers down her back to press against her waist, drawing her closer. His mouth touched hers again, a soft caress of lips and breath. A swirling, lightning-quick sensation rushed down the length of her torso to pulse in her lower body, and she drew in her breath sharply.

Circling her arms around his neck, tilting her head, she moved into the kiss with greater courage. She slid her fingers into the thick, silky waves of his hair, aware, in some detached part of her thoughts, of the tremor in her fingers and the insistent thumping of her own heart. His lips on hers were still exquisitely gentle, a little tentative, and she sensed some element of tension.

He drew back and she glanced up uncertainly. Touching a gentle fingertip to her cheek, he smiled a little wanly, ruefully. "I am sorry, my lady. You are promised to another, such as he is."

"Nay," she breathed. "I am promised to no one."

Subtle as a cloud gliding over the sun, something crossed his face, and he lowered his hand. Lifting his bow over his shoulder, he turned away from her.

"Go up to the cave," he said quietly. "I must go to the village, to see what news of the guards." Confused, Emlyn stood there for a moment. He turned and looked at her again.

"Go," he urged, his face impassive.

Emlyn turned to angle up the hill away from him. Like a warm touch between her shoulder blades, she sensed his lingering gaze as she climbed the slope. Several moments passed before she heard the soft crush of his steps through the undergrowth in the opposite direction.

Lilting through the twilight, the voices grew and faded, stronger as the singers climbed, fainter as they wended sideways. Emlyn peered out into the dimming light, through the tangle of trees and undergrowth that screened the cave entrance, curious and wanting to hear more of the music.

Through the slender trees, she saw him in the bluish twilight gloom, reclining against a hollow oak that had been uprooted ages ago, its great dried roots clawing at the lavender sky. Emlyn fetched her cloak and went out.

He glanced up as she stepped between the trees and beckoned her near. Heart quickening at the gesture, she went to his side.

"Listen, my lady." He held up a hand in the dusky light and slowly lowered it, resting his fingertips lightly on her forearm. His touch sent delicate shivers down her spine. "Listen." Faintly, like the chuckle of a brook or the silvery chime of fairy laughter, she heard the song. She cocked her head to listen. " 'Tis the young people of the village, out on May Eve."

"Aye." He slid down from the gnarly perch and held out his hand. "Come with me."

As Emlyn laid her hand in his, a light jolt danced through her palm as it touched his warm skin. Holding her hand firmly, he led the way past the cave entrance toward another outcropping of dark limestone, where a winding pathway, tufted with grass, slanted upward. He let go of her hand and stepped up.

Tucking part of her skirt into her belt, she followed, maneuvering the simple inclined track with little difficulty. Closer to the top, the way became very steep, and Emlyn exclaimed softly in frustration.

Thorne reached down and boosted her onto a wide, flat-topped crag. Emlyn stood up slowly, her chest heaving, slightly dizzy from the swift climb. The wind played fast and free with her cloak and hair and blew chill against her skin.

The view from the plateau was stunning. Approaching darkness washed indigo over sky, hillsides, and the forest that clustered against the slope leading to the dale far below. Stretched out like a long bowl lined with velvet, the dale floor was studded with farms and stone walls and cut by narrow streams, like deep folds in the velvet. The sides and ends of the dale faded in deep misty shadows.

" 'Tis beautiful," she said, spinning slowly around. The broad, flat crag was a checkerboard of stone and grasses, nearly as large as a small courtyard. Clouds sailed across the wide, darkening sky as the silver moon rose.

Thorne, behind her, placed a hand on her shoulder. "Up here," he said softly, "on foggy mornings, the mist covers the forest and dale like clouds come to earth. There is peace here, and power." He squeezed her shoulder and pointed. "Look."

A sinuous trail of light, the small sparks of distant torches, moved through the forest. "They gather branches and flowers for the May celebration." His fingers still rested on her shoulder, warm through her cloak.

She laughed. "If these girls and youths are like those near Ashbourne, they stay out the whole night of May Eve, and down a good deal of ale."

He smiled; she heard it in his voice. "And the groups break into couples, and more than flower-weaving takes place in the forest. Many a hasty marriage has been made in the weeks following the first of May."

Emlyn blushed furiously, remembering Maisry's words, and stepped away from the sheltering heat of his body. "Ah, there, hear it? They are singing again. And someone is playing a pipe." Gently she swayed to the melody formed by pipes and drums and dozens of bright, laughing voices, wafting up through the trees to the upper slopes.

Caught by the simple joy of the sound and the glorious wildness of the crag, she was also keenly aware of Thorne's steadfast presence behind her. Humming quietly, moving to the floating rhythms, her pale braids undulating softly, she knew when he stepped closer.

His fingers on her shoulder lightly turned her to face him.

The moon was higher now, a full globe behind him, and his tall silhouette loomed as he drew her forward until the tips of her shoes met his boots.

"Lady," he said softly, "do you dare to be about at night, on May Eve?"

Her breath quickened as he lightly stroked her upper back, his body a warm shield from the cool breezes. "I am not frightened," she replied.

He lowered his head, his mouth scant inches from hers. "Some enchantment might befall you," he murmured.

Her gaze was drawn to his mouth. An enthralling, delicious power began to awaken within her, as if she had discovered some deep, easy magic. "Ah, but I could weave a spell myself, if I had a maypole, with bright ribbons and flowers."

"You weave a spell now," he said, but Emlyn felt like she was the one caught fast. Raising a hand to her head, he traced along her silk-smooth hair until his fingers slid in to cradle the back of her head. With his other hand, he glided her toward him.

At the first feathery brush of his lips on her cheek, she tilted her mouth toward his, yearning to feel his lips on hers again. Tentatively, his lips touched hers and lifted, then touched again. Deep inside, her blood pulsed. She closed her eyes and parted her lips, and when his mouth covered hers once more, she thought she would melt like butter over flame.

Learning quickly, answering the pressure of his lips and the strong wrap of his arms around her, she slid her hands up to his shoulders and moved her lips softly, instinctively, beneath his.

His mouth met hers again and again, with growing strength and insistence. He crushed her against his body, his arms a strong, warm band around her. The silken dampness of the inner side of his lips sent strong rhythmic quivers cascading through her. A tremble began in her lower belly, and she pressed against the length of him, wanting the hard contours of his body to meld and fit to the softer recesses of hers, even through multiple layers of silk and wool and leather.

Breathless, she pulled back, then inhaled and plunged at

him again, pulling his face down to hers. He laughed softly and lightly touched his tongue to her lower lip. Her mouth opened readily to the warm, wet caress of his tongue. As she closed her lips tentatively around him, he explored her mouth with exquisite gentleness, holding her head between his hands.

Vaguely, she thought what a blessed relief this was, how easy. She felt odd, but somehow more focused than ever in her life, as if these breathless kisses brought her to a profoundly familiar place, to home, to where she belonged: with him.

One hand slipped down to trail along her throat until his fingers found the split at the collar of her cloak. His hand slid inside, feathering touches circling skin, brushing over silken fabric until his hand closed over her breast. Kneading gently, pressing against the hardened nipple that pushed against his palm, he kissed her deeply, arousing in the center of her body a sensation that was wholly new, wholly exhilarating.

She pressed closer to him, bending back her head and arching her torso toward him. Quick, light fingertips slid over her until her breasts began to ache. She only wanted more of his touch, of him, and felt no fear or wariness, only trust, and comfort, and a deep sense of ease and rightfulness.

Suddenly he moved his hands to grasp her shoulders. Silently they gazed at each other, breathing quickly. Her breasts rose and fell against his chest, the sensitive tips pinched slightly by the metal rings of his leather hauberk. With one hand, he tilted her head down into his shoulder, holding it there. She heard the heavy, solid rhythm of his heart.

"Sweet rood," he breathed. He stroked her head lightly, smoothing the wayward strands of hair. "I had best get you gone from here before something happens."

"Something has happened." She lifted her head to look at him.

"Aye," he said softly, "aye, and it should stop here. I am not one to tumble a maid on May Eve. Especially not a child-maid, betrothed already, who vows to be a nun."

She wanted to protest, to remind him again that she was

not promised to any man or to any convent just yet, but her thoughts were hazy and utterly confused.

"We stand on an open crag in bright moonlight," he went on. "If the villagers are out, then Chavant's guard may be as well. I know not what entered my thoughts, to take you up here on such a night. Or to let this happen." He let out a long breath, and stared down at her, frowning.

"Thorne—" She was halted by his stormy expression, apparent even in the darkness. Where she had enjoyed, even reveled in the wonder of their heated touching, he seemed to regret it.

In the moonlight, his eyes glistened, reawakening in her the same sweet, urgent burn she had felt when he kissed her. But that joy was overpowered by this sudden, unexplained rejection. The burn turned to a dull ache in the pit of her stomach.

He dropped his arms and turned, and she followed. Wordlessly, they made their way down the slope to the cave.

"Lady Emlyn." When he spoke, she stopped with her hand on the black cloth that covered the entrance opening and waited. "My debt to your family is genuine. I will not dishonor that promise." She turned to look at him, all her hurt welling in her eyes. With a soft, wordless exclamation, he reached out to touch her face gently, almost sorrowfully.

"I will see you safely to your uncle. We will leave on the morrow," he said. " 'Tis best, I think."

She tilted her face into his hand for an instant, then pulled away. Tears swelled her throat, and she could not answer. He did not want her in his life. Perhaps, for a moment, he had surrendered to the physical urges that she, too, had felt so keenly. But she realized now his feelings for her were based on an obligation from the past. Naught more than a debt to be honored.

Turning, she ran into the cave.

Chapter Nine

Standing in the shade of an old knotted oak, Emlyn watched the wreath of dancers spinning in the sun around the beribboned may tree, a tall sapling set in the center of the village green.

With crisscrossed hands, their feet tracing a circle dance, the girls were urged to quick and quicker footsteps by the breathy trill of wooden flutes and the staccato of the tabors. Beyond the village, the constant burbling rush of a wide, calm river lent a soft background to the music and raucous laughter and happy shouts that filled the sun-splashed green.

Laughing, Emlyn watched the girls make dizzy grabs at the long fluttering ribbons that dangled from the treetop. The dancers stepped around each other, weaving bright plaits with the red, blue, purple, and yellow ribbons. A little dog, excited by the music and the whirling dancers, ran into the group, barking and leaping, and had to be chased away.

Just after dawn that morning, Maisry had come to the cave, insisting that Emlyn join the festivities for May Day. Knowing that Thorne wanted her to leave for the abbey that day, Emlyn agreed. Maisry had lent her a linen wimple and an old homespun brown kirtle and apron to wear. She intended to claim Emlyn as her cousin, reassuring Emlyn that, once wimpled, she would look like any other married woman should Chavant's men be about.

The simple, snug headwrapping, worn beneath a coarse linen veil, even enveloped her brow and chin. "Some would hardly recognize ye," Maisry had commented. "Well, I would, but I am cleverer than most. The guards who seek ye would not know ye now. Men never notice details," she had said, laughing.

Now, watching the dancers, Emlyn's interest was caught

by something at the far end of the village green. A crowd of children gathered there, laughing and shouting.

"The Green Man is here!" they called. "Jack o' the Green!"

A tall, green-clad figure moved slowly through the village in the midst of a bouncing mass of children. Small arms reached up to him and waving little fingers spread for the treats they knew he carried under his leafy costume.

Emlyn narrowed her eyes, and nearly laughed out loud. An attempt had been made to disguise him, but Aelric was too big, too red-headed, and too graceless to pass as a mystical forest creature. Loping through the crowd with leaves stuck all over him, grinning merrily, his face was coated with what could only be Maisry's greeny ointment. On his head was a conical hat stuck with oak leaves, acorns, and buttercups, and his torso was hidden beneath a green basketwork tent.

Leaves and blossoms fell as he walked, exposing bits of the crude twig frame entwined with grasses, leaves, and flowers. With large green-coated hands, he gave out chunks of honeycomb and crisp little buttercakes to the children, who threw themselves on him, crushing the wickerwork mercilessly.

Smiling to herself, Emlyn turned to find Maisry. Tables had been set up under the trees along the riverbank, and Emlyn walked over, her mouth watering at the mingled smells. Trestle boards were filled with meat and vegetable pies, kettles of beans and onions, steaming loaves of crusty bread, wheels of golden cheeses, and jugs of ale and mead. Roasted chickens and geese were ready on wooden platters, and marinated pigs and a huge ox were being turned over fire pits.

As she joined Maisry and the other women near the tables beneath the spreading shade of the oak trees, Emlyn heard a rumbling, thundering noise. She thought, at first, that it emanated from the rushing river. Then a chill formed along her spine. She slowly turned her head toward the village green.

Burst as if from nowhere, four armored riders rode full force down the length of the earthen street, russet cloaks flying. Amid the fading squeal of pipes, they slowed and walked their horses across the green. Girls dropped their ribbons and fled, and the village men backed away from the horses' path as the riders reached the group of children clustered around Aelric.

Mothers called to their children in panicked voices. Aelric calmly shooed the children toward the trees and turned to face the riders.

The leader shoved back his mail hood. Emlyn recognized Hugh de Chavant, his dark eyes wobbling above his scruffy dark beard. She drew back under a shady tree, thankful for her wimple and the generous folds of Maisry's brown kirtle.

Chavant walked his horse up to Aelric, alone in the center of the green, and leaned forward to scrutinize him. Aelric stared back with steady dignity in spite of his ridiculous costume.

"Why were we not invited to the May celebration? Surely you knew we were about in the dale," Chavant said smoothly. He drew his sword and tilted the blade slowly toward Aelric until the sharp point rested against the leaves over his breastbone.

"We have spent months and more, searching for the Green Knight who haunts the borders of Lord Whitehawke's land," Chavant said. He pushed the sword point slowly up Aelric's chest until the tip disappeared into his collar of flowers.

"Be he demon or merely a man, we are sworn to catch him," Chavant continued casually, as the pressure of the sword tore through the flowery torque. Blood trickled from beneath the leaves and petals. Maisry gasped and covered her mouth with her hands. Beside her, Emlyn put an arm around her shoulder.

Chavant raised his voice slightly, not taking his gaze from Aelric's flat, even stare. "We have lately searched for the Lady Emlyn de Ashbourne as well. But no one within miles knows aught of her." He squinted his eyes at Aelric. "I spoke with you on this matter not a week hence."

Spurring his horse forward a few steps, he forced Aelric to move back, keeping the sword leveled at Aelric's neck, pressing until Aelric stumbled into the trunk of the deserted may tree. Red and yellow and purple ribbons spilled over his shoulders and caught on the leafy wickerwork of his costume.

"Tell me your name again," drawled Chavant.

"Aelric of Shepherdsgate, my lord."

"You are a farmer?"

"Aye, and a freeman. My house and land are leased from the abbey. I tend both my sheep, and some that belong to the abbey."

"What division of the sheep are yours?"

"This season, about one-third of the flock, my lord."

"So you have your own income?"

"A portion of what the wool brings is mine, aye."

"Do you pay rent to Wistonbury, or to Bolton?"

"Wistonbury, my lord." Aelric leaned against the slender beribboned tree, looking remarkably unruffled by his situation.

"My lord." One of the village men approached, a stooped old man with a grizzled white beard, who touched his forelock respectfully and bowed two or three times. Chavant rolled his eye in exasperation.

"Who are you?" he snapped.

"John Tanner, my lord," the man said. "Aelric here, he wears the leaves and such for the holy day, and for the little 'uns. I swear, as will we all, he is not the one you seek."

"Oh?"

"The Green Man, my lord, the Hunter Thorne, some call the creature, well, that one's a devil from hell's own fire. He cannot be found, my lord. He is not of this earth. The legend says he'll take yer head with his axe as soon as—"

"I know the legend!" Chavant shouted, and lifted the sword point from Aelric's neck to swing the blade flatside at John Tanner, knocking him to the ground. The old man rose stiffly and backed away. "I know the legend," Chavant grumbled.

He traced the sword point up Aelric's cheek and lifted the conical hat, dangling it on the end of his blade. He watched it spin lazily.

"Aelric the shepherd, are you the Green Man?"

"My lord, I wear this for the children on the May day."

"Liar." Chavant cast the hat into the air and pressed the sword point under Aelric's chin.

"Robert." Chavant spoke over his shoulder.

"Aye, my lord," answered one of the riders behind him. The three who had accompanied their leader had ridden over behind Chavant, watching the scene as quietly as did the villagers.

"Robert, we have found our Green Man. I saw him myself in the forest near this valley, on the day Lady Emlyn disappeared. Bind him hand and foot. I would hear what he has done with the lady." Robert dismounted, and the other guards strolled their horses around the hushed village green, swords drawn, eyes wary.

Aelric stood motionless as the guard bent and tied his hands around behind him, securing his wrists, then his ankles, to the slender maypole trunk.

Chavant leaned over to rest the tip of heavy blade at the base of Aelric's throat. Another trickle of blood ran onto the leaves. "Where is the lady we seek? Tell me, or I shall burn your carcass at this tree!"

Beside Emlyn, Maisry pressed Elvi's face into her skirts and held tightly to Dirk's hand, her bosom heaving, her face flushed.

"There must be no more of this cruelty on my account," Emlyn hissed to Maisry. "I will show myself." She stepped forward.

"Nay!" Maisry whispered emphatically, pulling her back. "He will come to no harm. Wait. We will be delivered from this." Maisry squeezed Emlyn's arm to hold her.

Looking at her in bewilderment, Emlyn stayed still.

"Where is the girl?" Chavant was shrieking by now. Aelric was silent, his gaze like stone.

"'Tis possible, shepherd," Chavant mused, "that my lord Whitehawke will spare your hide if the lady is safe, and has been shown proper respect."

Aelric tilted his head slightly to one side and leaned back against the tree, sliding his gaze off into the distance calmly.

Unable to watch more, Emlyn resolved to reveal herself. Watching Aelric's steadfast resistance, she realized that she could not allow the precious trust and friendship that she had found with Maisry and Aelric to be betrayed by her own cowardice. She stepped forward, her gaze riveted to Aelric.

But a subtle flicker in his flat expression halted her step, and she noticed that his posture straightened slightly. Intrigued, wondering what he had noticed, she waited.

"Tell me where the girl is, or by the rood, I will cleave your head like an apple!" Chavant raised his sword high.

Something zipped past Chavant's ear, droning like a bee, and grazed past his lifted hand. He dropped his sword with a sudden clatter. Splitting the tender bark of the young tree well above Aelric's head, a wooden arrowshaft quivered in the tree trunk, feathered delicately in green and black.

Chavant turned his head, and the others followed his gaze. Emlyn did, too, and sucked in her breath sharply.

At the crest of the long slope, a rider sat a horse draped in a fluttering green caparison. The horseman wore chain mail that gleamed like links of brilliant emeralds in the sunlight, and his leaf-woven surcoat, with its trailing mossy web, put Aelric's simple costume to petty shame. The rider's hair, beard, and skin glowed greenish beneath the emerald dazzle of his mail hood.

A longbow, clearly silhouetted against the light blue sky, appeared to be held by thick, heavily leafed branches rather than arms. The Green Knight pulled the string taut and aimed again, holding the arrow steady.

With a roar, Chavant wheeled his horse and waved for his men to follow. They raced across the village green, heedless of the villagers who dove out of the way. Within seconds the horses' hooves gained fast purchase in the soft green turf and rapidly climbed the steep slope.

The green rider lowered his bow. Then he urged his horse forward and shot along the ridge of the hill, away from the forest and the tall black crags, toward the upper part of the river that flowed down into the valley.

Slate floored the shallows like broad slick stair steps at a fast and dangerous curve in the course of the river. The green rider reached the bank and splashed rapidly through the swirling water, but Chavant and his men halted uncertainly. Once they saw how easily the creature's horse crossed, they entered the cold rushing waters slowly. The Green Knight was far ahead, a bright speck on the moors, when they came out on the opposite bank.

The Green Man rode full and fast across the moorland, past sparse boulders and straggling clumps of trees, up and over the gentle roll of countless hills. The guards followed, and the chase soon reached a brutal crescendo of speed, horses lathered and sweating profusely, their powerful sides working like bellows, their strong legs chewing up the heathery moor. Chavant and his men could not gain on the rider, who seemed to fly across the ground, a verdant blur smoothly clearing stones and bracken.

Just visible at the crest of a far hill, a group of standing stones leaned like the heavy bones of giants, pale in the sun. Heading straight for these, varying neither speed nor direction, the green rider disappeared over the swell of a hill. When Chavant and his men saw him next, he had reached the center of the henge, a stout, weathered skeleton of vertical posts and gigantic lintels.

The guards rode down an incline, losing sight of him until they came up again and headed for the stone cluster. Slowing, they finally hauled up on their reins altogether and stopped to look at one another in confusion.

The rider had vanished. He had ridden into the stone circle, but had not come out that they had seen. The surrounding moor, rolling but open in every direction, was deserted.

Chavant cursed loudly and walked his horse to a huge scarred stone slab, tilted at an angle against another stone. "Look here," he growled, gesturing toward the ground. Hoofprints were clearly marked in the center of the henge, where the inner circle was pocked with broken stones and low, scrubby undergrowth. No prints led outside again.

"He's melted away into the stones," muttered Robert.

Chavant cursed again, a guttural sound, and spat down onto the ground. He urged his horse forward to step slowly through the ancient rubble. Many of the huge slabs rested askew, some precariously tilted. The original design was obscured by collapse, the stones overgrown with ivy and furred with moss.

One huge menhir angled into the side of a grassy hill, deeply embedded at the top and sides; it must have fallen generations ago. Chavant stared at it for a moment, then shook his head and returned to the others.

"Damn him! 'Tis as if he's gone into the ground, or more likely, around the henge somehow," he said to Robert.

"Mayhap what they say is true, sire," Robert replied.

"What do you mean?"

"Mayhap the Green Man who haunts this moor is truly a demon, not a man."

Chavant snorted and looked around the circle of stones. "Whitehawke is a foolish man who has trained his garrison to his cowardice," he sneered. "He leaps in terror at the mention of a demon, like a woman who sees a mouse. But I believe the Green Man is a man, just that and no more. Though a clever bastard." Pulling at the reins to turn his horse's head, he stopped suddenly. "The old man in the village had another name for this green knave—Etienne, what was it?"

"He called him the Hunter Thorne, my lord," Etienne said. "'Tis an ancient name for the Green Man."

"The Hunter Thorne." He smiled. "Aye, to be sure, this fiend is risen from the ranks of the dead. He has been hunted and lost before, but not again. Mark me, Whitehawke shall be interested in this news. 'Twill be a most agreeable counter to the disappearance of his betrothed. Come on." Spurring his horse, he galloped away from the henge, followed by the others. Soon they were far across the moor, heading back to the village.

Behind the enormous monolith that canted into the hillside, Thorne stood jammed against the horse's shoulder in the black musty hollow between the stone and the earthen slope. He had remained still, hardly breathing in the cramped space as he listened and watched through a crack, softly stroking the horse's muzzle. Long after the guards' hoofbeats had faded and the ground had ceased to vibrate, he stood motionless.

Finally, reaching down until his fingers found an indentation in the stone, he pushed against it. The huge stone swung silently upward to balance again, as it had for centuries, on two vertical pivot stones. Ducking his head down to clear the heavy canopy, pulling the reins slightly to lower the horse's head, Thorne stepped out. Touching a corner of the stone, he moved away as it canted down to thud once more into the grassy mound.

A merlin glided in a graceful arc over the standing stones and landed on a high post with a soft flutter of wings, turning its unblinking stare toward Thorne. Pulling off the long gauntlets that were scaled with bits of bark and twigs glued to the leather, Thorne tucked them in front of the high saddle.

He adjusted the bulky surcoat he wore, every inch of the cloth tightly sewn with fresh and dried leaves and flowers, Maisry's careful work. He pushed back his mesh hood, the old armor tinted brilliant green, and ran his fingers through his dark, sweat-matted hair smearing a little of the green ointment that liberally coated his face. Tossing his cloak, an open web of torn green wool woven with greenery, back over his shoulders, he thrust his booted foot into the slender iron stirrup.

As the horse and rider moved at a leisurely pace over the rise and fall of the moors, the merlin soared, winging over the trees to disappear within seconds. A few minutes later, the rider crossed the river, and turned his horse toward the forest.

Though the image of the Green Knight had burned in her mind all day, Emlyn had found no chance to ask Maisry about him. The May Day celebration had ended in a grim, quick meal, and everyone had gone somberly to their homes. Emlyn had accompanied Maisry and the children the mile or so back to their cottage.

The simple rectangular house, built of fieldstone with a fat thatched roof and thick wattle and daub walls, was clean and well kept, the whitewashed walls of the main room glowing with smoky firelight from a large angled hearth. The boys slept now in the loft above the sleeping chamber, separated from the main chamber by a curtain.

Emlyn and Maisry sat in silent exhaustion on a bench by the hearth and awaited news of Aelric. Returning from his futile pursuit of the archer, Chavant had taken Aelric and some of the village men for questioning. That had been hours ago. Emlyn ran her fingers wearily through her hair, free of its constraining wimple. The dirt floor beneath their feet was carpeted with rushes, and she pushed at a few dried grasses with her toe.

"Maisry," she said softly, "'twas Thorne on the hill today, was it not?"

Maisry leaned her head back against the whitewashed

wall. Dark circles purpled and dulled her eyes. Sighing, she rubbed a hand across her brow. "Aye, my lady, 'twas he."

"What goes on in this dale, Maisry?"

Maisry sighed again. "Three years ago, Lord Whitehawke began to demand fines from the people who live in this dale, though we owe him naught. We are tenants of the monasteries. The monks have sued against the earl, but the courts have been mickle slow in proving or disproving the claim."

"Have you paid fines to the earl?" Emlyn asked.

"Nay, and those of us who resisted have been harassed by his guards. Over the years, barns have been burned and homes lost. We have been luckier than some. One year we lost a byre and a few chickens. Some have decided to go elsewhere, leaving their farms and sheep untended. That makes extra work for the rest."

"Has the sheriff done naught, or the king? How can the earl do this without check?"

Maisry shrugged wearily. "The king nurses some resentment toward the monks. Several years ago, King John and his sheriffs tried to drive the Cistercians from York, but the Pope ordered the persecution to stop. The king is not one to forgive, and so he and his sheriffs have turned a blind eye in this struggle between Whitehawke and the monks." Maisry left the bench to feed a few sticks to the fire. "For well over a year now, the matter has eased. 'Tis because of the protection of the Green Man."

"Protection? But he frightens everyone."

"Aye, just so. Thorne and Aelric, and lately a few others, have shared the task of playing the Green Knight. That way, they can appear in many places, and be seen often by Whitehawke's men. The earl believes tales told to children, I vow. The Green Man disguise has fooled Whitehawke and his men into believing that the land—the valley, the forests, the moors around here—are haunted."

"Truly, I cannot believe that this has kept them away."

"Men who have done evil will fear evil, my lady. Whitehawke has frightened many of his garrison, I hear, into accepting the haunt as real." Maisry used an iron poker to jab at the glowing embers. "Whitehawke must have a heart filled with guilt. He fears for the state of his soul, I think." She turned to look at Emlyn. "'Tis said that he killed his own wife, many years ago. Did ye know that when ye ran from him?"

"I have heard such a rumor," Emlyn murmured.

"Aye, well, no one knows but the man himself. He has been the cause of much sadness because of his tyranny, in his own lands and now in ours. And many deaths, I have heard, in the French wars, and then his lady wife. Mayhap those deeds torment him, and he fears the consequences. He must believe this demon means to take him to hell."

"He eats no flesh food, only fish, as a penance."

Maisry glanced at her curiously. "Truth to tell, my lady? 'Tis no surprise to me that he tries to make amends."

"Why does he not relinquish this land to the Church in payment for his soul, I wonder, and ease his soul that way?"

"Because he is greedy, even if guilt eats like a worm in his heart. 'Tis too great and rich a parcel, and too sore a temptation to have it in his grasp."

"Dear Lord. I must escape this family of de Hawkwoods," Emlyn said, shaking her head. "But I will not truly be free of them as long as the children are hostages at Hawksmoor."

Maisry placed a hand over Emlyn's fingers and squeezed gently. "God will guide ye in righteous action, my lady. I believe that He will take care of ye."

Emlyn laughed hollowly. "Either God, or myself must do."

Letting go of Emlyn's hand, Maisry turned her head suddenly. "Hark—Aelric comes," she said. Rising swiftly, she went to the door and unbolted it.

Aelric's huge frame, clad in the tunic and breeches that he had worn under his May Day costume, filled the doorway. Maisry clung to him with a fierceness that caused Emlyn to look away, wishing to give them privacy. Aelric embraced Maisry a long moment before releasing her and stepping into the room.

"Yer unharmed?" Maisry asked in surprise and relief.

"I am well, good wife," Aelric said, "though I cannot say as much for Chavant and the rest." He laughed, an odd note of pain mixed with mirth, and shuffled toward the fire. Hunkering down, he almost lost his balance. Maisry's brows snapped together.

Poor soul, thought Emlyn, he must be sore hurt. Bruises

swelled one eye, and crusted blood glazed his cheek and lip and creased his throat. His skin had a sickly green cast where the greeny ointment must have been rubbed off.

"Tell us!" Maisry demanded. Aelric grinned at her impatience. Though his face was lined with fatigue, his dark eyes twinkled with some secret pleasure.

"Ye shall hear all in a moment. Greetings, my lady," he said to Emlyn as he held his hands out before the flames.

"I am glad to see you safe, Aelric," she replied, as Maisry slipped past her to fetch remedies for Aelric's wounds. Noticing that the front door had been left ajar, letting in the cool night air, Emlyn went to close it.

Pushing against the solid wood, she felt a sudden resistance and peered around the door. A tall figure, cloaked and hooded, loomed in the entrance. Emlyn gasped.

Long fingers pushed back the hood, and Thorne cocked a dark eyebrow at her. "Might I come in, my lady?" he asked softly. His gaze traveled over her face, touching her eyes, her lips, her hair. Emlyn recalled the previous evening, his deep kisses and his sudden rejection, and color rushed into her cheeks, heating her face and throat. She swallowed hard, staring at him, knowing her eyes devoured his face, but she was unable to move.

His hand covered hers on the edge of the door, and the weight of his warm fingers stirred a subtle quivering in her belly.

"Emlyn," he urged softly, "open the door."

"Emlyn," he repeated. Feeling her hand, small and soft, curl beneath his, Thorne wanted to reach out and caress the downward turn of her lower lip. She looked away as if flustered and withdrew her hand, stepping back to allow him space to enter. Behind him, she swung the door shut and latched it.

He moved past her, unfastening his dark cloak and hanging it on a wall peg before he went to the fireside to squat down beside Aelric. When Emlyn sat near the hearth on a cushioned bench, his heart thumped strangely. Knowing she was so close, he wanted to turn to her, but he held himself still.

Her eyes, her subdued manner had told him that she still

felt the pain of last night's parting. He sighed deeply and rubbed his fingers over his face, the back of his hand already heated by the fire. These weeks with her had sorely tried his self-control. God knew how he had found the will to pull away from her lush sweetness last night; God knew how he kept his hands off of her this very moment. His desire for her had become an intense distraction. Though he had told himself that his duty was to fulfill his debt to her and let her go, he had not counted on wanting her like this, craving not just her soft, firm body but her keen mind and open heart as well.

He had lost a good deal of sleep last night, tossing on the pallet in Aelric's barn where he had spent the nights that she had occupied his cave. Thinking of her winsome face and trusting eyes, remembering the sweet burn of her body against his, he was unwilling to let her go. He had devised a plan, finally, that was simple yet bold, and potentially as dangerous as any venture he had yet tried. If it worked, he could help her and still keep her with him. All he would need was her consent.

"Good even, Thorne," Maisry said, entering the room. She went to the table and set out a small clay jar, linen cloths, a large jug and wooden cups. "Do ye share my husband's triumph? He is gleeful, though I cannot think why."

"Greetings, Maisry. I was not there, though I have heard the story," Thorne said, glancing up. "We met outside the village and walked back here together. Since Aelric wants to crow, I shall let him tell you how he bested Chavant." He tilted his head toward Aelric, who grunted as he rose heavily to his feet.

Maisry beckoned to her husband. "Come here and let me tend to ye while ye speak," she said. Aelric was soon seated at the table, head angled while Maisry cleaned his facial wounds with a damp cloth. Then she scooped up a fingerful of greeny ointment.

"No more of that stuff, I have had enough today for my lifetime," Aelric said. She rubbed it into his cheekbone. "Echh, go easy, my dove. It hurts," he grumbled.

She scrubbed at his lip with a wet cloth and dabbed the oozy green stuff at his mouth and throat. "And well it should. Bested Chavant, ye did, and then ye downed a full keg? Ye smell like a brewer's kitchen." Aelric laughed. Maisry rubbed the elder leaf ointment quite vigorously into his cuts, wiped her hands on the damp rag, and looked fiercely at her husband.

"Tell, Aelric," she said sternly, "before I best ye myself."

"I trow she could do it well, Aelric," Thorne said, chuckling. He shifted to settle his back comfortably against the bench Emlyn occupied, his shoulder only a breath from her knee.

"Harken, then." Aelric leaned his elbows on the table. "When Chavant and his men came back to the village, they were mad as boars to lose the Green Knight. They took me, and Richard Miller and John atte Well and John Tanner—this much Maisry and Lady Emlyn saw. We were taken to the mill and bound hand and foot. Chavant asked questions and we answered as before. Where is Lady Emlyn, what do we know of the Green Man, why does he harass Whitehawke's men." He paused for a moment, accepting the wooden cup that Maisry offered him, and sipped. "Water?" he choked.

"Good spring water," she nodded. "Drink it."

"Well, of course we knew naught to help him. John Tanner told the legend of the demon again, and Richard Miller agreed that Whitehawke must be at his wits' end concerning his bride, and was she pretty, for he might have noticed a pretty thing wandering about, though perhaps not a dung-faced woman."

Maisry screwed up her face in exasperation at that.

"After a bit, Richard Miller's eldest boy Henry came in, who helps his father around the mill. 'Twas fair brave of the lad, for he acted surprised to see us there, and then offered us ale."

"How say ye?" Maisry asked. "Ale? As if they were visitors, and not after murdering the lot of ye?"

"Aye, just so. Chavant must have had a powerful thirst, for he accepted. Henry came back rolling one of Christina Miller's kegs of new ale."

"Oh! By the saints," Maisry gasped, "Henry is a clever lad." She turned to Emlyn to explain. "Anyone in the village knows not to touch a drop of Christina's new ale unless it has been watered, for it has a punch like a donkey's kick," she said. "'Tis usually kept for Christmas and bride ale."

"Many is the fine strong man who has gone down, all unsuspecting, in the path of Christina's ale," Aelric said. "We who knew drank sparingly, with Henry filling the cups. Chavant and Robert, one called Etienne, and the fourth—ah—"

"Gerard," Emlyn said, speaking softly behind Thorne. He glanced at her. She did not look at him, and seemed tense and as keenly aware as he of the closeness of their bodies. He felt her gentle warmth near him, and had known each movement she had made, each breath she took, since he had arrived here.

"—Gerard, aye," Aelric continued, "well, they had a mickle thirst, and Henry filled their cups over and over. Soon Robert loosed our bonds, John atte Well produced a pair of dice, and we tossed bones with them all, and Chavant in the thick of it."

"Gambling with such a lot," Maisry said, "'tis not only a sin, but foolish, too. Chavant likely cheats."

"Aye, he cheats, because he cannot throw bones straight-like with that wild eye of his," Aelric said. "He got pouty after a bit, and John atte Well began to talk of the Green Man—"

"John atte Well talks so in his drink, he can go through the night and the next day," Maisry groaned, rolling her eyes.

"Aye, my dove, but none of us were as cupshotten as Chavant and them, for we knew the danger of Christina's best," Aelric said. "So John talked, and we all added some, and we told the finest tale ever spun in this valley, I vow. Frightening enough to curl the tail of the devil himself. How the Green Man haunts us mercilessly, takes our children and spoils our crops, and steals the lambs from the fields. Richard Miller said the green demon hangs upside down at night in hawthorn trees, and John Tanner said a man in his da's time had been beheaded by the creature." Aelric, well pleased with his tale, paused to look at his rapt audience. "One thing more, Thorne," he said.

"What is that?" Thorne asked, watching him carefully.

"Chavant did say to me, and he deep in his cup, did I

know of a man called Black Thorne, who might pose as the
Hunter Thorne."

"Aye—?" Thorne waited. He had not expected this as yet.

"I answered that I had heard of him, but that he was dead,
and could not pose as anyone unless 'twere a ghost."

Thorne nodded, blowing out a breath. "Aught else, then?"

"John Tanner said that the man must have been a thorn in
the earl's side for years," Aelric drawled.

Thorne shook his head at the poor joke. Emlyn turned to
gaze fully at him, and he looked up, his belly fluttering
oddly as his eyes fastened on hers. He shifted slightly to
lean his shoulder against her knee. She looked away, pressing her lips thin and flat; he sighed and shoved a hand
through his hair.

"Where are they now?" Maisry asked.

"Three are cupshotten and snoring on the floor of the
millhouse. Etienne relieved himself in the millpond and fell
in, so we pulled him out and left him on the bank."

"Mercy of God, what happens when they wake?" Maisry
asked.

"Likely their pates will ache badly," Thorne said, "and
they will leave Kernham ashamed of their poor effort to find
their prey." He looked at Emlyn then. "My lady, I must take
you away." Her wide eyes met his again. "When?" she asked
softly.

"If we go before dawn, we will be far away before any of
them crack an eyelid. You can be at Wistonbury by vespers,"
he said. She bit her lower lip slightly, nodding, staring at
him.

Her gaze heated every fiber of him, flaring an ember that
spread through his body and warmed his loins. He wanted to
reach out to her and fold her into his arms, feel her soft
warm curves meld to him. Above all, he wanted to amend
what he had begun last night and so callously ended. Now
that he had decided what course was needed, he sorely
wanted to ease the hurt he had caused her.

Her hair slipped over one shoulder, rippled golden silk
glistening in the firelight. Her eyes, large and round in the
smooth oval of her face, were deep blue spangled with gold
beneath her straight, serious brows. As she squared her shoulders, Thorne mused that for all her appearance of fragil-

ity, there was an underlying graceful strength in the way she moved and in the delicate, firm structure of her body. She had resilience of heart and mind, too, and thankfully so: she would need it if she agreed to his plan on the morrow.

"I will be ready, then, before dawn," she said. "My thanks."

"A debt is owed, my lady, and gladly fulfilled," he murmured, gazing steadily at her. God willing, Thorne intended to fulfill his debt to the breadth and strength of his being. But he knew the risk. This marriage that he planned could endanger both their lives and their hearts.

Chapter Ten

"Devil take it," Emlyn muttered, hopping briefly on one foot and casting a dark look at Thorne's cloaked back at least fifty paces ahead of her. Her leather pack weighed like a great stone on her shoulder, the heel of one foot was blistered, and the last time they had stopped to rest was mid-morning.

Thorne had set and kept a steady pace with his quick, long strides. An hour into their journey he was well ahead of her and had stayed there since, glancing back occasionally to inquire if she was tired. Scowling and blowing a wisp of hair out of her eyes, she vowed now to stop, with or without him.

Looking around her, she immediately forgot the pinch and rub of her boots and her irritatingly tireless companion. Throwing back her hood, she circled slowly on the sunny moor, ankle deep in early pink heather and buttercups. The high dark crags above the dale were far behind them, replaced by an even wilder beauty.

Ahead and to the left, a vast, serene moorland, dusted with pink blossoms and fringed by dark clusters of forest, rolled toward a flat silver river. But to the right, the open mouth of a gorge split the earth. Hearing muted thunder, Emlyn walked closer and peered down. A waterfall tumbled and rushed down one rocky wall to pour into a pool at the bottom of a narrow ravine, about eighty feet below her.

Thorne waited, swathed in a long brown cloak and deep hood that hid nearly all of him but his beard, boots, part of his left arm and the longbow and quiver suspended across his back. After a moment, he strode back toward her.

"'Tis Mercie's Force," he said. "A legend says this is a sacred place, tended by a fairy named Mercie. 'Tis good luck to drink from the pool, yet bad luck to carry water away from here."

"May we stop for a drink?" she asked, awed by the possibility that a magical creature inhabited the place.

"Aye," he replied, "'tis time we rested."

Emlyn followed Thorne as he walked down a twisting path of moss-coated slate that led down into the deep, narrow gorge. The high steep walls were a jumbled, haphazard pile of jagged rock slabs, slick with spray and furred with moss. Ferns sprouted in every crevice beside tangles of pink rock-roses and golden saxifrage. The force, not a very large waterfall, tumbled from the cliff edge, plunging and hissing over the mossy rocks to fan out in delicate lacy sprays and spill down into a wide pool.

"Oh!" Emlyn said, sitting on a jutting wedge of rock by the pool, across from the tumbling force, "'tis a fitting place for a fairy to live! Like being at the bottom of a deep well." She craned her head up to look at the cliff edge far above.

"A noisy well," Thorne said over the soft thunder of the falls. He dropped his bow and quiver and sank down beside her to dangle a foot over the lip of the rock.

Emlyn looked down. "Is it deep?"

"Quite deep," he said. "Are you thirsty?"

Emlyn smiled and nodded. Thorne swung his legs behind him and leaned over the edge. Scooping his hand down, he came up and brought his cupped fingers to her face.

She glanced at him, hesitating. He nudged his hand toward her chin. "Regretfully, my lady, I have no silver cup for you."

Leaning forward, she placed one hand beneath his and timidly touched her lips to his hand, sipping lightly. The water was cold and tasted slightly of him, wood smoke and leather and a hint of lavender from Maisry's soap. She kept her eyes downward. "My thanks," she said. He lowered his hand slowly.

He leaned down again and drank deeply from his hand, then rubbed his wet fingers across his face and through his wavy, unruly dark hair. Emlyn noticed how very much he looked like the baron, though she thought him far more handsome than his odious half-brother. Thorne's eyes were very green, a paler hue than the moss surrounding them. The set of his bearded jaw, indeed the whole graceful length of his body, belonged to a more relaxed man, more content in his life and heart, than Nicholas de Hawkwood had shown the brief time he had been at Ashbourne.

"We should eat here and rest, my lady," he said.

Emlyn nodded and loosened the thongs of her satchel. "Maisry gave us plenty of food," she said, spreading a cloth on the rock. She laid out a wedge of cheese, a loaf of dark bread wrapped in cloth, and roasted, seasoned apples and onions. "I have taken much of your time recently," she said, slicing bread and cheese with the knife he handed her from his belt.

He glanced at her. "Time given without complaint," he said.

"Thorne," she asked, "what is it you do in the dale?"

"I am a forest-reeve, my lady, so I keep a watchful eye, mostly, and see that not too many of the king's deer are taken, nor wild boars either." She glanced at him in surprise, knowing that the king's deer were not to be taken at all; apparently he turned a blind eye to a certain amount of hunting. "There are hunting rights to be granted to those who would catch smaller game. At times I discourage the cutting or burning of forest land, except by permission of the monks. And I make reports to my overlord on the state of the parcels and tenants. Since I am not the only forester in the dale, there is not an undue amount of work for me." He shrugged as he ate.

"Your overlord is the abbot?" she asked.

"Aye."

"You do not meet with Nicholas de Hawkwood?" she asked.

His eyelashes winged down. "Nay."

She frowned. "How is it that Whitehawke does not know of the forest-reeve called Thorne in Arnedale?"

The sudden flash of his crooked grin caused her heart to flutter. "The reeve is very careful, my lady, to avoid the earl. There are, as I said, other foresters there."

Finishing her meal, Emlyn gathered the remaining food and returned it, rewrapped, to her pack, and handed him back his knife. Easing up the sleeves of her gown, she stretched to scoop a drink out of the pool. The water felt cool and silky and wonderful, and she reached again to splash her face with wet fingers. Golden tendrils, loosed from her long braids, clung to her damp cheeks.

Thorne reclined on one elbow and watched her, his eyes steady and unreadable. "Think you, my lady," he said, "that your uncle can help you?"

She sat back, looking up toward the milky mist of the waterfall. "I hope so. None else can help me."

"If he appeals the betrothal to the Pope, 'twill be months before an answer is received. You need a quicker solution."

She shrugged. "Whatever I do will bring the wrath of Whitehawke on myself and my family. King John's anger as well, I vow." She shook her head slowly. "Mayhap 'twere better I had gone back to Chavant when he first searched for me."

"When I found you, my lady, you had a head injury," Thorne reminded her. "You could not have gone back then."

"But—wellaway, what is the use. The dye is set, the cloth is colored and cannot be undone. I have followed my heart in making this choice to go to my uncle." She picked at the folds of her cloak as she spoke. "My nurse Tibbie always says 'tis not in my nature to think, but to rush on, heart before head. Once again I have acted without careful thought."

Thorne sat up and tossed the last of his bread onto a far rock, where several small birds alighted to peck. "What is the wise choice here, my lady? Is it wise to marry a man known for his cruelty? Such a marriage would be like prison, or worse."

He turned and looked at her. "The wiser choice is to flee, as you do. You can better help your family from a position of greater safety. You protest an unfair order, even though it came from the king. 'Tis bravery I see in that, not unwisdom."

Emlyn listened, her head bowed. "'Tis you who have ever been the courageous one. You once went in protest against an unfair lord. And you do it still, as the Green Man." She looked up. "Maisry told me."

He nodded and did not seem to mind that she knew. "Those years ago, the lad you remember flew in Whitehawke's face as mean as any demon, with the full-blown anger of youth." He shook his head. "Heart, as you say. Not head. Not bravery, my lady."

"What of now—the Green Man?"

"That venture is out of necessity rather than valor." He smiled and touched her arm, pressing it gently, eliciting in her little shivers of warmth. "Be proud that you have the spirit to reject the king's orders," he said. "Right now, many barons do the same. King John has insulted and threatened and endangered his subjects, and will receive his due, I think. You rebel in your way against the king, just as his barons rebel."

"I have heard of this dispute between the barons and the king. I did not know that the king could be overthrown."

He withdrew his hand, and Emlyn immediately missed the penetrating heat of his touch. His voice became harder suddenly, and the edge sent a chill up Emlyn's spine. "Not overthrown, my lady, but controlled. King John's extravagances and cruelties must be—will be—curtailed. He must comply to the law, just as any subject of England must do."

"Can a few barons force this to happen?"

"More than a few. There is support from most of the northern barons and the younger barons throughout England as well. Lately some of those who have been most loyal to the king have promised to stand against him."

"Then this will happen for certain?"

He nodded. "They already gather in London en masse. There may be an attempt to siege London and begin civil war. Better, I think, to convince King John to honor the old laws of Henry the First. Then the king's signature is needed on a similar charter, rewritten to address current and future needs."

"I have heard of these old laws,'" she said. "My brother spoke of them, and my father once said that if the old charter were to be resurrected, King John would not be able to carry on in the manner that he has." She sat up suddenly, catching her breath. "Thorne—if the king agrees to these demands, will his previous misdeeds be annulled? Will retribution be made?"

"The barons will demand many changes, my lady. They mean to stop King John's methods of gaining revenue through ransom and kidnapping and imprisonment. Some retribution should be made to those—such as your family—made homeless and destitute by the king's actions."

"Then he will make up for the deeds he has committed?"

"Lives lost cannot be replaced, but estates and monies can be repaid, at least in part, to heirs. The barons intend to define these rights, so that John can no longer wield such abusive power over his subjects. There will be mention made, as well, of the plight of women, widows, and those forced to marry against their will." He cocked an eyebrow at her.

She furrowed her brow, thinking. "If a charter of liberties comes about, all could be made right for my family." She looked up at him, a new hope blooming inside her. Perhaps she had only to bide her time and wait for the barons to do their work. "Thorne, could this happen?"

"The charter is very possible," he answered in a careful tone. "A confrontation is bound to occur soon. By high summer, or autumn, there could be new laws in effect."

Emlyn sighed happily, hugging her knees to her chest as she perched at the edge of the rock. "We will be back in Ashbourne by autumn, or by winter at the very least!"

He put up the palm of his hand. "Nay, slow, my lady. King John is unpredictable. Even if he signs a charter, he may not keep his word."

"But he would have to obey his own charter! He might well retract the writ regarding my family. Guy will be free, the children will be returned, and my betrothal to Whitehawke will be dissolved." She smiled brightly at him, elated.

Thorne sighed. "'Tis possible that amends could be offered," he said slowly. "But I do not think it likely. Do not forget Whitehawke in this. He is a trusted favorite of the king, and does not support the barons' cause. Whitehawke gets what he wants, laws or no." Thorne leaned toward her. "Even if you cloister yourself, he could force you to wed him."

Emlyn frowned. "Even if I go to my uncle and the protection of the Church, Whitehawke could still marry me if he chose?"

"He can claim that right." He leaned very close; she had never seen lashes so thick and black, eyes so green.

"But there must be some way to undo that."

He looked at her for a long time. "There is but one."

Emlyn sat curled on the warm face of the rock, hearing, as if in a dream, the hissing waterfall and lapping of the pool, and the high chirp of birds nesting nearby. "Tell me," she said.

"If you married another before Whitehawke found you, he would then have no legal power over you." His voice was deep and low, thrumming in her ear over the soft rumble of the falls.

"How could such a marriage be valid?" she asked, her heart beating heavily in her chest.

A splash of colored deepened in Thorne's cheek as he glanced away. "To the Church, a marriage vow is stronger than a betrothal pact, however it is created." When he looked back, his eyes were the gray-green of a thundercloud before a storm.

Every pulse of her heart throbbed throughout her body as she returned his gaze. Thorne could wed her and annul the betrothal. The words hung unspoken in the air between them.

She lowered her gaze to the calm pool, feeling foolish for wanting him to offer. His rejection of the other evening still confused and hurt her, and she felt increasingly angry and unhappy over her hopeless situation. Her temper suddenly flared.

"Speak no more of these impossibilities!" she burst out. "Think you I know of some convenient suitor? Where is the man who offered to my father for me years ago? I know not, and neither do you!" She was on her feet now, shouting at him, her frustration of the past weeks finding a vent. "I have no choice but to follow my sister into the convent! Leave me be on this!" She jerked up her pack and stalked off toward the path.

Jumping to his feet, he grabbed her arm and yanked her backward, slamming her to his chest, crushing her breasts against his leather hauberk as he held her firmly by her upper arms. She pushed at him, near to sobbing with anger.

"I cannot leave it be so easily," he said, his face close to hers. "I will marry with you."

She blinked up at him. "You?" she echoed dumbly. Her

heart nearly jumped out from between her ribs. "You would?"

"Aye, I would," he said. His eyes gleamed with a tempestuous light. "Unless you would have none of a forester."

A host of reasons to wed him flashed fervently and incoherently through her mind. Unbidden, reasons why she should be cautious followed. She swallowed hard, and looked at him.

She had not seen Thorne angry before. His iron grip and his narrowed eyes alarmed her, reminding her of his half-brother Nicholas, and then of the cruel father they shared. Thorne's strong resemblance to the cold baron, and his anger with her now, touched off the rest of her temper.

"Do you think to fill your vow to my father this way? Or have you found a new way to attack Whitehawke?" The moment the words were out she regretted them.

His nostrils flared above the black hairs of his mustache. Then he pulled her even closer, dipping his head to cover her mouth with his, wrenching her head back, kissing her with none of the gentleness he had shown that night on the crag. Her body responded, though her mind was numb, and she opened her lips to his searching tongue. She felt the heated hard center of his body press against her. When a melting, dissolving sensation began in her body, with it went all coherent thought.

He suddenly pulled back, leaving her breathless and staring up at him with wide eyes. "The offer is made, my lady," he said curtly. "You have until Wistonbury's front gate to think it over." He dropped her arms and leaned over to pick up his bow and quiver. Then he sauntered past her toward the upward path.

They headed toward the river that flowed far in the distance, silver sparks glinting off its surface. To the right, a wide stream flowed back to the gorge; these waters spilled over the cliff edge to form the waterfall. Thorne turned toward the stream, across which lay a moor that met, at a lower point, the river that would bring them to the abbey.

Chuckling and flowing incessantly around rocks and stones, the stream followed a winding course back toward the edge of the gorge. Ferns, grasses, and slender trees hugged the edges of the beck, shading the streambed with a cool green curtain.

Thorne, his face obscured deep in his hood, stepped onto a rock covered with a scant washing of water. He began to cross, pausing briefly to gesture her onward. From his position in the middle of the gurgling stream, he could hear no other sound.

Emlyn glowered at his back, her mind still whirling from his angry proposal and heated kiss. Placing one foot carefully on the slippery stone, she raised her head, alerted by some indistinct noise that did not naturally belong to the trill and burble of the water. Shrugging, hearing nothing else amiss, she stepped down, wincing at the cold water that seeped into her thin leather boots and sucked at her hem. She lifted her skirts above the water.

Thorne had reached the far bank and she was climbing up when the first piercing shout rattled over the sound of the stream.

"Ho! You there! Stop!" Emlyn whipped her head around. From the side where she had begun to cross, three horsemen rode quickly toward the bank, wearing russet surcoats.

"Lady Emlyn de Ashbourne! Halt where you are!" one of them called. She recognized Gerard, one of the men in Chavant's escort, by the deep gravelly thickness of his voice.

Thorne turned, his feet slanted on the incline of the other bank, and nocked an arrow in his longbow in the instant it took for Gerard to shout. He raised the bow and pulled the string tight just as Gerard stepped his horse down into the stream.

"Come, Lady Emlyn!" Gerard called. Emlyn paused, stunned and alarmed. She saw Thorne set his legs wide, his eyes fierce. His extended arms held the longbow in a deadly still aim.

"Leave the girl!" Thorne warned in a clear voice.

"Leave you to the devil!" Gerard growled. In his hand, a crossbow gleamed as he raised it above the level of his horse's head. A shot tore out, just missing Thorne, who barely flinched.

"When I shoot, serjeant, I shall not miss," he said low.

In an instant, the other riders—Emlyn recognized Robert

and the one called Etienne—urged their mounts down into the stream.

Emlyn whirled to cross to the opposite bank, but realized that would lead them straight to Thorne. Instead, she ran downstream, splashing through the center of the shallow water, away from Thorne and the guards. Launching their horses forward, the guards followed her, churning noisily through the water.

The water reached only to her shins at the deepest point, and she held her skirts up, running with a fast, open stride. The leather satchel smacked rhythmically against her back, and wet hems slapped her legs. Rocks and pebbles in the streambed stung through the thin soles of her boots, but she ran on.

From the corner of her vision she saw Thorne on the bank, running alongside the stream, bow in hand. He shouted to her, but she could not hear him over her own loud breathing and the noisy splashing and pounding of the horses close behind her.

A hand clamped on her shoulder, slid off, and then grasped one of her thick, heavy braids. A ferocious pull nearly yanked her off her feet.

Stumbling, she struggled to keep from falling. Her knee struck a rock and she straightened, trapped by her braid. Pain burned through her scalp and her neck twisted as Robert pulled hard, dragging her toward his horse. Her linen headpiece came loose and floated into the stream.

Whirring past her head, an arrow slammed into the guard's chest. He cried out, dropping her braid as he fell from his horse. Emlyn lurched away, slipping and rising again, to run downstream. Gerard shouted for her to halt. She glanced back to see one guard lying facedown in the stream, and Etienne and Gerard still in pursuit of her.

One of them closed in, roaring at her to stop, reaching out just as the other man had done. An arrow caught him in the upper arm, and he screamed and pulled back. Another whine sliced the air by her head as a crossbow quarrel pierced the muddy bank. The bolt was meant for Thorne. She whipped her head around to look for him.

Behind a cluster of birches at the edge of the beck, Thorne ran parallel to her panicked downstream course.

"To the bank!" his words floated to her. "Run to the bank!"

Angling left, she dashed through cold, swirling water and over sharp slippery stones to reach the edge of the stream. She heard a horseman in pursuit. Another bolt slammed into the bank, splitting the gnarled root of a tree close to her foot as she scrambled up the embankment toward Thorne.

He reached for her hand and hauled her up beside him, turning to drag her with him. Not far ahead, the grassy bank ended abruptly as the stream poured over the cliff. Thorne and Emlyn neared the edge, skidded, stopped, and turned in unison, breathing hard.

The guards advanced at a leisurely, threatening walk, seeing that the runners were trapped. Thorne put his arm around her shoulders and stepped back a little, urging her with him as the horses came closer. Glancing nervously behind her, Emlyn saw only air and white spray, and heard the ferocious noise of the falls.

Below, the beck disappeared into a rushing, thundering mist. Grass and heathery blooms curled over the edge of the break. Emlyn looked at Thorne, who stood with the heels of his boots bouncing partly in thin air. He slid a glance at her, and she thought he jerked his head slightly. Nay, he could not mean it.

The men stopped their horses. Blood dripped from a wound above Etienne's elbow, congealing on his steel sleeve.

"So, bastard, you are the one who has taken Lord Whitehawke's betrothed," Gerard said.

"Serjeant," Thorne said, "the lady sought escape of her own will." Breathing like a small bellows, Emlyn stood beside him, held close in the circle of his arm, watching the guards warily.

"She is glad enough to be rescued now, I think." Gerard extended his gauntleted hand toward her. "My lady. Whitehawke will be greatly relieved to have you safe again."

Thorne squeezed her shoulder. She glanced up at him, and he tilted his head again, subtly, toward the cliff. She blinked. He meant for her to jump. She gaped at him.

"Lady Emlyn," Gerard growled. Emlyn looked nervously up at the guard, then back to Thorne.

Thorne murmured something that sounded like "now." His grip shifted to her waist and he stepped back over the cliffside, taking Emlyn with him.

Chapter Eleven

An instant later her feet hit a hard surface, jarring her ankles and slamming her forward onto her knees. She felt as if her stomach had flipped into her mouth. The leather satchel whacked against her, throwing off her precarious balance. Only Thorne's iron grip on her waist kept her from pitching backward over the lip of the rock.

"God on high, what are you doing?" she hissed.

"Saving us both. Can you climb down from here?"

They hunched on a wide ledge of rock about four feet below the cliff edge, high up on the gorge wall, barely a body length from the water that arched and roared over the edge. The spray hit her face like soft wet needles and blew loosened hair wildly about her face. Emlyn peered down and squeaked in dismay.

Lichen-covered rocks jutted out at odd, sharp angles, tumbling down to form one toothy greenish wall of the gorge. To one side, Mercie's force poured with a steady, muffled rumble over the rocks, plunging down to the deep pool. Above, shouts came as the guards dismounted and ran toward the cliff edge.

She took a deep breath. Once she was oriented, the height lost some of its threat. The inclined wall of the gorge did not appear to be even as high as the mural towers at Ashbourne. Moss-covered ledges would provide plenty of niches for climbing, and the slope of the escarpment would make the descent manageable. Besides, she thought, what else was left to do?

Gulping, she nodded. "Aye, I can climb down."

"Brave girl. Come ahead." He slid his legs and torso over the rock edge, grasping it near her toes. His feet found a sturdy support and he let go, dropping beneath her.

He looked up. "Now you." One of the guards screamed incoherently. "Do not listen to them, only to me," Thorne said.

She dropped down and slid, half falling to the ledge he was crouched on. He clambered down again, and she followed.

Slowly, they worked their way down the slick incline. Emlyn watched where Thorne placed his hands and feet, and then climbed after him, listening to his continued words of encouragement, carefully testing before she put her weight on any rock, her way a little altered from his because of her shorter arms and legs.

Gerard and Etienne peered over the cliff edge, shouting threats that faded into the noise of the water. Emlyn glanced up once to see the tip of a crossbow perched on the turf. A quarrel whistled past her to clatter away on the rocks, quickly followed by another bolt that almost caught Thorne's arm.

Thick, damp moss coated the slippery rock surfaces. Emlyn's face and hair and hands were misted and dripping from the spray. Once or twice she missed her footing on a slick lichenous mat. Against the rough green face of the gorge, the breeze played free with her cumbersome cloak and damp skirts and soggy braids.

When a bird flew past and startled her, she tightened her grip on the rocks and clung for a moment, breathing heavily, determined to quell the fear that roiled in her gut. She stretched her foot downward to go on.

Thorne seemed to descend effortlessly, his cloak floating out on the breeze, the quiver and longbow bouncing against his back. Whining quarrels cutting occasionally through the air seemed to bother him no more than buzzing bees. Struggling with her wet skirts and shorter limbs, Emlyn cursed under her breath. Looking down and glancing above made her dizzy, so she avoided looking anywhere but toward the next secure hold for her foot or hand.

As she extended her toe, a bolt pierced the folds of her mantle, fixing it to a crevice in the rock. Stretching to yank the shaft out, she nearly lost her balance. When the bolt refused to come loose, she began to panic.

Then Thorne was there beside her, gliding up to slip his

arm around her back. He plucked out the bolt and flung it away. Emlyn rested her forehead for a moment against the rock face, inhaling the musty smell of the moss, breathing hard, her hands and legs trembling.

He pressed her shoulder. Another quarrel sliced the air close to his back, followed by guttural shouts. Emlyn caught her breath in a frightened sob, not sure she could move.

"Easy, lady. Take off your cloak," Thorne said softly.

Unquestioning, she tried to unfasten the brooch. He reached over and ripped the garment away from her neck, breaking the pin. Clinging to the rock with one hand, he wound her mantle around the leather pack and flung them both into the ravine.

Peering down, she saw her things land on a rocky plateau near the waterfall. Thorne kept his cloak and bow, and she would have commented on that, but he had already dropped below her to continue his rapid, sure descent.

Relieved of the extra burden, Emlyn went faster. Soon climbing in tandem, they reached a flat ledge about two-thirds of the way down the gorge wall and squatted, looking up. The guards were no longer at the cliff edge.

"They will be coming down the path over there at any moment," Thorne said. "We will be easy targets. Can you swim?"

Emlyn nodded. "A little," she said. Hot summer days spent in Ashbourne's fish pond with Guy and Richard and Agnes had taught her a few basic skills.

"A little is enough," he said, taking off his cloak and heavy leather hauberk and dropping them, with his quiver and bow, to the same ledge where her things had fallen. "Come. Over the edge and into the pool."

She hesitated, glancing down, and then looked up at him, her eyes large with fright. She remembered that earlier he had mentioned that the water was deep enough for swimming. "But I cannot jump from here," she whispered.

"Emlyn. You must trust me," Thorne said urgently. "Worry not, think not, just do what must be done." He grabbed her hand and pulled her forward. "Feet first, take a breath. Go!"

Again, he left her no choice, no time to think. She had to go with him, had to trust his judgment and ability. Stepping over the rock ledge into empty space, her skirts belled out as she plunged into the sharp cold of the water. Surrounded, sucked under, she kicked her legs, but her skirts wound around her, pulling her down even as she fought to go up.

Slowly, as if in a dream, she looked up through the blue-green depth of the water. Distorted by the pond surface, the green walls of the gorge hovered overhead. Reaching up, she could not rise far enough or fast enough to break through the silent skin of the water. Stale air burned in her lungs.

Thorne came into her vision, his hair floating like a wild dark cloud around his face. He grabbed her arms and drew her up with him, pushing her toward the surface.

Sputtering, she exhaled and whooped in new breath, shaking her head, throwing an arm around Thorne's neck. He guided her along with him until she began to swim on her own and could follow his lead across the pool and straight toward the falls.

"Take a breath," he called, and when she did, he pulled her under the water toward the milky, foaming cascade. Diving down, they swam through the cold churning water and came up for air.

Gasping, sweeping her hair away from her face, Emlyn looked around in wonder. They were behind the force, which formed one sparkling, thundering wall of a narrow rocky alcove.

Thorne broke the surface beside her, clearing his hair out of his eyes, drops of water glistening like crystals in his beard. Treading water close to her, he reached out and pulled her to him, pressing his cheek against hers. Emlyn twined her arms tightly around his neck, coughing and wiping her face.

"Dear God, Emlyn," he breathed raggedly into her ear, "I thought I had lost you." His cool, wet lips touched her brow, her cheek, and clung to her mouth for a long moment.

With quick long strokes, he helped her swim to the back wall. Hauling himself up onto a narrow ledge, he half lifted her out of the water, then turned to toe along the ledge toward the gorge.

Shivering, Emlyn waited only a moment before he appeared again, carrying her cloak, the satchel, and his things. Beckoning for her to follow, he walked along the narrow, slippery ledge and bent to slither into a dark cleft in the rock.

She followed him into a natural tunnel, barely wide enough to squeeze through. The short passage opened into a tiny cave, dark but dry, where the noise of the waterfall was reduced. The low ceiling grazed Emlyn's head when she stood, and the walls tapered sharply. Thorne, too tall to stand upright in the cave, sat down against the wall.

Rivulets of water ran from her dress and pooled on the sandy floor when she wrung out her skirt. She sat beside him in the small, cramped space, her shoulder and hip pressed into his.

Thorne stretched out one long leg, and they sat together, both panting from exertion.

"Ugh," she said softly, after a moment.

"Aye," he agreed, "an ughsome feeling, this cold and wet."

"'Tis luck you knew of this cave," she said, her teeth chattering. He reached out his arm to draw her close.

"I did not know 'twas here. When I saw the crevice, I hoped there would be some space beyond it. Not much of a cave, but 'twill hide us well, I trow."

"What do we now?" she asked tremulously.

"We wait, my lady. I will go out shortly to see what has become of the guards." His voice vibrated, low and pleasant in her ear.

"Did you see them when you fetched the cloaks?" she asked. "Can they find us in here?"

"They were climbing down the path into the gorge then and are surely here by now, but they did not see me. Fret not, they cannot find us here. This place is too well hidden. As long as we are quiet and have no blazing fire to be seen through the waterfall, we are as safe as in a tomb."

Emlyn flinched at the comparison. "But night approaches."

"Aye," he said, barely whispering. "The guards may make camp in the gorge, for one of them is wounded."

"Must we stay the night here? 'Tis so cold."

"If we must, we can." He tightened his arm around her and she leaned her cheek against the soggy wool of his tunic, her body fitting comfortably to his at hip and thigh and shoulder. Thorne rubbed his fingers along her arm, and gradually her shivering began to lessen, though the cold was piercing.

From the tumbled pile of their things, he picked up his cloak and drew it over them like a blanket. Hunched in their chilly, soaking garments, they shivered beneath the dry wool.

In a moment, he sat up again. "Jesu," he muttered, "we must get dry and warm, or perish of this cold." Moving away, he quickly pulled off his wet tunic.

Silvery light from the tunnel entrance traced the undulating, muscular contours of his body as he stripped, wrung his tunic with fierce twists, and hung it on a jutting rock. When he bent over to remove his boots and breeches, she caught a glimpse of the side of his taut buttocks before she glanced away.

"Hand me my cloak," he said softly.

Her gaze shifted back to him, to the gleaming light that outlined his powerful legs and wide shoulders. Blushing heatedly, she tossed him the mantle. He quickly wrapped it around him, and crossed the cave in two crouching strides to drop down beside her.

"Now you must do the same," he murmured.

In the host of improprieties Emlyn had experienced of late, any one of which would have shocked Tibbie into apoplexy if she had known, this was by far the greatest. Not enough that she sat beside a nude man; now she would need to remove her own saturated clothing to don the dry garments in her bag. Wrapping her arms around herself uncertainly, she shivered violently and sneezed.

Thorne sat up. "Lady, you are chilled to the bone. If we are to survive this cursed night we must both get warm. Remove that sopping gown before you become ill."

He was right and she knew it. Turning her back to him, she reluctantly slid up the skirt of her gown to remove her boots and wool hosen. Tugging at the side laces of her gown beneath the cover of the cloak, she gave a half sob of frustration when she encountered stubborn wet knots.

Thorne reached out to undo the crisscrossed silken cords. She turned away from him, but he laid a hand on her shoulder.

"Let me help you," he said softly. His gentle tone eased her anxiousness a little. She lifted her arm slightly to give him access to the lacing.

His long, nimble fingers worked patiently. Emlyn watched the soft sheen of his dark head inches from her own in the dimly lit cave. When his fingers brushed against the subtle swell of the side of her breast, she found herself breathing raggedly, heavier.

Her thoughts were centered not on the danger of their predicament, with guards just outside looking for them; not on the half-mad marriage proposal she had received; but rather on his scent, on his touch. On the light graze of his fingers against the curving side of her breast as he undid the laces. On the scent of his damp hair, of warm male skin and the freshness of their cold water plunge. His breathing, too, was louder now, nearly in tandem with hers.

He touched her other shoulder, and she turned to allow him to undo the laces on the opposite side. Pulling her back against him, he slipped his arm over her chest to work at the second set of knots. Warmth radiated wherever their bodies touched. She thought his fingers trembled at the laces.

When her loosened gown slipped down over her shoulder, she felt his warm breath against her bare skin. Then, suddenly, his soft lips were nuzzling the back of her neck below the part of her heavy, damp braids, his beard tickling the skin there. Her heart seemed to plummet into her belly and bound back up again at the utter pleasure of the feeling. Instinctively she arched her back, and his hand came full over the softness of her breast. She might have moved, but her ability to reason was rapidly diminishing.

Then he turned her abruptly into his arms. Drawing her across his lap, he covered her lips in a melting, crushing kiss that suckled the breath from her. Winding her arms around him, she pressed closer to him, aching for more of his touch, for his warm solidity. The skin of his back was cool and damp beneath her trembling fingertips, and the puckered scar of an old, deep wound marred the smooth muscle there.

"Emlyn," he murmured against her lips, "marry with me."

She would have spoken but his tongue touched at her lips, the contact moist and hot and vibrant in the cold darkness.

She opened to its irresistible caress, moaning softly against his searching, pulling lips.

Thorne sank his fingers into her hair, loosening what was left of the tangled braids, and ran his hand along the damp, cool, silky length. Grasping a pillowed handful of its heavy thickness near the nape of her neck, he pulled her head back.

"Marry with me," he repeated hoarsely. His lips swept the gentle arch of her throat, his breath blowing hot into the neck of her gown, warming her damp breasts. The silken fabric slid full off her shoulder, and his long fingers found the buttersoft contour of one breast beneath her wet chemise. His palm pressed into the firmly ruched center, sending deep quavers through her body.

"Thorne—" she whispered, shuddering suddenly, only in part because of her chilled skin. What he asked of her, what his lips and hands and words were urging from her frightened her in part. Yet she realized that she trusted him now, so completely that she felt, with odd surprise, no need to cease his hands or his words. She drew a kind of strength from his solid, sure touch, and the sense of rightness grew within her.

"Marry with me," he breathed, and kissed her again, soft and clinging. Her lips began to tremble beneath his as she began to answer, but he sat back and looked at her, frowning.

"By the rood," he murmured, "your skin is like ice. We need to get you dry." Sitting back a little, he pulled off her cloak, deftly released the last of the side laces, and tugged her gown over her head.

A curious weakness had sapped any urge to protest. She allowed him to remove the gown. He skimmed her wet chemise up her thighs and quickly drew the clinging fabric over her head, flinging the garments away. Turning her, naked now, he cradled her snugly in his lap and pulled a cloak around them both. Her bare skin seemed to absorb an instant, simmering warmth from his skin, startlingly intense and profoundly welcome.

As he held her, her arm and breasts grazed the long wedge of hair that softened the taut surface of his torso. Against her hip, she could feel the rigid press of him, wholly exciting and strangely intriguing. She curled into his embrace, antic-

ipating more than simple warmth from him now, more than
simple kisses. Her heart pounded in her chest, and she was
certain, for a moment, that he could feel its strong beat, just
as she was easily sensing his.

"Are you cold, love?" he asked, as he tucked the cloak
closer around them, a thick, soft shield against the chill,
damp air.

"Aye so," she murmured, shuddering. He wrapped her in
his arms as a sultry heat kindled between and around their
bodies. Languorously he rubbed his hand down her back, his
other arm across her thighs, those fingers lightly caressing
the silken skin of her hip. After a moment he groaned softly,
his lips near her ear, a low whispered vibratto that spun a
melting whirlpool down in her belly.

"Emlyn," he breathed, "Emlyn. Marry with me." His lips
brushed along the skin of her jaw toward her mouth, erasing
all traces of reason from her mind.

"Wait," she murmured, "I cannot think—"

"Neither can I think well," he whispered, laying his
mouth over hers, gentle, breathless, nuzzling kisses. "God. I
cannot think at all." He lowered his head, and his lips moved
against the velvety skin of her upper breast.

As his fingers slipped over her hardened nipple, as his lips
found the firm bud, she arched and gasped low.

When he raised his head to kiss her mouth again, long and
luscious, the deep searing warmth offering a glorious comfort in the cold cave interior, Emlyn opened her lips fully beneath his, a swift moment of surrender amid the whirling,
surging sensations that overwhelmed her last rational
thought.

She roused beneath his subtle touches, like feathers, like
soft flame along her skin, slow and potent caresses that
stoked something fervid within her. His body was warm and
hard along hers, like a banked hearth, heating her skin and
awakening a kind of blood-fire that she had no idea how to
quell or control. She only went with it, willing and curious.

Kneading her breasts beneath long, gentle fingers, with
his other hand he answered the instinctive arching of her
body. Slipping between her thighs, his skimming touch
moved upward. At her sudden intake of breath, he drew her

head to his shoulder and moved his lips along her ear. "Emlyn," he whispered, "wed with me. Now. Here."

"Oh, God," she gasped, "Thorne—"

"Now," he murmured. His tongue and lips swallowed the little half sob that burst from her when his finger delved into the downy cleft, slick within, sliding upward. With firm, delicate motion, his fingers stoked the ember within until she sobbed wordlessly and tossed her head back, straining toward his touch.

Effortlessly, he turned her so that she straddled him, her breasts flush against his chest, their sensitive, awakened tips teased by the hair that feathered over his chest. His heart thudded a heavy pulse beneath hers; the rhythm blended with the rapid beat of her own heart, and merged with the soft thunder of the waterfall outside.

Lifting her for a moment, he set her down again, and pushed, firm and warm, between her thighs. A shift of his hips, a willing settle of hers, sheathed him, wrapped him just inside. She surged forward, stirring her hips, breathing deep and heavy with a need so strong that she nearly cried out for the want of it. Yet he held still; she sensed the subtle tension within him.

"Thorne—" she said breathlessly, pressing her lips to the side of his brow.

"Your answer," he whispered raggedly against the soft underside of her jaw. "I would have it now, than later. Wed me, now and here." Together, as one, they stirred again, pulsing, moistened, waiting. His hands pressed into her back and he leaned his forehead against hers, his breathing rapid and charged with intensity. She kissed his sweat-damp skin. At what moment he had begun to ask two questions of her, one with his body, the other with his heart, she was not certain, but she knew that both questions could be answered the same.

His hands slid to her hips, his fingers trembling. "Urge me to stop," he whispered, "and I will. But press me to go on, and 'tis done." Their breaths, a rushing echo in the small, damp cave, hung in the air.

His body pulsed, waiting, at the threshold of her own. He gave her the power to resolve the moment, here and now. Never in her life had she wanted something more than the dual union he offered her now, heart and body, soul and flesh.

"I will," she breathed. "Dear God, I will," she whispered against the satiny crown of his hair. She knew, with clear awareness, that the words came from her heart, not just formed from the sudden need-fire that had been kindled in her body.

He raised his head when she spoke. Taking her face in one hand, he looked at her, his eyes piercing in the darkness. "You will not regret this marriage, I swear to you," he growled. "I swear it. Do you believe me?"

She closed her eyes and nodded, lowering her head to rest against his shoulder. He smoothed the silky fall of her damp hair, holding her in an embrace, his chest moving heavily beneath her cheek. Then he pressed downward on her hips with exquisite ease. Lifting her head, she kissed him, pushing fervently with him until she gasped, a small cry of discovery and acceptance.

Her name on his lips changed to a wordless, hoarse cry as he plunged to find her deepest center. She bit her lip against the first quick objection of her inner flesh, but the pain soon dissolved into a sweet burn, soothed and heightened by each exhilarating movement. Shuddering, he wrapped his arms around her, and she wrapped around him, drawing him closer, welcoming his heat and fire and flow inside her, surging in cadence with him, like a stream of joy through her body.

He inhaled deeply, and she felt his breath ebb and flow within her, as if she breathed him and he her. As he subsided, breath and body, from her, the moment dissolved like a dream. She protested with a low moan. He kissed her, a slow caress, resting his cheek against hers for a long moment.

After a while, he nuzzled her damp temple, and drew the forgotten cloak up to cover them. "Dear saints," he whispered, "My thoughts are like mud right now. I near forgot that we are hunted."

She sighed, half in residual pleasure and half in dejection at his reminder, and looped her arms around his neck. "Do not go yet," she murmured, resting her head against his shoulder. He gently brushed her hair back from her forehead.

"Nay, love, not yet," he whispered. "I will not leave you, though soon I must dress and check on our friends."

"Thorne—" she said softly, rousing herself for a moment from the cozy temptation of sleep, pushing away the thought of the men outside, wanting no disturbance of the peace, the tranquility that she and Thorne had created between them. She lifted her head to look steadily at him, though he was but a silver-edged shadow in the darkness.

"Aye?"

"I trust you, sirrah," she said. "'Tis why I have agreed to wed with you."

"I know it well, love," he said, soft as a drift of wind. "And I promise that you will not regret that trust." His words blended with the noisy rush of the falls, and his lips took hers with gentle power.

He was freezing. Though the day had been mild, it was past twilight now and the air had a distinct chill. His clothing was damp and uncomfortable as he squatted on his haunches. Wriggling icy toes inside his damp boots, he blew on his fingertips and thought with strong yearning, and mild envy, of Emlyn, who slept sound and warm in the cave, dressed in the dry garments from her satchel; he had checked on her not long ago, and come back to watch again.

Squinting through the thick screen of ferns and bracken that shielded him from view, he peered across the width of the pool. The wounded guard, his arm bandaged, sat by a glowing fire in the fading light, roasting small game on a stick. The aroma wafted across the water to flare Thorne's nostrils, and his stomach rumbled sharply.

The other guard stood by the edge of the pool. Suddenly he shouted and bent down to the water for a moment. When he went back to the fire, he waved something in his hand.

Thorne watched, intrigued. The guards talked excitedly and passed between them a dripping white cloth. Frowning as he tried to place it, he remembered: when the guard had yanked on Emlyn's braid, her white veil had fallen into the beck. It must have floated over the falls and into the pool.

Pointing toward the cliffside and gesturing vehemently toward the pool, the wounded guard waved a hand in anger or frustration. The other guard walked over to stand looking into the pond, shaking his head and rubbing his jaw.

Apparently the guards believed that Emlyn, at least, had drowned when she went over the cliff; he had no way of guessing what they assumed about him. But he felt certain that the guards would stay the night in the gorge. Silently, hidden by the bracken, he crept back toward the falls.

He woke in the night, reclining uncomfortably against the rough stone wall. Beside him, Emlyn was curled in a small bundle, her hip against his thigh, her breathing soft and measured. Stretching his back and shoulders to ease his stiffening muscles, he was careful not to disturb her. Though the cave was miserably cold and black, the pewtery light that washed the edges of the tunnel opening heralded dawn. He sat back, his thoughts rushing quick as the steady waterfall.

Two days ago, he had received word that the barons gathered in London, and expected him to join them soon: the king had agreed, finally, to consider a new charter. He would be leaving in the next few days, but he wanted to see Emlyn safe first.

Whitehawke's guards had been persistent in their search, and although they might believe she was dead, a risk still existed. Even cloistered in an abbey, she could be found. He had little faith in her plan to retreat to a convent, knowing Whitehawke would haul her out of any place, short of the sanctity of a church, if he found her—unless she was no longer his betrothed.

Sighing, he glanced at the sleeping, peaceful girl, and his heartbeat surged. He would not tolerate knowing her wed to another, or shut away in a religious house. She belonged with him, and always had, since she had been a child. The pull he felt toward her had strengthened to an irresistible force, an inexorable destiny; reluctantly, finally, he admitted its power.

Eight years ago, when he had held and protected a trembling and brave child from danger, he had felt for the first time a selfless concern for another. For that one pure moment, he had known true honor, not the haughty idealism spouted by men like his father. Honor in its finest form, he had come to realize later, was close to love.

Somehow, beginning long ago, she had invaded the crevices that led to his inner self. This marriage to her would inevitably lay open his previous closed life; where he had always shielded himself from others, she had found access. She was in his life now, curled comfortably in his heart just as she curled beside him at this moment. But there was danger in allowing her into his life, and even more so into his heart.

Today, he thought, watching the dawn light begin to shine at the edges of the cave, there would be no time for a priest, no time for a proper wedding. The marriage must be made as swiftly as possible. A quick private vow could provide her legal protection from Whitehawke, could ensure some security for her when he left the York shire. Having bound himself to her and her family eight years ago, he would not fail them now. The children were safe at Hawksmoor, and he would see Emlyn safe as well.

Consequences would come of this marriage, surely, but he felt certain that he and Emlyn could last out the storm together. The gift was surely worth the price of the risk.

Since his conflict with Whitehawke seemed fated to continue, why not over this as any other matter?

He rubbed his hand over his face and shoved his hair back impatiently. Marrying his father's betrothed secretly was no honorable deed. Once again, honor seemed to confront and confound him. But he reminded himself that he had a full right to do this: as Thorne or as Nicholas, she was his by prior claim.

Years ago, as Nicholas, he had negotiated with Rogier de Ashbourne to marry Emlyn, never telling Baron Rogier that the offer was made in payment for the rescue of the Black Thorne one summer night. The arrangement had never reached final agreement because of Rogier's death. Then, when the king had promised Emlyn to Whitehawke, Nicholas had submitted an immediate formal protest, but had no written document to prove his claim. The word of a baron was not enough for King John.

At first, he had not thought overmuch about it, accepting custody of the children instead, and intending to keep a protective eye on his father's new wife. After he had seen Emlyn, and come to recognize her kindness and her pure spirit, the nature of the debt had been unexpectedly transformed.

Lately, wading in his mind through a morass of feelings, fear and yearning among them, and dread mixed with joy, he had suddenly discovered that he was as much in love, in his own reserved manner, as any fawning troubadour before his lady.

His hand, softly stroking, found the curve of her shoulder beside him in the dark, and he rested his fingers there as he thought. In finding his buried, innate ability to love, he had found his greatest cowardice: he could not endure her contempt for him, and so he held back the full truth from her. Had he possessed true courage, he would have already told her who he was, and would have patiently borne through her anger waiting for her understanding.

But he was afraid. He needed to win her heart before he revealed more about himself—may God forgive his deceit. If Emlyn knew the whole truth, she would not marry him. He was certain that she would despise him. And this marriage, if it were to be made, had to be done quickly.

God's teeth, he thought, as the discomforts of his rocky bed interrupted his thoughts, 'tis bitter damp in this cursed black cave. Best to be gone from here than to freeze our bones longer. Soon the guards will wake, and search anew.

Sliding down, he pressed closer to the inviting warmth of Emlyn's back. Resting one hand on her arm, he absently rubbed his fingers in small circles.

"If we could but have a fire, even a tiny one," she murmured. Her voice was husky as smoke in the dark.

"Are you very cold?" he asked quietly.

"Aye so," she said. "My fingers and toes feel like icicles. And you?" She sat up and turned to face him.

"Chilled through," he answered. Her face, just below his in the darkness, gave off a little shield of warmth. He inched his head toward hers, their foreheads nearly touching.

Her voice was glazed with sleepy laughter in the dark. "We sorely need a fire in this chimney-hole."

"'Tis not much larger than a hearth space, much as I like the closeness. 'Tis best we leave soon, my lady."

"How, with the guards outside?" she whispered, her breath

brushing his cheek. God, that sweet, soft face so close to his. He closed his eyes to revel a little in that dulcet warmth.

"With great caution," he murmured. Gently he laid a hand on the side of her head, sliding his fingertips over thick smooth hair, stroking his thumb along the slender line of her jaw. She felt soft and yielding. He suddenly yearned to gather that deep comfort around him, take succor from her as well as offer it.

He touched his lips to hers. More familiar with each other now, their lips withdrew and met, and again, stronger, until a kind of blissful tension grew in him. He tipped his head to kiss her more deeply, edging her lips with his tongue, wanting fiercely to dive into her warm wetness. When her mouth parted for him, he cupped her head in his hands and delved.

Her cloak was like a woolen cocoon scented with her sleepiness. Slipping her arms up around his neck, she sighed against his lips and snuggled against his still-damp tunic, wearing a dry gown that she had taken from her satchel. A web of blessed heat was spun wherever their bodies touched.

He leaned back with her against the cold stone wall, stroking the tangled gossamer strands of her hair. The comforting warmth lingered between them as she rested her head over his heart.

After a few moments she rose up to kneel before him, and he immediately missed her body as cool air filled the space between them. She touched slender fingers to his bearded cheek, her tousled hair silhouetted against the pale light of the tunnel opening, forming a silvery halo around her head.

"Thorne," she said softly. "You would wed with me to protect me against Whitehawke?"

"Aye, in part."

Her voice was husky, the barest whisper. "Why?"

He caught her fingers. "If we were wed, you would be mine to defend by right. No harm could come to you."

"You are a forester, yet you speak as if you have a fortress in which to keep me. I will not be the cause of any further war between you and Lord Whitehawke." She squeezed his hand. "I am sorry for what I said yesterday, that you would wed me to strike at him," she whispered.

He smiled ruefully. "Forgiven. Heed me, Emlyn," he said earnestly. "Think you a forester has so little to offer? I have land and a house of my own, away from here. You would be content as my wife. You would be safe."

"I had thought to be safe as a daughter of God," she said.

"By the rood, you are made for something more lightsome than dry prayers. You are not one for a convent—or for Whitehawke's cold keep." He gripped her hand in his. "Regrets so soon, lady? I have sworn my truth on this."

She was silent, furrowing her brow, looking down. He had seen her quick temper and her impulsiveness and her deep capacity for loving. Now he learned that she was a thinker as well. He had not known a woman to ponder so, like a man. He waited. Outside, the halo of light at the tunnel entrance began to glow.

"In my heart I feel that this is wholly right, though I cannot say why," she said finally.

In the shadows, he smiled, a lopsided grin that ignored the trained, severe inner voice reprimanding his foolishness, his lack of honor in this. He was pleased by her courage and intelligence. He knew no other woman so brave as to jump off a cliff and climb down a gorge, or one who would run in protest from an unjust betrothal, or wed a mere forester. But he knew that she thought herself to be timid and chaotic.

"No need to understand the urgings of your heart," he told her. "Remember, the Church patriarchs say the heart is the seat of our greatest wisdom." He tilted her chin up with his thumb.

She nodded again, and he kissed her forehead gently, then her lips, their mouths clinging for a long, breathless moment. Fierce and intense, a burning need for her nearly burst in his chest; to be with her, to know her safe and well by him always. The sensation overwhelmed him, swamping his reason like a wash.

"My uncle could marry us," she suggested.

"Your uncle would want to annul your betrothal to Whitehawke, or at least demand our banns be posted for three Sundays. There is a faster way." God, what a hurry he was in.

"What is that?" she asked softly.

"We will pledge in privacy," he said.

"Make vows without a priest?"

"God makes marriages, not man. If two people pledge with

body and soul, that bond is as strong as a priest could make. The Church regards clandestine marriages as valid."

"We declare ourselves wed, and we are," she said, frowning.

"If we mean it in our hearts and consummate it, 'tis done."

She looked up quickly. "Has the marriage been made, then?"

He shook his head and caught both her hands, cold and small, in his. "Not yet. We must pronounce words."

"I will not pledge with you in this dark, wet cave," she declared.

"Fair enough." He thought for a moment. "There is a place, east toward the river."

"Is it safe to leave?" she asked.

"Aye, if neither of us hollers like a drunken sot, or falls headlong into the guard's fire. They are sleeping sound, and I trow we can climb the path unseen. Gather your things, my lady." He pulled on his boots and stood to belt his cold leather hauberk.

Emlyn folded the damp things that had been spread out to dry, shoving them into her bag. She stood in the cave as he could not, with his greater height, and put on her cloak.

"I am ready, Thorne," she said.

"Aye, then, come with me." He knew the words to be true for his lifetime. Hope and fear and excitement rolled in his solar plexus, and he inhaled sharply. Sweet rood, what have I asked of her, he thought. She trusts me, yet knows not the whole man.

He stepped into the tunnel with Emlyn just behind him.

Chapter Twelve

Thousands of lilies, pale ivory-white, swayed on slender green stalks in the gentle breeze, the edges of their fragile petals tinted golden-pink by early sunlight. Feathering the meadow, the wild lilies spread across the field and clustered around the birches and oak trees that edged a small grove.

As Emlyn walked through the midst of the flowers, delicate leaves and petals caught at her hem, releasing their fragrance as she passed through. Heaven must be like this place, she thought.

A few steps ahead, Thorne stepped into the small, shaded grove, and Emlyn followed. Shafts of cool green light poured through the high arches of the trees, as if it were a graceful cathedral filled with green glass, filled with the musical twitter of birds and the gentle burble of water nearby.

A little spring emerged from an ivy-covered rock and tumbled into a shallow stream. Beside the water lay a broad, pale stone, fallen long ago. Lilies were everywhere, scattered across the sun-dappled grass, clustered under the trees, and clinging to the stream bank, their airy scent tracing through the grove.

Sunlight sliced through the trees in glittering beams, gilding Emlyn's hair and shoulders as she turned to place her leather pack on the ground. She watched Thorne lean his quiver and bow against a tree.

She felt shy now, here with him in this place, knowing what they meant to do. In the past hour or so as they had walked, each silent in their thoughts, she had mulled and worried this decision from every angle. A clandestine wedding was not as safe a choice as entering a convent, she thought, but it was perhaps a practical, even a wise path. More, she wanted it.

Convent life was cool and sacred, without the fire of touch, of lives merging. She knew that a kind of poverty of the heart threatened with Whitehawke. But to be in the forest with Thorne would be richer than any life she could imagine. In the past few days, and most especially since their passionate moments in the waterfall's cave, she had realized that she truly loved Thorne.

Perhaps she had not thought this through as others might, who would judge property and gold and position gained or lost. She reacted with her heart instead. If she were a traveler offered the warmth of a hearth fire, would she refuse it for the icy cold? Providence had offered her a gift; she would accept it.

Tall and lean, his long dark hair catching a sheen of light as he shrugged off his cloak, he looked like some powerful angel come down to earth, equally capable of love or vengeance. In his broad shoulders, wide stance, and easy carriage, in the steady gleam in his green eyes, she saw resilient strength and unwavering courage: a hero from a legend, even without silvery armor or an ancestry of honor.

Drawn like a lodestone to his steadfastness, she could not help but follow him. Earlier, while they had walked together, she mused that perhaps she sought her own inner strength through touching his; surely being with Thorne had made her stronger.

Turning around in the shaded grove, she saw him watching her. "'Tis a beautiful place," she said. "I have never seen lilies grow quite as they do here."

He stepped toward her. "The lilies have grown wild here as long as anyone can remember. 'Tis said that the blood of some Christian martyr was spilled in the meadow over there, and the lilies first sprung from that spot and spread, as flowers do."

Though it was still early morning, the day was warming quickly. She reached up to remove her heavy cloak. "We are close to the river here, are we not?" she asked.

"'Tis another two or three miles to the river, where we can hire a boat to take us to the abbey."

She glanced up. "We still journey to Wistonbury?"

"Aye, my lady." He placed his hands on her slender shoulders and looked down into her eyes. A curious, wonderful warmth began where his fingers touched her, and spread, tingling, throughout her body. "Our vows will ensure your safety should Whitehawke try to claim you. But you must stay with your uncle until the king has signed the new laws, at least. And I must go away, for a little while."

"But—what of us?" She frowned up at him. She had assumed that they would stay together, once bound by vows.

"We will be married, and none can put that asunder," he said. "But for a brief time, we must be apart." He lifted a silky tendril of hair away from her brow. "Trust me to come for you."

"Trust you," she repeated quietly. His eyes were the greenish-gray of stones in a streambed, his lashes thick black lace. "I trust you well."

"Aye." He bent down to kiss her lips, a soft, dry, pulling kiss, his beard tickling her cheeks. She leaned into the kiss, but he broke away. "Come. We have a vow to make," he said.

"Wait," she said. "I would prepare myself for my wedding."

"As you will. But hurry. We should not linger overlong." He walked through the screen of trees to the outer meadow.

Rummaging in her pack, she found her ivory comb and sat down by the edge of the stream to comb the stubborn tangles from her hair, and in a few minutes the shining soft mass swayed in delicate ripples to her hips. Then she took the fine blue silk gown from her satchel, slipped out of the gray wool gown that she wore, and laced the rumpled blue silk over her chemise.

Picking several lilies, she worked quickly to weave the stems into a chaplet for her hair. "I am ready," she called out, setting the flowered wreath on her head and standing by the edge of the little stream.

Watching Thorne walk quickly across the flower-strewn grass, Emlyn admired the graceful lope of his stride and the lean, muscular length of his body. He paused before her and slanted one black eyebrow, his eyes moving slowly up and down. She reached a hand shyly to her chaplet.

"Your beauty suits this heavenly place," he said.

Emlyn smiled up at him, feeling, for an instant, like one of the lilies opening up to the morning light.

"I have something for you," he said, holding out his hand.

In his palm lay a small ring of dark, dull metal. "A ring is appropriate, and will mark well our pledge. I pulled it off my hauberk and opened it to fit," he explained, "if you will have it, my lady, for I have none else to give you now."

"Aye," Emlyn breathed, "I will have it."

They moved toward the little spring that trickled from the rock, near the rectangular white menhir that slanted into the brook. "This place was once an ancient sanctuary," he told her. "See, there, the fallen altar stone by the spring. These waters are said to have sacred healing powers."

On an ivy-covered ledge beside the rock, small crudely carved statuettes of faded, cracked wood perched beside a few polished stones. "Those offerings were left long ago for some god or goddess of the forest," he said.

Emlyn dropped to her knees by the fallen stone and traced a fingertip along the faded runic designs of engraved spirals and crosses. She looked up and pointed beyond the tilted face of the stone. "Look there. A hawthorn tree, and next to it an oak tree—the oak, the thorn, the stone, the water, all come together here in this place. There was strong druidic magic here once."

"And still may be," he murmured. "Ancient druid magic was just a way to worship God, though the Church understands it not."

Emlyn looked at him in surprise. "You know of such things?"

"Some. The people of the dale often live by both Christian and pagan beliefs. Maisry surely does. The old ideas are harmless enough, and speak of the goodness of God's earth."

She nodded. "'Tis a blessing when people can both worship the Lord and love the ancient bounty of the earth, and see God in all of it."

Thorne knelt to face her by the ancient altar stone. "We make our bond in a holy place, then."

He captured her hands and wrapped his long fingers, warm and dry and strong, around hers. "Emlyn, I take you for my wife in God's eyes, forever. I pledge you love and protection, as my helpmate, for always."

Emlyn's blue eyes were caught in the depths of his mossy gaze. Words formed on her lips as if she knew exactly what to say. "I pledge unto you, Thorne, and I take you for my husband before the holy witness of God, his saints and his angels. I promise to love and care for you always."

"Our vow is sealed by this ring." He slipped the circlet onto her finger. "May our union be strong as this steel."

"And as continuous as the circle," she murmured. He lowered his head, and Emlyn leaned forward. Their lips lingered, warm and pliant, and he embraced her for a long, silent moment. "What offering shall we leave here?" he asked against her hair. "We will need the benisons of the forest gods as well as the saints, for what we have done this day." She glanced quickly at him, and he lifted the lily wreath from her head. "Ah, this will do for our wedding token."

He stepped away to set the flowers on the rocky shelf by the trickling spring, and came back to sit beside her at the edge of the stream.

"Take off your shoes," he said. He began to unlace the thongs that held his high boots snug against his legs.

"What?"

"Remove your shoes, and your hosen as well," he said, casting aside his own boots. Dipping his bare feet into the stream, he wiggled his toes, splashing a little as he waited.

Puzzled, she sat down and slowly did as he asked.

He splashed water at her, sprinkling her face and gown. Wrinkling her nose, she edged her feet into the shallow flow.

"It does feel nice," she admitted.

"Now come here and we will consummate the marriage."

"Thorne!" She stared, amazed at his callowness.

He smiled, a slight lift of the corner of his mouth, and held up his foot. "Here. Touch your foot to mine—just so— ahh, 'tis a tiny foot, lady wife, and so soft." He pressed his much longer sole against hers.

"There," he said, pushing a little harder, until she pushed back. He drew his foot slowly away, a caressing trace of his toes down her sole that sent deep shivers through her. "I suppose that will do it," he said.

"Do what?" She lowered her foot back into the stream.

"'Tis a way of sealing a marriage—the touching of bare feet serves as a consummation. Usually 'tis used in proxy marriages, when distance interferes with the wedding. But

'twill do for us. We must leave and travel fast." Pulling his
feet up out of the water, he wiped them with his hands.

"Oh," Emlyn said. She looked up. "Thorne."

"Aye?"

She held up her other foot. "Here, seal this one as well."

He laughed, then reached over and pulled her toward him
by the shoulders until she leaned against his chest. "Mayhap
we can linger in our wedding chapel for a few moments," he
murmured, and lowered his face to hers, his beard gently
grazing her chin and cheeks until his lips found hers.

Wrapped in his embrace, Emlyn returned the kiss. Her
heart set up a rapid beat, and an inner coil turned slowly in
her body, a strange, hot, melting blend of apprehension and
joy. She felt again that deep, powerful current whenever,
wherever he touched her. Each time she felt his touch, heard
his voice, the pull she felt between them was stronger, more
poignant, more certain.

She remembered that Tibbie had once haltingly explained
to her the duties of a wife in the marriage bed, although at
the time Emlyn had not understood how such an act could be
pleasurable, or how it could inspire the poems and songs of
troubadours. Tibbie had said, cheeks blushing fiercely, that
the act was tender and joyful, and that a woman's urges were
as hearty and healthy as a man's.

Last night, caught in his arms in the little cave, Emlyn had
felt the vibrant, irresistible power of those urges. She tilted
her head back, craving the return of those sensations, wanting the gentle flame of his touch so much at this moment
that her body seemed to fill with limpid warmth at the very
anticipation.

He traced soft kisses, tiny warm brushing contacts, down
her neck to the flushed skin just above the rounded neck of
her gown, and gently rolled her to the ground, where the
cool, fragrant grass cushioned them. His long fingers, still
damp from the stream, traced a feathery touch along her jaw
and down her neck. She closed her eyes, sighing as he
kissed her cheek, her ear, her jaw, then lifted her jaw to let
his lips brush lower until he teased at the neck of her gown.

Loosening the ribbons of her chemise and silk gown, he
dipped his fingers inside, sending her heartbeat into a
deeper, stronger rhythm. As the garments slipped from her

shoulders, his fingers found and explored the delicate, supple weight of her breasts, and his tongue, following, coaxed lightning shivers from her and sent them streaming down her body. Gasping softly, arching, she ran her hands through his long waving hair, her fingers seeking, flexing, pleading as he touched her. She felt as if she spun in a slow spiral, her breath and body entwining with his.

Thorne, she thought suddenly, fervently, I have loved you for years; but somehow she felt too shy to say it aloud, for the knowledge was too new, too precious. As he touched her, the hot, tingling glow that had already begun in her center spread outward in heated layers, in rippling, kindled waves, as if her soul rose up, beckoned by his touch.

He sighed and kissed her again and again, deep and deeper, his hands skimming over layers of silk, lifting them away. His fingers explored the lean length of her bare legs, drawing out the moment until he touched the nested threshold that he sought. As the small, fervent throb began to flicker under his coaxing fingers, she moaned softly against his lips.

Tugging at his tunic, suddenly yearning to feel his bare skin on hers, she shoved at his clothing until his torso pressed, hot and firmly muscled, against her cool skin. A vast relief washed through her, utter bliss at the feel of his body along the length of hers, solid, comforting and wholly pleasuring, each curve, each plane of her body melding to his.

He inhaled sharply when her stroking fingers drifted down along his left thigh. Taking her fingers, he lifted and kissed them, and then hastened to cover her questioning lips with his.

His hands slid down her back and slipped beneath her hips, and he drew her forward urgently, guiding her until she opened for him, lush channel yielding to silken core, cushioning his potent shuddering heat. Sighing, he buried his face in the soft curtain of her hair, where its satiny mass feathered over her shoulder. When his lips brushed her mouth, she opened there for him as tenderly as she welcomed his body into hers.

He urged her to move with him, an easy, supple rhythm at first, but the heated motion soon deepened and grew as the ember created between them became a firebrand, fervently ignited and eagerly tended. When his thrusts overtook the pace, when his breath quickened on her own, the simmering inner coil that had been spinning and pulsing inside her burst into a wild fire.

She surged with him in pursuit of a swirling, enticing vortex only glimpsed before. Meeting her, spinning through her like white flame, it whirled her awareness away. She grasped his shoulders, seeking the firm anchor of his presence, his strength.

Sweat-misted, he leaned his head to hers and exhaled, kissing her gently. She tilted her head and looked into his beautiful, kind, mossy-colored eyes, bright in the dappled light. Smiling, she reached up to push away an errant lock of his long hair.

Echoing his soft, breathy laughter, a ripple of pure love sang through her, like a cleansing wind after a storm. She had almost forgotten where she was, who she was. Until he frowned.

He angled his head, listening, looking away.

With a low curse, he slid from her, drawing the smooth silk down her legs. "Dear God. A fool's paradise, this," he murmured.

"What?" She could not seem to clear her thoughts.

He sat up with a heavy sigh. Adjusting his clothing, he reached for his boots. "Look, beyond the glade there. Birds. A whole flock, driven out of the woods to the west. Riders come through there, my love." He tossed her shoes and hosen to her. "We have miles to cover, and little time to get away."

Emlyn sighed, too, in gusty impatience at having their idyllic moments spoiled yet again. While he gathered their cloaks and his bow and quiver, she scuttled to the edge of the little stream and cleansed herself with cooling water before pulling on her hose, securing them with wide garter bands of embroidered silk around her thighs. Shoving on her shoes, she stood, wobbling, her legs unsteady beneath her.

Thorne moved to stand behind her, settling her cloak gently around her shoulders. His hands lingered at her neck, and he traced a finger around the shell of her ear and the line of her jaw. With his forearm he pulled her back to rest against his chest, laying his cheek on her hair.

"We will have our proper bedding, my lady wife, with none to hurry us through it," he murmured. He kissed her temple, a soft promise in his lips. "But for now, our marriage is made and cannot be put asunder."

Chapter Thirteen

A faint jingle, like tiny flat-toned bells, resounded beneath high gray stone walls. Emlyn peered warily from under her wide linen wimple, tucking her chin down as she sat on the bench next to Godwin. The soft murmurings of serving people attending to various tasks in the great hall continued. Hearing the jingle again, she recognized the sound of keys and looked up.

In spite of vaulted ceilings and lofty, elegant proportions, Hawksmoor's great hall seemed as cozy as a smaller room, filled with sunlight, embroidered hangings, petal-strewn rushes, and the warm gleam of polished oak tables and high-backed chairs.

Light poured from a row of tall, round-arched windows, spilling mullioned amber bars across the rushes on the planked floor. A huge fireplace with a high projecting stone hood dominated the far end of the hall, a roaring fire in its depth.

The jingling was louder now. Emlyn glanced toward the hearth end of the room. A woman entered through a side door, a heavy ring of keys jangling at her slim waist. Gliding to a chair near the fireplace, she sat, arranged her black skirts, and inclined her head toward the steward who had followed her.

"Lady Julian de Gantrou, the baron's aunt," Godwin murmured. Emlyn glanced up at her uncle, who leaned sideways toward her.

"Julian de Gantrou?"

"A countess, the widow of Earl John de Gantrou. Her sister was the baron's mother. I have seen Lady Julian betimes at the abbey, when she has visited Abbot John." Godwin rubbed his long chin thoughtfully, scratching at gray and white stubble. "The gateman said the Baron de Hawkwood would be away for some time. His lady aunt must be tending to matters in his absence. We shall have to present our request to her."

Emlyn nodded nervously, twisting her fingers in the ends of the black woolen cord that served as her belt. A little ivory crucifix swung from one looped end of the cord.

"Becalm yourself, and stay your hands. You are skittish as a squirrel," he said softly.

"Brother Godwin of Wistonbury," the steward called.

Godwin stood, a folded letter in his hand, and crossed the room, his black-cowled white tunic swaying with his lanky walk, his sandaled feet quiet on the rushes. Sunbeams careened off the top of his pink scalp and the fuzzy aureole of graying blond hair, and highlighted his keen blue eyes.

"God give you good day, Brother Godwin," Lady Julian said as he approached. She tilted her thin oval face. "Have we met?"

"Aye, my lady, in the scriptorium at Wistonbury."

"Ah, you are the painter! I purchased one of your shop's manuscripts for my daughter. Beautiful work. Welcome, Brother, to Hawksmoor. What brings you here?"

"My niece and I bring a letter from Abbot John," he said.

Lady Julian squinted the length of the room, where Emlyn sat demurely on the bench. "Your niece is a nun?" she asked.

Godwin cleared his throat. "Ah, er, aye."

"Come forward, Dame," she called, motioning Emlyn to the table, then gestured to a servant. A silver jug and goblets were brought by a woman who had been stoking the hearth fire.

Though the hall was pleasantly cool for late spring, the heat of the fire and sunlight made this end of the chamber quite warm. Emlyn, stifling in her close-fitting headgear and heavy woolen gown, had no wish to stand near the hearth. She paused next to Godwin, glancing curiously at the countess.

Lady Julian wore a black wool gown that was enlivened only by a long rosary of red jasper and ivory. A white headdress swathed her forehead and chin, and the delicate transparency of her skin showed only a trace of aging. Barely middle-aged, still with a lingering beauty, she looked more pious and severe than any nun.

"Prithee, refresh yourselves," the countess said, pouring a little red wine into two silver cups, which she handed to them. She peered at Emlyn. "Dame—?"

"Agnes of Roseberry Priory, my lady," Emlyn said. Godwin, swallowing his wine, began to cough and sputter in shock. Although he had a general understanding of her plan, she had not discussed her intention to use her sister Agnes's identity.

Lady Julian waited patiently for his spasm to cease, smiling vaguely. "Dame Agnes, welcome," the countess said. "How pleasant to have a sister of the cloth here. And a man of such excellent talent as well, Brother Godwin." She looked up at the tall monk, her brown eyes, deepset and hooded, aristocratic and obviously a little shortsighted.

"But," she continued, "I regret that my nephew is not here to greet you himself. He rode to London to join the northern barons in their meeting with King John. We do not expect him for several weeks."

Godwin set his cup on the table. "We had heard at the abbey that the Archbishop of Canterbury had arrived in London to gather the king and the barons together."

"Aye, he did so, after those disastrous weeks when the most rebellious barons attempted to siege London and force the king to their demands. Mayhap this meeting will be a move toward peace at last between the king and his barons."

"With God's will, we shall see greater wisdom from our king in future, if he accedes to the barons' wishes."

Lady Julian nodded once, an assured and superior gesture of agreement. "Tell me," she said, "about your letter."

"'Tis from Abbot John to either the baron or yourself, my lady," he explained, handing the parchment to her.

She accepted the parchment from him, but did not open it. "I have little ability to decipher words. Can this matter wait for the baron's return?"

Godwin shook his head solemnly. "My lady, the baron has lately been given custody of three children."

The countess lifted her slender dark eyebrows. "Aye."

"They are the children of my eldest brother, Rogier de Ashbourne. My niece, er, Agnes, is their elder sister."

The countess frowned. "And your request?"

"We wish to visit with the children," Godwin answered.

"Dame Agnes, you travel without another nun as companion?" the countess asked, peering up at her.

Emlyn blushed under the countess's frank, oddly squinted perusal. "My lady, I have dispensation to journey with my uncle." Godwin frowned slightly, and glanced away.

She knew her uncle was displeased with her ruse, though he accepted the need for it. Because he could not condone lying, he would tell no outright untruth, and so far had not: Agnes was indeed a nun, and the children's older sister, and his niece.

A fortnight ago, Thorne had seen her to the abbey gate, parting with a gentle kiss as she rang the outer bell. Godwin, surprised to see her, had agreed to help her regain the children, but urged her to allow him to petition the Pope. Unable to persuade him to swifter action, she told him of her marriage.

Concerned, fearing that she would try to extricate the children alone, Godwin had decided to accompany her to Hawksmoor. Only for a short visit, he had insisted. Agreeing that her safety was important, he had obtained a novitiate's garb for her.

His intention was to travel on to find Thorne. Clandestine marriages are legal but hotly disputed, he had told her. Now that the deed was done, a proper marriage should be performed.

"Where is your sister Emlyn?" the countess asked her.

Emlyn started, coloring faintly under the countess's open, curious stare. Godwin's cheeks showed two bright spots of color, but he turned a look of sublime innocence to the countess.

"She was given in marriage to Lord Whitehawke, my lady," Emlyn answered carefully.

The countess sighed. "Of course, you have been cloistered, my dear. I am sorry to tell you that your sister disappeared weeks ago on the way to Graymere Keep. Lord Whitehawke has been searching for her ever since, sending men out daily."

Emlyn glanced at Godwin, who avoided her eyes. "Disappeared?"

"Oh, by the Virgin," Godwin said, and murmured a Latin prayer. The countess bowed her head and folded her hands serenely. Emlyn flushed, glancing at Godwin, and belatedly did the same.

"We are all confident that the girl will be found safe," the countess murmured. Godwin nodded vigorously.

"My lady, may we see the children?" Emlyn asked.

"The baron is their guardian, but I will ponder the matter." Picking up the letter, Lady Julian rose from the table and looked at Godwin. "Brother, I would have a word with you."

Godwin followed her to a bench beneath a window. As the countess spoke, he listened carefully, nodding and glancing back at Emlyn once or twice. Anxiously twisting the long crucifix cord around her fingers, Emlyn waited.

"Lady Julian has her own request," Godwin murmured when he returned. Emlyn stared up at him, her breath in her throat. "The baron has a new chapel. The countess wishes to commission a wall decoration there, and promises a generous gift to the abbey in return. Since I will need an assistant, I told the countess of your abilities. You are welcome to stay as well."

Lady Julian swept forward, her hands folded over her ivory cross. "Baron Nicholas will be pleased that I have taken this opportunity to acquire the services of a goodly painter. He expressed an interest in decorating the new chapel, and mentioned some fine paintings done at Ashbourne." She smiled fully at Godwin. "He will be interested to meet the kin of his young wards, as well. Might I send a messenger to the abbot?"

"We accept the commission, my lady," Godwin said. "I would appreciate a messenger to Wistonbury, since I must request supplies. There is no need to write to Roseberry." A letter to Roseberry Priory could be disastrous, Emlyn thought, listening. Agnes was prioress there, and had no great sense of humor.

"A messenger will be sent to fetch your things, Brother Godwin," the countess said. "Rooms will be prepared for you, and the children will be brought to see you shortly. I will show you the chapel later, and we can discuss the project."

"Our thanks for your generosity, my lady," Godwin said.

"We may expect good work in return, I hope, Brother Godwin."

"The finest that we can produce." He smiled.

"Of course." She turned away, beckoning to the steward, and left the hall with him, murmuring instructions.

"My dear," Godwin muttered to Emlyn, "we must change our plans. This obligation could take months, and I will need your assistance for much of it."

Emlyn gazed up at him, chagrinned. Learning that the baron was not at Hawksmoor, she had felt relief, but now she felt a wrenching anxiety. De Hawkwood would surely return before they completed the work in the chapel. Intending to steal the wolf's cubs, she had become trapped in the wolf's lair.

A door opened at the far end of the room, and the children were ushered into the hall by Tibbie. Emlyn's concerns vanished like mist in the sun, and she held open her arms.

"Blessed be God! I have fretted day and night about ye, so I thank the saints to see ye safe, no matter yer name. Now tell me why, my lady girl, yer here with Godwin, and calling yerself Agnes." Tibbie raised her fuzzy brows reprovingly.

Seated on a stone bench with Tibbie, Emlyn held Harry and nudged her toe at a dandelion sprouting between the flagstones. The bench was set in a sunny corner beside a riotous summer flower bed. Bees droned past mounds of white marguerites and pink roses, fringed by tall, sweet lavender. Primroses crowded beside delicately tinted columbine blossoms.

Emlyn set Harry on the ground, where he wobbled off on bowed legs, his woolen shirt hiked up in the back over the bulk of his loose, dry breechcloth. He meandered a short distance and grabbed onto Isobel's skirt as she tossed a ball with Christien.

Tibbie leaned forward. "Tell me the whole of it!"

Hesitating, Emlyn pursed her lips and glanced at the children. Christien rolled the leather-covered ball to Harry, who picked it up and began to chew on it happily.

"All right," Emlyn said, "harken. But 'tis a grave secret."

Tibbie made the sign of the cross on her wide bosom. "By the Holy Savior, I will tell no soul."

"I am hiding from Lord Whitehawke because I cannot marry him. And I cannot trust his son. If the baron discovered me here, he would surely send me to his father. I intended to take the children away, but now Godwin has promised the countess that we will stay until the chapel paintings are done."

Tibbie flattened her hand on her chest. "Can ye truly refuse to wed that white-haired old goat?"

"'Tis impossible, now, for me to wed him. Tibbie—we must make certain the children understand I am to be called Agnes."

Tibbie nodded. "Easy to make a game of that. Why is it impossible for ye to wed the earl?" She gasped. "My lady! What happened when ye disappeared from the escort? Were ye . . . harmed?"

Emlyn sighed, watching Isobel take the ball from Harry and then hug him, covering his head with kisses until he pushed her away, screaming impatiently.

"Tibbie," she said softly, "when I hid from my escort, I met a forester who helped me." Squaring her shoulders, she shrugged back the wings of her veil. "And now, I am married to him."

"Ahh!" Tibbie shrieked. "What nonsense is this?"

"Hush," Emlyn urged, glancing at the children. "He is a kind, brave man. And our marriage vows annul my betrothal to Whitehawke." Tibbie's lower lip hung loose in astonishment.

"Holy saints," Tibbie said, recovering. "Holy, holy saints. I should have gone with ye instead of the little ones. What a loose-brained scheme this is. Ye wed a stranger?"

"He is no stranger," Emlyn said. "He is the Black Thorne."

"Eek! A dead man! An outlaw!"

Emlyn twisted her mouth in wry amusement. "Nay, dear, he is alive and well. We pledged sacred matrimony by mutual consent."

"By the rood," Tibbie murmured. "A clandestine marriage. What a devil of a tangle. Does Godwin know?"

"Aye, though he has not met Thorne. He wants to pronounce vows over us himself. But he says that such clandestine vows are valid in the Church, Tibbie. The betrothal is voided."

"And who has courage enough to tell the earl that? Holy jumping virgins! Married!" Tibbie glowered at Emlyn for a moment, then sighed heavily. "Yer vows came from the heart?"

"Aye, Tibbie," Emlyn replied quietly. "They did."

"I pray that however quickly made, this may be a blessing." Tibbie half smiled. "Ye need not tell me about clandestine vows, my lady. My father—yer mother's uncle—arranged a marriage for me with a knight who was fat and mean as a boar. I loved another, a young squire. The day the banns were posted, Thomas and I ran off and made our own vows, and consummated them as well. My family needed a full year to recover from the shock of it. And the knight was furious."

Emlyn leaned forward to hug Tibbie. "I did not know," she said. "Then you understand."

"Aye." Tibbie smiled ruefully. "We were young, as ye. I never regretted my boldness in choosing my own husband, bless his eternal soul. He died of a fever before I reached twenty-five years, and our daughter with him. After, yer mother asked me to Ashbourne, when ye was a babe," she added quietly.

Emlyn pressed Tibbie's round, roughened hand. "I am sorry for your loss, but glad you came to us, Tib. Pray for me," she said. "I would not regret my boldness, either."

"If this man is kind and trustworthy," Tibbie murmured, "ye will never have cause for regret."

Pushing open the chapel door, Nicholas closed it firmly against a soaking blast of rain. The interior of the chapel was cool and silent except for the steady beat of the summer storm on the copper roof tiles, and the rumble of distant thunder.

Dropping the damp hood of his cloak, he walked the length of the chapel, his boots scuffing softly on the floor stones, his black wool tunic, trimmed with silver braid, swinging against his calves. The cloth felt light and comfortable after weeks of heavy chain mail. At the altar, he dipped to one knee to whisper a prayer and light a votive candle, then rose to his feet and turned. He noticed the changes almost immediately.

On a sunny day, the chapel windows glowed with colored light, but this afternoon, thick purple shadows lingered in the corners. But there was light enough to see the half-finished paintings on the wall over the doorway: a row of figures sketched over a fresh coat of plaster.

Against the northern wall, a sturdy timber scaffolding, its platform about eight feet off the floor, was set up between two banks of tall arched windows filled with milk-white and colored glass. The wall area between the windows, once plain whitewash all the way up to the vaulted, stone-ribbed ceiling, was now covered with brightly painted images.

Intrigued, Nicholas strolled toward the scaffolding. Far above his head stood an armored Saint George, one foot on the back of a coiled green dragon. The saint's graceful, swayed posture seemed to echo and balance the arc of the slender windows. Vibrant color sparked the plain little chapel to life: deep ruby red for the saint's cloak and the cross on his white shield, brilliant grass green, crisscrossed with blue, for the dragon. Nearby, a willowy princess in a gown of yellow and blue thanked her rescuer with folded hands.

Nicholas had seen wall decorations at Westminster on his last visit to London, done by a well-known school; now, standing in his own chapel, looking at the bold color and fluid lines, he knew that this work could compete with the Westminster painters.

A movement from above caught his attention. Though he had seen no one when he entered, he stepped back to peer at the top surface of the scaffold.

A woman sat with her back to him, cross-legged in a loose gown of pale gray, her head covered in a wide white headdress that trailed over her slim shoulders and down her back. Leaning toward the wall, she held a long wooden brush in one hand, another clenched between her teeth.

Oblivious to his presence, she carefully painted tiny flowers beneath the princess. Beside her, a small collapsible stool held a motley jumble of clay jars, clamshells, brushes, and

paint-blotched rags. Three fat candles flickered to light her
work.

Nicholas frowned, wondering why his lady aunt had neglected to mention the new work in the chapel when he had
arrived late last night. He stepped toward the scaffold.

"Greetings, mistress," he said. The woman jumped and
squeaked, dropping the brush clenched in her teeth. She lost
her grip on the other brush, which flipped and came down
over the edge of the scaffold to roll toward his feet.

Bending down, he picked up the brush and rose. Wide
eyes under a big headdress peered at him over the edge of
the scaffold. Her face was indistinct in the deep shadows,
but he could see that she stared at him with her mouth open.

Stretching his arm up, he offered the brush. She reached
down a hand and snatched it back. He frowned again. "How
do you come to be painting my chapel walls, mistress?" he
asked sharply. He wished she would come out where he
could see her. A new torrent of rain hit the roof, rattling and
pounding, and the gloom in the chapel increased.

The woman cleared her throat, then spoke in a curiously
hushed voice. "I assist the painter, my lord."

"Who is this painter? Where is he now?"

"He was called to Lady Julian's chamber to perform a low
mass, sire."

"A mass?"

"He is Brother Godwin of Wistonbury, my lord."

Nicholas's heart thudded against his ribs. Of course.
Godwin the uncle, the painter-monk, must have come here
to speak with him about the children. He responded with a
cool, even tone. "I know the name. Who sent him here?"

"Lady Julian requested that he decorate the chapel, my
lord." She held back in the shadows, and her voice, barely
above a whisper, quavered timidly. He noticed that her eyes
were large, the neutral color of rain in the dim light, shaded
beneath the wimple that sat over her brow.

There was a sharp burst of thunder, and an instant of
lightning illumined the chapel, outlining the woman's face.
Nicholas narrowed his eyes. She looked like—his breath
caught in his throat for an instant. But now he saw that this
woman was clearly a nun of indeterminate age. He craned
his head to get a better look, but she ducked and turned

away to wipe her hands on the front of her coarse brown apron.

"Who are you, Dame?" he asked.

"I assist Brother Godwin. I am called Agnes," she said.

"You are a religious?" he asked. He needed a closer look. She bore too much resemblance; the mystery intrigued him.

Her headdress bobbed like a sheet flapping in the wind as she nodded. Then her head snapped up and she looked toward the door.

"Nicholas!"

He whirled as two women entered the chapel, sweeping back hoods sparkling with raindrops. Lady Julian nodded to him, and he bowed in return. "Good morning, Nicholas, I did not expect to find you here already," she said. "The weather is frightful."

"My lady," he said curtly. "Good morning." A muscle flipped in his cheek and he fisted one hand behind his back tensely. He had no wish to be rude, but he needed a few explanations.

A high moan and the strong stamp of a foot diverted his attention before he could question his aunt. The girl who had accompanied the countess stood in the open doorway, looking through silvery sheets of rain into the muddy courtyard beyond.

"Lady Julian, my jewels are in that chest over there, 'tis not a bundle of straw," the girl whined. Nicholas glimpsed drenched servants unloading baggage from a pair of wagons. "Here now!" the girl called out the door. "You shall be whipped unless you handle those chests with more care!"

"My dear cousin Alarice, your things traveled all the way to Hawksmoor from Kent," the countess said wearily. "Surely they will come to no harm between the bailey and the solar, but for some rain."

Alarice let the chapel door slam shut behind her and tossed her head. Beneath her fur-trimmed cloak hood, her hair was bright as autumn leaves, curling freely under a little cap of rose brocade and a white silk veil.

"Nicholas," she said sweetly, coming toward him and holding out her hands. Her rounded hips swayed in circles beneath her cloak, and generous curves peeked out, swathed in mauve sendal.

He bowed again. "Lady Alarice, I trust you are well."

"My back is a little stiff this morning. Likely 'twas my bed." She made a pretty moue of her mouth and arched her back, placing her palms along her hips. Her chest thrust and strained at the embroidered bodice.

Nicholas blinked. "I trow you feel the effects of riding in the van for so many days. My lady aunt will see to your comfort while you are here."

"Cousin Alarice, my apologies," the countess said. "Last night we offered you a poor, makeshift bed—you will have better tonight. 'Twas such a surprise to find that you had traveled north with Nicholas. Will you be with us through the summer? Nicholas has yet to read me your mother's letter."

"My parents wish for me to be here, my lady, as long as I may stay," Alarice answered. "All of Kent is so tense now. Papa was very concerned that I go somewhere safe, away from London. The king has been in a foul temper since he signed the charter in June, and my father feared for my safety."

"Lord Braye insisted that Alarice come north with me when he discovered that you and Maude were here," Nicholas said to his aunt, "though I cautioned him that the north might well be just as unsafe soon. King John is incensed about the charter, and all the northern barons will need to beware, I trow."

"Still, 'tis good news that the charter is signed," the countess replied. "As for Alarice, she is welcome here. Maude will be delighted to have a friend. If the situation changes, we can all leave Hawksmoor. My own castle is near to Wales, and quite secluded. We shall go there if the king has a tantrum."

Nicholas marveled at his aunt's ability to sort matters in her usual unperturbed way. He sighed and shook his head.

Alarice pointed a beringed finger up toward the scaffolding. "Nicholas, there is a nun up there," she said incredulously.

Lady Julian turned her head. "Good morning, Dame Agnes. Please meet my nephew, the Baron de Hawksmoor, and our cousin, Lady Alarice de Braye."

The nun, who had been intently cleaning brushes and ignoring them all, mumbled a polite greeting with a brief nod of her head. "Dame Agnes is from Roseberry Priory," the countess said. "She assists her uncle, the painter."

"I have already met Dame ... Agnes," Nicholas said wryly. "Though I did not know she was the painter's niece." Agnes of Roseberry. This, then, was Emlyn's elder sister. That would explain the resemblance.

"An artist nun, how unusual," Alarice murmured blandly, glancing around in a bored manner, clearly uninterested in artists, or in nuns.

"Aunt Julian," Nicholas said sternly, "I must admit to surprise when I entered the chapel this morning." Actually, he felt a little as if he had been punched in the stomach. If Agnes and Godwin of Wistonbury were both at Hawksmoor, then where was Emlyn? What in the name of the devil was going on here?

Obviously Emlyn had chosen to stay away, and had sent the rest of her family to demand the children. So be it: he was prepared to deal with their objections to his custody. But he needed to know that Emlyn was safe.

He pinched his lips together in a grim line, guarding his tongue against being sharp with his aunt. Arriving home after an absence of nearly two months, his patience keenly tried due to endless days of Alarice's spoiled, squirrel-brained company, he had expected the only change at Hawksmoor to be a settling in of the children, like prized cups polished and put in place.

Instead, he had found his organized, disciplined keep in a cheerful uproar. His soldiers were relaxed and laughing instead of efficiently tending to their duties, and his hall was littered with the evidence of children. He had crunched a tiny wooden cow beneath his heel at breakfast, and dodged Christien brandishing a wooden sword in the stairwell. A new puppy had bounded up the stairs behind the boy, and a litter of kittens was in the solar.

And now he found his chapel undergoing decoration without his opinion, and a veritable host of odd coincidences playing out around him, arranged at least in part by his aunt.

"I did mean to tell you about the chapel, Nicholas, but there were so many other matters to discuss last night when you arrived," Lady Julian was saying. "I knew you would not mind." She smiled and peered up at him.

He shrugged in defeat. "Hawksmoor bears no similarity to the garrison keep it was a few months ago, I assure you. We now have a passel of ladies, infants, nurses, pups, kittens, children's toys underfoot—what harm a nun and a priest?"

"Infants? Toys?" Alarice echoed.

Nicholas and his aunt ignored her, intent on their discussion. "Oh, Nicholas, dear, do not be in the doleful dumps over this, as Mistress Tibbie would say. You once said that paintings should be added in the chapel. When Brother Godwin came here, I knew his reputation and hired him immediately. I hoped to give you a pleasant surprise. We conferred on the design and decided that Saint George was very appropriate. And on the west wall he has planned a weighing of souls scene. Certes, if you disapprove, it can be changed."

"The design is fine, and I have no quarrel with the subject matter," he said. "Why, though, did Brother Godwin first come to Hawksmoor?" He glanced furtively up at the scaffold, but the slight gray figure had turned away to sort pots and brushes.

"He came to see the children, of course," the countess answered.

"Children?" asked Alarice. Her auburn brows frowned over eyes like pale green glass. "There are children here?"

"The king appointed Nicholas guardian to three adorable children," the countess said. "Brother Godwin and Dame Agnes are their relatives, so I asked them to stay as well."

"Must they live with you, Nicholas?" Alarice asked.

"The children? Until King John decides otherwise, they must," Nicholas said. The nun on the scaffold was setting down paint pots with loud force.

Nicholas worked the muscle in his jaw until it hurt. He had to get away to think. He turned to his aunt with a tilt of his head. "Please excuse me. I have much to attend to this morning." Spinning on his heel, he walked quickly out of the chapel and slammed the door.

Alarice pouted, smoothing her veil. "He seems displeased. Perhaps this fragrance is too overwhelming—'tis a special scent from the East, attar of jasmine," she said, leaning forward obligingly.

Lady Julian sniffed delicately. "Lovely, Alarice. Very exotic." They began to stroll toward the door. "Maude will be delighted to see you, if she can be found. She is often in the practice yards, spending time with the horses, though in such dreary weather one would hope to find her inside." She shook her head gracefully. "She can be a riotous child at times," she mused as they neared the door. The countess glanced back over her shoulder.

"Dame Agnes," she called, "the ladies will gather in my chamber as usual, shortly after the terce bell. Please join us."

"Aye, my lady," the nun replied, and ducked her head to continue working.

"Lady Julian," Alarice said, "will the chapel decorations be finished in time for the wedding?"

The countess stopped by the door. "Your mother sent word months ago that your father was interested in a marriage arrangement between you and Nicholas. Has aught else happened? Has Nicholas agreed, then?"

Alarice laughed, a delighted, confident trill that caused the nun on the scaffold to look up from her work. "Do not fret about Nicholas, my lady," Alarice said. "He will agree."

Still smiling, her cheeks dimpled prettily, Lady Alarice swung open the door and the women stepped out into the rain, pulling up their hoods.

Emlyn set the rest of the brushes and paint pots in careful order, her stomach churning all the while. She wondered why the giggling pratter of a young and obviously pampered girl should bother her. Then she sighed. If de Hawkwood married Alarice, the empty-headed nit would be the children's guardian as well.

She slapped a rag down onto the stool. If they wed, they likely deserved each other, two large egos, one cold and the other vain. But she would not have her siblings caught in that.

Taking a deep breath, she determined again to see this matter concluded. Throughout these past weeks at Hawksmoor, she had pleaded with Godwin to help her spirit the children away before the baron arrived home. Now it was too late for that. She would find another way; the Lord could not mean for her to lose them.

Sighing, she glanced out through the thick murky window glass, watching the rain turn the bailey to thick mud. Nicholas de Hawkwood's unexpected appearance in the chapel had shocked her badly. Her hands were still trembling, and her heart had not yet slowed. She had not seen the baron since those brief, unpleasant encounters at Ashbourne. When she had turned to find him standing there, her heart had nearly leaped into her throat.

Her first thought, surely the reason she was so completely shaken, was how strongly he resembled Thorne. Shared parentage was obvious. Yet the baron was grim and tense, his cheeks clean-shaven, his eyes gray and cold as steel. The long black cloak and tunic he wore had increased his stern demeanor. He had seemed as dark and stormy as the weather, with none of Thorne's gentle, relaxed air. Even his voice was deeper, sharper, with an irritating edge of anger in it.

Sighing again, she absently wiped at the moisture on the glass. Angels must have been with her this morn, for Nicholas de Hawkwood had not recognized her. He would surely have hauled her down from the scaffold and sent for Whitehawke if he had.

Rain sheeted against the windows. Wondering if it rained now in the dale, she imagined Thorne seated by Maisry's cozy fire, sipping ale and laughing with Aelric. She recalled the strong, secure wrap of his arms, the tilt of his bearded lip when he smiled, and the feel of his warm mouth on hers.

Dear God, she thought, leaning her head against the cold glass, she would sacrifice near anything to be with him. The longer she was parted from him, the more she felt a need for his calm presence, his protective arms, his reassuring strength.

She twisted the simple steel ring he had given her and squeezed her eyes shut against pricking tears. She saw his face in her mind with perfect clarity, eyes as green as moss, though she had seen them change color, quick as a summer sky turns with the storm, to a cold gray-green.

Then, unbidden, his image somehow blended with Nicholas de Hawkwood. A shiver twirled up her spine, and she shook her head to clear it. Alike as two halves of an apple, aye, and as different as steel and oak.

Gathering her skirts around her, she climbed down the scaffold. She needed to talk to Godwin. Grabbing her cloak from a hook, she slipped out of the chapel.

Chapter Fourteen

"We must." Emlyn hurried alongside Godwin as they moved through a vaulted stone corridor in the main keep. "Uncle, we must act soon. We cannot trust the baron. If he recognizes me, he might tell Whitehawke that I am here."

"Becalm yourself, my dear," Godwin sighed. "You wanted to be with the children, and now you want to leave. Faith and patience, and the way will become clear. Do you go to Lady Julian's chamber?" Emlyn nodded, and they turned a corner together.

"Uncle, you are content to stay for the paintings. But I cannot stay here now that the baron has returned. Have you sent your letter to the Pope?"

"I have collected my thoughts, but have not yet penned them."

"Pen them! By all means, pen them, and somehow I will find Thorne and we will take Tibbie and the children to Scotland. When you have heard from the Pope, then send word to us."

Godwin sighed, and stopped to look down at Emlyn. "My girl, harken to reason," he said softly. "Would you anger the baron, and the king as well? Whitehawke already searches for you. The baron would search as well, if you took the children. I beg you, use your head rather than your heart."

Emlyn pinched her mouth impatiently. "I will not fear men who use woman and babes to gain their ends. I have wits aplenty, and the strength of your canniness—do I not?—and Thorne's. The king's orders were made from mean greed. Now that the charter is law, 'twill be only time before the writs against us are lifted. Guy will be reinstated. We will go back to Ashbourne soon."

Godwin shook his head and sighed, rubbing his chin. "We cannot say what the king will do. And I fear your impulsive nature. What solution was your ill-timed marriage? Where is your protector husband now?"

When she opened her mouth to protest, he held up his hand. "Becalm yourself, and wait. I pray some provision in the charter will solve this for all concerned." He took her hands in his, covering them like a parent calming an overexcited child. "Trust in the Lord, my dear. What is your pressing need to whisk the little ones away? They are safe. Come, see for yourself."

He led her along the stone passage to a recess in the wall that was pierced by one small window, open to the breezes blowing in from the garden. The rainstorm had ended, and thin sunlight glazed the lush trees and plants. Near the orchard end of the garden, Emlyn saw Christien and Isobel join hands with Harry and a few other children. They skipped in an uneven circle, Harry toddling along to keep up, their giggles blithe and silly.

When Harry tumbled, he brought Isobel and two others down with him. One of the boys picked up a piece of fruit from the ground and pelted another child. Soon they were all gathering half-rotten crabapples and peaches, and the air was filled with projectiles. Laughter turned quickly to irate screams, until Tibbie barreled through the gate to scold and separate pairs of children and brush off muddy bottoms.

Emlyn smiled, resting her chin on her hand as she watched, having been admonished often enough by Tibbie to imagine what was being said. A fresh damp breeze fluttered the white wimple around her head. Godwin placed a hand on her shoulder.

"The children had a loving home at Ashbourne, God knows," he said. "But here they have freedom again. They may go outside the walls without fear, and they have the children of servants and knights to play with. Would you take that from them?"

Emlyn sighed. "I admit, I did not expect them to be content here. But they are my family, not kin of Nicholas de Hawkwood! Christien is not even old enough for fostering. I vowed to my father to keep them safe. They are hostages here."

"They are treated kindly here."

"I want what is best for them."

"What is best for them, or what suits you best?"

She turned to face him, stung by the truth. In seeking to obey her father's wishes, she had determined to take back the children, stirred by anger and her insistent conscience. Her siblings were in no danger here. And perhaps, she realized, they did not need her as much as she needed them.

"Watch and wait, my dear," Godwin urged. "Let God decide if you will stay or go."

After a long moment, she nodded, and the relinquishment that she felt was both painful and a relief. "I will try to remember what you say."

Godwin smiled, and patted her shoulder. "Trust, my girl."

The soggy weather had encouraged a larger gathering than usual in Lady Julian's bedchamber, the thriving center of feminine activity at Hawksmoor. Several women, wives of knights, had joined the countess, her daughter Lady Maude, and Lady Alarice by the time Emlyn arrived.

The cozy chamber, furnished with a curtained bed, chests, two fine chairs and a few low stools, was filled with chattering and laughing as Emlyn seated herself in a wide window niche, fitted with twin stone benches and deep cushions. Beginning her stitchery task of hemming a new shirt for Harry, she glanced at Lady Alarice and Lady Maude, who sat on the opposite bench, bent over embroidery frames and talking softly.

Much of the time sewing for the castle household, both functional and decorative, was done here whenever the ladies gathered. Garments were mended or embroidered, and bedding and linens were hemmed. Wall hangings, pillows, and other embroidery pieces, on which some of the women worked, were set up in wooden frames.

Emlyn glanced at the countess, who drew a needle in and out of a square of fabric, squinting, her stitches crooked. Lady Julian's vision was so poor that she usually had no idea what work the other women were doing unless she peered closely at the task in hand. Still, she had great appreciation for color and design, and loved stitcheries, paintings, and books.

Recently, Lady Julian had mounted the scaffolding in the chapel to examine Godwin's work at close hand, since she saw only blurred color and shape from the floor. Emlyn knew that glass spectacles were often available from skilled glaziers, and she resolved to suggest such to the countess or to Maude.

Maude smiled brightly at Emlyn, her brown eyes twinkling. "Little Harry has grown much since he has been here," she commented as Emlyn turned the shirt to finish the hem.

"Aye so," Emlyn replied, smiling. Maude was perhaps a year or two younger than Emlyn, with an open, friendly nature, a tall, sturdy girl with hair like warm mahogany, and her mother's eyes. Emlyn liked her immensely and found her honest and good-humored, interested more in hunting and riding than embroidery or silken gowns or the texture of her skin.

"Dame Agnes," Lady Julian said. "'Tis time for a prayer."

Maude groaned softly. "Mother, we prayed at terce, 'tis barely an hour past that."

Her mother looked sternly at her and folded her hands palm to palm. "Dame Agnes," she repeated.

Emlyn sighed inwardly and got down on her knees to murmur a brief Latin orison she had learned years before in the convent. After intoning the comforting, familiar words, each woman meditated silently.

Lady Julian presides serenely over all here, Emlyn thought, like a fond mother, or an abbess, with loving, pious discipline. Perhaps shortsightedness naturally turned one's thoughts inward, she thought, for Lady Julian certainly behaved more like an abbess than a countess, with simple dress, constant prayers, and a gracious nature.

Lady Julian demanded, in a gentle, persuading way, that the ladies stop their hands and minds several times a day for prayer and silence. At eventide, when households normally settled down to hear stories read by the lady of the castle, or to listen to musicians, Lady Julian insisted that all the ladies, married or not, retire to their beds for prayers. Maude was invariably disappointed with this nightly ritual. Alarice, having just arrived, would definitely be unhappy with it.

The countess smiled beatifically when the meditation was

over, and picked up a small leather-bound volume from a table.

"Dame Agnes, would you recite a few passages from Marie as we work?" There was a general titter of agreement from around the room in anticipation of the treat.

"Certes," Emlyn said. The *lais* of Marie de France were among her favorite stories. She opened the gilded leather cover of the little illustrated book, filled with simple pen drawings.

She chose the story of Guigemar, a knight who went hunting and fell into a curse, and began to read. Her slightly husky voice swept through the story, each pause filled by the crackle of the fire and the sibilant sounds of hands at needlework.

Guigemar shot a hind one day, she read, but the animal was magical. The arrow rebounded to strike the knight in the thigh. The stag cursed the man, saying that the wound would not heal until a woman gladly suffered, out of love for him, much anguish.

Emlyn blushed as she read. Her mind conjured images of Nicholas de Hawkwood in the forest at Ashbourne, with an arrow protruding from his thigh. She tried to dispel the memory. Only true love would salve the wound, she read. Indeed, she thought. Guigemar, at least, was lovable, not filled with seething anger.

When Emlyn finished the story, the countess dismissed the group of women to attend to their other duties, promising that they would meet in the garden later if the day remained clear.

Eager to get to her own project, Emlyn hurried along the corridor toward the solar that the countess had allowed her to use as a workroom. A narrow outer door opened onto the corridor, and she slipped inside.

A few weeks earlier, Lady Julian had asked her to complete some unfinished decorations in a book of psalms. Emlyn had been given free access to the little room that adjoined the baron's bedchamber, separated by a curtain from the unoccupied larger room. Now that the baron had returned, she wondered if she would be able to continue working in the little solar, which had become her favorite place at Hawksmoor.

Always filled with bright light and sweet fresh air from the gardens, always private and quiet, the solar was a haven for Emlyn, bringing privacy, scarce in any castle.

Peaceful silence greeted her as she crossed to the curtain and peeked rather furtively to make certain that the baron was not in his chamber. She had no desire to encounter him again.

The outer room was empty, though a fire blazed in the hearth and the rushes had been freshened. The baron's huge curtained bed, with carved posts and silk hangings of deep red, dominated the room. She thought the bed ostentatious, though it looked undeniably comfortable, deep and soft. Beside the bed, a tall iron candlestick, with three fat candles, sat on a low wooden chest. Two stiff-backed chairs were placed by the hearth, a chessboard set on a table between them. A pair of boots sat on the hearthstone.

Turning away, Emlyn sat before a long oak table placed beneath a row of windows. The room also held a narrow bed and a stool, yet the solar always seemed spacious because of the tall, arched, glassed windows, whose lower shutters she now opened.

The table surface, polished and gleaming with sunlight, held an illuminated book, weighted open by rocks at the corners. Several paint pots, which had come from her leather satchel, littered the tabletop, along with an ink horn, brushes, a quill, and soft rags. Emlyn rolled up her sleeves to get to work.

Lady Julian told her that she had purchased the little book from a binder's shop in London with several illuminations planned out but left undecorated. Emlyn had agreed to fill in the blank areas with pictures and border designs, but because she had to work in an already bound book, instead of on flat unsewn parchment sheets, the process was awkward and slow.

Bending forward, she examined the border she had painted the day before. A slender vine twisted around the text margin, adorned with delicate roses washed in pink: her signature border, which existed somewhere in every manuscript she had ever painted. This time, she had added tiny black thorns along the vine. Looking at the spines now tugged at her heart.

Dipping her brush in white lead mixed with carmine and ochre, she applied the flesh color to the tiny hand of God reaching down from the clouds toward King David, who knelt with his harp. Painting with deep concentration, she did not hear the door of the outer chamber open. Her head jerked up at the sound of horses tramping across the floor.

"Do stop neighing and stomping, Christien," she said. "You startled me so, I nearly blotted the paint."

Her brother galloped to her side and peeked over her shoulder. "Tibbie said you were here. What's that?" he asked.

"'Tis the hand of God, comforting King David."

"Where are the knights?" he asked.

"There are none, so far, in this manuscript."

"Well, I like knights. You painted lots in Guy's book. And Uncle Godwin has made a huge Saint George"—he lifted his arms high—"in the chapel. When I am grown, I shall have knights painted on my castle walls, as tall as the ceilings. You can do them if you like," he said magnanimously.

"Thank you. So you like Uncle Godwin's Saint George?" At his vigorous nod, she picked up a small square of linen, which she normally placed under the heel of her hand as she painted to protect the absorbent vellum from skin oils. Quickly, using a thin brush dipped in ink, she sketched a replica of Godwin's military saint, painting the details of his armor and adding a red cross to his shield. Christien watched in fascination and made eager suggestions on aspects of the armor, a subject quite dear to him. Emlyn, pleased and impressed by the extent of his knowledge, added pieces accordingly until the picture was done.

"There," she said, moving it to a corner, "When 'tis dry, you may have it."

"Thank you," he said. "Now, please, make me a dragon."

She laughed, and shook her head. "I have to finish my work here. But you may draw one if you like." She gave him another plain rag, a little brush, and enough suggestions to get him started. They conferred over his efforts, their heads close together, their backs to the door.

A brief cough, deep and masculine, brought their heads snapping up. Nicholas de Hawkwood stood in the inner doorway, one hand raised high, propped against the door-jamb, as he held the curtain aside. The silver trim on his black tunic glittered.

"My lord!" Christien cried, and bounced up from his seat. "Come see what my sister made for me!"

Stepping into the little solar, Nicholas leaned over the table. Emlyn kept her back turned, and slanted her head away, grateful for the generous shielding folds of the white head-dress.

"'Tis well drawn," the baron said to Christien. "Greetings, Dame Agnes. I was not aware that my private solar had been turned into a scriptorium."

Emlyn blushed fiercely, feeling the heat rise from her breasts to her hairline. Blessed Virgin, she thought, his voice has a velvety quality like Thorne's, but haughty, his words clipped and nasal. She turned only a degree toward him. The soft, snug wrappings swathing her throat and chin made movement less graceful, but she dared not show her face in the clear, full light of the solar, no matter how rude it was to avoid a baron.

"My lord, my apologies. I will move my things elsewhere if it disturbs your privacy," she said. "While you were away, the countess asked me to add some paintings in this manu-script, and suggested this room as a quiet place to work."

His hand came slowly over her shoulder as he reached out to touch the book, flipping the pages casually through his fingers.

"Ah, I see," he said after a moment. Emlyn felt the baking warmth of his torso behind her shoulder, felt the brushing weight of his arm over hers. "'Tis fine work. I was not aware that the de Ashbournes were all painters."

"My uncle and—myself, only, sire," she nearly whis-pered. "I trained at the convent."

He paused, his finger sliding gently along a decorated bor-der. Emlyn watched his clean, trim fingernail trace a cluster of thorns and roses, stop there, and move past. "Your work is excellent," he said. "Well. You may use the solar, then."

"Thank you, my lord." Please depart, she silently begged. His hand was perched on the table in front of her, his long fingers, dusted with dark hairs, fanning the pages of the book, his body warming her back. Her hand, with the steel circlet, rested on the table beside his. She tapped a finger nervously.

"Please, my lord," she said, "some of the paint is yet damp."

He withdrew his hand, slowly, almost deliberately grazing her shoulder in passing. At the contact, a shiver plunged, tickling, to her loins. Stunned by the feeling, she ducked her head, her cheeks reddening, her heartbeat rapid.

Christien reached out to pick up the cloth with the painted Saint George. "'Tis dry?" he asked her.

Emlyn nodded quickly. "Aye. You may take it, Christien." Trying to sound cool and ecclesiastical, she felt very rattled. Her brother held the cloth gingerly by a corner, letting it flap in the slight breeze that came through the open windows.

"Isobel will be so jealous!" he crowed, and scampered away, leaving the chamber as noisily as he had burst in.

Behind her, Emlyn felt Nicholas de Hawkwood's silent, powerful presence, felt the keen heat of his gaze upon her back. She flattened her hands on the table, afraid to turn around. The baron disturbed her enormously, threw off the rhythm of her breath, broke the pattern of her thoughts.

"Dame Agnes," Nicholas said, after a long moment. His voice, deep and low, thrummed in her body. The slight mocking tone with which he said her name reminded her of Whitehawke's insolent manner. "Will you and your uncle stay long at Hawksmoor?"

"Until the chapel work is done, sire," she stammered. "If we are welcome."

"Of course." He paused. "Your ring is quite unusual."

"I wear it for a vow, my lord," she whispered.

"A vow." The silence that followed was thick as honey. "Well," he said finally, his voice hushed, "I will no longer interrupt your work. Good day, Dame."

His footsteps crossed into the bedchamber with a purposeful stride. The heavy outer door was opened, then slammed hard against the stone frame.

Emlyn jumped in her seat. The baron was angry, but then

each time she had seen him he seemed to be angry about something. She shrugged, trying to shake off the powerful cling of his presence. At least, she thought gratefully, he had not recognized her.

Chapter Fifteen

Thunderclouds slid across the wide sky, the odd greenish light creating crystal-clear detail. Standing at the parapet, Nicholas could see well past the river that flowed beneath Hawksmoor's walls, over vast clusters of forest, far into the long green dale that rolled out below. The peaceful view was marred, a mile or so away, by plumes of slate-colored smoke.

"What the devil is that?" Nicholas asked as Peter joined him on the wall walk.

Peter looked out. "Beyond the river? A fire in a field."

"And what else lies there, beyond the smoke?"

"Looks like a broad stone wall." Peter squinted. "Jesu. 'Tis the curtain wall of a keep, just begun."

"Aye. My father's," Nicholas said. "On my land."

"But your boundaries are well marked by whitewashed boulders. Whatever he dares in the dale, the earl would not build within another's markers."

"Would he not?" He shot Peter a wry look. "Weeks ago I asked my father directly to cease work on that keep. But he has given no order for his masons to stop."

"Think you he has the king's permission to build there?"

"Nay, but with the whole realm on the verge of an uproar, he likely thinks this will be overlooked because he is one of the few loyals left to the crown. Damn. Fighting for that charter has changed little. 'Twill not even help me here."

"Surely the sheriff would intervene in this case, at least. Those walls are clearly on Hawksmoor land."

Nicholas huffed impatiently. "The sheriff of this shire has consistently refused to act against Whitehawke, and grows more blind and deaf each time my father rides into that dale."

"The king and his loyals in York still bear malice against the Cistercian monks," Peter said. "There lies their blind eye."

"Aye, that and a steady stream of Whitehawke's gold flowing the sheriff's way to keep the man ignorant."

"Your father's arrogance has no limit, my lord."

He nodded grimly. "Well I know it."

"I thought the forest extended more to the east."

Nicholas looked, wind whipping his long hair back from his face. "It did. 'Tis why we could not see the walls until now. Whitehawke has cleared a section of my forest for his keep. Even now it burns." He knocked a fist against stone. "This needs quick discouraging. I cannot allow my land to be invaded, burned, and built upon under my very nose."

"You do not mean to start a war with him!"

Nicholas turned, one eyebrow lifted. "Nay? Ah, chivalric sentiment forbids such dishonor. Quote me no codes."

"If you go down there with your troops, Whitehawke will retaliate, and knock at Hawksmoor's gates with his battering devices within days. You know full well he needs only an excuse to pursue what he has been eager to do for years—attack you full out in the name of some minor dispute."

Frowning, Nicholas scanned the clouds that dimmed the afternoon light. Indeed, he would do whatever he could to keep an attack away from his walls. Hawksmoor held precious treasure now, more valuable than Whitehawke or Peter realized.

Had he not been so angry, he would have laughed to recall Emlyn's disguise. He had recognized her quick enough, once he had seen her in the solar. For the nonce, he would remain silent until he knew quite what he wanted to do with her. Or to her, he thought irritably, relishing the temptation of shaking sense into her wimpled head. Now that she was here, and the children and his lady aunt and the rest as well, he could begin no outright war with his father. He would simply find another way.

"What will you do?" Peter asked him.

"I shall have a look, I think." A peculiar glint in his eye reflected the greenish storm clouds overhead. "I would like to know how close he is to my boundary stones. By the rood," he muttered, "a mickle lot of things have gone on

here in my absence." He pushed away from the parapet edge
and turned to stride quickly along the wallwalk, Peter keeping pace behind him.

The rider halted at the crest of a hill, pulling gently on
green-tinted leather reins, watching cloud shadows scud over
the verdant bowl of the dale. An acrid hint of smoke teased
his nostrils. He glanced toward a clearing, where a band of
pale limestone blocks formed high, smooth walls.

Masons and workmen climbed up and down on rubble
piles and wooden scaffolds, looking, from this distance, like
ants busy with crumbs. Some hoisted dressed stone in nets,
using pulley frameworks as high as the wall, shouting orders
back and forth.

A tall, white-haired man sat a creamy horse, surrounded
by a few of his guards, watching as smoke, dark as a breath
of night, rose into the stormy sky. Fields and forest edges
were being burned to make space for the castle grounds.

The rider urged his horse forward silently, the long green
caparison blowing back over his legs as he cantered down a
slope. Entering the greenwood, he rode swiftly toward the
partial wall of the new keep. When he was near enough to
the worksite to be seen by sharp eyes, he reined in between
the trees and sat, folding his leafy gauntlets over the saddle,
watching.

After a while, low thunder rolled through the darkening
sky. The workmen turned up their faces at the sound and
looked toward the earl. Chavant leaned over and spoke quietly to Whitehawke. Beside the earl's horse, a brown hunting
hound, wearing a spiked iron collar to protect him from
wolves and boars, pricked up his ears and whined softly.

The sky was ash-dust now, a ponderous color that sucked
the brightness from the greenwood and shadowed the pale
stone walls. Thunder broke overhead, heavy and loud. Without waiting for the earl's permission, the men scrambled
down from the walls and ran to safety inside a thatched hut
some distance away.

Whitehawke rode off with Chavant, the guards, and the
hunting dog behind him. As they cleared the work area and
moved through the deepening gloom, large spattering drops
of rain fell, and a new thundercrack sounded overhead.

Chavant glanced up nervously and called something to the earl.

The rain burst with its first energy, drenching forest and field and men in a beating downpour. Guiding his horse out of the wood, the Green Knight rode steadfast through the rain. Water flowed in rivulets from the densely woven foliage that covered his trunk and limbs. A stiff trim of spiked holly and hawthorn leaves fringed his hood, deflecting the rain from his face, and water beaded on the ointment that greened his skin. He rode forward smoothly, easily, a legend riding out of time and straight into the present moment.

Whitehawke reined in quickly, jerking his mount's head so violently that the animal neighed and raised up on its back legs. Chavant and the two guards pulled their mounts to a sharp halt.

The green rider lifted a hand, fingers trimmed with budding twigs, in greeting. Rain obscured the details of his appearance, but did not dilute the terror he quickened in those who saw him. Now the distance of a bowshot, he cantered forward.

A clap of thunder sounded again, muffled by the heavy spattering rain. The rider did not pause. Whitehawke and the others edged their agitated, prancing mounts backward. The hunting dog bared his teeth and growled, its menacing threat lost amid rain, and thunder, and horses thumping.

"Fiend of hell!" Whitehawke screamed. "Begone from here!"

Lowering his raised hand, the Green Knight leaned forward and urged his horse to a fast gallop, heading straight for the cluster of riders. They shouted in alarm and scattered as he ripped a path through the middle and shot toward the wall.

Whitehawke spat a command, and the dog leaped after the green-shrouded horse. Chavant and the two guards turned to chase behind, rain and mud and fresh clods thrown out from fast hooves.

The Green Knight neared the wall, leaping over the discarded stones that littered the ground. The unfinished end of the wall slanted down to the ground like a ramp, and the rider kneed his horse to take the incline in the pouring rain. The wall walk was slippery but very wide, and the horse climbed easily, cantering obediently over the layered straw and slate that covered the more complete, higher sections. The rider kept to one side, aware that the rubble which filled the hollow center of the walls had not yet settled and would not be stable.

Glancing behind him, he saw the approach of the dog and, farther back, one guard. He rode on, meaning to risk the dangerous ride along the wall walk. He gambled that the superstitious earl would consider the keep damned and abandon it. 'Twould save months of ineffectual legal action and orders to desist, which Whitehawke would likely ignore.

The hunting dog drew closer, frenzied enough to climb the ramped wall in the rain. Nipping at the green caparison cloth, wet and dragging low, the dog got a firm hold with his long teeth. Reaching to his belt, the rider pulled out his sword and sliced through the rain at the dog, who backed off abruptly. A clap of thunder boomed, followed by lightning, close and startling, its blue glint illuminating the green rider and the dog at the highest elevation of the wall.

Ahead the wall played out straight and then curved right. Beyond the curve, a wide gap loomed where a tower was under construction. Just at the edge of the gap, a pile of rubble slanted down to the ground. The rider spurred his horse ahead, meaning to take the rocky incline. Deep thunder slammed through his ears, and lightning crackled, dangerously close. He heard men shouting, and turned to see the guard riding the top of the wall in pursuit, sword raised, the dog close behind.

On the outer side of the wall, the tall framework of a pulley jutted up, its central wooden pole shaking in the driving rain. The Green Knight turned, just as a sharp needle of lightning hit the metal fittings of the pulley in a blue-white burst. The pulley careened into an unfinished portion of the wall.

Weakened by the rubble filling and unmortared stones, the wall collapsed, slowly at first, then more rapidly, until it dissolved in a trembling, roaring crash. Bits of rock spun off from the avalanche, and a loose fragment smashed into the green rider's head as he urged his horse down the rocky incline and away from the shattering wall.

Slipping and slithering in the pouring rain, he reached the

ground and spun the mount to gallop away from the great
trembling heap of the wall. Riding past the fields, where the
fires had been extinguished by rain, he disappeared into the
dripping shadows of the forest.

Nicholas accepted a refill of a golden, tart French wine
from a steward, and glanced toward Whitehawke, who sat
beside him at the largest table in the garden. Tossing back
his silky white hair, Whitehawke slurped steaming fish soup
and nodded at some comment Lady Julian had made.

Smiling grimly as he sipped his wine, Nicholas hoped that
the drink would dull the ache in his bruised head. He knew
that his aunt was making a valiant effort to be polite this
even. Though she could not abide the earl, she had arranged
the hastily concocted garden supper because he was a guest
at Hawksmoor.

Alarice, Maude, Peter, and Hugh de Chavant were seated
at the lord's table, facing several long tables packed with
knights and soldiers and servants. Nicholas settled back, attempting to listen to the three musicians who had been
quickly scoured from the surrounding countryside. He could
hardly hear the pipes and tabors above the din of the crowd.

Whitehawke and Chavant, with dozens of men, had ridden
unexpectedly into Hawksmoor earlier that afternoon. Fuming, swearing to slaughter the green bastard who rode the
moors, Whitehawke had told Nicholas what had happened
with no apparent sense of wrongdoing on his part. That land,
he said, was his to build on as he chose. Refusing to speak
further on the matter, Whitehawke claimed hunger and fatigue, and indicated that he expected a multiple-course meal
in honor of his arrival, no matter that he had given no notice.

Lady Julian had supervised the stewards and cooks in preparing a sumptuous summer feast in remarkably little time.
She had invited the knights and ladies, serjeants, and servants at Hawksmoor to attend, as well as Whitehawke's own
detachment of men. Nicholas, grinding his teeth in exasperation, had smiled politely and set himself to endure the feast
for his aunt's sake.

Several tables had been arranged beside the orchard. Apple and pear trees crowded nearby, drifting leaves onto white
tablecloths with each stirring breeze. The soft orange glow

of resinous torches placed around the garden settled down
over trees and flower beds, and over the heads and shoulders
of the diners.

A continual chain of servants ran to and from the kitchen
buildings, carrying platters of roasted meats, fish pies,
stewed vegetables, and sweet, delicate desserts, as well as
tuns of red and pale wines and kegs of ale. Losing the heat
of the day, the air was cool and moist from the recent rains,
and fragrant with smoke and blossoms and savory foods.

"Will you have the eels, my lord?" Alarice asked, tilting
her head prettily. "They are lightly stewed with garlic."

Seated beside her, Whitehawke nodded. Alarice scooped
up some of the slithery dish with a heel of bread and depos-
ited it on Whitehawke's square bread trencher. Since Lady
Alarice was of a lower rank than the earl, she had served
him each course.

So far, Nicholas noted, Whitehawke had kept her busy.
The earl had eaten generous servings of a spicy cheese dish,
followed by coddled mustardy eggs, cabbage soup, a fish
pie, boiled peas and turnips, and gingered plaice with a
strawberry sauce. Though he had refused the venison and
fruit pie, the smoked pork and the roast chicken, he had accepted herbed jelly and finely milled white bread. Now he
dug into the garlicked eels with appetite, eating juicy bits
with his fingers.

"Wine, my lord?" Alarice asked.

"Eh? What kind?" Whitehawke had drunk from each of
the wines and thick ales that had been passed along the table, urging Alarice to pour for him each time another con-
tainer appeared.

"'Tis raisin wine, my lord," Nicholas said, overhearing, as
Alarice tilted a silver jug with both hands to pour the dark
liquid into the earl's cup.

"Ah, raisin wine." Whitehawke burped into his hand.
"The best kind is clear as the tears of a nun, strong as a
house of monks, and hits the throat like lightning," he said.
Sipping, he set down the goblet and looked at Nicholas. "I
thought I saw a nun walking through your bailey earlier. An
odd sight."

"There is a monk newly arrived as well," Alarice added.

Whitehawke raised a white eyebrow. "Does Hawksmoor become a religious house?"

Nicholas sliced into a dish of stewed pears in wine sauce. "My lady aunt has commissioned some wall paintings in the chapel, sire. The monk came from Wistonbury to do them. The nun, his niece, assists him," he answered.

"Wistonbury?" Whitehawke frowned and reached for another sip of wine. "You would donate money to that abbey, even for painted decorations? The girl seemed a young one, I thought."

"Dame Agnes is the eldest sister to Nicholas's wards," Alarice offered. "She and her uncle have come to see the children."

Nicholas scowled at his cousin but said nothing.

"What? Another de Ashbourne? Rogier was a fertile cock. The eldest girl was shut away, was she not?" Whitehawke used his knife to lift another bite of seasoned eel. "I should like to question her about the Lady Emlyn."

"I have already done so," Lady Julian said firmly. "She lives a cloistered life, and did not even know her sister was missing. She is still missing, my lord?" she asked sweetly.

Whitehawke grunted in wordless annoyance.

"Do come to the chapel to see the paintings, my lord, before you leave Hawksmoor—when might that be?" Lady Alarice asked.

"We depart on the morrow," Whitehawke answered.

"The weather holds fair, I think," Alarice said. "I do hope the storms have passed, do you not agree, my lord?"

Whitehawke gnashed his teeth and flared his nostrils. "The thunderstorms have been violent of late."

"Thunderstorms can be very destructive," Nicholas said.

"Oh!" Maude interrupted. "We heard the most dreadful tale of a monster sighted after a thunderstorm near Buckden, with the head of an ass, a human torso, and charred monstrous limbs like long roasted turnips."

"A monster? More like some unfortunate villein learned the folly of riding out in lightning," Peter commented.

Lady Julian slid a wooden bowl toward Whitehawke. "Try the mutton stew, my lord," she said pleasantly. Nicholas raised his eyebrows; though he rarely saw maliciousness in his aunt, she seemed to reserve some for Whitehawke.

The earl shot her a hard look. "I take no flesh meat. As you know, my lady." He turned to Alarice. "But I will have some of the sallat," he said, and received a serving of lettuce boiled with raisins and almonds.

"The mutton is from Nicholas's own flocks," the countess said.

"Of course it is," Nicholas muttered. "With thousands of sheep, one hardly need purchase mutton on market day."

Whitehawke picked at the lettuce with his knife. "How fares your sheep farming, Nicholas?"

"We have done well this year. My seneschal reports more than fifteen thousand sheep on our estate farms. A great deal of the cheese and butter this winter came from our sheep, and the castle and the surrounding villages have used all the tallow produced. We have had orders from York and Lancaster parchment makers for skins. And I have lent flocks out to several farmers, who are now ready to give them back."

"Keeping how many?"

"I allowed them to keep half the lambs born during the two-year loan."

"Generous. But you set them up as sheep farmers that way."

"Aye."

"You will have too much competition in the wool market in a few years," Whitehawke pronounced, and sipped his wine.

"I think not. There is great demand for northern wool. But I will have farmers willing to aid my drovers when 'tis time for the flocks to be driven over the track south to market. And the whole area will benefit from the flourishing farms hereabouts."

"Hmmph. I have twenty-five thousand, last count."

"Impressive. All around Graymere, sire?"

Whitehawke stifled a belch. "Not all. I had the sheep counted on land that is mine by title. The crown still delays my rights to Arnedale, but my men counted the head there anyway, or what they could get to. 'Tis a matter of time before those farms are mine again."

"My lord," Lady Julian said, leaning forward. "That land belonged to my sister Blanche, and did not pass to you in the marriage arrangements. My father donated part of it to the monasteries, and the rest was my sister's, outside her dowry. It should have passed to Nicholas. 'Tis no wonder you have had years worth of trouble claiming it."

Whitehawke glared at her. "There is no proof of what you say, my lady. That entire strip of land—the western side of the valley from Wistonbury Abbey to the river that cuts in front of Hawksmoor—became mine upon my marriage to Blanche. The Church stole it from me, and I mean to get it back. The royal secretaries have been years over the job of finding the documents. I am sore tempted to go to London and tear through the account rooms myself. Your father filed the deed with the king's lawyers, Julian."

The countess drew a sharp breath to retort, but Nicholas laid a hand on his aunt's sleeve and squeezed gently. "Sire," he said, "that land, and those flocks, are the main support of two abbeys, and the livelihood of hundreds of villeins."

"The people will keep their living," the earl answered. "But I will have the land and the profit that has been due me these many years. The high holy monks can go back to their herb gardens and books. They have no business in the wool market, or on my land!" His face grew darker with each word.

Peter looked across Lady Alarice. "From what I have heard, my lord, this Green Man challenges your men to obtain their sheep counts and to travel the area at all."

Whitehawke stiffened. "God's throat, Blackpoole, I have no desire to discuss that here," he growled. "Enough to say the demon is soon vanquished."

Alarice gasped. "Demon, my lord?"

"A devil prowls that land, my lady, in the guise of a Green Knight," he said, smirking. "And I am determined to send him back to hell."

Peter leaned toward Chavant. "Mayhap the Green Man is seen about because he has acquired a taste for sheep. Try the mutton, Hugh." He passed the dish along.

Chavant licked his greasy lips. "The green bastard seems to have more of a craving for juicy little lambs, I think."

"Shut up, Hugh," Whitehawke snapped.

With a grunt, Whitehawke sat heavily on the bed and bent clumsily to pull off his boots. Nicholas, sipping hot spiced wine from a small wooden cup, leaned a shoulder against the wall. When they had left the feast, he had properly offered his father the use of his own bed for the night, and would have to search out a bed elsewhere.

Leaning slightly, sunk down in the deep soft mattress, Whitehawke ran his meaty fingers through his snowy hair and stared into the firelight. Even in the reddish glow, his eyes were pale shards of blue ice.

Nicholas could hear the faint whine of his father's breathing, like the susurration of heavy silk. He had heard the sound before, when his father was tired, or had been out in cold or rainy weather.

Whitehawke rubbed at his chest. "Did your steward see to that herbal potion?"

"Lady Julian had an infusion made from the herbs you requested. 'Tis there on the table."

Whitehawke reached for the cup and sipped at the steaming liquid, rubbing his breastbone vigorously. "Beshrew me, the only good thing Blanche ever did was create this remedy for my chest ailment. I am never without a decoction of this stuff, now." A raspy sigh turned to a deep belch. "My father had this same weakness of the lungs. 'Tis a trait of the de Hawkwoods." He glanced meaningfully at Nicholas. "Unlikely that you will ever develop it."

Nicholas clenched a fist behind his back. "You speak ill of my mother's honor, sire," he said in a low tone.

"At least we know who your mother is, since you crawled from that cursed space." Nicholas took a step forward at the remark.

Whitehawke laughed acidly. "Get no black mood on, now. I am too tired for it. We shall argue aplenty on the morrow, I am certain." He coughed again, wheezily, and lay back on the pillows. "Send in a servant to help me undress. Some pretty chit," he added, and rolled over, closing his eyes.

Nicholas turned away, breathing deeply to master his anger. In a moment, he heard sloppy snores from the bed. Sighing, he dragged the curtains shut around the bed.

Rubbing the back of his neck, Nicholas felt, sudden and keen, his own exhaustion. He had been plagued with a headache for two days, from the bruising blow to his head. Though he knew that he needed rest, he did not relish the prospect of sleeping in the garrison tower with drunken soldiers, or on the floor of the great hall, which was littered with the pallets and blankets of the castle servants and Whitehawke's men.

He yawned. The narrow bed in the solar next to his chamber would do well for tonight.

Pulling aside the curtain, he saw the small star of a low candle flame, guttering in a wooden dish on the table. He sighed impatiently. Emlyn—Dame Agnes, he thought sourly—must have come here during the garden supper, though Whitehawke's presence should have discouraged her from moving about the castle.

On other evenings he had been aware she was in the solar—the glow of candlelight through the thick weave of the red curtain, the scratch of brush or pen, a soft sigh, the quiet closing of the outer solar door. Some nights, he needed all of his self-control to keep from going through that curtain to be with her, to say what must soon be said between them.

Now, blowing out the flame and plunging the little room into darkness except for moonlight, he wondered why she would have carelessly left a candle burning.

Slender bars of moonlight slipped between the window shutters and fell across the room as he turned, yawning, toward the bed. He stopped in a half stretch.

Emlyn lay curled beneath the blanket, one hand palm up on the pillow. A breath escaped him and his heart thudded suddenly. His first thought was to get her away from such close proximity to Whitehawke. Remembering that several blasts of the Judgment Horn could not wake his father tonight, he sank to one knee beside the low bed.

She slept as deep and trusting as a child, lashes and brows dark against creamy skin, her mouth slightly open, her breathing gentle. The confining wimple was gone, and Nicholas touched the soft curling strands at her temple. In the pale light, her hair was a fine-spun, pearly silver. When she sighed and shifted beneath his fingertips, turning her head, her hair flooded over his hand, cool and fine as silk.

A wrenching desire grabbed at him. He inhaled slowly, drawing his fingers through the sleek curtain of her hair, aroused by its gossamer texture, by the warm cream of her skin, by her slender, graceful curves beneath the blanket. His shadow fell over her face and throat. She shifted again, sighing wantonly as his gentle fingers found her jaw.

Nicholas de Hawkwood should not touch this girl, he knew. But her husband could not help himself, and leaned closer.

His head spun with the amount of wine he had consumed at supper, with headache, with her nearness. Though his mind was hazed, his feelings were suddenly clear. He fervently wanted to abandon the ruse and adopt simple honesty. He wanted to hold her, talk to her, make love to her until she called his own name. Ignoring the sensible echo in his head that admonished him to stop, he bent forward and touched his mouth, wine-scented and spicy, to hers. Her pliant, warm lips clung to his even though she slept, her kiss so sweet that his loins ached and filled.

Breathless, his heard beating loudly, he felt like a drunk walking a bridge in the black of night, uncertain when his steps would plunge him into the waters below. He took the risk and kissed her again, deep and moist, allowing his fingers to trace along the smooth skin of her bared throat, feeling her pulse flutter beneath his feathery touch.

The muffled knock on the oaken door hardly disturbed him at first. He slid his fingers up to caress her jaw. When the knock sounded again, he reluctantly raised his head.

Emlyn groaned softly, opening her eyes to blink like a kitten in the moonlight, awake but not fully aware. Then, with a little breathy gasp, she reached up to rest her hand against his cheek.

He tilted his face into her palm and looked into her eyes, wrapped in the warm magic of her sleepy, bewildered gaze. Though his heart nearly thudded out of his chest, he willed her to see him then as he truly was.

"Thorne—" she whispered.

The knock sounded again. "Psst, dearie," Tibbie hissed loudly through the outer door. "Are ye sleeping in there?" The latch rattled, gave, and the door squealed open.

In one fluid motion, Nicholas stood and vanished like a phantom, slipping between the moon's blue glow and deep shadows. Emlyn reached out and gave a small cry. Cool moonlight fell across her hand.

Whitehawke's lusty, flapping snores echoed around the bedchamber as Nicholas came through the solar curtain and leaned his forehead against the wall, breathing rapidly.

Footsteps padded across the room. "My lady! Get ye gone from here," Tibbie said. "Have ye forgotten Lord Whitehawke is at Hawksmoor! Ye promised to keep to yer room!"

"Oh, Tibbie," Emlyn said, "I fell asleep. I dreamed—"

"The wine was strong this e'en," Tibbie was saying softly. "I am a wee cupshot m'self, but when I woke and saw ye not abed, I came to collect ye. Come to bed now, dear heart." Nicholas heard Emlyn's murmured assent, and the outer door creaked shut behind them, closing off Tibbie's whispered chatter.

A hint of the scent of rose soap lingered on the pillow, which was still warm and gently indented when Nicholas lay down on the narrow pallet. As he allowed sleep to drift through him, only one thought clung to his mind: he was finished with cowardice and deceit. On the morrow he would act on that decision, ready to pay the price.

Chapter Sixteen

"God's wounds! Out!" Whitehawke advanced heavily toward the fireplace, kicking angrily at a ginger cat curled up on the hearthstone. When a servant ran forward, the cat arched and hissed, darting lightly across the length of the room with the servant tearing after it. Whitehawke grunted and turned away to drain his morning ale, belching noisily and wiping his mouth on his hand. Transparent wedges of light spilled from the windows and shifted across the ebony gleam of his armor.

Nicholas slouched in a wide, high-backed chair before the fireplace, one leg stretched out in front of him, nursing a violent headache, a combination of wine and the bruise hidden beneath his hair. He would have wagered that his aching pate could not have equaled his father's after last night's feast, but the earl showed no sign beyond a deep irritability.

Swallowing watered morning ale from a silver goblet, Nicholas watched the activity in the hall, bemused. Should a cat wander into the great hall, no one bothered to shoo it out. Lady Julian and the other ladies were fond of cats, and the children enjoyed playing with the kittens they had been keeping in the solar. Whitehawke, however, saw merit only in dogs and hawks.

Hugh de Chavant entered the room just as the cat streaked in front of the doorway. A brown hunting dog padded in behind him. When a vicious, loud chase ensued between the hound and the cat, Nicholas squeezed his eyes shut, rubbing his temples against the jarring pain of barking and hissing.

Waving a corner of his russet cloak and moving clumsily in his full armor, Chavant somehow managed to chase the cat away from the dog and out over the threshold. He slammed the door shut and turned, his expression smug.

"Damned lickspittle," Whitehawke muttered, sloshing more foamy ale into his goblet from a clay jug. "Look how his eyes drift. Beshrew me, he can watch both doors at once. By Saint George, how does he handle a weapon?"

Nicholas opened one bleary eye of his own. "Hugh's eye wanders most when he is fatigued," he said. "You were the one made him the captain of your guard, my lord."

The earl grunted. "He is a cunning fellow betimes, though his wits have deserted him of late."

Nicholas glanced at his father. "Meaning—?"

"Meaning the lady is not yet found, nor the demon chased from the wood."

"The cat is gone, sire," Chavant said as he approached.

"I see that, idiot," Whitehawke snapped. "Foul beasts of the devil, cats. It must have slipped in here from the stables." He quaffed his ale, wiping his mouth with the back of his hand. The hunting dog loped over to sit beside Whitehawke, the black iron collar a peculiar match to his master's dark armor.

Chavant pulled off his leather gloves, stuffed them into his belt, and pushed back his mailed hood. Dark hair, trimmed high above his ears, lay in limp strings along his forehead, and the sweat and dirt of a hurried ride streaked his unshaven face. Nicholas knew that Whitehawke had sent Chavant, with several riders, out before dawn to search the moors and forests near Hawksmoor. He thought he knew why.

"Greetings, Hugh, arrived at last," Nicholas drawled. "There is cold ale in the jug." Chavant poured a cup and drank thirstily, his bulging brown eyes drifting apart as he set the goblet down. The hunting dog stood warily, spread its front feet, and began to growl at Nicholas.

"What the devil is the matter now?" Whitehawke said irritably. "Down, you infernal hound. The cat is gone."

"I know not, sire," Chavant said. "Down, Ivo."

Nicholas sat very still, his muscles tensed.

"Hey! Sit," Whitehawke said over the dog's harsh, thrumming growl. "Ivo! Sit!"

The dog lurched then, straight at Nicholas. Chavant leaped forward to grab at the collar, pulling the dog back and narrowly missing a mean puncture by the iron collar spikes.

"Remove him!" Whitehawke ordered. Chavant half dragged the dog down the length of the room, thrust him into the reluctant care of a servant, and returned.

"By the devil, I understand that not at all," the earl grumbled. He turned to Nicholas. "Well. We have come to Hawksmoor because 'tis close to where Lady Emlyn disappeared, and we have lately been in the dale searching again. Since you have been south lately with our good king," he stressed each word, looking stormily at his son, "you will not have heard the latest since Chavant misplaced my bride."

"She was taken by the Green Man, sire, not lost by us," Chavant protested.

"Whining changes naught," the earl said. "She is gone, and my betrothal has become a mockery. Tell my son the whole of it."

Chavant settled his uneven gaze on Nicholas. "You have heard the tales of the Green Man in the dale, my lord."

"Aye," Nicholas said slowly. He tossed the last of his ale down his throat and reached for the jug, filling his goblet again. "I have heard those tales."

"Most likely this Green Knight was responsible for the lady's disappearance. We have seen him since that day he took the lady from our escort in fog. Once we nearly had him," Chavant said.

"Saints preserve us from puddingheads," the earl interrupted with a sneer. "They grabbed a farmer dressed as Jack-o'-the-green for May, with sweets in his pockets and a leafy hat."

"You have admitted your own belief in demons, my lord," Nicholas said.

"Real creatures of hell exist, absolutely. We saw such a creature just last week, when he destroyed my wall," Whitehawke replied. "Hugh, however, insists 'twas only a man."

"The green bastard who brought down the keep wall was the same one that we pursued across the moor outside Kernham village. He is no hell-fiend, though somehow he disappears like one each time we see him," Chavant told

Nicholas. "He is a dead shot with the longbow. I think him a man."

"Bah," Whitehawke snarled. "The devil is behind this one. Lightning obeys his command. The wall of my keep collapsed when he willed it to. No man could do what he did that day."

Nicholas cut in. "Did you have royal permission to build there? 'Tis Hawksmoor land, as you surely know."

Whitehawke flushed deeply. "No time for a royal writ. John is in a frenzy over the barons' betrayal. And that parcel is not your land, but your mother's, and so mine, and an end to it."

"We differ on that. But you say the keep is destroyed?"

"Most of it is useless rubble now," Whitehawke said. "But I shall find another place to build. That glade is fair haunted."

"My lord earl," Chavant said, "I have told you 'tis a man."

"I know what you say. Tell your theory." He turned to Nicholas. "If I was not so firmly convinced that the devil is behind this creature, I might find this next very interesting."

Chavant cleared this throat. "My lord," he said to Nicholas, "lately I have given this matter a great deal of thought. Lord Whitehawke has a fierce enemy in the Green Knight."

"Chavant, get to it. You do naught quick," Whitehawke said. "'Twould take you a fortnight to tell a riddle." His white leonine head swiveled toward Nicholas, his pale gaze sharp. "Hugh thinks the Black Thorne has returned."

"Oh?" Nicholas said mildly.

Chavant's brown eyes slid crazily, one at a time, toward Nicholas. "The Green Man is called by another name in Arnedale, my lord. The Hunter Thorne."

Nicholas looked down at the golden froth in his goblet and willed himself to be calm. "You think Thorne is the Green Man?"

"The guards saw Lady Emlyn with a man, a forester or a villein, handy with a longbow. He held her captive when my men would have rescued her, and killed one of them. From the sound of it, he resembles Thorne. At the same time, the Green Man discourages our garrison from riding free in the dale, as Thorne did," Chavant said. "And the Green Man vanished like smoke, as Thorne could do. As Lady Emlyn and this man did weeks ago."

Whitehawke rubbed the short white stubble on his square jaw, making a tiny grating noise with his fingernails. "Though the villeins confirmed his death, Thorne's body was never found."

"But naught has been heard of the Thorne for eight years," Nicholas said, gripping the goblet.

"Likely he saw the wisdom in abandoning his attacks on my lord earl," Chavant said. "He may have traveled, fought in France or the Holy Land, or married and settled somewhere." He shrugged. "But now he is back to trouble us once more. If Thorne is the Green Man, then we deal with no demon."

"And if the creature is a spirit?" Nicholas asked softly.

Whitehawke tightened his lips and set his square jaw. "Then, by God, I will keep my distance. The devil rides far for souls. I should send a priest to decide this Green Man's nature." He leveled his gaze at Nicholas. "But if the Black Thorne is not dead, then I could have two enemies, a man whom I can fight, and a demon I cannot. No doubt the Lady Emlyn is held by one of them. My men thought her dead at one point, but there has been no proof of that. We will find her soon enough."

"Think you the Thorne challenges you again?" Nicholas turned his cup, examining the engraved pattern carefully.

"Possibly." Whitehawke turned to slump heavily in a chair. "God in heaven," he wheezed. "When I was younger, I had the spit and anger to fight the annoying pup. But now"—he shifted his large booted feet heavily. "I no longer have a desire to thunder around after the rogue. If he is out there, I want him dead, and no more of the dance to it." He sat up abruptly. "Chavant. Find them, the villein and the girl."

"Aye, my lord. We continue to search."

Whitehawke snorted in disgust. "I would have greater luck sending dogs to the task. I may yet do that."

Nicholas set his goblet on the floor. A peculiar prickling spread in his spine and his gut, and he stood up. "My lord," he said. "There is no cause to look further for Lady Emlyn."

"Why?" Whitehawke barked. "What do you know of it?"

Nicholas straightened his back and shoulders and forced himself to look into his father's flat, pale eyes with cool control. "She has wed another."

Whitehawke stood in one violent movement. "What!" he roared.

"There was a previous marriage arrangement when King John gave you his writ. An earlier promise takes priority."

Whitehawke's eyes narrowed. A hot, vivid stain crept into his cheeks. "Say what you mean," he growled.

"Lady Emlyn became my wife several weeks ago."

Chavant gasped. "'Tis a jest!"

Whitehawke took a step forward, his eyes glittering. "Explain yourself," he said menacingly.

"I had long owed a favor to Rogier de Ashbourne. In token of that, four years ago I offered for Emlyn's hand," Nicholas said. "No marriage was made because she was young, still in a convent. And at the time, the interdict, which the Pope had placed over all England for years, forbade priests to perform the sacraments. Later Baron Rogier died, but the heir had no chance to pursue the arrangement."

He clenched his jaw, bunching the muscles, waiting for his father to assimilate the shock. His glance slid toward Hugh, who drifted his hand to his empty sword hilt. "Stay your hand, cousin," Nicholas warned. "Your sword is safe with the porter."

With a clang, the earl's cup fell to the floor. Ale foamed slowly across the hearthstone. "What have you done?" Whitehawke said, his voice rasped with anger. "By God's eyes, you betray me! Cuckolded by my own son!" For a tense moment, Nicholas thought Whitehawke would leap and strangle him. But some iron control kept the earl still, though the muscles of his wide neck were red and corded, and his eyes became slivers of hoarfrost.

Nicholas faced his father, deep breathing and flared nostrils the only outward clues to his inner struggle against long-buried rage and fear. He fisted one hand by his side. "I wed her by my right as her first betrothed," he said. "She had run from her escort, to avoid marriage with you. She swore she would not go back, and was set on kidnapping her siblings from here. And I was certain that when you found her, she would no longer be regarded as your betrothed, but as ruined goods."

"Aye! I would toss her in a convent and lock her there for life for dishonoring me!" Whitehawke countered angrily. "I may still do that, by God!"

"She is under my protection now," Nicholas said.

"'Twas you took her from the escort!" Whitehawke accused. "Not some green monster, or this Thorne!" Hugh began to protest, but Whitehawke silenced him with a lethal glance. "Was it you who was with her at the waterfall, and killed one of my men?"

"But sire, the guards would have recognized Baron Nicholas," Chavant interrupted. He looked at Nicholas. "Did she tell you aught of that forester? Where did you find her?"

"She was in the wood, where she had run from your escort. Villeins had helped her in the forest."

"Then you know who aided her. You, or these villeins, can lead us to the Green Man," Chavant said.

Nicholas shrugged to indicate he knew little.

"By God's teeth," Whitehawke snarled. "Where is she now?"

"Safe enough, and no longer a concern of yours."

"By God, know that I will look into the legality of this. I think that chit can tell me what I need to know about Thorne. Give her over to me, or I will find her myself. Jesu!" Whitehawke spat. "Why did she run from the escort?"

"Your reputation as a lightsome helpmate is widely known," Nicholas drawled.

"God's eyeballs—" Whitehawke's face took on an ugly dusky hue, the roots of his scalp pink against the snowy strands of his hair. "You are your mother's son, are you not, to turn on me thus! I am roundly cuckolded!" He slammed his fist down on the table with a volatile curse. Chavant, leaning against the table edge, jumped away, bobbling his eyes warily.

"Trouble yourself no longer with the lady," Nicholas said. "I trow you never wanted her, but only took her for Ashbourne."

Whitehawke turned and looked at Nicholas for a long moment. Neither gaze wavered. "Ashbourne remains mine," the earl said. "No traitorous act can alter that." He crossed his arms over his chest and sat on the edge of the table, his breathing growing rapidly more labored and noisy. He shook his head slowly, rubbing his hand over his face and streaming his fingers through his lanky white hair. "By Christ! What would you wager, Hugh, that the king set this betrothal not as payment for my loyalty to the crown, but as a cruel jest against the de Hawkwoods."

Chavant nodded nervously. "I would not wager against it."

"Since the king was doubtless aware of my previous offer, such a jest would appeal to him," Nicholas said. "But since a first betrothal holds precedence, then, sire, who cuckolds who?"

Whitehawke's eyes narrowed to pale slits. "You have neatly remedied any injustice by your action. How you must have hated accompanying me to Ashbourne that day," he added slyly.

Nicholas, silent, kept his mouth a thin line, and kept his thoughts carefully in check.

Whitehawke looked over at Chavant. "This lady is fair, eh, Hugh, with a firm body and fire in her voice and walk. By my vices, 'twas lust moved me to accept that betrothal, I think. Though quick enough she showed her wicked tongue." He laughed, a short, mean bark. "You have made an ill marriage, Nicholas. She has no dowry, no lands, only a treasonous brother and a passel of worthless siblings. And for all her beauty, she will become a shrew who berates her husband. I am gladly spared that."

Nicholas remained silent, biting the inside of his cheek to keep from speaking. Whitehawke continued. "Well. Perhaps 'tis for the best. I keep the lands without the trouble of the spoiled child bride. Still, what you have done is reprehensible."

"A man who builds on another's land, or claims another's profits should not talk of reprehensible acts," Nicholas bit out. "A man whose wife dies an ignoble death should not judge others."

Whitehawke inhaled sharply, his nostrils flaring wide. "I have ever been within my rights, in all that I have done," he stated. "Cuckolding is unforgivable."

"Forgiveness is a hard lesson. I have yet to learn it."

"Now I know the true colors of my son and heir. But then, that has never been firmly established, has it?" Whitehawke glanced at Nicholas from the corner of his eye.

The silence in the room was as palpably cold as a winter dawn. "Nay, my lord," Nicholas finally murmured. "But how is paternity determined? Through trust. Faith. Love. Not virtues you are familiar with." He bowed his head mockingly.

"As I said, you are much like your mother," Whitehawke said. "Falseness is in your blood." He stood and picked up his leather gloves from the table, drawing each one on, slow and deliberate.

"We leave now," he said, his voice like iced steel. "When I have thought through your news, no doubt I shall speak to the king. Perhaps I will require damages for relieving me of my bride in this manner. Or I may challenge you to a jousting to the death. You will hear of my decision. Know, however, that you will never inherit so much as a burnt straw from me. For now, regardless of what else has happened, the harassment of my men by this green bastard, or Thorne, or whoever he is, will be stopped." He flexed his gloved fingers. "Yet it seems that mortal or no, this Green Man has more soul and guts than he who calls himself my son. Come, Hugh."

Abruptly, Whitehawke turned to leave the hall, his black cloak swinging about his powerful calves, his armor jingling stridently. As he pulled open the door, Lady Julian was advancing down the shadowed corridor.

"Bertran," she murmured politely as she entered the room.

"Good day, Julian," he clipped out, and slammed the door shut after him.

The countess blinked in obvious confusion at the affront, then moved down the length of the huge room. The flowing train of her dark skirts gracefully swept the rushes in a soft rhythm.

As he passed to leave, Chavant nodded at Nicholas. "My congratulations to you, cousin," he said, smooth and low. "Though poor as a mouse, your new wife is a delicate morsel."

"Say aught else of her," Nicholas growled, "and you will choke on your wagging tongue."

Hugh smiled. "Only allow me to thank you for clearing the way for me."

"Ah. As a cousin on my father's side, you hope he will declare you his heir in my stead. Welcome to it, Hugh. You are a worthy successor to Whitehawke's legacy."

Chavant looked momentarily puzzled, then lowered his brows menacingly as he understood the insult. He stalked away, nodding briskly to the countess as he passed her.

Lady Julian halted beside Nicholas as Chavant bumped the door shut, and folded her hands over her ivory cross. She looked up at her nephew with concern. "Another argument with Whitehawke? This one appears grave. Can I help, Nicholas?"

"Nay," Nicholas muttered, lips thin.

"Will you wish another sumptuous meal served this evening?"

"Hardly. Whitehawke departs now."

"I see. In some haste, and furious," she observed.

"Aye," he agreed. "With reason." He picked up his goblet from the table and sipped slowly.

"Why did he come here yesterday?" Her long-hooded eyes were pinched with concern.

Nicholas swallowed the tepid ale. He had had enough of confessing his sins, and his head ached cruelly now. He needed to tell Julian of his marriage, but it would hold for now. "To inform me that he continues to pursue the Green Man in the dale."

"And he continues to look for his betrothed, I suspect. He mentioned to me last even that when she is found, he will shut her in a convent. Though I cannot agree with his methods, others in such a position would have the girl beaten, or worse, and be well within their rights. A convent is a merciful punishment."

"She will not be found. And he wants no more female deaths on his conscience," he answered sourly. "He founded a priory, and does daily penance, and claims it enough."

"Is it, Nicholas?" she asked softly.

He turned to face the firelight, his glowing profile clean-shaven, his jaw held taut. "I am no avenging angel, Aunt. 'Tis not for me to judge."

Lady Julian placed her hand on his arm. "If what we love is snatched from us in one place, 'twill be restored in another. 'Tis one of God's most gracious laws."

Nicholas smiled, a mirthless twisting of his mouth. "Aye. And so you have been mother to me in your sister's place. I am always grateful."

"You are like Blanche—her eyes, her mouth. 'Tis a blessing to see her beauty in you. And I see Whitehawke there, as well. I always have."

He laughed, short and cruel. "My father does not see it." As if some overwhelming burden pulled at his shoulders and chest, he felt a dark heaviness and closed his eyes against it, rubbing his brow. Now his father's contempt for him had true reason.

"Will you help him find the girl?" Julian asked.

"Nay," he answered, "I will not." A muscle quirked in his jaw, and he could feel the cursed easy blush, which he regarded as his father's legacy, began to heat his cheeks. He turned his face away. As much as he trusted his aunt, he did not wish to confide in her yet. He watched the fire in silence. After a moment, Lady Julian quietly excused herself and left the hall.

Nicholas leaned a hand against the long slope of the stone hood, and with his other hand grasped the silver goblet tightly enough to distort the soft metal. His head throbbed, tense and painful, as he stared into the flames.

His thoughts were never far from Emlyn, even more so after his spiteful encounter with Whitehawke. Still, there was relief in revealing his marriage, no matter the risk. He had grown heartily sick of the whole play and both their ruses.

Witless fool, he thought, to have left her at the abbey. Riding on to London and Runnymede with Peter and half his garrison, he had felt a smug satisfaction that Emlyn would be safe until his return. He should have known she was too impatient to wait for Thorne's return.

Shaking his head in dismay, he downed the last foamy drops of ale. Her appearance in his own home had thrown him into utter confusion. He had hidden like a timid deer from the hunter, knowing the contempt she held for Nicholas de Hawkwood.

He was certain that Emlyn had not yet recognized him as Thorne. But he had known her in that ridiculous wimple. He grinned fleetingly. Guileless as a babe, she was, thinking her nun's garb hid her well. He had nearly guessed when she poked her head over the edge of the scaffold. Later, in the solar, he had heard the distinctive huskiness of her voice and seen the steel ring she wore. And he had deeply appreciated the black thorns on the rosebud vines in the manuscript.

That ability to paint had been unexpected, though. She had made no reference to any such training when she had been with him in the forest. Her unusual ability made him even prouder to be her husband.

He had come to love and cherish her, and he had made himself very scarce of late. He had combed back his hair, requesting a clean shave every other day, and he had paid careful attention to the timbre of his voice and the manner of his walk. Spending more time away from Hawksmoor than inside it of late, he had gone hunting and hawking and attended to details of his estate. And he had gone frequently to the dale, for days at a time.

Emlyn had looked at him once or twice, quite directly, her blue eyes, touched with gold specks, wide with curiosity. He had held his breath in those moments. But his cover was stronger than he had expected: voice, clothing, oiled-back hair and clean jaw, cool gray eyes, all changed from Thorne's. Last night, for a moment, she had seen him as Thorne, yet she thought it a dream.

He was well aware of the mutable quality of his eye color. When he was in a castle surrounded by stone walls, clothed in drab gray or black, or in steel armor, his eyes had a stony gray cast. Even his blue surcoat and cloak kept them grayish. But in the greenwood, when high, clear light flooded through verdant foliage, his eyes were green as moss.

Verifying it in polished steel mirrors and pond surfaces, he knew it to be consistent and reliable. His eyes reflected his environment and protected his identity. Thorne had deep green eyes; Nicholas de Hawkwood had gray. No man could change his eye color—unless Heaven gave him the means.

As Thorne, he had struck in a series of raids that constantly disrupted Whitehawke's supplies and escorts. Even now his hands closed into tight fists as he remembered how he had despised his father for insulting Blanche, for showing her such cruelty. Young and rebellious, vengeance had been his succor in the days when only violent soothing would do.

At first, lashing out at Whitehawke had been enough. Later, as it became more of a political struggle, Thorne became an unintentional hero. When Whitehawke began to harass the people of Arnedale in earnest, Nicholas, who had no tolerance for injustice, discovered more reason to sting at his father. Thorne quickly captured the admiration of the people of the dale.

No one had ever seen Thorne in him. He easily grew thick, dark beards, and his eye color was a protective, blessed screen that changed with his clothing and environment. Only Peter de Blackpoole and Aelric knew the truth.

Currently, to those in the dale, he was Thorne the reeve, a man with a common name, who worked for the abbot of Wistonbury. Indeed, as the baron, he met often with the abbot to appraise him of the situation in Arnedale. Not even the abbot had guessed.

At first, he had raided alone, but soon he began to find willing help among the villeins who despised Whitehawke's tactics. They had attacked the earl's convoys to steal grain, ale, wine, and occasionally a chest or two of gold. Keeping nothing, they had made certain that families in the dale received compensation from the earl's own stores.

As the earl grew bolder in his attacks on the dale, other barons made it clear that they abhorred Whitehawke's arrogant disregard for the law. Rogier de Ashbourne had been among the barons who had shunned Whitehawke at court and made public their contempt for his tyrannical, possessive demands. They had privately cheered the attempts of the young greenwood renegade.

But the current of distrust surrounding Whitehawke had not prompted the king to reprimand the earl, and had not eased the process of resolving the legal questions of ownership in Arnedale. The matter, quite simply, had gathered dust on the royal dockets and had continued to fester in the dale itself.

But the night that Thorne had been lung-shot had ended

his secret activities for a while. Hiding with Emlyn that evening eight years ago, he had finally seen where following his anger had led: innocents had been placed in danger because of him. The arrow that felled him had been like a reproving bolt from above.

Long weeks of recovery under Maisry's care had given him time to think. He had been selfish and impulsive, guilty of outright thievery and profound dishonor. In his fury with his father, he had lost cool logic, control, and a sense of valor. When he saw the wrong turn in his path, he had sought to correct it.

As soon as he was strong enough, he had gone to the village chapel and confessed to theft and failure to honor his father. He had made his penance and put Thorne to rest. Then Aelric had begun the rumor of his death, which quickly circulated.

Finally, a restraining order issued by the king, under pressure from several barons and the monks, had discouraged Whitehawke. But when the writ had expired, Whitehawke demanded the legal deed, a record of which apparently was lost somewhere in the vast roll depositories at Westminster.

The raids on the dale resumed and grew worse. Barns and homes were torched, forest land was razed. Hawksmoor, which came to Nicholas on his majority, was now peripherally threatened.

Late one night, Nicholas and Aelric had devised the ruse of the Green Man between them. With Maisry's help, they developed an elaborate costume, the first of many, and a fearsome creature was created. Glimpsed through a green halo of foliage, it would glide silent and threatening through a mist, or sit the crest of a hill. Armed with longbow or axe, a powerful guard for the dale, it had never had to directly attack.

So simple, so easy: the mere threat of losing one's soul to the demon had been frightening, and Whitehawke was highly superstitious. Perhaps guilt over his misdeeds made the earl sensitive to even the merest suggestion that he could go to hell. His fear of the Green Man was strong enough that he reduced his raids and pulled a number of his men out of the dale.

Nicholas blew out a long round breath and pushed away

from the fireplace hood. The situation in the dale would require some intense thought. Whitehawke rode there even now. Perhaps 'twould be best if the Green Man made an appearance or two, from a safe enough distance.

He knew he must speak with Emlyn soon. He had let it go long enough, and she deserved to know what had transpired today. Yet he felt that he had to ride to the dale soon. Another week or so would have to pass before he would speak with her.

In spite of his anger, Whitehawke had seemed surprisingly inclined to accept their marriage. Perhaps, as he claimed, he was glad enough to have Ashbourne without the burden of a penniless bride.

Nicholas would have been grateful, but he was afraid to trust his father.

Chapter Seventeen

"Not that one, the other—there!" Light as a silver bell, the voice that floated over the garden wall was off-tone with impatience. "Reach. Well then, go higher."

Having left the chapel, Emlyn was crossing the bailey on her way to the keep. Hearing her sister's voice as she passed by the garden wall, she sighed and altered her direction.

Beneath a tall apple tree at the far end of the garden, Isobel stood with her head angled back, her dark braids swinging gently. "There, Christien," she said, looking up just as an apple fell from above and hit the toe of her felt shoe. "Ow!"

Emlyn marched to the orchard. "Where is Christien?"

"There," Isobel said, pointing up.

A pair of brown leggings and small leather boots dangled far above Emlyn's head. Shifting around until she saw her brother's face through the green weave of branches, she placed her fists on her hips and tilted her head back. "Christien, come down!" she ordered firmly.

He squirmed around on the branch that supported him, extended his legs, and then peered down at her. "I cannot," he replied, his voice quavering. "I think I am stuck."

"Follow down as you came up," she called.

"My feet will not reach the branch below me. I will fall," he said plaintively. Frowning, Emlyn carefully assessed his position. The nearest lower branch was a good stretch away, and the limb to which Christien clung was slender and green. When he stretched out his leg again, Emlyn heard splitting wood.

"Christien!" she cried in alarm. "Slide back toward the trunk. Take hold of it and stay still. I will come get you." She began to hike up her skirts.

"What is the difficulty here?" Low and powerful and very close by, the voice caused her to whip around in surprise.

Nicholas de Hawkwood stood a few feet away, his face grim. For a moment, Emlyn was stunned by his presence; he had been away from Hawksmoor for over a fortnight, and though he had returned a few days ago, she had hardly seen him. And the brisk activity of men and horses in the bailey this morning indicated that he was headed out again, this time with a good portion of his garrison.

"Is the boy injured?" He strode quickly over to the tree and looked up.

"He is well and truly caught, my lord," she said, watching the play of his shoulders beneath a tunic of fine, pale gray wool, and the rich waves of mahogany hair that swept over his shoulders. Glancing briefly at her, he looked up again.

"However did he get up that high?" Nicholas sounded amused.

"We wanted apples," Isobel said.

"There are apples aplenty in the storage rooms, my girl," Nicholas said, moving around to examine the lay of the branches.

"I cannot get down, my lord," Christien called.

"Those are wrinkly ones from last season," Isobel said.

"Well, these are still quite green, and would give you the devil of a bellyache," Emlyn told her sternly.

"But some are red, and we wanted fresh apples," Isobel said. "Christien said he could get some. He is the best at climbing."

"Oh?" Nicholas's eyes twinkled as he looked up at Christien. "Are you a good climber, boy?"

"I—I thought I was, my lord," Christien replied hesitantly.

"Well, you shall soon show us your skill, for you will have to make your way down from there."

Emlyn turned to Isobel. "Run and find Tibbie," she said. When Isobel left, she turned to Nicholas. "I will go up and guide him down to safety, my lord. I can reach him easily."

He frowned at her, then looked up, exposing the strong line of his throat, dusted with powdery black stubble. "He can get down safe enough, I trow. I would not have you both injured."

"But he may fall," she said.

"Then he will learn not to take foolish risks."

She drew in her breath sharply. "He is only a child."

"And you are as protective as a mother wolf," he murmured. "Let the boy come down on his own. He is near fostering age."

Emlyn lowered her eyes, knowing the baron was right. Christien would be seven on his next birthday, and should be allowed his pride. She sighed and nodded.

Nicholas leaned into the wide crotch of the split trunk, his arm brushing against her shoulder, and tilted his head back. "Listen well, Christien. Slide down a bit farther . . . there. Now stretch your left foot toward that branch beneath you . . . nay, the other foot. Aye. Reach, lad."

Christien crept backward on the branch like a timid caterpillar. Emlyn squeezed her eyes shut for an instant, then quickly opened them to see her brother reach, miss the branch, then grab hold of the trunk to avoid failing. His swinging feet caught two apples and sent them thunking down toward the ground.

Emlyn stepped out of the way and bumped into Nicholas. He placed a steadying hand on her elbow while he spoke to Christien.

"Reach down with your leg, boy," he called. "Good. You must hang there, and jump a little. You can do it easily." He glanced at Emlyn. "If he looks to be in trouble, I will get him quick enough." His soft voice thrummed intimately in her ear, reverberating through her spine. The gentle pressure of his fingers on her arm sent tendrils of charged sensation all the way to her fingertips and toes.

Solid, tall and muscular, his body against her back felt comforting and safe. The subtle physical awareness that had begun with his touch on her elbow spread in minute shivers to her breasts and into her lower belly. His feathery touch was utterly, sinfully, subtly pleasurable. Though she knew it was improper to stand so close, she did not, could not, move away.

Whispers of a dream from a few nights ago clung to her thoughts: she had felt and seen Thorne, returned slow, luscious kisses, but he had become the baron just before the dream dissolved. Breathing in the sweet tang of apples and dispelling her wayward thoughts, she laid her hand alongside his on the curving trunk. Together they looked up at the boy.

"You are nearly there now," Nicholas encouraged Christien. "Just reach with your foot. You will not fall—you climbed all the way up there without mishap." Christien nodded nervously, and slid his torso off the branch to which he clung, stretching his toes to connect with the foothold. With a little leap, he landed on the lower branch and crouched there, hanging on.

"Excellent!" Nicholas called, removing his hand from Emlyn's elbow to applaud Christien's efforts. "Brave lad. Now make your way down again. Aye, like that. 'Tis easier from there."

Emlyn listened while Nicholas talked her brother down to a safer perch, grateful for his soothing, protective patience. She remembered when she had clung terrified to the slippery side of a rocky gorge, and had relied on Thorne's calm instructions.

Suddenly her concern and fear for Christien fled, leaving her with a single, shocking thought. She turned in wonder to look up at Nicholas de Hawkwood.

Dappled flakes of cool green light scattered over his head and shoulders as if he stood beneath a swirling, rising dome made of irregular slices of thin green glass. Looking at the underside of his jaw and at the upsweep of his coal-black lashes, Emlyn narrowed her eyes and imagined him with a beard.

Christien climbed to a lower branch with steadier control and began to clamber down toward them, chattering like a squirrel. Emlyn hardly heard him, her gaze fixed intensely on the baron.

Nicholas grinned and looked down at her. "By Saint George, the lad is no fledgling," he said, his voice warm with pride and touched with humor. "He did well." In the colored light, his eyes sparkled, fringed in sooty black, his irises as green as the buckthorn pigment she had used that morning in her manuscript. A soft grayish-green. Moss over stone.

"Mother Mary," she breathed.

"Oh, my sins and saints!" Hearing this, Emlyn tore her

gaze from Nicholas to see Tibbie hurrying across the garden with Harry in her arms, and Godwin and Isobel running beside her.

"The lad is fine," Nicholas called out, stepping away from Emlyn's side. Christien jumped down to the ground, grinning proudly. Tibbie breezed forward to gather him under her free arm, shifting Harry to one wide hip.

In a daze, Emlyn heard Tibbie scold Christien and Isobel. She heard Godwin lecture the boy about climbing and thank the baron for his help. As their words fluttered around her like the rustling, breeze-blown leaves of the apple tree, she remained silent and still, watching Tibbie and Godwin walk to the garden gate with the children.

Nicholas stood quietly beside her under the green canopy. She turned to stare up at him. Leafy patterns reflected in his eyes like light shining through emeralds. He glanced down at her, looking slightly puzzled. "Do you go to the keep, madame?"

"Your eyes," she said.

His smile faded quickly. "My eyes?" He glanced sharply upward at the crowning leaves. Then he swung his gaze full at her, a green intensity, keen and deep and completely aware.

"Green." She took a deep breath, the scent of apples nearly choking her. "Not gray. Green." Thorne's eyes. Thorne's voice, and hands, and Thorne's breath at her ear, a few moments ago, sending shivers along her spine.

He looked down at her and tilted an eyebrow. All pretense fell away between them in the lift of that brow, in the knowing cast of that look. Emlyn realized dimly that she had exposed her identity to him. She did not care. He hardly seemed surprised, seemed to know her without question, as she knew him.

A rumbling anger gathered within her, as if thunderclouds rolled full speed toward each other. Her heart hammered wildly. "'Twas you in the solar that night," she said. "You! Thorne!"

He sighed. "Lady, this is no place to—"

"What a simpkin I have been!" she cried. "A dunceheaded fool, not to have seen this!" Picking up her skirts, she stomped away along the flagstone path, passing quickly through the summer flowers, through fragrant, sunny patches of lavender and marigolds. She heard the scuff of his boots behind her.

His hand closed around her arm. "Emlyn," he said.

She whirled to face him, unable to think clearly. The revelation of who he was pounded at her mind and heart. She shook his arm off angrily.

"Emlyn," he said again. "I have known you from the first."

"Yet you said naught!" Embarrassment flashed through her in the midst of anger. Breath heaving, cheeks burning, she began to see that she had been manipulated into marriage, drawn into his trap. In marrying Thorne, she had married the baron. "Why have you done this?" she hissed.

"'Twas necessary," he said evenly. "I could ask why of you as well. That nun's garb is hardly an adequate disguise. Tibbie and the children must know."

"Of course they do," she snapped. "I thought you—the baron—would not recognize me." The words were bitter on her tongue. Her lip trembled and tears rose in her eyes, followed by a fog of fury that collected in her belly and rose into her throat.

Release was imminent, like a pot of stew about to boil and overspill the kettle's edge. She stepped toward him, breathing fast, her confusion almost painful.

His eyes softened as he looked down at her. "Emlyn, I—"

Reaching out suddenly, she slapped his face. Startled by her own action, she gasped and clapped her hand over her mouth. He stared down at her, his lips tightening, the imprint of slim pink fingers printed across his cheek, a slow flush collecting beneath the sting of her slap.

Gathering up her skirts, she ran through the open gate and quickly crossed the bailey to the keep. Running up the outer steps, she yanked open the heavy wooden door as it if were made of dry leaves, and disappeared inside.

Stunned only for a moment, Nicholas ran after her.

His iron-trimmed boots thundered on the curved steps. Ahead, he heard the soft shushing of her gown and shoes on the worn stone, past the level of the great hall to the upper corridor. At the last turn in the stair, he glimpsed her slipping into the nearest unlocked chamber. His. The door slammed shut in his face as he ran forward, blowing his hair back over his shoulders. He heard the iron bar scrape across the planking.

"Open the door!" he yelled, pounding his fist heavily against the oak and rattling the iron latch uselessly. Unless she lifted the bar, naught but a battering ram could force the door open. Turning, he ran to the solar door. Locked. He smacked at it with the fist of his hand and strode down the hall again.

"By God's feet!" he roared, thumping on the oaken planking. "Open this door!" From within the room, something hit the door with a resounding crash, and the wood reverberated under his hand. He cursed loudly, leaned both hands against the door and hung his head down between his arms.

There could be no worse moment for Emlyn to learn the truth about him. Nicholas had resolved, the day he had argued with Whitehawke, to speak with her, but he had left Hawksmoor the next day and had stayed away longer than he had planned. Nearly as soon as he had returned, the abbot of Wistonbury had sent a messenger requesting that he bring a garrison to the dale.

Now, severely pressed for time, he had neither the time nor the energy for a confrontation. Whitehawke's men, the abbot had written in his message, harassed the villeins with renewed ferocity. The abbot hoped that Nicholas could speak with the earl and discourage him until the bishop could send someone to negotiate peace.

Even now, his men were in the bailey preparing to leave. He had been there himself, until he had heard distressed voices in the garden. Through the little window at the end of the corridor he could hear dozens of horses stamping in the yard, and heard his men shouting over the faint jangle of armor and harnesses. He had not yet donned his chain mail, nor spoken with his seneschal about arrangements at Hawksmoor in his absence.

A movement in the hallway caught his attention. He turned to see Lady Julian and Lady Maude peering at him from the open threshold of the ladies' chamber, their mouths agape. He scowled at them, and their eyes popped wide.

Thunder of heaven, now tongues will waggle, he thought.

Well, the damage is done, and a hell of a ruin it is. Worse than Whitehawke's wall. He turned to bang both fists against the thick wooden door. "Open up!"

"Nay!" Emlyn screamed. "Swineshead! Sod you!"

Lady Julian gasped to hear such profanity from a nun. Maude pulled her mother back inside the chamber. Tense silence filled the dim stone-vaulted corridor.

Nicholas tipped his forehead against the wood and groaned. "Lady," he said quietly, trying to summon control, "let me in. If you will not, I must talk to you from out here. All will know what passes between us." He waited, his heart pounding fiercely.

After a few moments the bolt slid free. As he eased the door open, a blue and white jug sailed across the room, crashing into the jamb. Ceramic splinters tinkled onto the floor.

Shutting the door, he pushed at the pieces with his toe. "My lady, your temper is violent and your aim is lamentable. You missed me with a chess piece at Ashbourne, and near unmanned me with an arrow in the timber wood."

She stood beside the hearth, her fists clenched at her sides. "Would to God I had not missed that day in the timber wood! I wish the arrow had gone straight into your black heart!"

"Do you?" He stepped toward her.

"Aye!" She whirled away, and turned back again. "How could you do this? I thought Thorne—my husband"— she ground the words out between her teeth—"was away in the dale, keeping Whitehawke from the monks' land!"

"Well, I have not abandoned those duties," he said simply.

She glared at him, her narrowed eyes sparking blue and gold. "You are a snake! Have you lied to me in everything?" Lifting a silver goblet from a small table, she threw it on the floor, where it clinked and bounced, newly dented, against the hearthstone. She waved an arm wildly. "And is this the bit of land and the house you mentioned? A fine hole for a snake!"

He held up his hand and advanced slowly toward her. "Speak not of lies to me, my lady. You are no nun, and I am baron here, and have been for years. I would have told you who I was when the time was right to do it." She backed away as he came closer, and he flashed out his arm to rescue a second goblet from her hand, slamming the cup down on the table and glaring at her.

"The proper time to tell me was before you wed with me!"

"Would you have wed me, knowing that?"

"Never!" she snapped. Then a light in her eyes glinted, like a blue flint struck in the dark. "Ah, my lord. A clandestine wedding suited your purpose well, since I did not know who you were in truth."

"I meant no betrayal," he said firmly. "I meant to keep you safe from Whitehawke, and to honor——" He stopped, not ready yet to explain why he had a rightful claim to her hand in marriage. Let her absorb this first, and take the rest in time.

She stared coldly at him for a moment, her chest heaving like a soft bellows. "And I know why I did not see you as Thorne until today. These several weeks, you have avoided me."

"I have spent little time at Hawksmoor this summer," he admitted cautiously.

"Aye, and when you were here, you kept well away from me. When I entered a room, you left it, or spoke to me from behind, or in candlelight——"

"For both our protection, lady," he said. "And do not forget that when I came near, you turned away so that I would not recognize you. I had no choice but to speak to that wimple." With one hand, he flipped at the voluminous headdress.

"Then we have played each other for the fool," she said. Suddenly she stepped sideways. He reached out and grabbed her arm, spinning her to him as if she weighed no more than a pillow, and pinioned her wrist against his chest. Through the woolen gown, her body was warm and yielding along the length of his own, her heart thudding just below his.

"Is it foolish to love you, lady? For I do," he murmured, certain then that he spoke the deepest truth he had ever uttered. She stared up at him wordlessly, then flicked her eyes away. He thought he sensed softening anger in her long exhalation.

Though she resisted his grip, she responded to his nearness, her hips shifting slightly, her hands resting on his forearms. She arched her neck to meet his eyes, her jaw set, her eyes blazing like deep blue lakes in bright sun.

"Thorne or Nicholas, which are you?"

"Both, lady, and husband to you still," he murmured.

"Both, sir, and neither one trustworthy," she snapped.

"I have many reasons for my deceit, Emlyn, but you have only one, to steal the children from here."

She pulled against the strength of his grip. "Steal them? They are my family! Prithee say what you did at Ashbourne, sirrah, if not abduct children!"

"I obeyed my king!" he snapped.

"Aye, obeyed your king, and cuckolded your father as soon as you could!" The insult hung in the air, vicious and biting. He choked back a sharp retort, and felt a kindling flare of his own temper in the face of such bitter anger. Aye, he thought, he loved her well—but she could spark anger from a stone.

She looked up at him defiantly, her breasts rising and falling quickly against his chest. Two spots of color suffused her cheeks with a dusty, rosy blush and heightened her luminous eyes to azure flecked with gold, beneath dark, frowning brows. Nicholas thought of a painted carving of a furious, righteous angel confronting a miserable sinner.

"You are no honorable man!" she said accusingly.

"Nevertheless, you are wife to me," he growled. "Would you rather be my stepmother?"

"Neither! You had my trust. Yet you betrayed me!"

A muscle jumped in his cheek. "'Twas for your own safety that I wed you. I could not have spoken openly then."

"Would that I had seen to my own safety, and never met with you in the forest!" she exclaimed between clenched teeth, pushing against his chest.

Pinning her wrist firmly, he slid his other hand to her back and pulled her closer, until her toes scuffed unwillingly into his boots. "By the rood," he said, exasperated, and bent his head nose to nose with her, "you were the one said you wanted to be free of the betrothal. I saw 'twas done." He crushed her so tightly to his chest that she was forced to tilt her head far back to glare up at him. "You are my wife, lady," he growled, "and this game of ruse is finally over."

A blue flint in her eyes sparked an answering flame in his,

an ember long denied. Holding her tight against him, he swelled at the grazing pressure: so long without her, so often near her. His body surged, and he lowered his head to capture her lips.

She pushed at him briefly, then, with a little cry in her throat, relaxed her hand on his chest and tentatively returned the kiss, her lips trembling. Sighing into her slightly open mouth, he loosened his iron grip on her hand.

Emlyn broke the kiss and tried again to pull free. "Pray do not muddle my mind further. I cannot reason when you touch me." The inherent husky warmth of her voice had cooled to a brittle frost. "How could we be wed in truth, when your part of the pledge was false? You wed me to spite your father, to use our vows as a weapon against him."

"Nay," he said. "Nay." He placed his fingertips under her chin, soft and warm as the underside of a rose in the sun. His mind was muddled, too, by her warm, firm body pressed against his, and by his anger, fanned beneath her temper. "The pledge is valid, Emlyn. Private vows are a sacred pact. Who I am cannot undo what we said."

Closing her eyes at his touch, she turned her face to the side, her jaw trembling in his fingers. "'Tis honorable to release me from vows I spoke in ignorance."

Fury collected in his blood. He had risked much to keep her safe. "I will never release you," he said gruffly.

"This is no marriage," she whispered. "I married Thorne. Not you."

"There are reasons for what I did, Emlyn," he said. God, he thought, 'twill take time to tell all to her. He had no time left now; soon Peter would send a man to fetch him. He blew out a long breath of frustration. This revelation was exceedingly ill-timed. "I will tell you. But not now."

The shrill blast of a ram's horn sounded in the courtyard. "My men are gathered and armed," he said, loosening his grip.

Emlyn shrugged free and walked past him, pausing at the door to glance back, her brows slashing across her pallid face, her rose-colored mouth trembling. "Go, then," she said bitterly. "Save your explanations. I cannot countenance betrayal. Do not consider me your wife any longer, my lord." Yanking on the iron latch, she pulled open the door and left.

Nicholas sighed and shoved his fingers through his hair, feeling as if he had been whipped by some unseen lash. Instead of explaining and asking her forgiveness, he had held back the truth yet again, retreating to the secrecy that was his basic nature. They had both allowed temper to rule the moment. But something precious had been destroyed—her faith in him, in Thorne. Now she was certain that he was just as untrustworthy as his father.

He punched his fist into his palm, clenching his teeth. The ram's horn blew again. He should have told her who he was when she first came to Hawksmoor. Rather, he should have taken the risk and told her everything before they pledged. She might have listened, then.

Now, with deceit wedged between them like blocks of ice, 'twas perhaps too late. Sighing, he rubbed his brow wearily. He needed to reason this out, for he did not know how to gain back her lost trust. But he would not be here to work that riddle out and go to her. Judging from the abbot's missive, he would be gone for weeks.

Clawed hands and drooling mouths reached eagerly for the falling bodies of the sinners. Above the hell-fiends, a tall, willowy angel stood beside a pair of delicate balances, weighing the souls of the dead. Those without sin rose into heaven, shielded by the angel's rainbow wings. The burden of their misdeeds dragged the sinners, mouths distorted with screams, into the waiting arms of the demons.

Emlyn sat back on her heels and scrutinized her work, only vaguely aware that Godwin had left the chapel and the light was fading. She had painted no angels today. Demons were better suited to her present mood.

The sun had set, supper had been served, and Emlyn was still painting. She had no desire to see anyone, and had stayed the day in the chapel, whipping her brush over the plastered wall surface with determined strokes.

A few of the demons now had black hair and steel-gray eyes. Satisfied with the dark scowl on the bearded face of the last, she had created another with moss-green eyes and a malevolent glare. She had set its hoofed foot in a thornbush.

Stretching her stiffening shoulders, Emlyn tilted her head

critically at her picture. But her thoughts were not on the images. Her argument with Thorne—with Nicholas—repeated in her head, bringing remarks she should have said, or revealing some new aspect of his crime.

The sense that she had been utterly, boldly betrayed made her ill. Anger and tears this morn gave way by afternoon to a deep, empty sadness. Her eyes were swollen with tears. Earlier, she had sobbed openly, slamming around brushes and pots when she heard the clopping thunder of the garrison riding out of the bailey. Godwin, no doubt confused because she refused to explain her behavior, had finally left.

The light was very dim as she climbed down from the scaffold and went to the altar to whisper a prayer to the Holy Virgin, pleading for guidance. Votive candles sputtered on a wooden shelf beside the altar, and Emlyn took comfort in the simple, familiar act of lighting a candle. Inhaling the odor of smoke and wax, she watched the pure, tiny flame.

When the chapel door creaked open, she turned to see Tibbie's short, squat outline in the doorway. "Dearie? Are ye in here?"

"Aye, Tibbie, here."

Tibbie waddled across the chapel. "Tsk, m'love, Godwin did say ye were painting like yer fingers were afire with it, and sobbing as well." Kneeling on the cold stone beside Emlyn, Tibbie murmured a short prayer, then lifted an eyebrow meaningfully. "Say me what happened, my lady."

"What mean you?" Emlyn asked warily.

"Wellaway, what do I mean! The ladies are buzzing like bees in a field of daisies. They say ye and the baron shouted at each other in his bedchamber. Lady Julian flopped like a cold fish in the doorway, I heard."

Emlyn sighed. "So everyone knows," she said.

"Some do. Lady Maude and Lady Alarice and Margaret de Welles were discussing it at supper. When ye did not arrive at table, the talk grew even more curious." Gentle candlelight smoothed the seams in Tibbie's fierce expression. "The Lady Alarice thinks he wants ye fer his mistress."

"Hah! That would be simple."

"Then he's discovered who ye are!"

"Worse," Emlyn muttered. "The baron is my husband."

Tibbie gasped. "By the Virgin! How many do ye have?"

"Oh, Tib." Emlyn half laughed. "The baron is the forester I wed." She lowered her eyes. "I am ashamed to say I did not know him until this morn. He was somehow different, before. Bearded, and . . ." Kinder, she thought. Gentle and caring, with eyes green as hawthorn leaves.

"And did he know ye, in yer nun's wimple?" Tibbie asked. Emlyn nodded sheepishly. "Well, I count him no dunce. Ye've not fooled any who knew ye, my lady."

Emlyn scowled. "Well." She paused. "I do not think the marriage is valid. He has betrayed me."

"Wed is wed, dearling, if ye consummated it."

Blushing a deep rose, Emlyn remembered bare feet at the pool, and much, much more. She hung her head, feeling ashamed and helpless. Part of her wanted Tibbie to remedy this as she had solved her childhood dilemmas, but she knew no one could help her—except Nicholas. "Oh, Tib," she whispered miserably.

Tibbie stood and paced away, then turned back, frowning thoughtfully. "Yer baron surprises me, I admit. He is older than ye, and seems not one to act rash. But I like him well, for he has a gentle way with the children. I trow he has a loyal heart." She fisted her hands in her hips. "As I see it, the Lord of Heaven has provided ye a fine husband. Would ye rather have the earl?"

"You mean the Lord works in mysterious ways." Emlyn sighed.

Tibbie nodded vigorously. "He will find a way to release ye from Whitehawke. That one is yer only trouble, methinks."

"Only trouble!" Emlyn exclaimed, dismayed. "I was tricked into marriage! I do not wish to be the baron's wife!"

"Yer choosy, betimes. Do not forget that he is yer forester, as well. Did ye ask him why he fooled ye so?"

She lowered her eyes. "Nay. I was too angry to hear it."

"Aye, well. Some knots are slow to unravel. The man is steady, and so the reason must be steady as well. There's much honor in that one."

Emlyn shot Tibbie a wry glance. "Hmmph. But I know not when he will return, nor where he has gone."

"I hear he rides to Arnedale at the abbot's request, to talk peace with Whitehawke. The earl has begun new attacks on those poor farmers in Arnedale. He has threatened to burn them all to the ground." Tibbie shook her head. "Rather the earl should look to his holy salvation and let go the claim, I say."

"Whitehawke has a stubborn, vengeful nature," Emlyn said. "Oh, dear God. What if there is a skirmish between Nicholas's garrison and his father's?"

Tibbie slanted her a curious glance. "Ye worry yer baron will come to harm? Men will struggle over land and wealth like babes over sweets, and there's naught women can do to change that. Trust the Lord to protect yer love, my lady. If ye would fret, then dread what his father will do when he finds ye two are wed," she pronounced, nodding sagely.

"I am befuddled by this, Tib."

The nurse leaned forward to pat Emlyn's hand. "Well and I know it, my lady. But only wait. Let not anger break the holy bond between wife and husband."

"I feel no such bond with the baron," Emlyn murmured. "Once I did with the forester, but I am not sure now."

Chapter Eighteen

Swaying from a high tree limb, the figure burned bright and hot, a roaring torch fanned by late summer heat. Villagers circled below the straw effigy, joining hands and softly chanting. Dark smoke sullied the azure sky and dissolved over the green and gold bars of the harvested fields stretching beyond the village.

Nicholas shifted in his saddle and glanced uneasily at Whitehawke, noting the peculiar glint in his father's pale eyes as he watched the burning. They sat their destriers on a low slope overlooking the village green, accompanied by several guards from each garrison.

During the fortnight that Nicholas and his men had been encamped in the dale, Whitehawke had not mentioned his son's marriage, and indeed had barely spoken to him. Nicholas had been surprised to receive a summons to join the earl in the village.

He turned back to watch the slow swing of the blazing effigy. On Saint Bartholomew's Day, following an ancient custom, a humpbacked, ugly straw creature dressed in rags was dubbed Old Bartle, carried around the village three times and hung in a high bare sapling. Once the pitch-soaked straw was ignited into a fierce torch, the villeins chanted verses, danced, and feasted, in part an homage to some long-forgotten pagan harvest spirit.

Aelric was among the villagers, a head taller than anyone else, with Maisry and their sons beside him. Nicholas saw Aelric grin and laugh at some jest, nodding to his wife as the people meshed their voices in a singsong chant.

> "At the crag he dressed in rags,
> And blew his horn at Hunter's Thorne ..."

Curved sheep horns sounded, eerie and hollow, mingling with the crackling flames and the continued chanting.

"Old Bartle is burned, and this day I send a warning to the Thorne," Whitehawke told Nicholas abruptly. "Look there." He gestured toward the steep valley wall.

A group of Whitehawke's guards rode down the long, grassy, hummocked slope toward the village, ten or twelve in a rapid flange, russet cloaks brilliant in the sunshine.

One of the guards carried a long bundle across the front of his saddle. Galloping into the village, he flung it down beneath the flaming Bartle and rode past. Squinting, Nicholas saw another crude effigy of straw, this one wrapped in green rags, its arms and legs and head decorated with thorny branches.

From a position on the slope, a crossbowman loosed a flaming bolt toward the village green. A woman screamed as the shaft slammed into the green-clothed effigy and ignited it.

Whitehawke cantered past the village church and rode in a slow circle around the burning effigies. His glossy white hair blew back from his high forehead and wide neck, and his black cloak whipped out. Stopping, he slid his pale gaze around the circle of villeins. His formidable presence demanded silence. A child's cry was hushed by an anxious mother.

"Bartle is burned to cast out evil amongst you," he called. "So, too, I burn the Thorne and the Green Man. His evil has long haunted this place. I will show you favor should he find his death here. This land is mine to keep, and I am your lord. Harken to my words if you would have my good will." Lifting the reins, he cantered away, riding past Nicholas and the guards.

"The Thorne is finished," Whitehawke said confidently as Nicholas drew up beside him. "They will protect him no more."

Hearing the rising rhythm of the chant once again, Nicholas glanced behind him. Voices drifted through the hot atmosphere, sunlight laced with smoke.

> "At the crag he dressed in rags,
> He blew his horn at Hunter's Thorne
> At high hill's end he made an end ..."

Aelric ran through the circle carrying a bucket of water, and tossed the deluge onto the strawman that was Thorne. As the people cheered and laughed, Aelric laughed, too, rich as a great deep bell. Someone trilled a pipe, and the dancing began again.

With an amused quirk on his lips, Nicholas turned away.

Summer faded quickly, falling away like the garden blooms. Most of Hawksmoor's harvesting and tallying and preparations for winter were completed under Eustace's supervision in the baron's extended absence. Nicholas returned only three times within a period of several weeks to consult with Eustace and Lady Julian. Each time he left at first light, always riding out with more men than when he had arrived.

Emlyn avoided him completely when he first returned. Sharply aware that he was in the castle, she kept to the chapel and to her chamber. He left at dawn. A few weeks later, he rode in again, well past dark. The next morning she overheard his deep chuckle in the garden as she walked past, and heard Alarice's light response. Emlyn hurried away and stayed in her room the remainder of the day.

Tibbie urged her to approach him, but Emlyn refused. Confusion and anger had formed a sullen lump in her heart. She would not speak to him until he came to her, she told Tibbie stubbornly; 'twas his betrayal, and so his place to make amends.

Late in September, he returned again one afternoon and stayed through the following day. Searching for Christien after breakfast, Emlyn walked into the great hall. Nicholas and Lady Julian stood together near the hearth, in earnest, quiet conversation.

Emlyn halted her steps as Nicholas turned and saw her. He stopped in mid-sentence, gaining a curious glance from his aunt.

In spite of the length of the room, his eyes fastened to hers with keen intensity, and his cheeks flushed. She thought she saw distinct longing in his glance. Her heart beat rapidly, and she stood there, willing him to speak. But his expression hardened, and he turned away. Her own face reddening, she fled the hall.

At first angered and hurt by his betrayal, over the weeks

that he was away from Hawksmoor she gradually began to wish that he would come to her and explain his deception. But during his brief visits, he never spoke to her.

She wanted to understand, to know why he had manipulated this deceit. Where did the calm, loving forester she knew mesh with the cool, remote baron? When Nicholas had turned away from her in the hall so abruptly, Emlyn had felt, in spite of her own resentment, a blow of utter and complete rejection. When they had argued, she had told him to no longer consider her his wife.

Now she began to fear that he had taken her at her word.

While cold autumn rain pattered on the chapel roof, Emlyn and Godwin finished the Weighing of Souls scene. With only a few minor areas left to paint, Godwin decided that his part in the chapel decoration was complete. He told Emlyn that he would return to Wistonbury soon.

"Abbot John will wish me back," he said. "There are many manuscripts to be done in our scriptorium. 'Tis well past time for me to go." Outside the barbican gate one cool morning, Emlyn hugged him fiercely, and stood with Tibbie and the children as he rode away on a fine new donkey, a gift from Lady Julian. Godwin carried the payment for the chapel work in a pouch tucked under his belt. The coins were to be given to the abbey, since Godwin could accept no money for himself.

Blowing frosty huffs of air and pulling her cloak close, Emlyn looked fondly at the children as they waved at their uncle. They had grown so much that Lady Julian had ordered seamstresses to make new clothing, and had commissioned a cobbler to cut new leather shoes to fit their larger feet.

Christien was taller and thinner, stringing out like a sapling, his moods bold and boisterous. Emlyn recalled that Guy had grown along the same pattern. Isobel was taller, too, though she would always be small like Emlyn. Her natural uncertainty was lessening, though she still relied on her brother's lead. Harry was walking and running on sturdy legs, although it would be awhile yet before he wore breeches beneath his tunics.

The children were well cared for at Hawksmoor, as loved

and cherished by the household as if they were the lord's own. Much to her chagrin, her siblings had found exactly the kind of life she had meant to provide for them herself. Removing them was no longer a question; they were happily settled as Nicholas's wards. Emlyn knew that their welfare was assured.

Her status in the baron's household was not so certain. With the chapel almost finished and her uncle gone, she had less reason to stay on as Dame Agnes. She kept to the nun's disguise, though, since only Nicholas and her family knew she was Emlyn. Needing to be with the children, whose light, joyous energy helped her own somber feelings, she stayed silent.

Unsure of her status as Nicholas's wife since their quarrel, she was not about to expose her identity yet. If Whitehawke found out that she was there, she feared what he might do in his son's absence. Originally she had used the ruse to get into Hawksmoor to take the children; now, she clung to it as protection from Whitehawke.

Often, she lost sleep turning in her bed until the small hours, thinking about whether to stay or go, to trust Nicholas or remain wary, whether to approach him or wait for him to speak.

One night she dreamed of a hawk who had become trapped in the thorny tendrils of a flowering vine. In struggling to free itself, the hawk destroyed the pink roses and golden primroses that somehow had sprouted together from the vine. She had awoken from the dream with tears in her eyes, desperately wanting Thorne's arms around her.

Cooler autumn weather changed the routines of summer. Because of the earlier darkness, Lady Julian relaxed more often her rule that dictated that the ladies should retire at sundown. Emlyn read or told stories to an increasing number of listeners, including the ladies, and servants and knights who lingered after supper to hear the tales she recited before a roaring fire in the hearth.

A small group of children, including Christien, Isobel, and a few of the knights' sons, came to Emlyn each day for lessons in reading, writing, and a little mathematics. To her surprise, Harry showed an interest in books and letters, and she would give him a stick of chalk and a piece of slate while she taught the other children. But more often, Harry ran on straight chubby legs, chattering blithe half sentences as he roamed the keep and bailey with a maidservant in close pursuit.

Each morning in the ladies' chamber, Isobel worked diligently at stitchery pieces with Tibbie or Emlyn or Lady Maude, her stitches neat and careful. Christien rode his pony with sharp skill now, and spent a good deal of time in the stables, or watching the men practice in the tiltyard, or catching frogs in the garden pond with the other boys.

Soon the apples were picked in the orchard, and on Michaelmas, the servants and the garrison knights and villeins gathered in the bailey for gurning, when contenders took turns making a horribly contorted face through a plow collar. The winners were awarded bushels of apples. Christien delightedly took his turn, to the rousing cheers of the crowd. Emlyn heard more than one person remark that day that had Peter de Blackpoole been there, the winners would have been smartly challenged.

By mid-October, Emlyn had nearly finished the chapel decoration. Having completed the little psalter, she spent time repairing minor flaws in other manuscripts. Lady Julian then asked her to decorate the whitewashed walls of her bedchamber, which were already delineated with red lines to imitate blocks. Emlyn, grateful for a task to justify her stay at Hawksmoor, added borders of delicate, colorful flowers.

All was peaceful, but for the occasional bitter comment from Alarice, whose obvious displeasure at Emlyn's continued presence sometimes grated on everyone. Even Lady Julian, one afternoon, was so exasperated that she asked Alarice to cease her pestering and pray for a sweeter nature. Emlyn did her best to avoid Alarice's sharp, sour tongue, and closed her ears to the girl's boasts concerning what Alarice considered to be an imminent marriage proposal from the absent baron.

Losing herself in her duties, Emlyn stayed away from others as much as she could. A part of each day went to teaching the children, reading stories, and stitching handwork. Every day she thought of Nicholas and prayed for some resolution of her dilemma, or at least from her unhappy plague of indecision. Continuing to wonder what course she should take, she took none.

She did not know why Nicholas stayed away so long from Hawksmoor, and Lady Julian rarely mentioned what her nephew was doing. Emlyn had managed to glean from household chatter that he and his garrison were camped in the dale, acting on behalf of the abbey monks, discouraging Whitehawke's aggressive methods of convincing the villeins that he was their lord.

Lady Julian had never mentioned the afternoon that Emlyn and Nicholas had shouted at each other like fishmongers. Lady Maude had kept silent as well, and Emlyn had noticed that any allusion to the topic had dropped among the women. Only Lady Alarice retained a malicious curiosity.

Moving a slender brush carefully along the bottom edge of a completed pattern frieze of blue and gold diamonds, Emlyn painted a red line, her tongue caught between her teeth in concentration, her brow furrowed. When the chapel door swung open, several moments passed before she glanced up to see Lady Alarice.

"Dame Agnes," Alarice said, shoving back her marten-trimmed hood. She narrowed her green eyes. "Your uncle left weeks ago. I expect that you will return to your abbey soon."

"I have dispensation to stay with my brothers and sister for as long as they need me, my lady," Emlyn answered cautiously.

"So unusual for a nun to stay alone, outside her abbey," Alarice murmured, tilting her head.

"Greater freedom is commonly accorded for family circumstances, my lady. And my mother's cousin Tibbie is my companion here." Emlyn turned back to continue the delicate decorative line.

"Surely you have privileges in the outside world that most religious would never dream of," Alarice said. "Privileges of the bedchamber, as well."

Emlyn stopped. "Pardon, my lady?" she asked.

"Do not linger at Hawksmoor waiting for the baron to return," Alarice said. "He will show you no more attentions."

Emlyn sighed. "If you will excuse me, I have work to do." Trembling, she walked over to climb the scaffolding.

"I intend to speak to the countess," Alarice said, her voice ringing cold and clear. "'Tis past time that you returned to your convent. Your siblings are the baron's wards, and do not need you. Any priest could educate them. The chapel is finished, and ready for our wedding. When the baron returns, our banns will likely be announced." Alarice walked to the tall arched doors. "We shall be wed just past the New Year, I think."

"So soon? I wish you blessings, then," Emlyn said sweetly. Though her stomach tensed with anger, she kept her expression placid as she rummaged among the painting supplies.

Alarice slammed the door as she left. Emlyn flung down her brush and put her face into her hands. Soon, she told herself, soon she would not need this cursed disguise. She wondered what kept Nicholas in the dale, wondered when he would return. She desperately wanted an end to this.

Remembering Thorne's voice, his low chuckling laugh, recalling the secure feel of his arms around her, her eyes filled with tears. Whatever else was confused in her heart and mind, she still needed and loved Thorne. She fervently wanted to be with him, living simply in the cave, together, happy.

She sat straight up, her eyes wide. Had a beam of light burst through the chapel roof straight from heaven, she could not have seen the truth with better clarity.

Thorne was not gone. Nicholas could not so completely change his personality with his clothing that there would be no trace of Thorne, the man she had come to trust and love. Some inner voice would have warned her if he had been full of secret malice. If they were one and the same man, so be it. The man she loved was contained somewhere within the man she did not know.

She blinked in surprise at the utter simplicity of it. Until this moment, she had not accepted him fully. Loving only part of him and denying the rest had torn her apart. She felt a glimmer of forgiveness wash through her and gather strength. Peace would come, she now knew, when she opened her heart to all of him.

Wiping at her cheeks, she straightened her posture, her breath quick and light. She was wed to a man whom she loved, even if he had turned out to be the baron she feared. Alarice could not usurp her as baroness, and Emlyn felt sure that Lady Julian would not dismiss Dame Agnes in Nicholas's absence.

As soon as Nicholas returned, she would confront him, would accept no more avoidance from him. She would see an end to this.

Bursting through the tent flaps, Peter pulled them shut behind him as a howling, soaking wind whipped the cloth. Rivulets of water rolled down his armor as he swirled off his dark green cloak, and cold spray spattered the low central fire so that it hissed and smoked. He poured a cup of ale and sank down onto a narrow pallet with a gravelly sigh.

"God's bones," he groaned, wiping his wet face, "I have need of a roaring hearth fire, an eight-course meal, and a steam bath. Nine days of this sodding rain. I think my armor has rusted to my skin."

Nicholas looked up from his seat by a small table, where he had spent more than an hour deciphering the cramped lettering of several documents and listening to the pounding beat of the rain. "Your rounds for the day are complete?"

Peter sniffed and cleared his throat. "As far as we were willing to go. No one is about in this wretched weather, though a farmer a league away claims that ten of his sheep are gone."

Nicholas sighed. "Likely they are in Whitehawke's soup pots with someone's missing turnips." He shoved aside the parchments, reached for a wooden goblet half filled with ale, and leaned his elbows on the wooden table. His head felt as though it were crammed with wet wool. Like Peter, he was thoroughly tired of cold feet and wet clothing and lumpy mildewed straw mattresses.

Rains and cold mists had persisted for days. All the tents were filled with mold and mildew, not just this one. The pavilions, set up in two camps at one end of the dale since late summer, no longer served as a bold temporal monument to aristocratic power. Some leaned sadly, the proud bright silks beaten by winds and rain, tattered, soaked, their colors bleeding into the earth.

Most of the men had developed coughs or aching, rheumy joints, and had begun to care more about getting garlic in their soup than about which farmer Whitehawke's men had threatened that day. Nicholas heartily wished that this sojourn were over.

Peter waved a hand toward the embroidered, soggy entrance flaps. "I cannot recall what a solid wall looks like. Think what lovely hands wrought the stitchery on this pavilion. A shame we are not at some tourney and likely to see some of those maiden hands." he grumbled, sipping his ale. "Thunder of heaven, we have been here for weeks."

"Longer than we thought to be. Still, the dale is not yet burnt to rubble," Nicholas replied, shifting the parchments beneath his fingers and choosing a particular folded document.

Peter rolled his eyes. "'Tis not our presence that has discouraged burning in the dale, but the wet hand of God."

Nicholas huffed in amusement. "Aye. Aside from patrolling, and disputing the claim endlessly with Whitehawke, we've done little else. He refuses to move out, and so we stay."

"How went your meeting this morn? We heard naught but shouting as we rode past the pavilion."

Summoned to Whitehawke's tent after the arrival of the royal messenger, Nicholas recalled the volatile hour that had followed as they discussed King John's latest plans for both of them.

Although Whitehawke had made no direct reference to Nicholas's marriage since their argument at Hawksmoor, he continued to treat Nicholas with a frozen courtesy bordering on spite. Not overly surprised by his father's reaction, Nicholas assumed that the earl was biding his time, checking legalities and forming some planned reaction, probably total disinheritance. Today, Nicholas had attempted once again, at the abbot's request, to discuss the issue of dale ownership with Whitehawke. Now he clenched his jaw muscle at the sour memory.

"He talked of naught but his honorable right to the land until 'twas all I could do to keep from throttling him," he told Peter, and poured himself another cup of dark ale, the double-brewed stuff sent to him a few days earlier by the abbot. He quaffed it down.

"Honor? And where is the earl's honor in this, I wonder?" Peter mused.

"Where indeed. Now he orders the abbey to relinquish the land once and for all. He declares his right to burn them out if they do not acknowledge him." Nicholas laughed. "His right!"

"Between your garrison and the rains, he has been unable to carry out his threats. Biding his time until we leave, I vow."

Nicholas flipped the dangling ribbon on the letter he held. "His men still prowl like roaches through grain, looking for Thorne or the Green Man."

Peter laughed. "A futile search, my lord."

Nicholas shrugged. "He is not yet discouraged. And now he has chosen another site for his damned fortress. He hangs on to this dale like a starved dog gnashes a bone."

"He has given up one quest, though." Peter raised a brow at Nicholas. "Why has he ceased to look for Lady Emlyn? I think you know something of it, my lord, though you say naught." He shot Nicholas a mildly resentful look, and sneezed. "Aye well. So here we sit, two camps politely riding rings around the farms and forests and moors, waiting for the bishop's delegates to wend their lazy way over here from York. Even the arrival of Archbishop Walter himself could not solve this. Some action must be taken."

Nicholas flicked a glance at Peter, his eyes as gray as the rain. "What do you suggest?"

Peter shrugged casually. "If the earl saw the Green Knight again, a taste of fear might send him home."

Rubbing his unshaven jaw, Nicholas frowned. "I want no one else to take the risk, and I have not been free since we came here." He tapped the parchment against the table. "Besides, such a move may be unnecessary. A royal messenger came in today. Whitehawke has been called south by the king."

"Has the legal claim been decided, then?"

"Nay. John is far too preoccupied with his own troubles to worry about Whitehawke's squabbles up here. The king calls him to Rochester Castle to join his men. And if the earl values his life and property, he will depart immediately."

"Rochester? Reginald of Cornhill holds that for the king."

"No longer. A group of rebels took it easily. John is furious, and apparently has his smiths working on siege engines. He advances with his most loyal men surrounding him."

"Not a good sign for the rest of the barons, then."

"Aye. I wager he has plans beyond this siege. He swore last summer to wreak revenge on whoever took part in what he thinks was his attempted downfall."

"At first he seemed amenable enough, giving up a few castles that he had withheld from their rightful owners," Peter said. "What of Guy de Ashbourne? Was his inheritance among them?"

Nicholas shook his head. "Nay. I recently inquired on that. John made only those few gestures of peace while he waited for word from the Pope on the question of the charter."

"Well, he is not known for fairness, whatever the law."

"'Twill only worsen from here. Whatever happens in the south, we northerners may soon be arming against our king."

Peter stood and began to pace. "He has chosen a likely place to start his little war against his cantankerous barons. But the baroncy has no organization, no field army—" He shook his head. "If the king moves north, he will strike the barons one by one."

Nicholas waved the parchment, from which dangled a royal seal. "He has already begun his attack. This writ was delivered to me this morn. Pope Innocent sides with the king, and has annulled the Great Charter. He has also excommunicated those of us who had any part in the rebellion. John must be pleased."

"Jesu! An interesting strategy. Threaten the enemy's soul?"

"Fear of eternal damnation works miracles. John will strike each baron however he can." Nicholas tossed the parchment onto the table. "War comes, Perkin. But for the nonce, the bishop's party will refuse to meet with Whitehawke if an excommunicated baron is present." He shrugged. "I am anathema."

"At least we can leave here," Peter said gratefully.

"Though your lady aunt will fret when she learns the state of your soul."

Nicholas dismissed that with a brief wave of his hand. "'Tis no great matter to obtain a reinstatement. Either I will pay for it in good coin, or wait until the Pope pardons the rebel barons. That, at least, we can be certain will happen eventually."

Peter laughed ruefully. "Lady Alarice will be distressed as well. She hopes for a wedding when you return, my lord."

Nicholas blew out a breath and tapped his fingers on the table surface. "Bones and saints," he muttered, then sighed and picked up his goblet, swirling the frothy liquid inside. "I must speak to you concerning this matter of my marriage."

Peter looked surprised. "You plan to offer for Alarice?"

"I do not intend to offer for anyone. I am already wed."

"What!" Peter crossed to the table in three strides.

"To the Lady Emlyn."

Peter, shaking his head in disbelief, reached for his goblet. "Thunder of heaven. Give over some of that double ale you've been hoarding. I would strengthen my blood to hear this."

Chapter Nineteen

Harry was teething. Shifting his solid, warm weight to her opposite hip, Emlyn walked across the room yet again. In the curtained bed, Isobel slept beside Tibbie, who snored in loud exhaustion. Christien lay curled on a small pallet on the floor.

The children had fallen asleep despite Harry's noisy fussing, and Emlyn had convinced Tibbie to rest as well. Though Harry had slept for a little while, he had awoken to cry again, tugging at his ears and pulling at his hair.

Noting his pearly, swollen gums several days earlier, Tibbie and Emlyn felt only time was needed. But time brought little improvement. Thinking it might be the earache, they soothed him with warm poultices and drops of warm garlic oil in the ears. Now, though, Emlyn knew another molar was bursting through.

"Come with me, cabbage, we shall go out," Emlyn sighed.

"Out, out," he repeated tearfully while she wrapped a thick woolen blanket around him and fastened her own cloak.

With well-swaddled Harry in her arms, she slipped down the silent, dark corridor and made her way through doors and up steps until she stepped into the cool night air, high on the battlement that encircled the curtain wall.

Harry's attention was, thankfully, caught. He gripped her neck, pointing here and there as Emlyn strolled with him. A guard passed by them and nodded briefly. Other such night strolls had accustomed the guards to seeing her on the wall walk in the deep of night.

Emlyn showed Harry the stars in the black sky, and the white moon shining like an apple wedge above the highest tower. Harry chattered blithely, but after a few minutes began to whimper and bite at his fingers. She reached into her sleeve for the piece of clean leather that Tibbie had rolled and soaked in sweet wine.

As Harry gnawed and sucked at the leather, Emlyn strolled along the wall walk. When he quieted, she leaned her head against his and sighed, looking up at the sprinkled stars. Nicholas had been gone for so long now that she feared he prolonged his sojourn, in part, simply because she was still at Hawksmoor. She missed him greatly, even as she dreaded the inevitable encounter.

She understood that he grappled with a troubling situation in the dale, and she also realized that King John's taste for revenge could become a great concern over the next few weeks, and possibly a real threat to Hawksmoor. The charter signed in June had not solved England's tumultuous political situation, and the baroncy, who had hoped to see the charter honored, might soon be forced to defend their homes and lives against the king's rage.

Lady Julian had recently mentioned, when the ladies had gathered in her chamber, that Nicholas had been excommunicated. Emlyn had listened in dismay, for excommunication was an unspeakable horror. When one's soul was outside the grace of the Church, it was cut off from holy salvation and unprotected from the devil's power. For a knight, death was never far away, especially now, with such uproar in the country.

In her arms, Harry began to sing in his high soft voice, and Emlyn laughed to hear the sweet, simple words. The wind ruffled his golden curls and lifted a lock of her hair, loosened beneath her hood. She heard the scrape of a boot behind her.

"What is this? Two new members of the wall guard on duty? Our enemies must beware." Hearing the low voice, she spun around to peer into the shadows, and gasped.

Nicholas stepped away from the tower doorway. Emlyn paused uncertainly where she stood, her heart thumping under her ribs.

He came nearer. "My lady," he murmured, sliding back the hood of his dark cloak, worn over a long tunic. A cool breeze wafted the scent of wood smoke and horses toward her, and blew his hair across his cheek and brow. He stopped an arm's length from her.

She leaned Harry against her hip. "Greetings, my lord," she said carefully. "I was unaware you had returned."

"We rode in just after dark," he said.

"Then you are here briefly, as before?"

"I am back, my lady," he said quietly. "For good and all."

Her heart thumped a stronger pace. Though she had come to regret her angry words to him, the hurt of his betrayal came rushing back, keen and sharp as a blade pushing at her breast. The low, honeyed rumble of his voice, so familiar, seemed to vibrate in the center of her belly.

Her heart fluttered like a silly flapping hen, and she could not catch her breath. His voice, the lean shadowed planes of his face, and his silent, watchful expression all exerted some subtle power over her mind and limbs, mingling a sense of pleasure and pain. She felt misery, joy, and utter confusion.

Gazing up at him in the moonlight, she wondered if he would reject their marriage. Easy enough to cast a clandestine marriage pledge aside, she thought, if he desired to do so.

"Well, my lady," he said, "I will bid you good night."

"My lord—" She took a little step forward, groping for something to say, wanting him to stay, wanting to talk to him, yet fearing the painful matter between them. "Did you see Maisry and Aelric in the dale?" she asked. "Are they well?"

He nodded. "Well and hale, though Whitehawke's men have been threatening their farm along with the other parcels."

"'Twas why you were gone, I heard," she said.

He was staring down at her, the moonlight casting a sheen on the crown of his head. Harry whimpered in her arms, and she shushed him, glancing back at Nicholas.

"Aye, 'twas why I left and stayed away so long. The abbot asked me to encamp my men for the welfare of the villeins, until the archbishop could send an envoy."

His manner seemed relaxed, without the tension and anger she had come to expect from the baron. The wind played freely with his hair, but he never took his eyes from her. Standing there in the crisp moonlight, without his armor, with his hair blowing loose and his face unshaven, he was more Thorne than Nicholas. Her heart pounded insistently.

"The bishop's priests—they came?" she asked.

"Aye, but they took too long about it. Whitehawke left before they arrived."

"Then naught has been settled," she said.

"At least some measure of peace exists now, if only because Whitehawke is absent. With winter approaching, the archbishop will send no one else to travel so far in bitter weather, and Whitehawke refuses to go to York."

"When this is settled, and likely in the monk's favor, will your father accept the judgment?"

"Will he learn that arrogance and tyranny do not gain him what he wants? I know not." He shrugged. "More likely he will direct his fury to some other matter." He hesitated, as if he wanted to say more.

Harry began to cry in earnest, and Emlyn swayed in a little rhythm, patting his back and shushing him softly.

"By the saints, what troubles the child?" Nicholas asked irritably, tense and clipped, like the baron she knew.

"New teeth are sometimes painful," she said. "What does the king say of Whitehawke's actions?"

"King John still makes no decree, which galls my father no end. The king turned it over to the courts and has done naught since. Now that the archbishop has involved himself, he will be the one to settle this, if a peaceful resolution is possible," he replied, raising his voice a little over Harry's fretting.

Harry let out a loud wail, and Emlyn bobbled him up and down, distracted. A lock of hair worked its way out of her lopsided hood and fell into her eyes. She blew it back in exasperation.

Nicholas reached out a hand to Harry's head. Tiny blond locks curled gently around his fingers. The child quieted for a moment, the leather roll dangling from his wet lips, as he stared up at Nicholas. "The air is quite chilled. What the devil are you doing out here past matins?"

"Harry disdains sleep for now, my lord," she answered. "Night walks are sometimes calming."

"You look pale, even in moonlight," he said, frowning down at her. "Have either of you slept this night?"

She shook her head. "Nay, but he will tire soon."

"Come." He took her elbow and quickly pulled her along to the tower door. Lit by orangey, fat-spitting torchlight, they went down the circular tower stairs. He drew her relentlessly along through the shadowed, musty corridor, until they reached his bedchamber. Harry was unaccountably quiet, perhaps surprised by their swift progress through the halls.

Nicholas guided her inside his chamber and shut the door. Firelight sent soft amber shadows dancing around the room, and she smelled fragrant applewood smoke.

"Well, give him to me," he said behind her.

She turned. "My lord?"

"Will he not come?" He lifted the child easily out of her arms. Harry did not protest. "Come, boy, see if you can tire a seasoned knight." He jiggled Harry, who emitted a watery, hiccupy giggle. "I will sit with him awhile. Go and rest in the solar." He lifted one brow. "Or rest in your own chamber if such proximity makes you ill at ease," he added coolly.

His remark did not escape her, and she flicked her eyes away. "My lord, 'tis woman's work to sit with fussing babes."

"Is it? I have known Aelric to sit with his boys when they are ill. Is the child—er, dry?"

Emlyn felt the breechcloth under Harry's tunic. "Aye."

"Then go. 'Tis barely past midnight. I am not tired, and have much to think about. Lulling the child to sleep will be no great chore."

Wondering if he knew what he took on, Emlyn pursed her lips. Her thoughts were decidedly foggy and her eyes felt pinched and heavy. "I am tired," she admitted. "Just an hour, then. When he falls asleep, lay him somewhere safe so that he will not fall."

"I know they climb like ferrets. Now go." He turned away to sit in a high-backed chair in front of the fire, settling Harry on his lap.

Emlyn paused, her hand on the door latch. Then she turned and crossed the bedchamber to lift the solar curtain.

She awoke, blinking, in the dense blackness of the solar and sat up. Through the shuttered windows, she saw a faint crack of moonlight. Dawn had not yet come. She had slept only an hour or two at the most.

Pushing aside the curtain, she peered into the firelit bed-chamber. Hearing soft rhythmic sounds from the chair that was turned away from her, she stepped into the room.

Nicholas snored gently, his head tilted against the high back of the chair, his eyelashes black crescents against his slightly flushed cheeks. Emlyn thought his face quite startlingly beautiful in repose, strong and perfectly made, like a statue of a saint, gently colored and almost beatific. She realized, with a curious twinge deep inside, that she had never seen him asleep.

His hand rested on Harry's head, long fingers caught in the pale curls. The child slept as if Nicholas's chest were a cozy pillow, his cheek mashed against the dark tunic, his mouth lax and drooling slightly.

Emlyn smiled and touched Harry's warm, slightly sweaty head. Then her hand drifted lightly up to Nicholas's hair, grazing the wavy dark locks in a soft caress. Neither one awoke as she bent to scoop Harry up and settle his limp, solid weight against her shoulder. She glided toward the solar and laid him gently on the cot, covering him with her cloak.

Unable to relax, she went to one of the windows and parted the shutter slightly. Blue moonlight spilled over her hands and face, and her hair blew back over her shoulders. Her heart pounded and her stomach turned nervously as she thought of Thorne—or Nicholas—so close, only a few steps away.

A deep, poignant ache insisted that she had lost him through her hot declaration that she could no longer be his wife. Though she regretted her impulsive temper, she also recalled why she had been angry: he had proven shatteringly untrustworthy.

Sighing, she rested her hands on the rough stone ledge. He had shown her a kindness that was unexpected. But he was fond of Harry, and concerned for him. He had not asked forgiveness, or mentioned aught that stood between them. He had remained remote toward her, but she had responded to his presence in every fiber of her body.

Suddenly she heard a soft shuffle behind her. The curtain opened quickly, iron rings jangling in the heavy silence.

Startled, Emlyn gripped the window ledge, but did not turn. His boots scuffed softly as he crossed the wooden floor. She sensed the warmth and rhythm of his body behind her. Her shoulders tensed delicately and her heart pounded.

He stood so close that his breath stirred her hair. "Emlyn," he murmured. "Give me leave to speak or not, we must talk." His voice thrummed in her ear, blending the gentle tone of the forester with the clipped decisiveness of the baron.

An ache of frightening intensity flooded her. The desire to whirl and press into his arms was so strong that she tightened her body against the urge. She did not know whether to speak, or flee, or spin into his embrace. Taking a deep breath, she let it out slowly, keeping her head turned from him.

"Once I believed you to be Thorne, an outlaw, the forester I wed most willingly," she said softly. "But then you became a stranger to me." She closed her eyes against a rush of anguish. "I know not how to smooth this rift between us." Behind her, she sensed the warm, solid block of his body, and she bit back a sob.

"Do you want to mend this?" he asked softly.

She caught her lip between her teeth, her back still to him. Aye, she thought, aye, I do. But she remained silent.

His fingers suddenly gripped her shoulders. "Emlyn," he said. "Look at me." He turned her forcefully, and she raised her eyes to his. A slender shaft of moonlight made his eyes seem luminous as silver. Tall and broad-shouldered, clad in a long belted tunic of dark wool, his long hair brushed his shoulders like raven's wings, and his shadowed jaw was firm and stubborn as he frowned down at her.

"Harken to me," he said quietly, "before you condemn me."

"Enlighten me, then," she said. Dear God, she thought. Part of her wanted to be pulled into his arms, but his hard grip on her shoulders seemed to speak of anger. "I would know why you betrayed me."

"Four years ago, 'twas I asked your father for your hand."

Emlyn stared up at him, her eyes widening at his unexpected words. "You? My father wanted me to marry you?"

"Aye. But 'twas during the Interdict, and your mother desired that you finish your education in the convent, perhaps because of your painting skill, of which I was unaware. Assured of the pledge, I waited. But your father died. What he did with the letter of intent we signed, I have no idea. Your mother had passed, too, and Guy was captured before I could approach him."

Emlyn listened with a dawning sense of relief, of pure joy, but she feared to give it rein. He had been false before. She had to be cautious. "I was told naught of this," she said. "How do I know 'tis true?"

"Here is the truth of it." He let go of her shoulder to reach to his belt, pulled out something tucked in it and extended his hand. A small ring lay in his open palm.

She picked up the ring. One small garnet, set between golden dragon claws, glinted in the moonlight. "This was my mother's," she breathed softly. "How do you have it?"

"Your parents gave it to me as a token of intent." He gently took her hand and slid the garnet onto her slender finger, next to the steel circlet. "I do owe you a ring, my lady."

She cocked her head, thinking, narrowing her eyes at him. "Why did you ask for my hand, years ago?"

He looked steadily at her in the cool milky light, and he smiled, a lopsided tilt. Emlyn's heart lurched. She knew that smile so well. She had missed it.

"I once pledged my life to you and your family."

"Aye," she breathed.

"A husband protects his wife. He is obligated to look after her family as well."

"Aye." Her voice was near a whisper. He stepped closer, his eyes never wavering. She tilted her head back, caught in his gaze. "But Lord Whitehawke—"

"He will come to accept this. But I regret that you thought I wed you only to strike at him," he said quietly. "There was no other way. I could spare you from Whitehawke by pledging with you myself. But I could not tell you who I was, not then." He ran his fingers through his hair, blowing out a breath. His eyes crinkled with amusement. "You would not have married me. Truly, I think you would have killed me out of ire."

Their gazes touched and held. Emlyn no longer wanted to flee. She felt like a hare pinned to the trap, yet somehow glad of the end. She leaned in toward the smoky depth of his eyes.

"Look at the muddle I find myself in," he said huskily. "I have kept my ruse secret for years. Now you have entered both lives, and disrupted both. And I find myself asking for more of this sweet, dangerous disruption."

He raised a hand to cradle her head, his fingers stroking lightly beneath her ear. Gathered into his embrace, she went, resting her head on his chest. His chin, warm and slightly prickly, pressed against her temple.

Anger and disharmony slipped away as if they had never been. Closing her eyes, she felt a wash of sheer joy in his arms. Listening to the deep velvet of his breath, she felt him as Thorne; he spoke, and with each word he uttered, with each breath he drew, Thorne and Nicholas blended completely.

"At first I admired you, the beautiful, brave child," he said. "And I knew marriage would pay an important debt." He streamed his fingers through her hair, sending slow, languid shivers down her spine into her lower abdomen. Only Thorne had ever touched her like that, she thought.

"I did not know then that you would mean so much," he continued. "But when I met you again, I came to cherish you. Your spirit," he paused, smiling against her cheek. "Your sharp temper. I could not let my father have you. I would not see you shut away. I would have done anything to keep you in my life. Anything, Emlyn." He breathed out softly. "Even lie to you, and risk your hatred when you discovered me."

"I do not hate you," she whispered. "I could not."

Almost lazily, he stroked the silken tendrils of her hair, then thrust his long fingers into its cool mass, pulling her head back to look at him. She was unable to quell a delicate shiver.

"I need your forgiveness," he said gruffly.

She looked at him for a long moment. "You are not

Thorne, and yet you are," she said. "When I learned you were the baron, I thought Thorne was lost to me."

"Not lost to you, my love," he murmured, lowering his head. "Never lost to you," he whispered.

His warm breath smelled of wine and cinnamon as his mouth clung gently to hers. The comforting brush of his lips, soft as silk, warm as heated wine, changed to a moist, sweet demand.

His lips withdrew. "Emlyn," he said huskily, "I have loved you for years. Only now am I seeing how much, how long that feeling has been with me. I need your forgiveness."

She circled her arms around his neck, and the last bitter core that had sat hard in her heart began to melt like wax.

"'Tis yours," she whispered. What had not been forgiven, held in some angry reserve, suddenly dissolved like shadows in light. The depth of what she felt in that moment humbled her. Where she had feared malice and betrayal and coldness from him, he had offered only love. She tilted her face, and his mouth covered hers in a deep, almost desperate kiss, warm and urgent and enduring.

"Nicholas," she whispered against his lips, "I have loved you since I was a child." She kissed him firmly. "Both of you, I trow. Only promise me that I will come to understand all this."

"We will speak more of this," he murmured, his lips against the corner of her mouth, the curve of her jaw, his fingers delicately tracing the line of her throat, "but not now."

She caught her breath as his feathery touch moved down over her throat and shoulder. His long fingers slid over the soft wool of her gown to round the full contour of her breast. She caught her breath as her nipples ruched, tingling and aching beneath his whispering touch.

Groaning softly against her mouth, he put an arm beneath her and lifted her in his arms. She pressed her cheek to his.

"Nicholas," she murmured against his soft earlobe. "Harry—"

"I let him sip a little French wine," he whispered. "He will sleep well until morn."

He carried her through the curtained threshold into the snug warmth of the bedchamber. A circle of golden firelight spilled over the wide bed as they sank into deep feather mattresses covered in red samite and overlaid with silky furs. Nicholas reached up to draw the curtains shut; the firelight penetrated the delicate weave in places, enclosing them in a warm gold and red cocoon.

With quick, breathless movements, they drew away each other's garments and flung them aside, slid back the coverlets, and glided into a warm, close, breathless embrace.

As he kissed her with a growing urgency, Emlyn gave into the need to savor his nearness after so long without him. Her fingers grazed the dark cloud of hair covering his chest. She leaned forward to kiss his shoulder, inhaling his warm scent, redolent of leather and spices, smoke and sweat.

Her hands skimmed over his chest, caressing the warm, muscular surface of his hard torso and the taut contours of his hips. She touched his back, exploring, gently circling the scar that Thorne had received eight years ago. Her fingers drifted down to touch the round, smooth weal on his thigh, left from the arrow wound that she had given him only months ago. Lowering her head, she softly kissed the pink scar in loving apology. In one smooth, flowing motion, she glided her body over his hard belly and chest, raising her head to meet his lips with hers, wrapping herself in his embrace, sinking into kisses that flowed over her like warmed honey.

His fingertips moved over her throat and shoulders, warm and lambent, easing across her body, his touch so featherlight that she felt only the sweet influence of their grazing contact. Sighing, sliding her fingers through the dark silk of his hair, she arched with burgeoning pleasure as he kissed her soft skin, suckling and swelling each breast in turn, the contact nurturing to both of them. His touch was tranquil and slow, every movement a gentle solace, cleansing, healing, renewing, dissolving the heart-wounds that lay between them.

His fingers drifted down over her supple curves, turning her to the rousing will of his hands. With smooth and exquisite motions he stroked her hips and abdomen until she parted with a welcoming moan, and his fingers stirred her tiny quicksilver flame into limpid glowing strength.

Taut as a golden bowstring that trembled for release, she wrapped her limbs around his waist, pleading with her body for his sweet supple weight and yielding to it. Silken and warm, he thrust, then glided into her.

Moving to a compelling rhythm of heartbeat and breath and muscle, she yearned to meld her body, her very soul, into a rich blend with his. Pressing closer still, pulling his firmness deep inside, she surged toward the pulsating, incandescent center within her. Shivering against her, he drove breath and body into hers with sudden urgency, until her inner cadences flowed with his, released at last.

Shifting, sighing, they drew slowly apart with small cherishing kisses. Crackling flames carried the sweet tang of applewood as she curled close to him, resting, wanting the peaceful silence to carry through into her sleep. The gentle fusing of their bodies and spirits, through expressing profound love, had created forgiveness, washing away the feelings of betrayal that had wedged between them earlier.

She slept for a while, waking in the deep gloom of the hour before dawn to Nicholas's brushing kiss on her shoulder. They loved each other again with exquisite gentleness, so leisurely that the sun began to stream through the shutters as they gave and received dulcet, honeyed satisfaction.

Later, her head resting on his bare shoulder, the red silk coverlet over them, she traced a finger in circles over his chest. "Will we tell, now, of our marriage?"

"Aye," he whispered into her hair, "we will, this very day."

"'Twill be difficult, Nicholas."

"I am with you, love," he said, shifting to look at her. "Our marriage will gain acceptance, now or with time."

"But your father—"

He place a finger over her lips. "Worry not over him just now. There is still much we must speak of, you and I."

She nodded, watching him in the bright shadows of the curtained bed.

He traced the contours of her face. "Your eyes are blue as lapis, and sprinkled with golden dust."

She laughed. "And yours are gray as stone and green as frogs," she teased. "Changeling husband, I do not know what color to call them. But I know you now, whatever your name."

"As it should be," he said. "Now, Dame Agnes, rise up and dress quickly. We have matters to attend to. I will not be called a blasphemous sinner for bedding a nun."

Chapter Twenty

Nicholas folded the parchment closed and sighed, rubbing the back of his neck with his hand. Wat's missive, like every message that had come to Hawksmoor of late, mentioned King John's activities: the king now pushed north with his mercenary troops, threatening to overthrow every rebel castle in his path.

Wat also had sent news of Whitehawke. Tossing the stiff parchment onto the table, Nicholas stood, stretching the tension from his neck and shoulders. Peter waited patiently, leaned back in a chair, his legs sprawled comfortably before the hearth.

Beyond the tall shuttered windows in the great hall, the wind chorused like distant wolves, and frozen rain pattered against the window glass. Not a time of year to run battle campaigns, Nicholas thought; yet he doubted if the usual custom of truce during winter would persuade the king to forgo his revenge.

He flicked a somber glance at Peter. "Wat writes that my father has obtained another royal writ to confirm his ownership of the Ashbourne properties. He takes steps to disinherit me, and declares his betrothal to Emlyn annulled because of her disgraceful behavior."

Peter nodded. "Still, you and your lady have the luck of angels, my lord. Whitehawke has been remarkably docile, even so. But for Lady Alarice, your marriage has raised few brows, in spite of the rather odd circumstances."

"True. Lady Julian gave us her generous approval. And the servants and villeins view life in simple, pragmatic terms. She was a nun, now she is the baroness. They might chuckle over a cup of ale at eventide, but they accept and ask no questions. Only Alarice, as you say, has been discontent. But I trow she will be leaving us as soon as the weather allows. Her father, I hear, negotiates with Chavant."

Peter rolled his eyes expressively. "Holy saints! Chavant and Lady Alarice?"

Nicholas shrugged. "She brings a sizable dowry, and a fat inheritance someday. For myself, I would not wish to tell the lady news of her suitor," he said wryly.

"Nor I," Peter agreed. "But how is it, my lord, that your father hardly disputes your marriage to Lady Emlyn?"

Nicholas shrugged. "I am not sure what he has in his mind. Come spring, I may be invited to a tourney to have my head lopped off by my offended sire. For now, other matters concern him, since he has been with the king at Rochester Castle."

Peter sat forward. "Wat sent news of Rochester?"

Nicholas nodded and stared into the hearth blaze. "The siege is over. King John had forty bacon pigs slaughtered, and his men used the fat to fire the walls and undermine a corner tower late in November. He was ruthless there. Prisoners were chained, some were mutilated. He hung a childhood friend." He sighed heavily. "He is mad with rage, and moves north on a path of war with his foreign army. He will be in Nottingham by Christmas."

"Good Christ," Peter murmured, frowning. "He moves quickly. What then of the rebel barons in London? 'Tis said they spend most of their time drinking and playing bones."

"Aye, but they want very badly to bring John off the throne, and have tried whatever legal means available. Naught can come of it. He counters every move too cleverly."

"The York landholders were summoned by the rebels weeks ago to discuss these matters, yet you did not go."

"I will not join them in offering the English crown to a French prince. My support of the charter is well known. Beyond that, I will not further ally myself with the rebels against this unpredictable king."

"John is a sly coward," Peter agreed. " 'Tis surprising to see him at the head of his army for such a long campaign."

"He would most enjoy treating his barons like those bacon pigs at Rochester, I trow, and be done with it. But, since

the northerners lack the unity of an army, 'tis each for himself now."

"The northern barons must either surrender outright, buy
the king's favor, or lace their helms for war."

Nicholas nodded grimly. "Aye. I have given the matter
much thought, Perkin," he said quietly. "I will not surrender
Hawksmoor. We will fortify our walls immediately." As he
gazed into the hearth, feeling the searing amber heat flicker
over his face, a hard resolve forged in his gut. He would defend his home and family to the utmost of his power.

"I will never ransom my castle gates," he said softly.
"Look you to your sword, my friend."

Emlyn's arm ached from waving, and her cheeks were
bright from the bitter cold. She gripped the reins of her
chestnut mare and glanced at Nicholas, who rode Sylvanus
at a leisurely walk. He twisted in the saddle to wave again
toward the villeins who clustered along the snow-crusted
roadside. During their long ride around the countryside, he
had tossed coins from a leather pouch and called greetings,
knowing many people by name. They, in turn, showed him
the respect and easy friendship of villeins toward a good and
fair lord.

Squinting her eyes, she scanned the bright expanse of
snowy moors, shining in the sun like overturned bowls of
white glass. Ahead, the gray walls of Hawksmoor Castle
loomed strong and solid. The hall would feel warm as a
bakehouse compared to this snapping icy chill. Eager to
reach home, she spurred her horse.

Early that morning, after everyone but Nicholas, who was
still excommunicated, had attended Christmas mass in
Hawksmoor's newly decorated chapel, the baron and baroness and a small entourage of guards had begun a circuit of
the frozen roads that etched the moors north of Hawksmoor.

In spite of the cold, villeins came running everywhere
they went, shouting and laughing, catching the silver coins
and handing up fresh bread and mistletoe and holly for luck.
After a few miles, Emlyn and Nicholas had accepted cups of
hot spiced cider from an innkeeper, and had turned their escort for home.

"Have you any doubts remaining about your welcome

here, my lady, set them to rest," Nicholas said, smiling. "Our Christmas procession is cheered loudly enough to show their approval."

Emlyn looked at him, her eyes glowing with a sparkle put there by cold, sunlight, and happiness. "I vow I felt like a bride as we rode past, sirrah," she answered lightly, "but 'twas likely your largess of coin that widened their smiles most."

"Nay, love, though the coins were welcome, 'twas you they cheered," he said, and turned to wave as a woman called enthusiastically to them.

Emlyn settled in her saddle, recalling the noisy, colorful blur of the past week, and the increasing demands on her as the new chatelaine of Hawksmoor. But her duties had been very pleasant, including the supervision of the hanging of garlands of fresh holly and ivy and lengths of bright silk in the hall.

The huge Yule log had been dragged into the hall by seven men, placed into the hearth, and ignited to burn until Twelfth Night. They had hosted a feast to feed hundreds of castle servants, knights, and a steady stream of villeins.

Yule gifts were exchanged among the family. Emlyn gave Nicholas a small painting that she had made on wood, of the Holy Virgin, with Saint Nicholas on the reverse side of the panel. He had been well pleased with the gift, and she had loved his to her: a belt of gold links, set with several oval-cut sapphires.

Then he had whispered, to her great curiosity, that his other gift would be presented later. Blushing, she had laughed and kissed him, thinking that he referred to spending another magical, tender night in his great red-curtained bed.

Weeks earlier, he had helped her to find gifts for the children. Christien had received a yew bow with arrows and a quiver, and Isobel a bracelet of carved amber that had once belonged to Lady Blanche. Harry was gleeful over a set of small lead knights on wooden wheels. But the most delighted recipient of all had been Lady Julian, who had been given a pair of tiny gold-wired spectacles that Nicholas had ordered from a glazier's shop in York.

The children had stayed up until their eyes were bleary

with fatigue and excitement. Harry had found a bean in his
cake, and had been proclaimed, amid raucous laughter, King
of the Feast. He had ruled wisely enough, until he broke
down in a tyrant's tears and had to be removed to bed.

Still smiling at the pleasant swirl of memories, Emlyn
clicked her horse ahead to cross over Hawksmoor's drawbridge and under the wide arched portcullis grille.

Grooms ran forward to take the horses. As Emlyn was being helped down from her mount, an older steward came
stiffly down the outer keep stairs and approached Nicholas,
murmuring low.

Listening to the old man, Nicholas frowned, nodded
quickly, and tossed his reins to a groom.

Emlyn's puzzled glance went unnoticed as Nicholas whispered a quick word to Peter. Then he spun on his heel and
went toward the keep, running up the steps.

A man in mud-spattered armor and red cloak stood before
the hearth, gazing into the huge, flaming Yule log. His beard
was grizzled and gray and his face showed harsh lines of exhaustion as he accepted a cup of steaming spiced wine from
a serving girl. Nicholas strode quickly toward him, and the
man turned.

"Wat!" Nicholas smiled, clapping him on the shoulder.
"Christmas greetings, man. Emlyn will be well pleased to
see you. When did you arrive?"

"My lord baron," Wat said. "No more than an hour past.
I have arranged what you requested."

" 'Tis done then?" Nicholas asked sharply.

"Aye, my lord," Wat said, nodding.

Accepting a leather-sleeved cup filled with hot wine from
the servant, Nicholas dismissed her with a brief nod. He
sipped the steaming liquid gingerly, then glanced at Wat.
"And the parcel?"

"Handed over to your seneschal, Sir Eustace."

"Good." He exhaled, long and low, as if releasing a burden long held. "Have you had difficulty at Ashbourne?"

"Nay, my lord. The king's path goes north, but not west.
We are spared his wrath by our location and Whitehawke's
ownership."

Nicholas lifted an eyebrow. "I see you wear the red of the

de Ashbourne baron, and not the russet of Whitehawke's men."

Wat shrugged. "I wear whatever cloak I choose, now that I am no longer Ashbourne's seneschal."

"What say you?"

"Whitehawke sent word that he had appointed another seneschal upon his arrival at Graymere."

"He has come back north? I had not heard."

"Aye, he sent a missive to me last week. But I had heard from you long before then. By God's wounds, my lord, I was much pleased to learn of your marriage to Lady Emlyn. Your father must be livid, my lord, if I may say."

"A long story, which you will hear soon, Wat. Rest your bones, and tell me word of the king." He leaned a hip against the table while Wat sat heavily on a bench. "We heard that he was in Nottingham at Christmas with his mercenaries."

"Aye, my lord, and 'tis said he rode out of there with the fury of hell in his soul." Wat sipped at his wine and shook his head. "He sends his foreign routiers out in packs, like wolves to the kill, to take rebel castles wherever they find them. Attacking, burning. He has met with little resistance, and goodwill—coin, my lord—is extended him everywhere. He accepts or not, as his wont goes."

"What is his route?"

"Steadily north. Rockingham, Belvoir, and Doncaster among others have surrendered. Castles and towns are throwing open their gates to him to avoid the inevitable. Any castle that refuses him entry meets his army and siege machines. He collects ransom fees like a clerk at tax time."

"Where is he now, then?"

"Last I heard, Pontefract, perhaps York by now, my lord."

"Then he is not so far from Hawksmoor."

The door swung open at the far end of the room, and Peter looked in, then advanced to greet Wat. Shoving back his mail hood and propping a foot on the bench, Peter listened as Nicholas summarily told him Wat's news.

Intrigued, full of questions, Peter leaned toward Wat to discuss the king's northward rampage. Propped against the table edge, Nicholas sipped the remainder of his wine and lifted his eyes around the room to study the graceful swags of greenery looped above the mantel and windows and door frames.

Traces of laughter and joy still lingered in the room for him, as tantalizing and warm as snatches of a pleasant dream. The gigantic, fragrant Christmas bush, made from a wheel-shaped framework of green boughs hung with apples, pears, nuts, and silk ribbons, was suspended from the rafters over the center of the long chamber. Filling the hearth, the Yule log glowed orange and black, crackling and snapping out its light and warmth.

Nicholas felt loathe to give up this recently acquired taste for peace and family, and return to the grim business of war and snarling disputes that had become the norm in England lately. Still, there was no choice for it. Sighing, he turned back to listen to Wat and Peter.

"Does the king follow a planned route?" Peter asked Wat.

"He heads for Berwick on the Scots border, knocking down each stronghold that stands along his path," Wat answered. "Alexander of Scotland moves into England, and John is determined to stop his progress at the same time that he swears to wipe the rebellion from his realm."

"Evidently Alexander smells the rotting carcass of England beneath his nose," Peter observed.

"As does Philip of France," Nicholas said. "John invited the French to help him quell the rebellion, and soldiers and knights have come over in herds. So many, I have heard, that with the proper leadership, they could wrestle England to the ground. Or so the French would hope."

"What a stew John has made of England," Peter said. "Little wonder that outsiders seek the chance to invade. They see us torn amongst ourselves, withdrawing support from our own king."

"Aye so. The man is brilliant in his own right, but more impetuous than any rebel. A wise council and limitations such as in the charter were all that was needed. But this has gone too far, now. Once angered, he does not cool easily. He will see us pay by coin or castle or life," Nicholas said, shaking his head. "A stew, as you say. Wat—the king's army is mostly French?"

"Aye, my lord, as well as Gascons, Brabantines, and Flemish."

"Ha," Peter said. "If John is lax with the payroll, he will have a mutinous bunch riding at his back."

Wat lifted an eyebrow and looked at Nicholas. "They say the king travels with his entire treasury on packhorses."

Nicholas whistled low. "A large purse for a journey. He trusts no one, then."

Peter pushed away from the bench and went to a side table to fetch a cup of wine. "Some of his most loyal supporters are swinging to the rebel's side," he said. "Arundel, York, the earl of Surrey. There are others as well."

"Not York now," Wat told them. "He has offered John a thousand marks to ride past Alnwick Castle."

"Whitehawke is among those who still support the king regardless," Peter said.

Nicholas nodded. "Thus ensuring the safety of Graymere Keep. I misdoubt the king will come here, either, but we are fortified to the last man, and the battlements are prepared for any attack. But—Peter, I want you to take several men and escort the ladies and the children to Evincourt."

"To the countess's castle near Lancaster?" Peter asked.

"Aye. They will have better safety so far west. John cannot cover the whole long bowl of England in one winter's trek. You will have returned before aught has happened here. If anything does," Nicholas added. "With God's luck, we will see no fighting here at Hawksmoor."

Peter cocked an eyebrow. "Your lady wife will be greatly displeased if you send her away."

"She has been displeased with me before," Nicholas drawled.

At the sudden sound of the latch scraping on the door, Nicholas glanced around. Emlyn, still wearing her outercloak, her face wind-chapped and rosy, stepped into the room, pulling off her rabbit-fur gloves as she moved gracefully down the length of the room, her long cloak sweeping the rushes. Winter sunlight turned her braids to smooth golden flax beneath the gauzy veil.

She tilted her head suddenly, and a brilliant sunbeam flooded across her translucent cheek, setting the golden flecks in her blue eyes to dancing. Nicholas felt a swirl of warmth in his loins as he watched her, and then a stronger surge, beyond physical excitement: complete, surrendering love.

And anticipation. In the next few moments, he would present her with a yule gift that she would not soon forget.

As she advanced the length of the sunlit hall, her cloak whispering on the rushes, Emlyn could see only the arm and back of the visitor who stood partially obscured by Nicholas and Peter, all three with their backs to her. Another messenger, she decided, one in the long stream of riders dispatched to and from Hawksmoor in the past few weeks.

She saw that the man was wide as a barrel, wearing tarnished steel and a dark red cloak. News from Ashbourne; her heart quickened. Pulling off her gloves as she came forward, she saw that Nicholas beckoned Peter close and murmured a few words.

Peter gave him a startled glance and left the room quickly through a side door, without even a courteous word or nod to her. That, she thought, was most unlike Peter.

Halfway across the room, she called, "My lord, I was told we had a visitor—" She paused in midstride, recognizing the grizzled hair, the dark-eyed, heavy-jowled face as the man turned. Her smile faded into openmouthed shock.

"Wat!" she cried. The gloves hit the floor as she picked up her skirts and hurried forward. "Wat!" Running toward his opening arms, she hugged him fiercely. "Dear God! How is it you are here? Is aught wrong at Ashbourne? What then of Guy?"

"Ashbourne is safe," Nicholas interrupted. "My father has released Wat from his duties there. I think that we have need of such an experienced soldier here at Hawksmoor, if Wat will consent to stay." Emlyn smiled up at Nicholas, her arm wrapped around Wat's thick forearm.

Wat bowed his head. "Thank you, my lord. I gladly accept." His voice was deep and warm, his solid, unassuming manner reassuring. Emlyn realized how much she had missed him.

"Sir Walter brings word that the king advances toward York with his army," Nicholas said.

She looked at him in alarm. "North? Might he come here?"

"That we cannot know, my lady," Nicholas said, his eyes leveling into hers, serious, but with a curious silver light in them. "But for now, there is another matter for your concern."

"What is that?" she asked, as the side door opened and Peter returned, his fair-skinned face a bit flushed. A man came in behind him. Emlyn's hands flew up to cover her mouth.

He was tall, thin as a reed in a drooping brown tunic, his blond hair, streaked with brown, swinging long and untidy over his brow and wide, bony shoulders. He stood a few paces away and looked at her, then turned his hands, palm up.

"Oh, God," she breathed. Tears started in her eyes. "Oh, God." She took a step forward, hesitating, her heart pounding fiercely, her breath constricted. Then she ran the last few steps into his arms.

"Emlyn," Guy said.

Wrapping her arms around him, she could feel the bony outline of his ribs through the tunic, and she sensed his fatigue, almost a frailty, as he embraced her. Her brother had been like a blond bear, more muscular in build than Nicholas, as strong as men twice his breadth. He had been known for his solid strength, but Emlyn could have lifted his weight now. "Guy," she breathed, her tears wetting his bristly golden chin. "When—?"

"I was released in November," he said. Emlyn noticed then the gaunt hollows in his face and the purplish crescents beneath his blue eyes. Creases lined his mouth, and the somber set of his eyes and jaw made him seem much older than when she had last seen him over a year ago.

"My lady," Wat said, "Lord Guy arrived home at Ashbourne as weak as a newborn, and needed time to recover strength to travel before we could come to Hawksmoor."

"But why did no one tell me that he was free?" she asked, puzzled. "Wat, you wrote to Nicholas."

"I did know, Emlyn," Nicholas said. "But I said naught of it at the time." She turned her wide, questioning gaze to him. "Guy was quite ill, and insisted on our silence until he could come here himself to be with his family."

"You have been ill?" She looked up at Guy.

"He greatly needed food and liquids and rest," Wat explained. "He was near starved to death in that dungeon cell."

Emlyn gasped. Peter nodded grimly. " 'Tis a common method of King John, my lady. Starving a prisoner is more economical than keeping him well-fed. Many have died that way in the king's prisons. John has been known to call it accidental, and apologize for his forgetfulness."

"Dear Lord," Emlyn breathed, "how cruel. But how is it you were let go? The king refused to reinstate you because of the charge of high treason."

"Any charge has its price these days, for John," Guy replied. "And 'tis thanks to your lord that my price was paid."

She whipped her glance around. Nicholas had been quietly watching them, his eyes a muted grayish-green, glowing above deeply rouged cheeks. That blush, evidence of his vulnerable discomfiture, brought a smile to her lips. She had taken in so much joy in these last few moments, she wondered if 'twere possible to burst with it. "Nicholas? You paid the ransom?"

He nodded briefly, his eyes locked with hers. "I would not pay ransom for my own castle, as I have said. But there was no other way to see Guy free. The king persisted in his charge of treason. Only his purse showed any sense, in the end."

Guy laughed. "I congratulate you on your fine marriage, sister. I could not have arranged better for you than this man."

Holding out her hand to Nicholas, she answered. "I would have accepted no one else," she said as his long, warm fingers closed possessively over hers.

"Again I say you nay, Emlyn. The king cuts a wide, bloody swath up the length of England. I want you removed from danger." As Nicholas strode rapidly across the bailey, Emlyn hurried in his wake, clutching her cloak closed against the bitter morning chill.

"But Hawksmoor is too far west for the king to bother with us," she insisted. "You told Peter so last even." He shot her an exasperated glance and entered the stable, Emlyn on his heels like a hound.

"We have been separated through most of our marriage," she argued as they entered the warmer, straw-insulated stable. A yawning groom, piling up fresh hay with a pitchfork, threw a startled glance at the baron and his lady, then pulled at his hood and hastily left.

"Do not ask me to leave you now, Nicholas," she continued.

"Emlyn, the king puts to the torch, each morn, the very house in which he slept the night. True, he may never reach this far west, and Hawksmoor will likely go untouched," Nicholas conceded over his shoulder. He advanced down the central aisle with Emlyn close behind, their steps muffled by thick straw. "But King John is not a predictable man. If he bears enough malice toward me for my hand in the charter, he will send his routiers to burn me out. He knows I will pay no fee to gain his lenience."

"Why should he single you out, when there are others closer to his route? He is at Pontefract, you said."

Nicholas halted in midstride, and Emlyn collided into his back. He turned and grabbed her by the upper shoulders. "And on his way to York, which is not so far from here, even in the dead of winter. The weather has not been so fierce as to make the moors impassable. Think, Emlyn. Why might he come here?" He shook her a little, and her hood slipped back as she scowled up at him. "Think. Who has the king's ear?" he asked.

"Whitehawke," she said. "But your father would not do that. Even he would not betray his own son."

Nicholas looked steadily at her for a moment. In the pale light that cascaded through the wide entrance of the stable, his eyes glinted with the same steely sheen as his hauberk. "Would he not?" he asked coldly.

"Nicholas," she said, touching his arm, hard muscle sheathed in cold metal beneath her fingers. "Whitehawke will soften to our marriage, given time. For all his anger, he seems a pious man. He does penance daily by forgoing meat, he has founded an abbey to pray for his soul, he—"

Nicholas laughed, a loud, harsh bark. "Know you why he constantly seeks to placate God?" He tightened his grip on her arms and tilted his face toward hers, his expression as fierce as if he faced a warrior rather than his wife. Emlyn pulled back, drawing in her breath.

"N-nay," she said in a small voice.

"Because he fears eternal hell for murdering my mother."

"Nicholas," she whispered. "Nay—"

He turned away from her abruptly, rubbing his temples wearily. In one of the dark stalls, a horse nickered softly.

"He accused my mother of adultery," he said over his shoulder. "He imprisoned her, and she died there."

Emlyn put a trembling hand to her lips. Though she had heard the rumor, she had not thought in terms of such shocking cruelty. She had assumed Blanche's death was some kind of accident for which Whitehawke had been blamed.

Stepping forward, she put a hand on his cloaked shoulder. He angled his head away from her in taut rejection. She understood, suddenly, how stubbornly he held on to his hatred and anger. As if the onslaught of his pain tore through in her own breast, she took a deep breath against its weight, and realized that he had never allowed healing to take place within his heart.

Tears moistened her eyes as she moved to stand in front of him, leaning her forehead to his chest. Beneath cold, unyielding steel, she felt the gentle movement of his breath, the strong, steady throb of his heart. Though he rested a hand on her upper back, she felt a tension, a distance, in him.

"You never spoke of this," she said softly.

"Now I have," he said coldly. "A man who murders his wife for adulterous behavior, with no proof of her sin, has no shred of honor. Naught would gainsay him from betraying his son."

"But she died imprisoned. He did not kill her, she died while there, of illness, perhaps."

He stared above her head. "I was seven years old," he said woodenly. "I was sent to live at Evincourt with Lady Julian and her husband. Whitehawke had placed my mother under what he claimed was a genteel confinement, such as many a lord has given his wife. Some men see no harm in locking up their wives for a spell. But Whitehawke found her dead one day." He swiveled his eyes down to hers; the chill gray gleam in them pierced like a blade. "Know you why he eats no meat?"

" 'Tis his penance," she whispered.

"My mother died of starvation."

"Dear God," Emlyn said. Deep inside, her belly turned with shock and dismay. She felt sick. "He suffers much guilt, to exact a similar penance on himself."

Nicholas huffed out a short breath. "As if 'twould help."

Emlyn stared up at him, seeing the dark sprinkle of stubble across his cheeks, the beautiful, muted colors when the clear light shone through his eyes, and the deep hurt that lingered in the depths of his glance. "You were very young," she said softly, "to lose your mother. No wonder you bear such hatred for him."

" 'Tis hard no matter my age, Emlyn. 'Twas senseless and cruel. And the sentiment I bear him is not one-sided, as you have seen. He has hated me since I was born, I think. He would betray me to the king in the blink of an eye."

"But there are times when he has shown courtesy to you. He has seemed to accept our marriage with little argument beyond disinheritance. You have said that oftentimes he disinherits you with one hand and pulls you back again with the other. That seems more like fits of anger than hardened hatred."

"He disinherits me because he does not truly believe that I am his blood son," he said. "He accused my mother of adultery several times over the years, and doubts my paternity. And he has never let me forget that uncertainty of his."

"Nicholas—" she began, but he silenced her by pulling her to him in a sudden, fierce embrace. Soon he relaxed his hold and rested his cheek against her smoothly braided head.

"Emlyn," he said gruffly, "this matter between my father and me cannot be eased quickly. Honor thy father, the priests teach us. 'Tis the hardest task I have ever had, and I am not capable of meeting it."

"You can, Nicholas," she said gently.

"You are the very soul of loyalty and honor, Emlyn. Did you know? I have watched it in you, so ready, so easy. Loyalty to family guides you and shapes you. You are angered by injustice as I am, but your anger never festers to hate. Would that I could learn from you." Stroking her hair, he traced his fingers down to lift her chin, looking at her evenly. "But for now, try to understand what exists between

Whitehawke and me. Even your sweet, earnest nature cannot mend this rift."

He lowered his lips to hers, and his gentle kiss touched that deep place in her that always responded so fully to him. She sensed that his turmoil had been quelled and set away once again, far from her reach.

"Harken to me," he said, his lips warm against her forehead. "You must leave Hawksmoor for now. I must know you safe, Emlyn."

Drawing back, she looked in his eyes, like mossy flecks over glinting stone. "But I cannot leave for yet a few days. The village priest asked me to attend Twelfth Night mass in his church. As your baroness, and because you are banned from mass still, I must accept. Then, my lord—if you promise to keep safe—I will go meek as any good wife to her husband's will."

"A few days, then. I will vow anything to hear such obeisance from you." He smiled wanly, a crooked lift of the corner of his mouth.

She wrinkled up her nose. "Alas, my lord, you will not hear it often from me, so honor my request ere you do."

"We have bargained like this before, I recall," he said. "See to your packing, but leave my windows in peace."

She laughed, remembering. "My lord, I would not disturb the windows here, for I will soon return."

Nicholas smiled, then brought his mouth down to hers in a crushing, searing kiss that tore the breath from her and sent waves of pleasure from her hairline to her toes. He slipped a hand inside her cloak to stroke the curve of her waist and hip, moving up to round over her breast. She gasped at the powerful surge of desire that quickened her breath and pulsed through her lower body, filling her with lush readiness. "Sirrah," she whispered, half laughing, "we are in a stable."

"Aye," he growled, and traced his lips along her cheek to meet her mouth again greedily. "Think you the stable boy will be back soon?"

She shook her head and circled her arms around his neck, pressing her body eagerly to his.

Chapter Twenty-one

A cold, wispy blanket of fog curled around the village, blurring the already uneasy distinction between white-shrouded earth and pale sky, as Emlyn and Alarice emerged together, shivering, from the portal of the square Saxon-built church.

Bidding the priest farewell after Twelfth Day mass, they hurried to their horses, where a groom waited to boost them into their saddles. Nearby, six armed guards were mounted beside a covered van, driven by a servant, which held the children and their nursemaid. Once the ladies were mounted, the group moved out onto the crusty ice-rimed road to travel the few miles back to Hawksmoor.

Emlyn took up the reins of her chestnut mare. "Set us a quick pace, William," she said to the young serjeant who headed the escort. "More snow threatens before long, I think." Nodding agreement, he gestured the group forward.

" 'Tis fearsomely cold and damp of a sudden," Alarice said with a tight little smile.

Smiling back, Emlyn reminded herself that Alarice had shown some effort to be kind lately, talking to Emlyn after a long, resentful silence and smiling at Nicholas once again. Any grudge she bore regarding their marriage appeared to be in the past. Cool, polite friendship seemed to be offered.

When Alarice had asked to accompany Emlyn to the church for the Twelfth Day mass, Emlyn had suggested that they ride their horses and leave the van for the children and their nursemaid. She had felt a need for some vigorous exercise, but now the raw, bleak weather made her long for the comfort of hearth fires and thick enclosing walls. And leaving Nicholas so that she could fulfill her duties as baroness had little appeal, since she was to depart for Evincourt the next day.

Excommunication had kept Nicholas away from mass, but the priest had appreciated Emlyn's attendance. Saying that it boded well for the new year, he thanked her for the tithes of salted meats and cheeses, as well as several bundles of fat beeswax candles she had brought as New Year's gifts to the church.

Glancing back at the van, where the children peered out from under the canvas shelter, she made a face of mock consternation. They waved back, cozy and giggly under layers of furs, hot bricks at their feet. Betrys, a dark-eyed, broadly built girl who tolerated few antics, had removed them from mass early because of some errant silliness. Hearing the high giggles now, Emlyn judged that their wayward energies were still much in force.

Ahead, through torn and gauzy fog, the road dipped and curved over the moors. A subtle uneasiness crept through her again as she glanced nervously at the blurred wintry landscape.

King John's relentless mercenaries were nowhere near this place, she told herself, though she still felt an uncertain foreboding. The ceaseless talk of war and defensive strategies that she had been hearing at Hawksmoor must have affected her nerves, she thought.

The pale, heavy sky and a cold tension in the air warned of an imminent snowstorm. A trip of a few miles was completely safe, she thought. Snow would not fall until later. Shivering, she urged her horse to a faster gait. The green and white de Hawkwood banner flapped briskly atop a pole attached to a guard's saddle, a symbol of the protection and privilege she had as the baroness of Hawksmoor. No harm could befall them today.

On the winter-bleak moors, the fog thickened to fleecy white at every dip of the road. Had she known the extent of the chill and fog out on the moors, she thought, she would have left the children at home. Now, she only wanted to get home to Hawksmoor.

Misty shadows appeared on the white rim of a hill, resolving into a party of at least thirty riders advancing toward them. When Emlyn saw the russet cloaks of Whitehawke's garrison, she clutched at the reins, her breath catching in her throat.

The sudden silence was filled by the steady crunch of hooves on the ice-crusted snow and the snorting of horses. Coming forward, the leader held up his hand.

Halting, William murmured a quiet order to his men. They guided their horses to form a cautious, protective arc in front of the two ladies and the van.

Emlyn squared her shoulders beneath her heavy overcloak and steadied her horse. Beside her, Alarice sat tense and silent.

Hugh de Chavant cantered forward and stopped in front of the serjeant, glancing sharply at Emlyn and bowing his head. "My lady baroness," he said. His eyes flickered restively toward Alarice. "My lady. New Year's greetings to you both."

"Baron de Chavant," Emlyn answered. "Why do you halt our escort? 'Tis bitter cold and we have young children with us. Whatever business you have can be addressed within walls. You may either accompany us to Hawksmoor, or ride on."

Chavant smiled, showing long yellowed teeth. One eye seemed to wander toward William. "My lady, allow me to accompany you to Graymere Keep to meet with Lord Whitehawke, at his request."

"Tell him to take up the matter with my husband or with the courts," she said curtly. "Let us pass."

"My lady, I must insist that you come with us," Chavant said.

"Baron de Chavant," the serjeant interjected. "Lord Whitehawke has no authority here on Hawksmoor land. For you to ask such of my lady is a challenge to arms, my lord."

Chavant sighed mildly and looked away for a moment, as if thinking. "So be it, then," he said smoothly, and gave a quick signal to his garrison. Far outnumbering Emlyn's guards, they spread out to surround the escort like long arms, their heavy metal helmets and nasal guards obscuring their faces.

With a nearly physical jolt, Emlyn realized that Chavant and his men meant to enforce a confrontation. Her heart

lurched into a rapid beat. She wished again, desperately
now, that she had not brought the children along.

"For Whitehawke!" Chavant yelled, raising his sword.

"To arms!" William bellowed. "For Hawksmoor and Saint
George!"

Descending on the small escort, Chavant's men scraped
their swords free. Emlyn heard the awful, sibilant whistle of
raw metal slicking through cold air as the first blows
clanged and smacked, echoing eerily in the fog.

Wheeling her horse, she cantered back toward the van,
maneuvering through the jostling, roiling haunches of battle-
trained horses, all larger and steadier than her own agitated
mare. Alarice, her face pale with alarm, swam past in the
chaos, her palfrey circling out of control. Turning again,
Emlyn saw a russet-cloaked guard knock the van driver
senseless with the side of his broadsword. Reaching down,
he grabbed Christien out of the wagon, tossed him over his
saddle and spun away.

Screaming, unable to wedge her horse closer, she watched
in disbelief and panic as two other guards quickly snatched
up Isobel and Harry, and then dragged a screaming Betrys
out of the wagon. Dumping their captives over their saddles,
they galloped away, shielded by a thrashing row of
Chavant's soldiers.

Emlyn's shrill screams mingled with the children's cries
and with the harsh ring of steel slamming steel. She felt a
sudden, strong compression around her waist, and gasped as
a mesh-clad arm yanked her brutally from her horse.

Shoved facedown over another horse's shoulders, she
fought for breath as the high saddle pommel pushed cruelly
into her ribs. Struggling, screaming incoherently, she could
see nothing, though she heard metal blades crushing into
wooden shields and grinding on mailed limbs. A heavy hand
pressed down on her back.

She elbowed her captor sharply where his surcoat split at
the crotch. He grunted, and then the cruel weight of his fist
slammed into her jaw. Raising her head, thinking she was
going to vomit, she went spinning into a soft, deep blackness.

* * *

"Blessed be God," Lady Julian said, her hand clutching her throat, "how do you mean, gone? How can this be?"

"They are taken, Aunt," Nicholas answered curtly, his face drained of color as he led a weeping Alarice down the length of the great hall.

Alarice nodded, half swooning against Nicholas, her hair disheveled, her veil askew, her eyes swollen with tears. He seated her in a chair by the hearth and handed her a cup of wine that sat on a nearby table. As the girl drank, he closed his eyes, fighting back a powerful rising fury.

Alarice, accompanied by William, two guards, and the concussed driver, had ridden into the bailey less than twenty minutes past. Breathless and agitated, they had quickly told what had happened out on the moor. The driver and the two guards, also injured, had been led away to have their wounds tended, and Nicholas had asked William to come up to the great hall with the others.

Standing by the hearth while Alarice sipped her wine and sobbed out the details of the attack, Nicholas listened. His fingers fisted and flexed, aching for a sword. Deep in his gut, anger roiled toward Chavant. This cowardly attack must have had Whitehawke's approval. He expected, by the style of the raid, a ransom demand, but he was puzzled. Whitehawke likely needed no coin; what, then, could he want? He swore under his breath, and inside him, rage and fear flamed together, fueling each other.

He glanced at Peter, who stood nearby with William, and at Lady Julian, who fingered the beads of her rosary necklace as she listened intently. His gaze swung back to Alarice, whose tearful voice sobbed out the rest of the story.

"By Christ!" Nicholas suddenly shouted, slamming his fist against the table surface. "I will have Chavant's heart on a platter for this!"

Alarice straightened in the chair, her eyes growing wide.

"I understand it not," Peter said. "How did Chavant know that Lady Emlyn would be at the village church?"

"No coincidence, be sure of it," Nicholas snapped. He rounded on Alarice. "Did Chavant say aught of how he came to be there?"

"N-nay, my lord," she stammered.

"William?" Nicholas swiveled his intense gaze.

"I heard no mention, sire, though I thought it very odd at the time that he seemed to be laying in wait for us."

"Alarice!" Nicholas exploded, turning to her.

Alarice leaped nervously to her feet. "My lord," she whined, " 'twas not meant to happen thus!"

"Alarice!" Lady Julian gasped. "What—"

"I intended to ask if Emlyn had sent word ahead to the village that she was coming out this morn," Nicholas growled.

"I know naught of any messages." Alarice's eyes slid away.

The odd cast in her green eyes reminded him, curiously, of Hugh de Chavant, and the back of his neck prickled suddenly. He moved slowly toward her. "What is it you know?" he demanded.

She stepped backward as he came relentlessly closer. "N-naught, my lord," she choked.

Peter slid smoothly toward her from the other side, both men closing in on her. Lady Julian glided silently forward as well.

"Lady Alarice," Peter said, "has your father settled your marriage portion yet?"

"Sweet Jesu," Nicholas said. "I had forgotten. Chavant is your betrothed now."

Eyes fluttering, head swiveling between the two men, Alarice looked like a wild, trapped bird. "Hugh—Hugh told me to do it," she blurted. "He urged me—" She turned suddenly, as if to run.

Nicholas reached out and grabbed her by the arm, yanking her toward him. "What have you done!" he shouted. "What in the name of God have you done!"

"Sent word to Chavant to tell him when Lady Emlyn would be outside the walls," Peter said.

"Alarice," Lady Julian began, "did you meet with Chavant those times you went out riding?" Alarice nodded mutely, biting her lip at Nicholas's hold on her.

"I did not think he would take the children," Alarice sobbed out suddenly, curling forward, limp enough that Nicholas was forced to hold her up. She laid her head on his chest, her tears wetting the wool of his tunic.

"Oh, Nicholas," she sobbed, "I wanted to be your wife.

You knew that. Emlyn did not deserve you—she lied, sinned, humiliated Chavant. He said he and your father had a right to punish her." She threw her arms around his neck. "But not the children," she sobbed, "not the little ones, too."

The thought of her betrayal was nearly too much for him to endure at this moment. His whole body seemed to vibrate with anger. He ripped her hands away from his neck and grabbed her so tightly by the upper arms that she winced with pain.

"God's eyes!" he shouted. "Are you mad, to hand Emlyn to my father like this? He will kill her for disgracing him, just as he killed my mother!"

His fingertips whitened with pressure, and she cried out, trying to twist away. Cold, numb fury filled him as he thought of Emlyn treated like his mother had been. His body and heart felt as if they had transmuted into cold-forged steel. He was hardly aware that he was hurting Alarice.

"Nicholas," Peter said quietly.

Lady Julian laid a hand on his arm. "She is but a girl." He let go then, pushing Alarice away in disgust, shaking off his aunt's hand impatiently.

Alarice stumbled back a step, lowering her eyes, sniffing heavily. "I am remorseful," she whispered. "Truly, Nicholas."

"Remorse will gain you naught here," he growled.

Lady Julian glided silently past him with a sweep of her black skirts. "I will send for a priest, Alarice," she said, her voice cool and precise. "You must confess, and do penance. And we will pray together for the safety of Emlyn and the children." Alarice nodded, blubbering, as Lady Julian led her away.

"Jesu," Peter said softly, shaking his head.

Still wrestling the bestial strength of his anger, Nicholas took a deep breath, "Summon the garrison to ride out," he barked, and stalked out of the hall.

"By the throat of God," Nicholas said, "King John is here."

Mounted beside him, Peter stared through the white afternoon light. Powdery snow dusted the tiny red-gold curls that escaped from his mail hood. "Aye, 'tis the king's standard above Whitehawke's. And a mickle number of guardsmen on the parapet."

They squinted across the fell toward Graymere Keep, which rose high and solid on a crystalline rise of snow-coated rock, its slanted base surrounded by a frozen moat and backed by a steep cliff. Inside the curtain wall, the old keep jutted up like a mammoth block of stone, a newer hall dwarfed beyond it.

Nicholas swore softly. "Even had we a thousand men behind us, we could not attack with the king inside. No telling how many mercenaries are in there with him."

"Not to mention, of course, that attacking now would be a blatant act of treason," Peter drawled.

Nicholas narrowed his eyes to dangerous steely slits. "My lady wife was stolen this morn, and I will have her back safely, king or no. Jesu! John's presence tears my plans. Am I supposed to walk in there as the former heir and ask politely?" Shaking his head, he swore again in an utter, black sense of frustration.

The frantic ride to Graymere, with a hundred men thundering behind him, had filled Nicholas with an urge to fight, like a bellows builds a fire to a roaring pitch. Now, sitting at the edge of a wood that rimmed the meadow fronting Graymere, Nicholas watched the king's banner flutter over the battlements and felt powerless, halted by the king's presence as if slammed into a wall of stone. He clenched his jaw in anger. If his father stood before him this very moment, Nicholas could not answer for the consequences.

With Peter and Eustace, Nicholas had gathered much of his garrison, including William, who insisted on going. Primed for battle, they had ridden to the site of the capture.

Three guards and the young groom lay out in the still, silent cold, hacked like so much meat, reddened flesh and steel dumped in the snow. Nicholas had left a dozen men to gather up the bodies and transport them to Hawksmoor.

"Damn Chavant to hell," Nicholas muttered, watching Graymere through eyes pinched with tension. "Damn my father as well."

"What does Whitehawke want with Lady Emlyn?" Peter asked. "And why take the children, for the love of saints?"

Nicholas surveyed the castle through the screen of winter-black trees and bracken, noting the frequency of the guards that paced the battlements, adding up numbers as if he clicked an abacus in his mind. The king's men alternated with Whitehawke's guard; he could see the different colors of their cloaks.

There was no way he and his garrison could directly attack and not lose the better part of their group immediately. And they had no siege machines to batter the gates or walls, no means to dig beneath and undermine the towers. The parapet guard nearly matched his own in number. God only knew how many were inside.

After a time he turned to Peter. "Why did Whitehawke take them? Because only Emlyn can give him the man he most wants."

Peter nodded in sudden understanding. "Black Thorne."

"Aye so." Nicholas straightened. "Mayhap Whitehawke shall have him. In exchange, of course, for what I want."

"You cannot mean to give up the Thorne," Peter said, shocked.

"What choice have I?" Nicholas countered quietly. "In order to free my family—" He stopped. The word that fell so naturally from his lips threatened to take his breath, to tear his heart open. His family. Setting his jaw determinedly, he continued. "I wish to see my family safe, and I will risk my life for the privilege." Emlyn and her siblings had come into his solitary life like a gift bestowed on him by heaven's own benevolence. He would not give them up easily, now.

"Your lady wishes to see you alive, my lord. You would do best to think with your head and not your gut," Peter said.

Nicholas shot him a look and opened his mouth to speak, but quickly snapped it shut, frowning off into the distance. "Hold. What is that, beyond there?" He gestured.

Peter glanced in that direction "A supply wagon."

A four-wheeled wagon lumbered over a nearby road, a speck of wood and hides that grew larger as it approached the castle grounds. "One man. Are those barrels of ale?" Nicholas asked in surprise.

The wagon creaked and shushed across the snowy meadow and halted in front of the gate. Shouts, too faint for Nicholas to hear, were exchanged between the driver and the porter, and then the cumbersome wooden drawbridge hovered and thumped down to span the icy moat. Like a hellmouth opening, the iron teeth of the portcullis pulled up slowly to receive the wagon, then swallowed it quickly, slamming shut again.

"A tradesman with ale?" Peter frowned. "Whitehawke must be hosting a Twelfth Night feast for the king."

Nicholas turned to his friend and grinned slowly.

"Nay," Peter said, holding up the palm of his hand. "Nay. Think of the risk. Once in, how could we get them all out? We cannot smuggle in a hundred men to help us fight our way free!"

Nicholas scanned the snow-blanketed countryside and the high-walled enclosure of the keep. His eyelids blinked rapidly as an idea formed in his mind. Appealing. Ridiculous. And possible.

"Come," he said to Peter. "We must return to camp. I need to send out men to scour the villages."

"My lord," Peter said warily, "what plan are you hatching?"

"I am not entirely certain. But we will need tablecloths and baskets of bread. And mayhap some wine or ale."

"A picnic?" Peter looked at him in amazement.

"Certes, a picnic. I am hungry." Nicholas laughed out loud as he turned Sylvanus's head and walked the horse deeper into the lacy black tangle of the winter forest, away from the meadow's edge. He smiled without humor as he snapped the reins. "Aye, hungry for the taste of Chavant's blood on my sword tip."

Chapter Twenty-two

No foul pit, but a prison nonetheless, Emlyn thought. The dim bedchamber was deathly cold in spite of a low fire in the hearth, and a guard stood outside the bolted door. Faint but constant, she could hear the raucous sounds of the feast that continued in the great hall.

Casting a glance at the curtained bed where Betrys slept with the children, Emlyn drew her cloak snug and walked to the window. Though her ribs ached and her jaw was sore and bruised, no amount of fatigue or discomfort would convince her to rest.

After a long, cold, pounding ride to Graymere Keep, they had been led to Whitehawke's newly built chamber hall, and up to this bedchamber near the gallery that overlooked the great hall. A guard had brought bread and watered ale and had bolted the door.

That had been hours ago. Then, quite late in the afternoon, they heard the first thrumming of the pipes and drums as the Twelfth Night feast began in the great hall.

The children had been distracted from their fear, hunger, and boredom by the sounds. Emlyn told them a story and divided the bread between the children and Betrys, only swallowing a dry mouthful herself. Finally she and Betrys had coaxed them to sleep on the deep, dusty feather mattresses.

She lifted the shutter hook, letting in cold air and pale lavender light. Snow feathered down in gentle spirals, and the sky seemed tinted with an amethyst wash. Breathing in the fresh, damp air, she peered out into chill silence.

The chamber hall was built directly into the outer curtain wall. Rough-hewn limestone stretched down to a slanted base, which met the frozen moat far below. Beyond the moat, a steep ravine tumbled away to the black depths of a river. From where she sat, Graymere Keep seemed suspended in an icy ring of water on a base of jagged rock: an impenetrable, inescapable fortress.

She remembered that Nicholas had once mentioned Whitehawke's new keep, built over a steep drop that no army could scale. The older Norman-built tower keep was in the center of the bailey; she vaguely remembered seeing it when they entered.

There was no possibility of escape here. Sighing, she closed the shutters and went to the hearth to sit on a low stool.

She stared into the weak flames. Surely Nicholas knew of the capture by now, and would be on his way to Graymere, enraged and ready for battle.

Whitehawke must intend to keep them as hostages, but why? His fury toward Nicholas must have led him to this. Emlyn was afraid to ponder what else he might attempt.

Closing her eyes, she prayed, and the whispered Latin phrases calmed her a little. After a time, she heard the outer door bar shift, and the door creaked open. Emlyn leaped up to stand straight and firm in the bronze light.

Glancing briefly at the closed bed curtains, Whitehawke walked toward her. His black tunic merged with the shadows and his long white hair reflected the warm light as he stood before her, his pale gaze piercing and flat. The odors of strong wine and oily torch smoke lingered about him. She had not seen him since Ashbourne, and the force of his presence was startling. Raising her chin to return his stare, she tried to quell her fear.

"Lady Emlyn. Your quarters are comfortable?" His voice was a deep rumble, his tone mild.

" 'Tis freezing in here, and the children are hungry, though thank God they sleep for now. Is this how you treat your guests?" she snapped.

"Not usually," he said, towering over her. "God's teeth. I will have you know that the imbecile Chavant gave the order to take the children, not I. Seizing babes is for cowards."

"And for kings."

He tipped an eyebrow. "Such insults are treasonous when spoken within hearing of your king."

"What mean you?"

"King John arrived this morn. He sits at the feast in the hall below this room."

Fear and anger spread like hot poison through her body. She clenched her fists. "Does he know you make prisoners of your son's family?"

"Prisoners? Nay, my lady. You are my daughter-in-law, and will be staying here for a little while."

"Where will the king go when he leaves here?" she asked, suddenly remembering Nicholas's suspicions regarding his father.

He stared at her, his eyelids hooded. "I have no idea. The king comes from sacking the rebels at Pontefract. Since I am one of his most loyal men, he chooses to rest here for a day or two. Do you wish an audience? Think you he will show leniency to the wife of a rebel baron?" He smiled, wolflike and dangerous in the flickering firelight.

"I have neglected to congratulate you on your marriage, my lady," he added. Then, quick as a snake, he grabbed her by the shoulders, forcing her to look up at him. "You were to be my bride. Mine," he said, his hot breath reeking of onion and decay with every wheezy exhalation.

"Nicholas had the prior claim, and took it," she said.

"Where were you those weeks we searched?" he demanded, his voice clotted with anger. He shook her. "You betrayed me! Your absence was a humiliation to me!"

"I—I stayed with villeins, my lord," she said.

"The Green Man? Or did the Thorne keep you?" She winced at his painful grip. He was so much larger than her that he could have lifted her from the floor with no effort. "You stayed with the one who took you. Did you whore yourself for him?"

"My lord," she said, pushing against his powerful arms. "Do not speak to me thus. I did not wish to marry you. When Nicholas offered, I married him, as my father had arranged."

"I am not some snot-faced young suitor for you to reject!"

Her jaw hurt, she was hungry and tired, and her shoulders ached from his grip. "Let go of me," she said irritably, pummeling at him. "Let go!"

He opened his large hands suddenly, and she stumbled free, rubbing her arms and glaring up at him. He hovered over her. "How dare you reject a betrothal arranged by the king!"

Her own anger and discomfort flared like a wall of flame. "I am no sword blade to be used in your war!" she yelled. "You and your son have each wielded me against the other! The king regarded me as just one more sheep to be handed over with Ashbourne! I have been abducted, tricked—" She realized then, with a burst of horror, what she almost said, and mustered her composure. "I am full and proper wed to Nicholas. His offer was accepted by my parents."

"Nicholas wed with you to grind the blade at me, misdoubt it not. Why else wed so quick? You do not carry his child that I can see." He narrowed his eyes. "Where did you hide? And how did he find you when my men could not?" He paused, and then raised his eyebrows as the truth dawned on him. "Of course. He had the children. You went to him."

She remained mute, allowing him to make his suppositions. He nodded, continuing. "But I am not here to rail against you for marrying my son when you were promised to me."

She blinked in surprise. "What do you want, then?"

His blue eyes were shards of ice. "The Black Thorne."

"Thorne?" Her voice sounded wooden, half-witted.

"My men saw you with him at the waterfall. Tell me where he can be found."

She stared dumbly at him. "I know naught of such a man."

"Do not be a fool," he warned her. "By the devil, I scoured half the York shire looking for you—so I could find him! You know where he hides himself in that dale." He reached out and grabbed one loose, uncombed golden braid, drawing her toward him as if he held a leash. "Tell me where to find his lair, my lady, do you wish to see the light of another day!"

"Nicholas will come for me," she said, wincing against the pull on her hair. "He and his garrison will knock at your gate!"

"He would not dare to attack this keep with King John here. And you will be dead ere Nicholas sees you again, if you do not speak! Give me the Black Thorne!"

"Villeins saved me. I know of no Thorne."

"Tell me," he said, his voice rough as crushed stone, his grip tight and sharp on her braid.

"I met villeins only. And all the forest looks alike to me." Two spots of livid color stained his cheeks. "You lie."

"I cannot help you."

Letting go of the plait, he struck her across the face. Stumbling but keeping her balance, she raised her eyes defiantly.

"I cannot help you." She cradled her throbbing cheek.

"You can and you shall. The bratlings will stay here under guard. Your silence will harm them, my lady. Remember that. Give me what I ask, for their sake."

She stared at him silently, breathing hard, her mind whirling. Nicholas and the children were each threatened, whether she stayed silent or spoke. She had to risk that Whitehawke would not actually harm children. She said nothing.

Grabbing her arm, Whitehawke dragged her across the room to the door and pulled it open.

"Mayhap you will not care for our *donjon*," he said, and shoved her across the threshold into Chavant's waiting arms.

Icy bursts of wind whipped at her cloak as Chavant hauled her across the bailey like a recalcitrant mule. An eerie half light was cast by gently falling snow. Whitehawke strode ahead briskly, crossing the yard, passing soldiers and servants without a word.

Rising from the center of the bailey like a monolithic stone box, the old keep blocked the wind and the milky light. Emlyn stumbled up the steep, crumbling steps and entered the darkened doorway, pushed by Chavant. Whitehawke lifted a burning torch from its stone socket just inside the door, and mounted a flight of curving steps ahead of them.

He spoke over his shoulder, "This tower keep was built over a hundred years ago. We use its rooms for storage now." His tone was mild and conversational. "If we are ever besieged, our attackers would run short of supplies long before we would. Every room is packed with stores—sacks of flour, barley, oats, and beans. Barrels of cured meat and salted fish. Tuns of wine and ale, and water enough to fill a pond. Resin torches, candles, blankets—enough to keep us for six months or more."

Listening as she went, pushed upward by Chavant's prodding hand at her back, Emlyn negotiated the steps carefully, stumbling a little over the dips and bumps in the worn stone.

At the third and uppermost level, Whitehawke stopped at a door. "One chamber here is not used for stores." She heard the shrill scrape of a key, and the door creaked open.

Shoved inside the room, she pulled back her hood and looked around. Beyond the pool of light created by Whitehawke's torch, she saw only shapes and degrees of darkness.

"Chavant," Whitehawke said, "get down to the hall and see to our lord king. Bring word if he needs my attendance."

Chavant nodded and left, shutting the door. Whitehawke turned in the center of the room, holding the torch high. "But for dust, this room looks just as it looked then."

Her eyes adjusted to the dimness, and Emlyn saw a curtained bed, a high-backed chair, a table, a wooden chest emerge from the shadows as the torch swept in slow circles. A large tapestry hung on one wall, and the wall opposite was pierced by a slender arrow-slit window.

Thick dust coated every surface. Cobwebs spun delicate, lacy bridges between the table and the bed, the canopy and the wooden rafters in the ceiling. Emlyn's nose twitched, and she coughed.

Whitehawke set the torch in an iron sconce high in the wall, then strolled to the table and ran a finger along the dusty surface. "She spent her last days here."

Cold, fleshy bumps rose along Emlyn's arms. "Lady Blanche?"

"Aye," he said gruffly. "This was her favorite chamber in the days when we lived in this keep. She would watch the stars here, of a night."

Emlyn stepped closer. "You speak of her with affection."

He blew out a mirthless chuckle. "I admired her beauty. She had eyes like silver, hair like ebony. She had a sharp mind for a woman, and could read and cipher like a priest. She had good knowledge, as well, of plant medicines." He shrugged. "But women are weak and untrustworthy creatures. She betrayed me. Humiliated me."

"She gave you a son, she ran your household," Emlyn offered.

"Blanche betrayed her marriage vows. She had a lover, though she would not admit it. I knew the man, a knight. I confronted them, challenged him to a tourney. Julian can tell you this."

"I have heard none of it," Emlyn murmured.

"I knocked the man from his charger and killed him. Then I went home and shut my wife in this room."

"You imprisoned her."

" 'Twas not unheard of. Even King Henry shut his Eleanor up to keep her hands from the reins and quell her tongue. I locked her in to teach her humility. And I sent her son to her sister."

"What happened to Lady Blanche?"

"She starved to death," he said flatly. "Here in this room." He rubbed a hand over his face and hair, wildly, as if scrubbing at something. Snow light from the window picked out shining peaks in his hair, like demon's horns. "Before a week was out."

"My God," Emlyn breathed. She knew of people who had fasted for ten days and more and been no worse for it. Others, though, were more fragile, and suffered ill after a day or two.

"I eat no flesh. I fast often. I had a convent built."

"You regret your cruelty, my lord," she said. "The priests say God forgives those who repent."

He turned to stare at her. "I have no regrets," he snarled. "Her death was her parting insult to me. She died rather than admit her adultery, out of spite. I ask no forgiveness from God. I was in the right."

Emlyn blinked at him, confused. "Then why do you forgo flesh food? Why the convent?"

"Priests' advice for the sake of my eternal soul. I do not regret the punishment I gave her, but Blanche showed me a final humiliation. Her death keeps me from heaven." He pounded a fist on the table. "Do you hear? She keeps me from heaven!"

"Lord Whitehawke." Emlyn held her voice firm, though her heart beat rapidly. "My lord, do not commit another such act. Let us go. Send the children, at least, back to Hawksmoor."

He paced the room, and she realized that he was very

drunk from his Twelfth Night feast, for he swayed and shuffled at the turns. "Nay," he said, shaking his head. "I cannot
let you go. You, too, have betrayed me, and caused me humiliation."

He crossed the room and grabbed Emlyn's face in one
large hand, his meaty fingers cold on her skin, his grip
forcing her head back. "Give me my enemy if you would be
free."

"I have said I cannot help you."

His fingers pressed deep into her jaw, bruising the skin.
"No woman will ever best me again." He was panting now,
and reached a hand to rub his upper chest, though his grip
on her face grew tighter. "Give me the Black Thorne!"

She met his glare with her own, silently, her breathing a
soft rhythm between his noisy exhalations.

"Why such loyalty, lady?" he drawled dangerously. " 'Tis
misplaced. You owe fealty to your husband, and to the bratlings in the chamber hall." He shoved her then, violently,
and she fell back, crashing down onto the bed. The straw-
filled mattress rustled beneath her, raising a cloud of mold
and dust.

"Stay here, then," he bellowed, "and think on Blanche's
fate!" His dark height towered over her, and he raised his
hand. She winced away, covering her face, listening to his
hoarse breathing. After a moment, he turned and went to the
door.

"Soon you will see the wisdom in speaking. You are
stronger stock than Blanche. A time without sustenance will
clear your thoughts, as any holy fast will do."

He opened and then slammed the door. Emlyn heard the
key rotate in the lock. Leaping from the bed, she ran to pull
at the ring handle set in the door.

"Nay!" she screamed. "You cannot!" Beating on the door
until the soft flesh of her palms was bruised, she heard only
silence. Thick walls and three levels of chambers stuffed
with sacks and barrels absorbed sound like a tower of
feather beds.

After a while, Emlyn crossed to the window. Freezing air
soothed her heated face. Beyond the beveled stone frame, the
sky shimmered with infinitesimal layers of falling snow.

She extended her arm out the deep-set, narrow aperture,

able to reach no farther than her elbow. Tiny flakes fluttered and melted on her palm, cold and fresh and pure. Far across the courtyard, faint sounds from the Twelfth Night feast drifted, muffled by the silent, thick snowfall.

Chapter Twenty-three

"Christ's trews, our friendship is at an end for certain," Peter muttered. He squirmed on the cart seat and adjusted his gauzy veil. "I swear, my lord, next tourney that is given, I will win enough land to leave your service at last."

Nicholas looked over his shoulder as he leaned forward and slapped the reins. "If we live through this, I shall give you the land myself and be glad to see you gone. An old grandmother could not gripe more."

"An old grandmother would not have had to shave off a mustache for a friend's cause." Peter picked at the folds of his skirt.

Nicholas cast his friend a side glance and pinched down a smile. "Mayhap not. But I am too tall to be the wench. Brush up those charming red curls of yours, and we will gain admittance without delay."

"This is a witless scheme," Peter complained. He spread his knees and propped one boot upon the side of the cart.

"But costumes are always welcome on Twelfth Night."

Peter grunted sullenly. "Go milk cranes."

"You have armor and weapons beneath that pretty borrowed gown and cloak of yours. Remove the female clothing as soon as we are in, and out of sight, if it makes you feel better."

"I feel a twatling fool," Peter muttered.

"Well, even with that tender babe's face of yours, you still need this darkness to pass as a woman," Nicholas said, urging the slow ox forward as they lumbered closer to the castle walls. "Think you the gatesmen would admit two armed knights?"

"Nay. But the miller and his wife, bringing ale and baskets of fresh bread for the feast, will be inside in a trice."

"Aye, and the ruse had better get us in. I paid near the miller's income for a year for this wagon, and the same all round the village for the bread and ale and clothing. Straighten up, would you, and sit as becomes a woman. We are near the drawbridge." Nicholas pulled the hood of his cloak down to shadow his face in the reflected light of the thick, rapid snowfall. Soft drifts covered the ground and piled on the parapet and against the base of the castle in gracefully tapered shapes, nearly glowing in the darkness.

"Ho! Gateman!" Nicholas called heartily.

The gateman answered with a suspicious query, and Nicholas gestured broadly to his cart. "Thomas Miller, with the fresh loaves my lord Whitehawke did order from the village for this even's feast."

"Yer late to be bringing it," the gateman growled. "Who's that with ye?"

"Me wife," he called back. "She and the village women baked as quick as they could on short notice. Mayhap we're late, but we're here and expecting payment from the steward. And I have two kegs of double ale."

"Double ale, is it?"

"Aye, Kentish, too. Sent by the innkeeper."

Permission was quickly given, and the drawbridge groaned and thumped into place. Guiding the cart across the bridge, Nicholas was stopped beneath the portcullis vault. The gateman, stepping out, stated that any weapons were to be left with him. Nicholas shrugged and lifted his cloak to show he had no sword or knife at his belt. Beneath the long cloak, he wore a dark wool tunic, with thick hosen and sturdy boots wrapped to the knees. His hair straggled in his eyes, and with his grimy hands and stubbly beard, he could only be taken for a villein. Beside him, Peter clutched a blue cloak over the gown and his armor beneath it, and simpered as best he could. The gateman nodded and waved them into the bailey.

Once inside, Nicholas jumped down and came around to assist Peter, whose red-gold curls peeked out from under a plain veil. A soldier winked, smiling in the torchlight. Peter scowled and turned away.

Servants came forward to help unload several large, deep, reed-woven baskets piled high with round loaves of bread, carrying them toward the chamber hall. As other servants struggled to unload the clumsy wooden ale kegs, Nicholas took up the last basket himself.

He and Peter set off across the bailey toward the chamber hall, their boots shuffling through gathering drifts. Torches flickering on tall spikes gave the bailey an unnatural light and threw giant halos out into the swirling, flurrying snow.

"Witless," muttered Peter.

"Quiet, you cretin," Nicholas growled. "Once inside, we will find Emlyn and the children, get them out, and then judge our next move, whether to summon my garrison or leave as we came in."

"A noddy-headed plan. Attack and rescue, there's a scheme."

"A pity you never took to the forest life," Nicholas murmured. "Outwitting my father is much preferable to an attack in certain circumstances." He tilted his head meaningfully, and Peter glanced across the courtyard.

The far end of the bailey looked like a horse fair. More than two hundred horses stood inside a makeshift enclosure. Dozens of armed guards milled about, while grooms darted back and forth with feed bags, blankets and currying brushes. The armorer's building, and next to it the blacksmith's, were both alight with stoked firepits and blazing torches, and full of noise and bustle as stacks of swords and lances were greased and repaired, broken harnesses were reinforced, and horseshoes were shaped on the anvil.

Outside the armory stood two huge war machines, a wooden catapult and a rolling battering ram suspended by massive chains on a framework, their giant superstructures powdered and piled with fresh snow.

Peter whistled low. "Jacky Softsword and his traveling players," he said.

"Aye, a bloody army, and best avoided."

They ducked their heads deeper into their cloaks and hurried toward the hall at the back of the bailey complex.

"Since we must deliver the bread," Nicholas murmured, "we shall search the chamber hall first. If they are there, our plan has a good chance of success." He shifted the heavy basket and shot a cautious glance around the bailey. Thank God, no soldiers cared to bother a tradesman and his wife.

They easily gained admittance to the hall by handing fresh loaves to the watchmen. Inside, warmth and light and noise assailed them from every angle. Candles and torches gave off golden light and a thin, pervasive smoke filled the air, stinging Nicholas's eyes. He inhaled the tantalizing aroma of roasted meat and savory spiced dishes, and though his mouth watered, he felt no hunger, only cold vengeance.

The long, high-ceilinged hall teemed with men, most of them drunk, all of them eating or drinking or talking loudly. The humming din of hundreds of deep voices nearly drowned the lilting music played by a troupe of musicians at one end of the room. Nicholas noted that no one, beyond the king's personal guard, wore weapons. Such could not be allowed during a feast, especially when the feasters were primarily soldiers on respite from battle.

Nicholas saw the king at the table on a raised dais, a dark head and bejeweled fingers waving and gesturing in animated boisterous conversation. He saw Whitehawke there, too, and turned quickly away.

Moving toward the stairs with Peter in his wake, he thought the upper chambers a likely place to search. If he had to upturn every stick in the castle, he would find them.

A group of soldiers spotted them and reached for the bread that was piled up in the basket. Nicholas complied, careful to keep his head down, though with his hair mussed and hanging in a tangle in his eyes and his face unshaven, he doubted anyone would look closely at him and see Nicholas de Hawkwood.

Behind him, Peter slapped away a lusty hand. Nicholas turned to the soldier who persistently pulled on Peter's cloak.

"My wife, sir, if you please," he said, filling the man's hand with a crusty loaf and nudging Peter toward the stairs.

Edging their way to the gallery, they rounded the broad stone pillar and slipped up the steps.

"By all that's holy," Peter hissed, "to be caught like this before the king and hundreds of soldiers would be hell's own punishment!" He tore off the veil, cloak, and gown, and stuffed them in the basket. "I will take my chances in armor," he muttered, adjusting the lay of his mesh hauberk and pulling up the heavy hood to cover his hair.

"There are enough mercenaries here, with different surcoats and armor, that you can pass for a routier," Nicholas said, "but for God's sake put your sword away."

Sliding the sword from his scabbard, Peter slipped it into the long, deep basket, pulling a fold of the cloak up to cover it. "Now, my lord, where are they kept?" he asked.

"A question for the saints, I trow," Nicholas replied. "Mayhap we should search the upper floors and work down." Reaching the gallery level, he hesitated, and then started up the steps again.

"Hold!" Peter whispered. "Look there—at the end of the gallery. A guard stands by that door."

Nicholas edged around the curve of the central stair pillar. "Aye," he murmured low. "Shall we ask him how he fares?"

"Ho, serjeant," Peter called, striding down the corridor. "I am sent to relieve you. Have you eaten at the feast, or had any of the double ale that has just arrived?"

The soldier blinked at him in surprise. "Nay, I have only had some wine." He frowned. "Lord Whitehawke sent you here?"

Peter leaned forward. "Aye, and me a king's man. But we are under orders to cooperate with Whitehawke while we are here. And he is drunker than the devil on Lammas night. Astonishing that he even remembered what is up here," he said, and jerked his head toward the door.

"They're all asleep, quiet as a tomb," the serjeant said.

"Good, good. Less work for us, eh? Ah, here is the miller, newly come with fresh bread," Peter said heartily. The guard looked toward Nicholas, who came down the hall carrying the basket. Peter grabbed the serjeant around the neck, pulling tight, while Nicholas yanked the sword out of the basket and struck the hilt against the man's head. With a low groan, the guard slumped over. Peter bent to arrange him in a seated position by the door, then picked up the guard's wine cup and tossed the contents in his face.

"Cupshot," he said distastefully.

Nicholas put his mouth to the fine crack between the oak door and the stone jamb. "Emlyn!" he called in a loud whisper. He tilted his head, waiting for a response. He did not relish breaking into the wrong room. "Christien!"

Soft footsteps padded on the other side. "Christien is sleeping, sir," a small voice replied.

"Isobel! Are you well? Are the others with you?"

"We're fine, my lord. Have you brought food? I'm hungry," she said plaintively.

"Stand back, my girl." He lifted the heavy drawbar from its stone rests and slid it into the storage place beside the door. Pushing the door open, he and Peter slipped inside.

Isobel stood by the bed, shaking Betrys awake. Christien bobbed up, blinking sleepily, and the nursemaid shrieked and grabbed Isobel to her.

"Hush, girl," Peter said to the maid. "We are taking all of you out of here. Quietly now, ready the little ones." Betrys nodded and began to gather the children's cloaks and shoes.

Nicholas stood by the door, his brow creased into a deep frown as he watched them. A muscle in his jaw worked rapidly. "Where is Lady Emlyn?" he asked in a quiet, severe voice.

Christien looked up. "She was here, but Lord Whitehawke took her, my lord."

"Took her where?" he demanded, crossing the room.

Betrys knelt before Christien, pulling a cloak around his shoulders. "We know not, my lord. 'Twas hours ago he took my lady."

"My lord," Christien said, jumping nervously while Betrys fastened his cloak snug under his throat, "I know where she is. In the dungeon."

"Dungeon?" Nicholas asked sharply. He knelt, eye level with the boy. "Tell me what you know."

"I was awake, but they thought me asleep. He asked her to give him something, a thorn, I think he said, and she said him nay. He hit her, and she said nay again, and then he said she would not like his dungeon. And he took her away."

Nicholas closed his eyes for a moment, drawing in a deep breath and letting it out slowly. "Thank you, Christien." He stood and turned to Peter. "If she is hurt, he will not last a day, father or no."

"Well enough. But we have a task here first."

Nodding brusquely, Nicholas went to the window and opened the shutter. He scanned the walls below and to each side, striving to see through the swirling snowstorm. Sweeping at his wildly blowing hair, he turned around.

"We can only try. Give the signal."

Peter gathered a few of the floor rushes, went to the hearth, and lit them into a spitting, blazing torch. At the window, he thrust out his arm and waved the flame, then released the burning rushes to fall and flutter with the snowflakes.

Nicholas turned to Betrys, who had tied the silken strings of Isobel's cloak and now leaned over the bed to wake Harry.

"Hold," he said softly. Betrys looked up. "Go gently. Keep the babe well asleep, if you can."

Betrys understood. "He is a noisy mite," she said.

"Remember the apple tree?" Nicholas asked Christien. "This will be easier by far, you need only stay still. You are a brave lad, and we shall keep you safe." Christien sat curled in the deep basket like a babe in a womb, blinking his eyes rapidly and nodding. Nicholas tugged at the net of hempen ropes he had woven about the bottom of the basket, and pulled firmly on the longer ropes that would lower it. "Ready, Peter. Are they there?"

Peter peered out the window. "Aye, I think. The snow is very thick."

Dragging the basket toward the window, Nicholas leaned his head out. Wind whipped his hair and icy flakes of snow bit at his face. "By God's teeth," he said, "this approaches a blizzard!" He looked down. "Look there. On the moat."

Below them, a cluster of snowdrifts seemed to move along the moat's frozen surface, near the brink of the cliff. Through the feathering snow, because he knew what to look for, Nicholas could discern the shapes of several of his men, hunched over, covered with white tablecloths. They scuttled along and stopped beneath the window, where Peter waved a lit candle.

"Picnic, indeed," Peter said, and blew out the little flame. "Interesting use of table linen, my lord."

"Queen Matilda once escaped from a tower this way, I have heard," Nicholas said. "Seemed a good idea, I thought, with snow in the air." He looked down again. "Eustace and the others would not be on the ice if 'twere not solid through. They can go back along the moat, and the ravine will be no threat. If they can see where they go, in that storm," he added.

"The ropes we smuggled in the basket should be long enough to lower them," Peter said. "The drop looks about thirty or forty feet. But the wind is strong, and this boy weighs no more than a goose feather."

Nicholas nodded, glancing around the room. Then he looked back at Peter. "Give me your hauberk."

Peter frowned. "Warming stones, or a few books—"

"There are none in here. The mesh weighs a bit more than the child, yet takes up little space. 'Twill help fight the winds."

"Aye, so." Peter sighed, and began to untie the laces between his mesh hood and his short-sleeved hauberk, wriggling out of it with quick assistance from Nicholas.

Clad in his quilted linen gambois and mesh leggings, Peter squatted down and settled the springy, jingling mass of steel rings around the boy's feet. "Pray ask Eustace to send this back up," he said. "Your sister will have need of it."

Christien nodded. Nicholas picked up a folded white tablecloth, also smuggled in the basket, and tossed it over Christien, lifting the corner for a moment.

"Saint Michael be with you, boy," he whispered, smiling. "You are about to feel like you have angel's wings."

Christien smiled tremulously, with a wide, trusting gaze that wrenched at Nicholas's heart. Working together, Nicholas and Peter hoisted the basket to the edge of the window, then squeezed and compressed it through the aperture. Slowly, they began to pulley it downward, tugging the ropes taut as they fed them out the window.

"Jesu," Peter grunted as he pulled, " 'tis a mickle dangerous thing to do, with a child."

"By the rood, Perkin, well I know it." While his muscles contracted with the effort to keep the movement of the basket slow and steady, his gut contracted with a dread that near overwhelmed him. He would have done this any other way if he had seen a choice. The danger in which he had placed these children terrified him; yet it was, he knew, a fear based on love.

Half a year earlier, these children had been like pups underfoot to be stepped over or around, not requiring his attention. But gradually, somehow, each one had gained a personhood. He wanted them safe, as much as he wanted their golden-haired sister safe.

He shook his head against his distracting thoughts, and concentrated on his task. While Peter held the rope steady, he pulled hand over hand toward the window to peer out.

"Nearly down," he said, his hair tearing back away from his brow in the wind. "Without the hauberk, that basket would have swung like an oak leaf."

They felt a stiff yank on the rope. Nicholas peered down again. "They have him," he said, his throat closing over the words. "He is safe. Ho, here comes the basket."

Within a few minutes, they had Isobel curled in the nest of mesh armor. Harry, awake but by some miracle silent, watched them with wide eyes as he was placed in Isobel's lap and covered with Peter's cloak.

Whispering words of encouragement, Nicholas bent down to the little girl, who wrapped her arms fiercely around his neck. He kissed her glossy dark head, touched Harry's back gently, then covered the basket with the white cloth. Betrys, her eyes glazed with nervous tears, bit on her fist as Nicholas and Peter lowered the basket again to the ground.

When it returned, Peter grumbled that they had neglected to send back his hauberk. Next they fixed a rope sling for Betrys' plump bottom, draped the last white cloth over her as she gripped the rope, and shoved and pushed until she was through the window.

When she had been lowered, Nicholas hauled the rope back up, and spoke without looking at Peter. "You go next."

"Nay. I'll not leave you."

"I need you outside the castle with Eustace and the garrison. When I find Emlyn, we will go out in the miller's cart. We came in as two, not three," he reminded him.

"Know you where the dungeon is?"

"I shall find it. Go, before the storm worsens."

Peter stared hard at Nicholas, then sighed, and scratched his head, standing armorless but for his leggings, in his long padded undertunic and boots. "Without my hauberk, I feel strangely naked. Ah well, I came in looking like a mummer's churl. I may as well leave in a similar condition," he said, shrugging.

Nicholas laughed. "Take my cloak," he said, handing it to him, "and your weapon as you depart the castle." He reached for the sword hilt, which stuck up out of the basket.

"Nay, my lord," Peter said. "You may have need of a good blade." Nicholas nodded, and jammed the sword into his belt.

"Tie the rope to that pillar and toss it out. I can climb down, I think," Peter said. The rope was soon fixed around a freestanding pillar that supported the low ceiling arch. With one of the pale linen bed sheets wrapped around him like a concealing cocoon, Peter was soon ready. He clapped Nicholas's shoulder.

"We will watch for your signal," Peter said, and leaped up to wriggle through the window. A few minutes later he had joined the others on the ground. Nicholas leaned at the window and watched as the white-clad group, obscured by swirling snowflakes, scurried off toward safety in the direction of the forest edge.

Shoving the empty basket and remaining rope into a corner, he opened the door and peered out into the darkened corridor.

A cacophony of snores reverberated around the great hall and echoed into the open gallery level. The earlier blazing torchlight from the hall had reduced to a coppery glow; the feast was over and the castle was bedded. Closing the door softly behind him, Nicholas rested one hand on his sword hilt, stepped over the collapsed guard, and set off in search of the dungeon.

Chapter Twenty-four

Tiny flakes of snow fluttered and fell in the darkness as Nicholas emerged from a door on the lower level of the chamber hall. Glancing warily around, he moved like a wraith along the shadowed base of the curtain wall, his steps muffled by feathery drifts of snow.

With cautious exploration, he had discovered that the chamber hall had rooms filled with drunken and exhausted sleepers, and a few storage rooms, but no dungeon cells. Most of Whitehawke's soldiers and servants and the king's mercenaries lay sleeping on pallets scattered everywhere, even in the corridors. Those few remaining awake were noisy enough to give him ample warning as he slipped through the halls and out of the building. Deciding that the mural towers were likely places to keep prisoners, he headed for the nearest tower.

Once inside, he followed the curved stairs upward, finding no lower level. Investigating each of the three floors carefully, he found only empty guard rooms and snoring men. The strong drink in Whitehawke's guest cups had made his search uncomplicated so far, he thought, as he slipped outside. Three other towers, explored in a similar fashion, yielded nothing.

Hesitating just inside the fourth tower, he ran cold fingers through his dampened hair in frustration. Hearing voices above, and the clanking thud of iron-trimmed boots on the stairs, he went back outside to press into a dark corner. The door swung open nearly in his face.

Three guards emerged from the tower and set off across the bailey, murmuring indistinctly. Then one whooped, a gleeful echo, and scooped up a handful of snow, tossing it at the others. A few snowballs danced back and forth among them as they crossed the yard.

Catching the door, Nicholas eased back into the tower and moved stealthily up the steps, through the profound silence that filled the cylindrical space of the stairwell.

On the first level, a door left slightly ajar opened quietly beneath his hand. The scant light of a glowing brazier cast long shadows, illumining the head and shoulders of a man at the table, bent over a parchment.

Outside, faintly heard, the guard whooped again. The man at the table glanced up, then slowly turned his head.

Curling his fingers around the slim hilt of the long dagger tucked at the back of his belt, Nicholas stared into the surprised, uneven gaze of Hugh de Chavant. Making a quick decision, he stepped into the shadowy room.

"What do you want?" Chavant demanded irritably. "There are no sleeping quarters here for villeins. Begone from here, man."

Nicholas crossed the room so fast that Chavant barely had time to rise from the table. The knife flashed and the glistening point rested against Chavant's throat as he stumbled back, half falling against the bench. Nicholas leaned over him, a glaring, shadowy, unkempt wild man, his hair dangling in damp, snow-dusted strings over his brow.

"Who are you?" Chavant rasped. "What do you want?"

"Where is she?"

Chavant blinked at him, then narrowed his eyes. "My God," he said slowly. "I know you. The Black Thorne."

Nicholas pressed the blade tip closer. "Tell me where the lady is held. Your throat is soft as any pig's belly, I trow," he hissed. "Call out to your guards, and they will slip in your blood. Where is Lady Emlyn?"

"God's eyes!" Chavant said suddenly. "Nicholas! I thought you were the—"

"Answer my question, Hugh," he growled.

"Your lady is well, my lord. But I cannot say where she is held. Whitehawke would be loathe to see her go just yet."

Slowly Nicholas drew the point across Chavant's throat, raising a thin scratch. Blood welled in tiny drops. "I seek no courtesy from you and I return none. You seized my wife and the children like a true coward. Give her up to me now, or my troops will destroy these walls."

Wincing at the sting of the cut, Chavant flared his nostrils. "Whitehawke has shut her away until she says where—" He inhaled sharply as he studied Nicholas. "Ah," he said, "By the rood. I believe the Black Thorne has come for her after all. You—"

Nicholas grabbed a handful of chain mail, hauling Chavant up to a seated position, pressing the blade close. "By God, I feel inclined to slit your craven throat here and now and find her myself. I make no meaningless jests. Where is she held?"

Chavant whimpered softly, sweat on his brow. "Please—"

With swift strength, Nicholas hoisted him to a standing position and wrenched him around to trap one arm behind, resting the knife blade just under his ear. "Take me to her. Now."

Chavant stumbled forward as Nicholas pushed him toward the door. "By God," he said, "you have been the Thorne all along. Your father will be greatly disappointed in you."

"An improvement, then, in his opinion of me," Nicholas said as they descended the curving steps.

Stepping meekly through the outer door, Chavant started across the bailey. They slogged through fresh snow piled in blowing drifts. Ahead, a bulky cluster of wagons took on the shape of a ghost-white hill.

Biting cold snapped at Nicholas's ears and nose and filled his lungs. The dagger felt like silver ice in his hand, numbing his bare fingers.

"Christ's arse," Chavant said, his words blowing back to Nicholas. " 'Tis bitter as demon's milk out here. Your garrison would never attack in such weather. Horses could not make it across the moors."

"My garrison stands ready and close by. Snow will not hinder them. If they do not hear from me within a certain time, they will advance on Graymere."

"Fool! King John is here."

"I know that. But the king's presence is not much of a deterrent, since he may already plan to ride for Hawksmoor when he leaves here. What matter, then, where the battle is fought?"

Bursting out of the swirling snow, something whacked Chavant full in the side of the head. He threw up his free arm and folded to his knees, collapsing forward. Another snowball rushed between them. Nicholas struggled to keep hold of Chavant as they went down in the deep snow. Nearby, he heard laughter quickly change to shouts of alarm, and footsteps shushed through the snow toward them. Regaining his balance quickly and half standing, he dragged Chavant to his knees.

"Stand!" he ordered.

"Guards!" Chavant yelled. Nicholas dropped the dagger and yanked at the hilt of Peter's sword just as he was broadsided by two men. His knee plunged into a cold, deep snowdrift, but he managed to clear and swing the sword. With a ragged scream, one of the guards fell away from him, clutching at a wounded thigh.

Nicholas leaped to his feet in a wide, swaying stance. The other guard drew his sword and faced him, competent enough with the broadsword, but without subtlety. Even in the darkness, Nicholas saw the opening and plunged forward with the force of his weight, feeling the sickening crunch of rib bones as the blade penetrated the unprotected area beneath the guard's arm.

Before he had a chance to swing again, he was rammed from behind and tossed like a sack of grain. Several guards held him down; he could not tell how many piled on him. Their weight pressed his face and body flat in the snow. Struggling for breath, he turned his head to the side. His arm was pinned and the sword was torn from his numb fingers. Shouts and thundering footsteps seemed to come from every angle as he lay in the frozen, powdery depth, pushing futilely against the weight of those who held him down.

"Bring him to his feet," Chavant snapped.

Nicholas was hauled upright. Guards seemed to circle everywhere nearby. Two men held his arms, angling them behind his back, pulling forcefully on his frontal chest muscles. A mailed fist grabbed a handful of Nicholas's long hair and yanked his head back. Someone tilted a sword tip at his throat, ensuring that he made no move.

Chavant stepped forward. "Well, then," he sneered, "I have snagged the prize for Lord Whitehawke." He jerked his head to one side. "Take him to the hall, and guard him well. And send someone to wake the earl."

As Nicholas was led away, he thought he heard a voice, sweet and high, call his name. The faint sound was lost in the cold whisper of the wind. Turning his head to hear, the blunt end of an axe smashed into his cheekbone. Stars blazed in his eyes.

"Emlyn!" he answered, screaming out into the night as he was dragged relentlessly forward. *"Emlyn!"*

The stone wall was slick with a thin layer of ice beneath her fingertips. Emlyn raised on her toes and leaned as far into the deep-set window niche as she could, straining to see.

Shouts and the solid clang of steel had drawn her to the window. Craning her neck and peering down and left, she could glimpse movement below. An amorphous shape rolled in the yard beneath the keep, finally recognizable as two men engaged in a vicious sword fight. Several guards ran through the bailey, converging on the two who fought.

The guards jumped one man and wrestled him to the ground. He struggled as they jerked him to his feet. When someone yanked his head back, the snow light gave his face a pale clarity.

Emlyn's eyes widened. "Nicholas!" she screamed, but her voice seemed to fade against the snow and wind. "Oh, God. Nicholas!" The guards pulled him out of sight of the arrowslit.

"Emlynnn!" The poignant, anguished cry wrenched her very soul. She felt utterly, painfully helpless. Sobbing bitterly, she slid to the floor, covering her face in her hands. Tears drenched her face and her shoulders collapsed inward.

Whitehawke would soon discover, she thought in a panic, that his son was Thorne. The awful destiny that Nicholas had teased, time and again, had finally come to him. She feared that Whitehawke, in his rage, would kill Nicholas.

Even as she wept, she realized that Nicholas would maintain his calm, steady courage no matter what course Whitehawke took. Best, she thought, to try to do the same.

But no such bravery dwelled in her, she thought miserably, wiping her eyes with the back of her hand. The only flashes of courage she had ever felt had burst from no more noble place than her quick, hot temper. She had always struggled with her fears.

Thinking of Nicholas, she could almost feel his strength flow into her, palpable and warm. Straightening, she drew a shaky breath, her need to be with him growing even more urgent.

Somehow, she would leave this tower and find Nicholas and the children. Hawksmoor's garrison would be coming soon to aid them, she was certain, and they could get away from here together.

Thrusting to her feet, she sniffed and turned to pace. Nicholas would tell her to think and then act, not fret. She could not sit and weep while her husband and family suffered.

While she could try to free herself, she would have to trust to God and the saints for the rest. Faith, honor, courage, hope, all these, she had been taught, were virtues cut of the same cloth, the fabric of inner strength. That was what she sensed, had always admired, in Nicholas. If 'twas within her, too, then now came the test that would find it.

Going to the door, she passed her hand slowly over the flat, bolted iron lock. The original latch was a simple iron pin that pivoted, pulled by a leather thong. The lock below it must have been added when the chamber was converted to a prison.

Earlier, Emlyn had tugged on the latch pin and the iron ring in the center of the door until her fingers were bruised. Still, she thought, with the right tool, the lock could be forced open.

She determined to tear apart the chamber, if necessary, to find some object that would break the lock. Hoping to find scissors or a knife or some other metal tool in the wooden chest beside the bed, she went to it and knelt down, pulling at the lid until the stiff hinges creaked open.

Chapter Twenty-five

Bitter, bone-cracking cold, like death, like hell's own ice, crept into his limbs. All around him darkness, and an eerie, flat silence. This would be his eternity: the cold, the dark, silence without end, and total helplessness.

Nicholas awoke with a start, and shook his head to dispel the clinging misery of the dream. A dream that echoed his reality—pitch-black, and freezing cold. The chamber was the same one that had held the children, but the low fire had extinguished, allowing the damp, bitter chill to settle in, while more cold seeped through the window shutters.

He lay on the floor, ankles and wrists bound tightly with ropes. Blinking, he looked around, unsure how much time had passed. But he doubted that Whitehawke, once informed of his capture, would let him lay here long. The light through the shutter cracks hinted at early dawn.

He had not come along to this chamber easily, and the process of dragging him here and binding him had given him, in addition to the bruised cheek, a swollen, tender lip and a couple of very painful ribs. He lay curled on his side, now fully alert, and breathed deeply to conquer pain, thirst, and hunger. His mouth felt as scummy as old rushes. He wished, quite simply, that he had eaten before he came here. He wished he had a cloak.

Chavant had ordered that Nicholas be taken to the only chamber in the overcrowded castle that housed no other guests: the room where the children were kept.

Erupting into a fury upon discovering that the chamber was empty, its only guard apparently passed out drunk, Chavant had whipped Nicholas across the face with the end of his mailed glove. Then he had stalked off to find

Whitehawke, grumbling to one of the guards that the earl was being detained by the king.

Now, bending his legs as he lay on the floor, Nicholas tried to grope for the small steel dagger tucked in his boot, but could not reach it with his wrists bound behind him and his ankles tied. Finally he lay on his back and lifted his legs, shaking them until the blade eased out of his boot-top and thunked down onto his chest. Then he dumped it onto the floor and shifted to grasp the wooden hilt with his long fingers.

Sawing laboriously at the thick hempen ropes, wincing as he nicked his hand once, he manipulated the thin sharp knife until he felt less resistance in the ropes and scratchy tendrils touched his arms. The work was not near finished, for the ropes were wound three times or more around his leather wristbands.

Once he had the use of hands and feet, he would get free of the chamber, even if it meant calling in the guard to use the dagger blade on him. Emlyn was here somewhere, and he meant to find her. All the better if he could get out before Whitehawke returned to delay him, he thought cynically.

The problem that remained was what had gotten him into this thick soup in the first place: where was Emlyn? He had lived at Graymere as a child, and did not remember a dungeon. And the design of the new hall and older towers did not allow space for such cells.

Struggling, lurching, writhing, he managed to sit up and scoot over to lean against the bed, though his ribs paid him with such pain that he regretted the movement afterward. He creased his brow as he wielded the dagger behind him. Where had Chavant been leading him when he was set upon by the guards? They had been crossing the bailey toward the old keep, and beyond it, to the remaining two mural towers.

But there was no dungeon, he knew for certain, in the old tower keep, where the living quarters had been when he was a child. Built like its Norman counterparts, high and block-like for defense, it rested on a stone foundation with a few storage rooms below, a massive limestone coffin set on end.

Still, Christien had said dungeon.

Nicholas stopped sawing and nearly dropped the knife. The boy had said "dungeon"—in English.

Whitehawke might have spoken to Emlyn in French. The
Frank word for keep was *donjon.*

Sweet Christ! Emlyn was in the keep.

A rumbling blend of voices and booted feet sounded out
in the corridor. He slid the dagger beneath the bed just as the
draw bar was lifted noisily and the door was thrown open.

"You are not my son!" Whitehawke roared, his face a gri-
macing mask, his hair flying wildly around his head. He advanced toward Nicholas, arms stiff at his sides, hands fisted
with barely controlled rage. "No son of my seed would thus
betray me!"

Nicholas tilted his head back to stare up at Whitehawke
calmly. "My lord," he said, "I believe, to both our misfortune, that I am your true son."

Whitehawke backhanded him, and the blow set his
wounded lower lip to throbbing. Nicholas probed it with his
tongue, tasting salty blood. Whitehawke glared down at him,
wheezing heavily.

"Pull him up," he snapped to a guard. Yanked roughly to
his feet, Nicholas clenched his wrists together, thankful for
the moment that the loosened ropes were not yet sliced
through.

Turning away, Whitehawke scrubbed his big hand over his
face and hair. Chavant entered the room and edged over to
Whitehawke to murmur quietly.

Whitehawke rounded on Nicholas. "Where are the children?"

"Gone to play in the snow, I trow," Nicholas said.

"He's removed them, no doubt," Chavant said. "How did
you do it? Where are they, and where are the men who aided
you?"

Nicholas cut him a contemptuous glance. "The children
are safe. Would that I had found Emlyn before I found you."

Whitehawke advanced toward Nicholas. "I swear to you,
boy, you'll not see your lady again in this earthly life. How
many men do you have outside these walls?"

At the earl's threat toward Emlyn, Nicholas clenched his
jaw muscles. "Hundreds by now. The rest will come as soon
as the moors are passable."

"None will come without a signal, I think. And you will

send no sign now. Likely you lie, as you have lied to me for years. Jesu. I have harbored a viper in my own nest."

"I have spent little of my life in your nest, my lord."

"Why have you done this?" Whitehawke demanded. "God's eyes! You the Thorne! I thought to catch myself a villein ripe for hanging—and instead I find you! You smear the name of de Hawkwood by your actions!"

"What dishonor I have was learned at my father's knee, who murdered my mother when I was a child."

"I have proven repentance times over for her death. She betrayed me. I do not forget that."

"Still, your mistreatment of her was not the whole part of why I took to the greenwood when I was a youth." Nicholas leveled a glance at Whitehawke.

"Why, then?"

"An entire dale has suffered for years due to your greed, my lord. Barns and homesteads have been burned, profits stolen. Little by little, parts of the dale have surrendered to your tactics. You began this relentless pursuit of the monks' land when the king decided to persecute the York monks. Even the king desisted when the Pope threatened him with excommunication. But you did not cease your persecutions." He glared at his father, feeling a hot, angry blush creep up his neck to stain his cheeks. "None could talk reason to you. I tried, barely in my majority, as have others over the years, Rogier de Ashbourne among them."

"The York monks paid no taxes for years," Whitehawke snapped. "King John ordered their flocks be removed from the forests. I merely aided in the execution of those orders!"

"The king gave free rein to his sheriffs to search out the monks' flocks, and harry the farmers who tended them," Nicholas said. "You took to those orders like a starving dog to meat."

"I had reason to pursue those monks. That land was part of Blanche's dowry," Whitehawke said. "It is mine now!"

"Why, then, have the courts never produced the documents to support your claim?" Nicholas countered. "Were that land owned by another baron, you would have had a war to fight. But monks can do naught against sacking and burning, and the theft of their profits. So I chose to help them."

"You had no right! The monks should have given up the land years ago," Whitehawke growled. "You were once persistent in your efforts to stop me. Then we heard of your death."

"The first time your men captured the flocks and the wagon loads of fleeces on the way to market, so that you could sell them as your own—that, my lord, was the year I began my forays into the wood. Soon I had several good men with me from the farms and villages around. We destroyed your supply wagons when we could. What profits we could steal back were distributed among the villagers, and the rest was given to the monasteries in your name."

"My guards had you in their grasp once, but you escaped."

"Aided by a demon wolf," Chavant said from behind Whitehawke.

Nicholas smiled thinly. "Baron de Ashbourne heard that the Black Thorne had been captured and was being taken south to Windsor, to the king's justice. He sent his own captain of the guard, Sir Walter de Lyddell, my lord"—he tilted his head toward Whitehawke, knowing he would recognize the name—"to free me." His smile grew into a grin, lopsided and very painful. "The baron's son and daughter helped, and their white hound as well. 'Twas where I first saw Emlyn. I offered to the baron for her hand because of that night."

"Good Christ. I am surrounded by traitors," Whitehawke said in disgust.

"Beneath your very nose, my lord," Nicholas agreed.

Whitehawke stepped closer, and Nicholas could smell foul breath and hear the faint airy whine of his father's breathing. "You seemed to have conceived a fierce attachment to these villeins," Whitehawke spit out. "What, then, do you know of this Green Man?"

"I know, my lord," he said slowly, "that the Green Man would take your soul to hell the moment you laid a hand on him."

Growing pale, Whitehawke backed away. "Your actions are a travesty of honor."

"Ah," Nicholas said. "Here, then, is the proof of our

shared blood. There is no honor in the father, and none in the son."

"Enough!" Whitehawke yelled, his cheeks reddening. "I live by a code of honor you young curs do not understand! And by God, I will soon have Hawksmoor to my own! That land was a part of Blanche's property settlement, and was meant to go to my legitimate issue. Which you, most likely, are not."

"Try to gain my land, my lord," Nicholas said quietly, "and see what loyalty a son has for a father."

"I have already seen your loyalty. Son of my body or not, I gave you a name and saw that you were reared as a knight. I allowed you to take your mother's inheritance. But now that you have been disowned, you will hold naught through me!"

Behind his back, Nicholas fisted his fingers in mounting anger. The urge to burst his bonds and throttle his father now, this moment, was so strong that he broke out in a misted sweat. "Hawksmoor is rightfully mine through my mother. Touch it, and I will have cause to kill you."

"We will let the king decide what to do with you. He may solve all of our difficulties." Whitehawke shook his head, his breath loud and wheezy. "Bah. I should have murdered you, her spawn. Then you would not have lived to betray me so."

Flaring his nostrils, Nicholas drew in a slow breath, mustering the control he needed. He could feel his cheeks burning, flushed bright. "Julian swears that my mother had no lover. And I was near seven when you murdered Blanche for adultery. How is it you can insist that you did not father me?"

Whitehawke shot him a hard look, but paced away and back again. "Women are temptresses by nature, so the Patriarchs teach us. Even a married woman cannot be trusted alone with a man. Before you were born, I was gone for over two months with King Henry. When I returned, your mother had a courteous friendship, she called it, with a young baron. I accused her then of adultery, and she denied it. I chose to believe her." Nicholas waited, his heart pounding uncomfortably in his chest. Though he had asked, he did not want to hear of the hate and anger between his parents. He felt slightly sick.

"Blanche was with child," Whitehawke continued. "She said she discovered it while I was gone. But when you were born, I counted back the months. Likely not mine, I said, though the midwife claimed the child was born well before his time." He shrugged. "But I had reason to doubt your mother's word."

Nicholas remembered hearing how tiny and weak he had been at birth, not expected to live because he was born too soon. He looked away for a moment, listening to the ragged whine of Whitehawke's breath.

"Several times over several years, I found her with this man," the earl continued. "Talking only, singing some, but I suspected falsity. Years she maintained this friendship, even after the man wed another. Finally, I could stand no more insult." He whirled to face Nicholas. "I challenged him, won the tourney, and locked her up." Nicholas remained silent in a kind of fascination, wanting him to stop, and wanting him to go on.

"She was held in her favorite chamber—no hardship there. I simply wanted her to admit her wrong. I would have sent her to a nunnery. I might even have forgiven her, had she asked. She did naught but return silence to me, and refuse most of the food that was brought to her, eating less and less. Then, after a few weeks, she asked for a priest, though she would not speak to me. Her stubbornness enraged me. I ordered no more food sent, no visitors, until she begged my forgiveness."

"Did she beg?" Nicholas asked dully, lowering his head, his hair swinging down to shield him.

"I went to the chamber after a week." He paused for a long moment. "She was dead."

Nicholas felt exhausted. He wanted suddenly to drop his eyelids and sleep a very, very long time. His father had starved his mother to death, and he was the product of that cursed union.

Somehow he knew that he was Whitehawke's son, knew it with every bone and fiber in his body. Honor had always been his most tortured struggle. Tainted blood told in time.

* * *

Emlyn sipped the hot drink, feeling its heat run down into her empty stomach. Holding the small wooden bowl in the palms of her hands, she glanced around the chamber. Another moment, and she would get back to work; for now, she wanted to enjoy her resourcefulness. She had started a fire in the little hearth using the torch that Whitehawke had left; she had found something to assuage her painfully empty stomach; and if she had not yet opened the lock, she was at least working toward that end.

The results of her productive day showed in the chaos of the chamber. As morning light grew into midday, Emlyn had dumped out the contents of two wooden chests and a few small coffers, looking for any sharp tool that could break the lock.

Blanche's possessions had been stored here, since this had been her private chamber. Clothing of all kinds, woolen kirtles and silk gowns, chemises, veils, hosen, littered the floor. Stacked and tumbled nearby were small carved-ivory boxes; shoes, silver belts and buckles; gold and silver brooches and an amber rosary; three books, a psalter, an herbal and a bestiary, all beautifully illuminated; several candles; and a leather case containing quills and a ram's horn, its ink dried to powder.

One lead coffer had contained several painted earthenware jars stoppered with wax over cork, each carefully labeled in painted letters and symbols. Curious, Emlyn had pried open a few seals and found dried herbs, still potent by their fragrances: chamomile, mint, and rosemary; fennel, rosehips, and bramble leaves; baneberry root for lung ailments, and willow bark and meadowsweet for pain; hawthorn and foxglove, both powerful and poisonous.

Earlier, Emlyn had collected falling snow in a small brass jug. After a while, she had enough to melt for drinking. The henap served as a pot for the fire, and she sprinkled mint leaves and rosehips into the heated water, knowing that the chamomile would only increase her thirst. Removing the hot jug with a cloth, she had been well pleased with her ingenuity.

The steaming infusion was enormously comforting. She sipped at it and watched the low fire. Lady Blanche's embroidery frame had burned down already, followed by the legs of a little wooden stool that she had pulled apart. With whispered apologies to the spirit of Lady Blanche, Emlyn had tossed in carved boxwood combs and two distaff rods for spinning, a twig basket, and a pair of wooden clogs. Wooden bowls lay stacked with other items that looked as if they might burn well.

With light and warmth and drink, she felt calmer and thought more clearly. So far, her captivity had been spent in greater physical ease than Whitehawke had obviously intended for her. She refused to think what it would be like once her few luxuries ran out. By then, she would have escaped, she thought firmly.

But the lock still held. A pair of scissors, an iron-pronged candlestick, a lead belt buckle had all been tried to no avail. She had gouged and scraped without result.

Tearing apart the contents of the room had proven a good antidote for too much time. Engaged in rummaging, with constant apologies to Lady Blanche for overt curiosity, Emlyn had examined the books and admired the jewels and other fine things. Expecting some response to the tendrils of smoke wafting from one of the old keep's chimneys, she had heard no footsteps on the stairs.

From the narrow arrow slit, she had watched as servants cleared the snow with shovels and brooms, while soldiers passed back and forth continually. High above a castle full of activity, she felt a strange sense of isolation.

Setting down her bowl, she went to the wooden chest beside the bed, meaning to replace Blanche's things, and to sift through them once again, in case she had missed some useful implement.

As she lifted the awkwardly heavy lid, it slipped from her hands to fall against the wall, which was covered by a wide embroidered hanging. The lid pushed against free-floating linen.

Puzzled, Emlyn stood and peeked around the edge of the fabric. Where she had expected to see solid wall, she found a tunnel-like space, dark and cold. Excited, she grabbed up a lit candle, then lifted the heavy embroidered curtain and stepped into the dank, musty interior.

Damp chill, and a faint unpleasant odor, permeated the enclosed space. The uneven surface of the stone wall was slick with frozen moisture. Shivering, Emlyn felt her way forward and followed the turn to the left.

Since the tower chamber had once been a private room for Lady Blanche, it did not surprise Emlyn to find that it was fitted with a privy. At the end of the angle, a wooden seat with a round hole in it was placed over a narrow opening. A small window spilled a thin beam of light across the plank. Fresh, cold air swirled through the tunnel.

Emlyn set her candle in a little niche, where the melted wax from long-ago candles had formed a high, hard relief. Climbing up on the seat to peer out the window, she saw another angle of the bailey.

The blacksmith's thatched open-sided building, brightly lit, reverberated with the clang of iron tools. Two large siege engines, freshly brushed of snow, stood outside, and just beyond was the long, large stable, where the yard was thick with soldiers. She heard the chapel bells ring out the hour of nones, sweet and clear. With the bailey so close, and yet so far, she felt like crying from sheer frustration.

Squeezing her eyes shut for a moment, she prayed fervently: Dear God, please, please help me. Nicholas is still alive, I feel it. I have to be with him and the children.

Opening her eyes, she scrutinized the window. Merely a gap left unfilled between two stones, the space was hardly wide enough to admit an arm or a head. Had it been large enough, she would have attempted to climb out. She had heard of many such escapes, in stories and in fact. The privy disappointingly yielded nothing for her until she needed its services. Sighing, she turned away and stepped down from the planked seat.

Remembering the candle, she reached up to the niche, and her fingertips grazed the smooth wax. The candle fell off the stone shelf, hit the seat and rolled into the privy hole.

Emlyn peered into the hole as the flame flickered and went out. She heard a bouncing, tapping echo all the way down.

She stared into the black chute for a long time.

There was a way out of the tower after all.

Be careful how ye pray, Tibbie had always said; ye might get yer wish. Emlyn paced back and forth in front of the hearth in agitation. Her prayers had been answered, but she was not certain she liked the solution.

Privies, she knew, were basically long shafts that led to cesspits below a building. Sometimes the shafts were built on a slant, as at Ashbourne, connecting to privies on other levels in the building, all feeding downward. Others were simple and straight. At Ashbourne and Hawksmoor, as at most castles, leftover washwater was dumped regularly to keep the shafts clean. Workmen were hired to clean out the cesspits, and the exorbitant fee they demanded was always paid.

With relief, Emlyn realized that the cesspit for this keep would be clear, since the building was used only for storage now. Besides, anything disagreeable would be covered with snow.

Before the tumbling candle flame had gone out, she had glimpsed the chute, which appeared to be barely wider than her shoulders and a straight drop. She was small and slender and could probably squeeze down along its whole length.

"Gaillard," she muttered to herself, twisting her fingers anxiously as she walked to and fro. "They did it at Château Gaillard. And they were armored men, much larger than I am." She remembered hearing a story of the conquest of King Richard's impenetrable fortress, Château Gaillard, in France, which was lost when a group of French knights entered via the privy shafts. That clever infiltration began the downfall of one of the finest castles ever built.

Emlyn whirled around the room. Better the privy shaft than starvation here, she told herself. Better the privy shaft than lose the chance of finding Nicholas and the children.

She went over to the pile of clothing in the middle of the room and began to sift through the tumble. Refusing to dwell on the more frightening aspects of her plan, she concentrated firmly on what she must do to get out.

Chapter Twenty-six

"Greetings, Baron de Hawkwood," the king said as he crossed the room. Whitehawke and Chavant followed with ten or twelve soldiers. Someone kicked the door shut.

"My liege," Nicholas said. Standing with the ropes still tied around his ankles, he worked the muscles of his feet and legs to keep an upright balance, and looked down at the king.

Shrewd, round dark eyes regarded him. A full head shorter than Nicholas, King John had short-trimmed auburn hair, a square jaw made more angular by a neat, close beard, and a powerful trunk with wiry, strong limbs. Nicholas was reminded of a monkey he had once seen, cunning, watchful, and nervous.

"We have heard from Lord Whitehawke of your indiscretions. We find them curious indeed." The king turned to Whitehawke and grinned. "Your pup gives you much trouble, by God. Not properly heeled, eh?" Whitehawke returned a stone cold look, but John seemed unperturbed. He looked at Nicholas. "Do you admit to being this renegade called the Black Thorne?"

"I do, my liege."

"And may we count you among those northern barons who have crossed with us?"

"You may, sire." Nicholas regarded him steadily.

"Then you have two crimes against you. But our displeasure can be rectified, at least in part."

"My liege?" Nicholas knew what was hinted.

"A token of your good intentions would be welcomed." The king tipped his head slightly, touching his fingertips together.

"Sire," Nicholas said, "as you are no doubt aware, I am in

jeopardy of my life at this moment. Imprisoned, you understand."

"Aye?" The king looked puzzled.

"Sire, my pockets are empty," Nicholas said, shrugging.

John threw back his head and laughed. "A man who attacks his own father is either without sense, or brave beyond measure. And since your sire is Whitehawke"—he lifted his shoulders eloquently—"you are undoubtedly brave. In recognition, then, we will offer you a choice—will you be executed as an outlaw, or for high treason as a rebel?"

"An outlaw, sire." A hope glimmered in Nicholas's mind.

"Very well. So be it."

"My lord king," Nicholas said. The king raised his eyebrows. "There is a law, my liege, regarding any outlaw who evades capture for at least a year and a day."

John frowned. "God's bones, so there is. An obscure law made by the Conqueror decrees that such a man shall be pardoned forever." He glanced at Whitehawke. "How much time has passed since the first time you captured this man?"

Whitehawke ground his teeth. "Eight years, my liege."

John's delighted grin hooked his brows into a demonic angle. "By God, Whitehawke, this is better than any mummer's diversion you might have arranged for our snowbound sojourn here. Because we so enjoy a jest, we will go along with the play." Smirking, he turned to Nicholas. "Very well, then, de Hawkwood—we pardon you of your crimes as a forest outlaw."

"Thank you, my liege." He let out a slow breath. Take what is offered and deal with the rest later, he told himself.

"Since we offered you a choice, it seems that you have managed to escape with your life." John turned to Whitehawke. "God's teeth, this is good! You do us a favor with your little family war. Word will be spread of our leniency today with a rebel baron." He glanced shrewdly at Nicholas. "But we do not forget that you remain accountable for acts of treason."

That, unfortunately, was the rest. "Of course, my liege."

John's stare was like a dark, cold pit. Nicholas saw no more mercy there, and then, suddenly, not much interest either. The king turned away. "Whitehawke, as soon as the weather permits, we will depart Graymere. This man should be detained for treason. Other than that, how you handle your rebellious offspring now is not our further concern."

"Aye, my lord king." Whitehawke bowed, his face a peculiar shade of mauve beneath his peaked snow-white hair. The king whirled sharply and left the room, his guards close behind him. Sliding an angry glance at Nicholas, Chavant left with them.

Whitehawke paused, waiting for the room to clear. He turned to Nicholas. "You handled the king in a clever manner. Snowbound as he is, he has not had a good frame of mind. The luck of your outcome is a plain amazement to me—I paid a heavy bag of coins yestereve for such a show of goodwill. You received it for naught."

Nicholas blinked in surprise, having expected another tirade from his father. "John enjoys our little play, as he said."

Whitehawke stared at him, his eyes like pale quartz in the dim light. "Though you have escaped a sentence of death, you and I have much to reckon between us."

"Aye, we do." Nicholas returned his gaze evenly.

"I have asked the king to declare Hawksmoor forfeit due to your crimes. It reverts to me." Whitehawke lifted his chin slightly and looked at Nicholas through hooded eyes. "And I believe I will bestow that property on my new heir."

"My lord?" A cold feeling spread through Nicholas's gut.

"Chavant is a nephew of mine, after all. And you are disavowed, and will be imprisoned for a long time. A little more of my gold lining the king's pocket, and I can arrange to have you transferred to Windsor's dungeons. No one has ever come out of there alive and sane, both."

"Hugh at Hawksmoor?" Nicholas laughed harshly. "My garrison would never accept him, or your decision. Hawksmoor will not be yours or his. Just as the dale has never yet fallen into your palm, no matter how long or hard you have tugged at the tree."

Whitehawke gazed at him for a long while, then drew a long, wheezy breath. "I swear," he said softly, "there have been times that I have wished you were my son. Whatever lack of judgment has brought you to this fate, you have a heart of iron. You do not back down. That takes courage and wit."

"Truly, my lord," Nicholas replied. "I will not back down where you are concerned."

Emlyn pulled at the last knot with a satisfied tug. The makeshift rope was strong and would hold. She would soon discover if it was long enough. Pushing the soft, heavy mass of colored fabrics out of her lap, she stood and flexed her hands, stiff from tying the fat knots.

Again she had felt an obligation to apologize to Lady Blanche. Silken gowns, chemises, woolen tunics, hosen, and embroidered belts now formed one long colorful rope. She had also added the dusty linen sheets from the bed.

Carrying the clumsy length back into the privy, she lifted the heavy planked seat a little and tied one end of the rope around the front edge. As she dropped the bundle into the privy hole, the bright mass of color slipped sibilantly down into the dark shaft. Tugging on the well-anchored knot, she felt certain that the bulky cord would hold her weight.

Her preparations made, she went back into the tower chamber to wait until full darkness, not eager to emerge from the privy chute into a yard full of soldiers. Smiling in satisfaction, she heated the last of the melted snow and added another pinch of mint. Nicholas could not have done better, she thought, were he caught in this very tower himself.

Truly bold action was an exhilarating feeling; she felt like an Amazon of legend. She straightened her shoulders, relishing the comparison. A thrilling sense of power, only glimpsed before in her life, filled her with confidence.

The bumbling girl who had shot a baron inadvertently could not have carried out this plan, no matter how sharp her temper, she thought. Hiding or disguised, she had relied on Thorne and Godwin to help her. Now she acted totally of her own accord, with courage and firm purpose.

When she had poured the hot infusion into a bowl, she settled down by the hearth and reached for a small book that she had found among Blanche's things, grateful to have a diversion until darkness came.

Flipping through the pages, she saw lovely decorations and brilliantly colored half-page paintings. The book was a collection of short prayers and psalms with a calendar of

holy days. On the last page she found an inscription, dated
1180, a few years before Nicholas's birth, that gave
Blanche's name.

Her attention was caught by a picture inside a larger letter
initial B, at the beginning of a Latin verse, where the tiny,
graceful figure of a woman knelt with her hands in prayer.
Though not meant to be an exact portrait, the woman's delicate face and pinkened cheeks were exquisite, and long
black braids rippled over her blue gown. Nearby, a white
hawk sat on a branch, an allusion to Bertran de Hawkwood.

Emlyn studied the little image of Blanche de Hawkwood
for a long moment. As she leaned forward to sip at her
drink, the book slid from her lap. When she picked it up, she
saw that the binding was loose, and that the back board of
the cover, made of thin wood covered in gilded leather,
gapped oddly.

Curious, she poked at the gap, and felt a thick, crackly lining. Tucked inside the leather was a folded parchment sheet,
which she drew out gingerly. Cramped, neat handwriting in
French covered the verso side, with a round red seal at the
bottom. On the reverse side were unevenly written words in
faded brown ink. She saw immediately that the signature
above the seal, dated 1178, belonged to King Henry. Emlyn
frowned as she waded through the complicated French text.
Her attention was riveted by the names she read there: Baron
Robert de Thorneton, of Castle Wilcott in Cumberland, and
his daughters Julian and Blanche.

The document concerned the parceling of lands belonging
to Baron Robert. Certain portions were officially donated by
the baron to two designated abbeys in York, in memory of
his late wife. Other portions, the locations described in detail, were given to Julian and Blanche, to be held in their
own right and not to be included in dowries, in memory,
again, of their mother.

Emlyn's heart pounded as she smoothed the old vellum
with trembling fingers. Here was the deed to the dale, the
land that Whitehawke coveted so fiercely. Blanche must
have hidden it.

A few words were scribbled in a bottom corner beside the
royal seal, written in faded brown ink that matched what she

had seen on the back. Emlyn read aloud, her voice soft but husky.

"Land rightfully mine I leave to my son Nicholas. Blanche, la comtesse." A tiny signature below the sentence read "Wil. Clerc, priest."

Emlyn sat back in amazement. Lady Blanche had even ensured a witness. The document was genuine and had to be legal. Nicholas and Lady Julian, not Whitehawke, owned the dale with the Monks.

Stunned, she turned the page over.

"Mi chere soune Nichls." Emlyn had to concentrate in order to decipher the letters and to understand the words, a curious mix of French and English. Most texts were written in French or Latin, and she could read those very well. Little was written in the vernacular, the spoken language that she and most of the nobility spoke, a blend of Norman French and English.

"My dear son Nicholas," she translated aloud.

"I am told that you are with Julian and John. This pleases me.

I have asked for a priest, for I feel my days will be few. Pains in my chest plague and weaken me. Bertran thinks my will equal to his. He is wrong. Tomorrow I will beg his forgiveness for a sin I never made. This I do to see you again, my sweet son.

But I shall not live to see you a man. I pray Bertran will not disavow you unfairly in his unfounded jealousy. May God be with you.

Keep this little book in memoriam.

B. cmtsse."

Tears misted Emlyn's eyes. Lady Blanche was no adultress. The letter proved that she fully intended to live, even by confessing falsely, in order to be with her small son. More, Emlyn suspected that Lady Blanche had not died of starvation.

Among the contents of the glazed apothecary jars, from which Emily had taken the mint for her infusion, were willow bark and meadowsweet, used for pain, and hawthorn berries and foxglove flowers, remedies for heart ailments.

Weakened by hunger and a poor heart, Lady Blanche could easily have died from even a normal dose of hawthorn and foxglove, which were dangerously strong. The little jar with dried purple foxglove had been nearly empty, Emlyn remembered.

Carefully folding the parchment, she slid it back into its hiding place. During her rummaging she had found a pouch of soft chamois trimmed with silk. She fetched the purse, fit the book inside it, and wound the silk cords around her belt.

The arrow loop still admitted gray daylight and cold air into the chamber. Shivering, Emlyn fastened her cloak, and began to pace the chamber anxiously. From the bailey, she heard distant snatches of laughter and occasional shouts. When darkness came and the castle was quiet, she would escape.

A persistent dizziness plagued her, a result of lack of sleep and lack of food. Laying across the rumpled, dusty bed, she drew her mantle around her like a blanket, intending to rest lightly.

The thunderous rhythm of galloping horses startled Emlyn out of a deep sleep. Rubbing her eyes, she dashed to the window, dismayed to find that she had slept through the night.

Golden dawn light on the crisp surface of the snow, and the red and gold cloaks of hundreds of armored riders created a dense, colorful picture. The king's troops streamed across the white-crusted bailey in a wide body to channel beneath the open porcullis gate. Embroidered banners flew ahead of the king, whose purple cloak lifted in the wind as he passed through the gate. Looking back, he raised and then lowered his arm, not in farewell, Emlyn saw, but in a signal.

As the teeming mass of horseflesh and armor emptied through the gate to thunder furiously across the wooden drawbridge, twenty or thirty soldiers split off from the group. Each rider held a glowing, spitting torch.

Emlyn watched, horrified, as the soldiers rode through the bailey, flinging their torches toward the thatch-roofed buildings that clustered beneath the walls. The flaming brands whipped through the air like spinning gold stars, igniting the roofs.

"Dear God," Emlyn breathed. King John had given an order to fire the castle. Even as she comprehended, shocked, what was happening, one of the torch-carriers peeled off from his group and rode directly toward the old keep, tossing his flame. Emlyn peered down, but could not see where it landed.

The riders circled the bailey until they had discharged their torches, then galloped beneath the portcullis. Barely a few moments had passed. The king and his routiers were gone.

Hot orange flames had erupted in several places at once, and thick smoke drifted up like charcoal-tinted clouds. Though the thatched roofs were damp with snow, bright flames burst from the drier places, and had already begun to lick inside the buildings. The pungent, stinging odor of smoke filled the air.

Kitchen fires often plagued castles, and wells were usually strategically placed for that reason. Emlyn heard shouts in the bailey as servants and soldiers ran back and forth from the wells carrying sloshing buckets of water. Others grabbed shovels to fling snow in an attempt to smother the flames.

She could smell smoke, acrid and stinging, inside her tower chamber. Running to the locked door, she pressed her face to the wood. The strong odor came from the stairwell.

The keep was on fire. Certes, she thought, the routiers would make certain that Whitehawke's stores burned. She sat atop a ready torch, made of barrels of wine and ale, and hundreds of sacks and baskets of dry goods.

Running back into the privy, she took hold of the taut rope fastened to the seat, whispered a quick, frightened prayer, and lowered herself into the round hole. Bracing her feet against the side, she inhaled as if she were slipping underwater and resisted the urge to pinch her nose shut.

Clinging firmly to the long rope, she inched down into dense, cloying darkness. With the makeshift rope pressed between her feet, as she had learned years ago when she and Guy used to climb ropes in the stable loft at Ashbourne, she moved further down. The blackness was alarmingly oppressive. A faint stench lingered, but not of smoke. The odors here were old and unpleasant, imbedded in mortar and stone.

The cold breezes wafting up from below were still fresh, and she moved down.

The fat tumble of rope swayed with her movements in the narrow shaft as her back slid along one wall and her knees and feet brushed the opposite side. Repeatedly, her long braids snagged in the stone cracks, and her skirts hampered her, making the difficult task even more awkward.

What she had not anticipated, as she descended further, was the slimy coating on the walls. Thick oozy molds, in some places quite fetid, clung wherever she touched stone. Her nose clogged with the musty stench and her throat grew irritated. When her head pressed into something spongy, she jerked away.

After a while, her shoulders and hands began to ache. The purse knocked rhythmically against her thigh, and the weight of her heavy cloak and her thick braids strained her neck.

Braced against the wall, she paused to rest, and briefly thought of her frenzied descent with Thorne in the gorge. That day she had been nearly paralyzed with terror. But now, even in this dark slimy shaft, she felt a surprising sense of calm. Necessity and firm purpose enabled her to squelch her fears. Breathing hard now with the effort of descent, she thought of the children and Betrys, locked up in the chamber hall. If the fire reached there, who would see that they were removed from danger? She had to get to them and find Nicholas, and the need spurred her on. Hawksmoor's garrison would undoubtedly arrive soon, but the snowy moors would greatly delay them. The castle could be a hollow black shell by the time they arrived.

The molds that poisoned the air were making her ill. She must have descended over halfway by now, she thought. Slipping one foot down the silky folds, she toed into empty space.

Her heart lurched. The knotted rope was not long enough to reach to the bottom. Groping madly in the dark, she climbed upward a little in a sudden panic.

Dangling like a caterpillar on a branch, she peered cautiously downward, and was greatly relieved to see the floor of the cesspit, though she could not easily judge the distance. A wedge of light, swimming with motes, filtered in from one side and sliced through the thick shadows below.

Her hands and shoulders burned fiercely. She would not be able to cling much longer. A formless, needy prayer, thoughts and images only, rushed through her mind. Then she let go.

An instant in midair, and her forearms and knees struck solid bottom. Rolling with the momentum of her fall and the natural slope of the floor, she lay for a long time without moving, until her lungs gradually filled again and her head stopped spinning. Inhaling, she smelled smoke laid over a malodorous stench similar to compost and dried manure; the ground beneath her was frozen hard and slightly crunchy, a rounded pile of something indefinable. She sat up quickly.

A few feet away, the bright outline of an ill-fitting slatted door emitted streams of light. The shock of her descent still quivered in her bones and muscles, and she stood cautiously, then opened the little door and stepped out into the bailey, pulling up her hood.

Sunlight and smoke and freezing air hit her all at once. Blinking away stinging tears, she stood transfixed by the uproar as servants, soldiers, women and children ran in every direction, yelling orders, carrying water buckets, hatchets or shovels. Some screaming, some carrying their belongings or their children, a throng of people streamed toward the gate.

Near the portcullis, Emlyn saw Whitehawke mounted on his white destrier. Even as her belly clenched in fear, she knew that he would not see her amid the confusion. Armored and helmetless, he called out orders to the soldiers gathered by him. Chavant, mounted beside him, directed a group of serjeants and servantmen toward the stables.

Flames were devouring the roofs of the stable and kitchens, and the smithy had begun to burn. Ugly, thick curls of smoke spiraled up, and cinders and glowing sparks drifted through the air, capable of igniting new fires elsewhere.

She looked up to see smoke pouring from the arrow loops of the old keep. Stepping hastily away, she nearly bumped into two men, who ran past carrying water buckets.

Emlyn broke into a run. The children were locked in the chamber hall. Somehow, she must get them out and find Nicholas.

She ran past high piles of cleared snow, gleaming like molten gold as dawn and fire reflected off the glossy surfaces. Servants stood atop with shovels, flinging snow onto the smaller blazes. Further on, sparks had ignited the walled garden near the hall, leaving the bare-branched orchard trees black, flaming torches.

Emlyn ran faster, rubbing stinging cinders from her eyes and coughing into her fist, toward the chamber hall.

Smoke, increasingly pungent, traced through his nostrils, but he could not determine the source. Puzzled, he also heard distant shouts and heavy footsteps in the corridor. By the commotion in the great hall at dawn, he had already surmised that the king and his troops had departed.

But something else was happening now. Briefly, Nicholas wondered if Peter and Eustace had decided to attack. Then he guessed, with an acute twist in his gut, that King John had torched the castle as he left.

After his visitors had left yesterday, he had made quick work of the ropes around his wrists and ankles. No one had been back since. Even with his limbs free, he had been unable to find a way out, and had finally rested for part of the night. He had been awake for a long while, stalking the perimeters of the room, investigating every niche, chest, and coffer, and listening to the increasing uproar outside his door.

Glancing at the bright sliver of sky at the window, he saw smoke drift past. Best, he thought wryly, to be gone from here.

Preferring to ambush the next guard who came in, rather than going out the window on bed sheets and prayers, he had armed himself earlier with a tall iron candlestick, whose wicked tripod base and sharp candle prong made a formidable weapon.

Shifting the candle support in his hands, he spun and tossed it, exploring the length and uneven weight distribution. Just a question of time before someone opened the door. Nicholas grasped the candlestick confidently in his hands and waited.

Emlyn hurried through the chamber hall as simply and

freely as if she had lived there all her life. Each person she passed, soldiers or servants, ignored her or glanced incuriously as they rushed outside. There was a strong smell of smoke in the hall, but no evidence of fire that she could see. With her head tucked in the shadow of her deep hood, she slipped up the stairs.

Hesitating, she walked slowly along the gallery toward the bedchamber, relieved to find it unguarded. The heavy draw bar was stuck fast in the struts, and she strained to dislodge it and set it aside. Easing the door open, she stepped into the dim room.

And walked into a whirlwind of motion. Instinct ruled and she ducked, throwing up her hands to defend against something that came whirring down out of the shadows. She screamed.

Some heavy object hit the floor, thunking painfully against her foot. Then she was caught up in strong arms, and pulled fiercely into Nicholas's embrace.

"Oh, God, Emlyn!" he said breathlessly into the side of her hood. "Emlyn! How—"

"Nicholas!" she cried, clinging to him. "By the Virgin, you are here, and safe." The warm haven of his arms closed around her, and she sank against his chest, listening for a blissful moment to the simple, strong beat of his heart.

She lifted her face and his lips slipped over hers, roughened with thirst, tender and fierce. Emlyn embraced him, desperately needing to touch him, to feel his touch and hear his voice, to know him real and alive and unhurt.

"Where is the guard?" he asked against her cheek.

"There was none," she said. "Oh, Nicholas, the castle is ablaze. The world has gone topsy-turvy. King John's routiers fired the castle at dawn. They just tossed torches—" She quickly told him what she had seen.

"Whitehawke has been mightily betrayed, then, for he thought himself among the favorites."

Emlyn peeked around his shoulder and saw the empty chamber. "Nicholas," she said slowly, "where are the children?"

"Safe, sweeting." He offered his brief narrative.

Her hood slipped back as she threw her arms around his neck and whispered her thanks.

"They are likely back at Hawksmoor by now," he said, and bent to nuzzle his face into her hair. "Aaauggh—" he gasped. "Bloody saints. What rotten hole did you crawl from?" He put a hand up to his mouth. At her look of dismay, he dropped it. "Where did those bastards lock you? I thought you were in the old keep."

She glanced up at him, a little hurt. A slight stench wafted through the air as she stepped forward. "Oh, aye," she said, "I was in the upper chamber, but the door was locked. I had to climb down the privy shaft to get out."

"You did what?"

She grinned proudly. "I escaped out the privy shaft."

Nicholas raked his fingers through his hair. "Jesu," he said, "you are an amazement." He reached out and pulled her to him again, bringing his face close to hers. "A malodorous, wondrous amazement. Come here, my love." Though his mouth tasted sticky and sour, and her own odor lingered unpleasantly, the tender familiarity of the kiss sweetened all else.

He broke away to look at her, his eyes glittering like bright steel. In the dim light, with his bristly stubble, tangled hair and purpled bruises, he looked wild, strong, and strangely vulnerable. Emlyn put a finger gently on his cheek.

"You are hurt," she said.

"I am well enough," he said, wincing a little at her touch. His crooked half grin told her that however, wherever, he might hurt, he chose to think naught of it.

He stroked his fingers along her jaw. "At times these past days, I never thought to see you again." His body grazed hers, and Emlyn felt a delicious, languid heat at the brushing contact.

"And I you, my love," she whispered, splaying a hand on his chest. His heart thumped softly beneath her fingers.

Frowning, he lifted his head to sniff exploringly in the air. "We must leave here. The smell of smoke is stronger."

"None stopped me as I came in. With caution, we can get to the gate and join those who are leaving." Distracted by his nearness, she traced her hand in gentle circles on his chest.

Nicholas watched her with a bemused expression, and tilted his face down to hers. "Best we leave soon, or I shall give into a very lustful temptation to put that bed to its finest use."

Circling an arm behind her back, he fitted his hips to hers, and the warm weight in the core of her body dissolved into an eager yearning, molten and trembly. His turgid arousal pressed against her lower body, and she gripped his shoulders as an urgent desire nearly buckled her knees.

He groaned softly against her lips. "Dearling, though I am loathe to say it, 'twould be too great a delay." He took her elbows and put her away from him, wrinkling his nose briefly. "And by my troth, you do reek, lady wife."

"Nicholas," she said, placing a detaining hand on his arm. "There is something I would tell you—"

"Later, my love, we must go. Hurry!" He opened the door and pulled her along with him, into a corridor filled with smoke.

Chapter Twenty-seven

The castle complex, encircled by the high curtain wall, lay curled like a great dragon belching flame and smoke, and pungent charcoal-colored clouds rolled furiously overhead as Emlyn and Nicholas ran out into the bailey. Hurrying beside Nicholas, every exposed inch of Emlyn's skin felt the scorching, suffocating heat, as if the wintry chill did not exist here.

The stable had collapsed, a ferocious, flaming pit. Beyond that, the kitchen roof beams were crashing to the ground, pulling the weakened stone walls partly down.

"Hounds of hell! The chapel!" Nicholas called.

Emlyn looked up. Crowning the chapel was a gleaming, swirling mass of rainbow color, like sliding oil. "What is it?"

"The roof is made of sheets of tin. They're melting."

"Jesu," she breathed, as he hauled her forward once again.

They stumbled into the crowd that condensed and shoved toward the gate. Graymere was home to hundreds of soldiers, servants, craftsmen, and their families; now it seemed as if most of them pressed forward at once in a frenzied, shouting, jostling body.

Jammed into the crowd and carried along like driftwood in rushing water, Emlyn gripped Nicholas's arm, determined not to lose him. Bouncing up on her toes, she tried to see over the heads and shoulders in front of her.

Whitehawke, his white hair a signature banner, guided his horse ahead of a group of armed, mounted knights, who led their destriers under the gate, delaying the exodus of the crowd of people behind them. Looking for Chavant, Emlyn saw him riding with the garrison. She gestured, and Nicholas nodded.

"They leave with the landed knights," he said over the din. "The rest of these people must fend for themselves." Someone stumbled next to him, and he turned and bent over to pick up a small, lost, dirty-faced, crying boy.

Reassuring the child, promising to find his family, Nicholas carried him easily in one arm as they moved slowly under the portcullis arch. Once outside the castle walls, the mass of people drifted apart into smaller groups.

Villeins from the near countryside were filtering onto the rolling white meadow that fronted the castle, coming in wagons, on mules and plow oxen, or on foot, to see what help was needed and to find family members. Women gathered near a fire, over which was hung a large iron kettle full of steaming soup. Others tapped barrels of cider in a wagon, handing out drinks from deep wooden ladles.

Emlyn's mouth watered at first, but when she looked in another direction, her throat nearly closed with anguish and shock. Bodies lay clustered on the bare snow, or on blankets or cloaks. Some writhed in pain with burn wounds; others were still as cloth dolls. Women knelt among them, applying snow or ointments to wounds, and offering liquids.

Looking around again, she saw that Nicholas had walked away, carrying the boy toward a crowded hay wagon. When a woman reached out, he lifted the child into his mother's arms.

Watching, Emlyn felt a surge of love flow through her, from the top of her head to her toes, a warm, tingling, nurturing rain of profound gratitude that Nicholas was safe and unhurt. With a sudden sense of clarity, she admired the grace and power of each simple movement he made as he found a blanket and wrapped it around the boy, and she relished every nuance of his deep, gentle voice as he spoke to the child's mother.

She stood staring as if he were the only person in the snowy meadow. Then he turned, and his eyes met Emlyn's across the short distance. He raised his arms, and she ran toward him.

Cradling her against him, he stroked her hair as they stood wrapped together, heedless of the confusion and commotion that surrounded them. They turned to face the burning castle. Though the flames had tempered in some spots, dark smoke still billowed and belched from within the walls. Graymere would be a blackened, hollow shell by nightfall.

"My lord," said a voice behind them. Emlyn whirled.

"Peter!" she cried.

"My lady," he said, bowing his head. He glanced at Nicholas. "I am heartened to see you both safe." Though his voice was calm, lines of exhaustion were etched around his blue eyes. Coppery bristles sparkled as he rubbed his chin and looked at the castle.

"You walked out of the jaws of hell, my lord."

"Aye so," Nicholas replied wearily.

"What of the children?" Emlyn asked.

"Snug at Hawksmoor by now and likely being treated like saints arrived from heaven." Peter gestured toward the trees, where a long line of Hawksmoor's garrison waited, armed and mounted. "We have been mickle worried about you both, and disputing the best time to attempt a rescue. For the meanwhile, many of our guards have been helping with matters out here."

Emlyn noticed then several green-cloaked guards moving among the crowd, finding spaces in packed wagons, boosting people onto horses, and hitching harnesses. Her breath swelled with pride, and beside her, Nicholas nodded his approval.

"Whitehawke and his men rode off as if hellhounds were after them," Peter remarked to Nicholas.

"Aye, intent on claiming Hawksmoor for Hugh's inheritance. When better than now, when they have no roof for their heads?"

"Thunder of heaven," Peter muttered. Emlyn glanced up to see the quick look that Nicholas and Peter exchanged.

"I will go with you!" she exclaimed. "I can shoot a bow!" The flush of her Amazonian escapade was still with her, and she hardly heard Peter's muted groan.

Nicholas turned pewter-colored eyes on her. "You, my lady, will go to Evincourt as planned, since the king still proves unpredictable. Your taste of adventure is over, Emlyn. I would have you safe and know where you are. A stitching needle would be a goodly thing for your hands now, rather than a weapon."

Her mouth dropped open. Nicholas took advantage of the

sudden silence. "My lady," he nodded, "I will see you in a few weeks. An escort will be given you." He strode briskly away from her toward the trees where his soldiers waited.

Stunned, Emlyn hesitated a moment too long before she took off after him. He had already leaped up into Sylvanus's saddle by the time she reached him.

"Nicholas!" she cried, remembering the little prayerbook that weighted the purse at her belt. "I must speak to you!"

Someone tossed him a green cloak, and he wrapped it around him. Steadying the restive prancing of the war-horse, he looked down at Emlyn. His eyes, reflecting the cloak, were now the cool green of bottle glass. She would have placed a detaining hand on his boot, but his gaze stopped her.

"See that my lady wife is given an escort," he called out to one of the guards. "The rest of you will ride out with me."

"What will you do?" she cried in alarm.

"There are matters to be finished, lady." Yanking the reins, he turned the horse and rode off, signaling to the others.

Feathery spray churned from the horses' hooves as they thundered and glided over the snowy moor. Hair flying out like dark silk, his cloak lifting behind him, Nicholas vanished in the white distance, headed west for Hawksmoor.

Fuming with a hot blend of anger and fear, Emlyn watched with snapping blue eyes until he disappeared over the rim of a hill.

"My lady." William, who had defended her bravely outside the village just days ago, cantered his horse over to her. "We will depart now," he said.

Mounted on a strong gray stallion and wrapped in another of the thick green Hawksmoor cloaks, Emlyn had taken the time to sip a long draught of cider and eat a hunk of bread dipped in stew. With a little sustenance, she felt clearheaded and determined as she looked around at the twenty guards who waited for her.

Sighing at the prospect of yet another escort ready to lead her away from Nicholas, she realized that she had been separated from him far too much. His orders condemned her to weeks of cloistered waiting, protected from the king, but isolated from Nicholas, and perhaps from news of his fate.

A wise wife obeyed a husband's judgment, the Church taught, and she knew 'twas best to support the ladies and children who would arrive later at Evincourt. Nicholas did not want her with him. Though some women had followed their men into battle, they had been royalty or ladies of pleasure. And certainly, her taste of men's affairs of late had left her longing for the serene comforts of a peaceful home.

William waited, puzzled by her silence. She shifted in the saddle, and the little purse bumped against her abdomen. Its insistent weight decided her. Nicholas must have the deed.

Pulling sideways at the reins, Emlyn dug in her heels. The gray responded with a glorious surge of speed, tearing west across the hills.

"My lady!" William called.

Snow caught delicately on her eyelashes and dusted her cloak. Emlyn brushed at her eyes with one hand and pressed on beside William, fighting a numbing, painful fatigue. She wanted a hearth, a soft bed with hot, hot stones, and a bowl of steaming soup. Her fingers had nearly frozen with cold until she had borrowed a pair of leather gauntlets, overlarge but warm, from one of the guards. Breathing out puffs of mist, flexing her fingers inside the heavy gloves, she looked up as the escort rounded yet another white-blanketed swell of moorland.

Impulsively heading for Hawksmoor, she had been ill-prepared for hours of hard riding. When the snow had begun again, she almost wished that she had sent the prayerbook to Nicholas via one of the guards. But she needed to bring him the truth herself. Now, having set both the pace and the direction, she would not complain about the bone-deep chill, an aching fatigue, or a ferocious, dizzying hunger.

She rode on over the wild, white, airy moorland, with twenty men pounding a faithful rhythm behind her. Crossing slick stones to ford a broad stream, they turned for Hawksmoor.

Moving steadily along a sweeping descent where the cold winds cut like strong, sharp steel, Emlyn ducked her head and pulled her cloak tighter. Not only was the air raw with cold, but the dimming light would soon fade entirely.

Finally, distant but visible through flurrying snow, Hawksmoor's crenellated walls rose at the far crest of a long white hill. Dense forest covered the slope and reached back toward the moorland like long, dark arms.

Fringing a wide clearing, the trees were draped with snow and hung with icicles. Farther down the immense sweep of the incline on which she sat, Emlyn saw Nicholas's garrison, their green cloaks unmistakable, heading for the clearing.

Beyond them on the moor, approaching the stretch of land that backed up to the castle, she glimpsed the russet cloaks of Whitehawke's guard, like autumn leaves scattering over the snow, as they hastened toward Hawksmoor. Spurring the gray, she urged him down the rolling contours of the slope.

Just then, a small party of men galloped out of the forest to angle across the snowy moor toward Emlyn and her escort. Emlyn slowed, and William caught up to her.

"Who are they?" she asked him, watching them approach.

"Men from Hawksmoor, my lady, though I do not recognize them two in the lead, with their red cloaks."

Emlyn squinted, then suddenly leaned forward to furrow the gray through the snow. "Guy!" she screamed as she rode. "Guy!"

She nearly toppled from her horse in her haste to embrace him. Guy caught her, hugged her, and set her back in the saddle.

"Emlyn! What do you here?" he exclaimed in surprise.

She smiled breathlessly at Guy and at Wat, who rode up beside them. Wat, his nose red with cold, frowned at her. "You should not be here, Lady Emlyn. 'Tis no place for a woman. The baron means to catch Whitehawke before the earl reaches Hawksmoor."

"How is it you knew to come here?" she asked him.

"When the children were returned from captivity—they are well, my lady, and full proud of their adventures," he added, "we posted extra guards on the battlements. Whitehawke's men were spotted not long ago, with Nicholas and his garrison coming hard behind them. We rode out, taking that shortcut through the wood, to see what aid we could bring. I, for one, am anxious to draw steel against those who seize children."

"Emlyn," Guy said reprovingly. "You are supposed to be on your way to Evincourt. Lady Julian and the others are readying to leave as well, though Whitehawke's approach has disrupted those plans."

"I must speak with Nicholas first," she said. " 'Tis very important."

"Here, then, is your chance," Guy said, looking beyond her.

She whirled to see Nicholas pounding toward them, his scowl as dark as a thundercloud.

"Emlyn!" he roared, pulling up beside her. "Get you gone from here! Have you any notion of the danger?"

"Nicholas, I—"

"William!" He turned away from her impatiently.

"My lord, she tore after you," William called as he rode up. He shrugged. "Would you have had me truss her up?"

Nicholas emitted a sound that was as close to a bear's growl as Emlyn had ever heard from a human. Angry pink blotches stained his darkly bristled cheeks. Defiantly, she locked her eyes with his flashing glance.

"My sister has changed, my lord," Guy mused. "I recall a quiet girl content with painting and stitcheries. Always a hot temper, I trow, but never so rebellious."

"Rebellion is a craft. I learned it from a master," Emlyn said between her teeth, glaring at Nicholas.

His eyes were a sharp gray-green, penetrating hers as he answered Guy. "Marriage has made your sister into something of the lioness," he snapped.

"God help you, my lord," Guy said. "Especially should you have cubs." The look Emlyn turned on her brother might have melted his armor. Guy lifted his brows and raised his hands.

"The only way to deal with a lioness is to be firm in the face of her temper," Nicholas said dryly. "Emlyn, my men will take you from here immediately. And aye, trussed and chained, if need be." Looking at Guy and Wat, he nodded. "Come with me." Jerking the reins, he turned his horse's head.

"Nicholas!" she said hotly. "I must speak with you!"

"Later," he growled back over his shoulder. "Get you gone from here! Now!" He kneed his horse and rode away.

Emlyn drew a breath and huffed it out. Tears burned in her eyes at the piercing sting of his words, even as she filled with an answering burst of anger. Her lower lip trembled. Fatigue, hunger, and disappointment threatened to cave in her hard-won resolve. She inhaled sharply, fighting for control.

A hand rested on her shoulder, heavy and comforting. "He is alarmed by your presence here," Guy said. "He loves you well, to be so incensed. Whatever your news is, hold it for now. Your husband must know you safe, or he cannot apply himself to the task ahead. Go with your guards, Emlyn, and keep safe."

Mutely, she nodded. Guy smiled encouragingly and turned away with Wat and the others to ride after Nicholas. Sniffing, Emlyn guided her horse toward the upland moor and her waiting escort.

"My lady," William said. "We will take you on to Evincourt."

"Then I must ask that one of your guards give my husband this—" She reached for the little purse at her belt. " 'Tis greatly—" She stopped. "William, what is it?"

The serjeant was staring off into the distance, and she heard the other guards mutter among themselves. "Look there," William said, pointing.

Whitehawke's garrison had stopped on the white expanse of moor. Squinting through the snow flurry, she saw Whitehawke move away from the group. Nicholas's men halted uncertainly and fanned out in a curve formation, waiting and watching as she did.

Then Nicholas rode forward alone. Puzzled, Emlyn walked her horse closer, moving down the slope. She watched as Nicholas met with his father and appeared to exchange words. Then Whitehawke lifted an arm and pointed toward the trees.

At first, the rider who emerged from the earthy brown tangle of the forest looked like another guard from Hawksmoor. But the green he wore was brilliant and saturated, coloring horse and rider both. Emlyn gasped, and covered her mouth with her leather-gloved hand.

William edged his horse nervously forward. "My lady—"

"Go, William, you may be needed there," she said. "Leave two men with me. William—pray give me a weapon. Should I need to defend myself, I can use a bow or a dagger. An upright bow."

He hesitated, then motioned for a guard to hand her a bow and quiver. "Better that you run like a doe for cover, my lady. The baron will have my head for this."

Shouldering the bow, she slung the loop of the quiver over her saddle. Beneath her, the gray shifted uneasily. "This is my decision, not yours. I would know the fate of my husband and brother before I leave here. Give me that much, at least."

"Aye, my lady," he answered reluctantly, and rode down the slope with most of her escort at his heels.

Narrowing her eyes to see, she leaned forward, and the gray moved under her. She hardly noticed that she rode downhill. What she saw far ahead had riveted all her attention.

As if a lodestone pulled her, she was drawn forward. The men of Hawksmoor and Graymere both moved back as if to distance themselves from the green rider. Emlyn rode slowly through a thick silence, hearing only the soft shush of the horses' hooves and the icy rattle of wind and snow through the treetops.

Emlyn halted the gray the length of an arrow shot behind Nicholas, unnoticed by him. Her eyes wide, she saw only the Green Man who rode out of the wood.

Chapter Twenty-eight

"Christ's curse," Whitehawke rasped.

Nicholas had halted Sylvanus beside Whitehawke's stallion, watching in silence as the Green Knight rode slowly toward them, emerging like a garish ghost out of the swirling, light snow. The huge horse, as wide at the shoulders as a bull, taller than a destrier, glowed a paler green than the rider on its back.

"'Tis not you," Whitehawke said slowly. "By all that rules hell, this one is real!"

Nicholas looked at his father and returned his gaze to the rider who approached them. Behind them, every man sat silent.

Biting wind spit snow into Nicholas's face as he narrowed his eyes. This had to be Aelric, he thought. Somehow his friend must have heard that the garrisons were gathering on this part of the moor.

The demon rider came steadily closer, and raised an arm that looked like oak. A huge axe gleamed in his long, knotty fingers.

For a moment Nicholas squeezed his eyes shut to clear his vision. The creature looked so eldritch, so elementally powerful that he doubted his own sanity. No wonder men had been fooled by its appearance; the devil could not have devised a more convincing apparition than this one.

Then he recognized a few accoutrements that could only have come from the locked chest in Thorne's cave: the emerald-glazed armor and leggings, and the green leaf-woven netting for a cloak.

But real, springy moss seemed to sprout from the creature's head, glistening as green as his skin and beard. Fresh bright leaves were woven into every available place, crown to toe, bursting summery growth in winter.

Small berries and tiny white flowers cascaded and fell with each step of the horse, leaving a green trail of blossom and foliage in the snow. Leaves and flowers rioting over the creature's arms and shoulders and cloak were as fresh and lush as any in May. The Green Knight's presence hinted at a sylvan otherworld, spoke of new, verdant life in the midst of winter's bleak death, of potent magic beyond the rhythm of seasons.

The creature halted, still far enough away that particular details were blurred by the powdery snowfall and the fading light. Fresh, tangy fragrances drifted briefly on the chill breeze. The Green Man began to canter in a deliberate circle, riding as if the passage of time had slowed, stretching out the few moments in the stillness.

Nicholas had never seen the Green Man as Whitehawke had seen him. The overall effect struck like a thunderbolt out of a snowstorm, magnificent and terrifying. He turned to look at his father. Whitehawke stared wide-eyed at the spectre, his face chalky, his eyes gray as old ice.

Whatever Aelric meant to do here today was bravely done, and could cost the man his life, Nicholas thought. He shifted his glance around the clearing. The soldiers sat their horses as still as knights carved from marble, each man looking as if he saw a vision from Hell. Even Chavant stared and sat his horse as if paralyzed.

Turning his head, Nicholas saw Emlyn behind him.

He swore under his breath and looked quickly away, his thoughts tumbling. Then he shifted in his saddle and motioned cautiously for her to come nearer. If she had to be out here, he wanted her by his side, where he could protect her.

He felt that need because he knew that she held something precious within her: she loved him. She had acted bravely and impulsively out of her concern for him, first by escaping the tower, and then by following him here. Uncertain that he deserved such loyalty, such devotion, he knew that he could return love to her a thousandfold and still have more to give.

If he did not leave this moor alive, whatever part of him that was good and pure, that had been shaped by love, would survive in her memories, or, pray God, in his nurtured seed within her. Nicholas de Hawkwood would continue better than he had lived, with the impurities stripped away. He desperately wanted her safe, to preserve her life, and to save a part of his.

Emlyn walked her gray horse in between Whitehawke's creamy stallion and Sylvanus. Nicholas saw that she was not afraid; she knew the Green Man. Her beauty, in that instant, nearly startled him in its purity and strength, reflecting a serene faith, a total lack of fear that glowed from deep within. She sat the gray in the lush whiteness, rosy-cheeked, her golden hair spilling over the green cloak. Catching his glance, she smiled a little and moved her hand toward him.

She offered him a book. Frowning, puzzled, he accepted it.

The Green Man continued to canter in a circle, wide enough to include Whitehawke, Nicholas, and Emlyn as the stable point at the center. With a ponderous, deliberate rhythm, the green hooves laid a fresh track in the snow, scattering leaves and berries and blossoms as he rode.

Whitehawke gasped and inhaled sharply. Nicholas turned. The older man's face had gone the color of the light that now deepened over the snow: a cool, pale bluish hue, close to the color of death. Nicholas drew his brows together in concern.

Around them, the circle had been drawn three times. The spell held long enough for the Green Man to canter away as he had come, pounding, quick and magnificent, back to the wood.

Suddenly a cry broke through the trancelike silence. "Kill him! Fools!" Chavant galloped across the clearing. "Kill him! He is mortal!"

A few soldiers stirred to ride behind Chavant, though most still seemed to feel the strange lethargy of the past few moments, or else waited for Whitehawke's reaction.

"Emlyn! Ride to my men!" Nicholas called over his shoulder. Glancing at Whitehawke, he saw that the earl sat motionless on his horse, staring blankly into the forest where the Green Knight had vanished. Spurring his mount, Nicholas chased after Chavant.

Followed by several of his men, including Guy and Peter, he dashed across the clearing. Chavant charged forward into the bracken, screaming furiously after the vanished green rider.

As Nicholas drew near, Chavant turned with an anguished, frustrated cry and raised his sword high. Guy and Peter and several others hovered nearby, ready to defend their lord. When a few of Chavant's men leaped over the bracken, the Hawksmoor men went toward them, engaging in a melee to lure the guards away from Nicholas.

Chavant weighted his sword in his gauntleted fist, pulling against the restless turning of his horse. "Now face me, my lord," he said. "Swords on horseback is honorable combat. Face to face, hand to hand. Unlike the longbow you have wielded in the past." They circled each other, maneuvering among bracken and slender tree trunks, dredging through deep, powdery drifts.

Nicholas remembered training with Hugh de Chavant when they had been squires together. Chavant's wandering eye perceived movement in a faulty manner, and he had no high skill with sword or bow. But he was cunning, and used his wits to make up for what his vision failed to provide. Nicholas recalled also, as he carefully sidestepped Sylvanus, that Chavant never fought fairly.

Neither time nor experience had improved Chavant. He made the first swipe, swinging too far to one side. Nicholas parried easily, blocking the downward return swing and galloping past.

They swung the horses for the return. As Nicholas rode near, his heavy blow met Chavant's blade with a jarring slam. Chavant kicked out with his heavy boot at Nicholas's leg. Dancing the horse away as if the animal were a part of him, blood and bone, Nicholas lunged again, and this time his quick blade found Chavant's shoulder and a weak place in the armor. Blood darkened the russet surcoat.

Chavant smiled, a thin grimace, as he countered the next push of Nicholas's blade. "I am Whitehawke's heir now," he grunted.

"You will never have Hawksmoor!" Nicholas growled.

"I will! You have played us all for fools. Thorne!" He whooshed the blade through the air as he spat out the name, and Nicholas neatly blocked.

The two horses jostled side to side as the men fought, and

Chavant grimaced, unwittingly warning of another blow, and swung downward. Nicholas easily knocked the blade away, but the arc of his swing chopped his long heavy sword into a tree trunk.

Pulling the weapon free, Nicholas spun as Chavant, both hands wrapped around his sword hilt, swung with all his strength.

Nicholas ducked, kneeing his horse forward as Chavant's sword whistled past. Grunting with the momentum of his own swing, he spiraled to swipe his blade at Chavant's raised arm, slicing through the mesh-covered bicep. Screaming like a raging boar, Chavant lunged for Nicholas, knocking them both to the ground.

Catching the brunt of Chavant's head like a battering ram to his midriff, Nicholas was hurled onto the frozen ground. His lungs emptied like collapsing bellows beneath Chavant's heavy armor-clad weight. Striving to climb to his feet, scrambling for his fallen sword, he saw that Chavant had grabbed a blade and stood over him, raising his arms to strike.

With a small cry, Emlyn rode the gray forward, reining in near the wood's edge. Hearing the ugly clang of metal on metal, she saw that Nicholas and Chavant were locked in combat, twisting toward each other like knights in tourney. She gasped, realizing the disadvantage that Nicholas had without armor or helm.

Then Chavant leaped, knocking Nicholas to the ground and grabbing up a fallen sword. Emlyn screamed a warning, and spurred her horse closer. No one was near enough to Nicholas to help him. Chavant grabbed a sword up and raised it just as Nicholas rolled to come to his feet.

Without thinking, she had already notched an arrow in the bow. Turning her shoulders, lifting the bow and drawing the string tight along her jawline, all in one movement, she only thought: sweetly, on a breath. Then Chavant raised his sword to strike downward.

She let go of the string. The shaft raced up and then down. Emlyn stared in shocked silence as it hit its mark.

The blade cut clumsily to one side as Chavant fell. Nicholas gained his footing easily and glanced down, then up, looking around perplexed. Guy came up beside him, holding Sylvanus.

"God's bones," someone said behind Emlyn, "I think you killed him, my lady."

Emlyn turned to see William and the escort circled protectively behind her. "He did go down," she said.

"Your arrow struck his neck. A truer shot could not have been made by any man I know." William beamed at her.

She drew a shaky breath and turned her horse to ride away, sickened by what she had done.

Ahead, Whitehawke sat in the saddle, his shoulders hunched oddly. As she came close, a frisson of fear ran up her spine. Why had he done nothing, ordered no men in pursuit or attack?

"My lord?" she asked.

He turned, his pale eyes flat and glazed, then leaned slowly forward over the high front of his saddle.

Nicholas dashed past her on Sylvanus. She was startled by his sudden appearance; in turning away, she had not noticed that the short battle had ended with Chavant's death.

He leaped off his horse. "Help me get him down!" he yelled.

William and another guard dismounted to help Nicholas ease Whitehawke to the ground. Emlyn scrambled down from her horse and dashed through the snow to fall on her knees beside Nicholas.

"Loosen his armor!" she cried, tearing off her gloves to fumble with the leather strips that attached hood to hauberk. Nicholas slid his hands beneath hers to pull the chain mail away from Whitehawke's wide, fleshy throat.

A hideous noise, somewhat like the high whine of an arrow, alternated with a gurgling sound in his chest and throat. He repeatedly seemed to gasp for air and then choke.

"What is it?" Emlyn cried. As she lifted his head, his hair spread over her hands like cold silk. She angled his head against her thighs, sensing that he needed the incline to breathe.

" 'Tis the illness in his lungs," Nicholas answered her.

"Send someone to fetch Maisry," she said.

"No time." Nicholas snatched off his green cloak and threw it over Whitehawke. "We must keep him warm," he said. "The cold air makes this worse. Peter!" he called, as he searched through the folds of Whitehawke's cloak and patted the black surcoat as if looking for something.

"What are you doing?" Emlyn asked. In her lap, Whitehawke gasped loudly, striving for breath.

Nicholas looked up at Peter. "He always carries a remedy with him. A vial, or a packet of herbs. Look in his saddle." Nodding, Peter ran to search the saddle pouches.

"My mother had a treatment for his lung ailment," Nicholas explained to Emlyn. "He has a decoction of it made regularly."

Whitehawke's skin was the color of stone. He formed a word with his lips.

Emlyn leaned forward. "Priest," she repeated.

Nicholas reached into his tunic, drew out the prayerbook that Emlyn had given him, and handed it to Whitehawke.

Grasping it, the earl coughed, and a horrible whine began in the barrel of his chest, traveling upward.

"Oh, God," Emlyn whispered. "Is there no way to help him?"

"Here," Nicholas said, catching a small jar that Peter tossed to him. Prying loose the wax seal, Nicholas held the jar to Whitehawke's lips and tipped a thick liquid into his mouth. The older man swallowed, coughed, and swallowed again.

Tears heated Emlyn's eyes to see such strength and fire brought down to such a state. She wondered if he would die. "My lord," she said. "My lord, there is something you should know."

"What?" Nicholas said. She held up her hand to silence him.

Whitehawke looked at her. "The Lady Blanche did not die of starvation," she said to him. "I found a letter, my lord, in the tower. She was dosing herself for a heart illness. Lady Blanche planned to reconcile with you the next day, my lord. Either she took too much of the herb unwittingly, or her heart stopped."

Emlyn grasped his hand firmly in her own. "She did not mean to die, my lord. Neither did you kill her. Her heart was very weak, and she knew it. She wanted to live as long as she could."

"If 'tis true, sire, then you are free of the sin of her death," Nicholas said quietly.

Whitehawke drew a breath, a sibilant rustling noise, and looked at Nicholas grimly.

Emlyn leaned forward. "My lord," she whispered, "the lady wrote also that you have a son. He is a man of courage and purpose. A good man, my lord."

She raised her eyes to Nicholas. His gaze deepened with comprehension, and his cheeks suffused with a bright stain as he looked down at his father.

Whitehawke coughed again, the wheezing burble softening. Grasping the prayerbook to his chest, he glanced at Nicholas and opened his mouth, then closed it again, stubbornly set.

"I have often acted out of anger, my lord," Nicholas murmured. "Aye, and without honor. I beg your forgiveness."

"My temper," Whitehawke rasped. "You have my temper."

Emlyn brushed the pale hair back from the earl's head with trembling fingers. The loud insistent whine that had sounded in his chest was fading. Whitehawke inhaled shakily.

"The herbs are helping," she said.

"If he has the strength now, we should move him to a warmer place," Nicholas said. "Peter! Arrange for a litter!"

Whitehawke stirred. "Nay. I will not go on my back," he barked hoarsely. "Get me to my horse."

"But my lord—" she protested.

"Aye, my lord," Nicholas said. Helping Whitehawke to sit, he boosted him to his feet. Wavering, the earl pushed Nicholas aside and made his way stiffly to his destrier. Two of his guards assisted him into the saddle.

Once mounted, he glared down at Nicholas and Emlyn, who had moved to stand near his horse. A diluted ferociousness still gleamed in his pale blue eyes.

Silently he offered the prayerbook to Emlyn. She took it, watching him with wide, uncertain eyes. She was certain that the moment of gentling she had seen just now in the earl had been genuine. Whatever else happened once Whitehawke discovered the truth about the deed to the dale, she thought that some measure of peace could be established at last.

"My lady," Whitehawke said, "I have not shown you the courtesy you deserve. Accept my apologies."

"I will," she said. "My lord, you are yet weak, and have need of a healer. And 'tis a long way to Graymere, with no roof for your head there."

"Go on to Hawksmoor," Nicholas said quietly.

Whitehawke looked at him. "You would welcome me there?"

Nicholas passed his gloved hand along the stallion's creamy neck. "I once told you that forgiveness was the part of valor I could not learn," he said. "But my lady wife has tried, I think, to show me that family is one of our most valuable gifts. If we are fortunate enough to have such ties, they should be respected, my lord, not destroyed."

Emlyn looked up at Nicholas in wonder, and placed a hand on his arm. He covered her hand in his, looking at his father.

"Your lady is loyal and strong-willed," Whitehawke said gruffly. "Your mother was that, too, I see it now. Would that Blanche and I had not both been so stubborn. We destroyed each other."

"You are welcome at Hawksmoor, sire," Nicholas said. "We have much to discuss, you and I, when you are recovered."

Whitehawke nodded. "I would see this letter, my lady."

"My lord," she said softly, "you shall see it."

Whitehawke nodded and turned his horse, riding slowly toward Hawksmoor, followed quietly by his garrison.

Nicholas took the book from Emlyn's hand, flipping briefly through the pages. "I remember this little book, I think."

"She meant it for you," she said. Nicholas glanced at her questioningly.

"Lady Blanche left the deed to the dale in there."

He opened the cover quickly, snatching a glove off with his teeth, extracting the folded parchment and scanning it in the winter twilight.

"The dale belongs to the monks, and to you and Lady Julian."

"I see so." He refolded the page and slid it back into place. " 'Tis best if the monks are given the entire parcel. I think Julian will agree."

Emlyn nodded. "She will be pleased. Nicholas, was it truly Aelric we saw today? What will become of the Green Man now?"

"Aye, 'twas Aelric. He saved our lives, I trow, with his magic. And if my mother's deed is legal and true, which it appears, there will be no more need for the Green Man, except on May Day to hand out sweetmeats."

Smiling at that, she turned her head to see Whitehawke riding far across the moor. She felt a twinging stab of sympathy for him, with his notion of honor fast crumbling. "I feared that your father might die without knowing the truth of Blanche, or of you," she said. "Whatever else he has done, he greatly values that state of his soul."

"He is too fierce to die yet, though he has lost much honor of late. This morn he was mightily betrayed by the king he has loyally supported. If death were preferable, he would be gone now." Nicholas ran his fingers through his tangled, wind-whipped hair, suddenly looking very tired. She leaned her forehead gently against his chest, and he stroked her hair.

"Emlyn," he said after a moment. "Was it you shot Chavant?"

She nodded miserably. "Now I am the one who carries a terrible sin. I will never touch a bow again," she said, her face muffled against his chest. "I only wanted to save you."

"Aye so, sweeting," he said. "But look there."

She looked where he pointed, at two Hawksmoor guards kneeling beside Chavant's body in the bracken. "Oh, God," she choked, placing a hand over her eyes.

"Emlyn," Nicholas said insistently. "Look."

She opened her eyes. Chavant sat up, rubbing at his neck. Nicholas chuckled. "Your arrow just grazed him. He has a nasty cut on the side of his neck."

Emlyn stared, and breathed out in relief. "My aim is not so true, after all—thank God."

Nicholas wrapped his arms around her, the green cloak enveloping them both. He rested his cheek against the top of her head. "I would have it no other way," he murmured, "for I, too, bear the scar of one of your wayward shots."

Emlyn made a soft sound, part sob and part laugh, and raised her head, watching as the guards helped Chavant to his feet. "What will happen to Chavant now? You will keep Hawksmoor, certes, but will your father rename you his heir?"

"Chavant might stay with my father, or go to his own holding. Or he could ride with the king; I hear 'tis possible to gain quick wealth in John's service these days." Nicholas shrugged. "I care not who my father names his heir. Hugh is welcome to it. I have you, my lady, and Hawksmoor. I am content."

"Oh, Nicholas," she breathed. A sudden rushing joy welled in the center of her body and set her heart to a quick, thumping beat. She wrapped her arms around his waist beneath the green cloak and hugged him. "I do so truly love you. I have loved you for years, since I first sat in a tree with you. There is no hero in any tale of chivalry who can compare to you."

He laughed softly, hugging her, and was silent for a moment. "My dragon has been my own father. Honor thy father," he mused. "I have not fared well with that, Emlyn. Pray God my father and I will come to understand each other in time. But the chance for honor there is lost, I fear."

"Nay," she said. " 'Tis not lost. Honor dwells in the heart. Yours is filled with courage, aye, and with love, would you but see it. Even for your father, my lord."

"You have taught a rebel a little notion of what makes true honor," he murmured. "You, and your family that has become my own. Do you know that the children are finer than gold to me?"

" 'Twas a fortuitous assignment that the king gave you, those months ago, to seize babes for hostaging."

"Aye so. And you," he tilted her chin with his finger and looked down at her. "You, my lady, are more precious than my own soul." In his eyes, she saw a muted, beautiful gray-green, the blended colors of winter and spring. Then his lids drifted shut and he kissed her, as gently as the snowflakes that fell on their cheeks, his lips warm as sunlight.

"Now, my lady wife, since our king still rides his terrible

path up the length of England, will you go to safety at Evincourt?"

She looked up at him. Not for a long, long while, would she endure another parting from this man. "Oh, aye, my lord," she answered, "but only with you."

Epilogue

"Hurry, Godwin, ye'll never make it at that pace," Tibbie gasped as she rushed ahead of him down the corridor. "My lady will not wait longer. Oh, dear saints, that it should come to this," she muttered, her fingers flying in a rapid cross over her bosom. They hurried to join Nicholas, who stood outside the door to his bedchamber, tapping an impatient foot.

"My lord, my lord," Tibbie said breathlessly. "Yon Brother is arrived, finally."

"In here," Nicholas directed, throwing open the door and stepping inside after them. As Tibbie pulled Godwin toward the bed, he fumbled for the small cross suspended from his belt.

Emlyn reclined against several pillows, her face flushed brightly, her sweat-darkened hair wound in a thick, untidy braid. Breathing in a heavy, pronounced rhythm, she slid her hands in slow, deliberate strokes over the great mound of her belly, which was hidden beneath the rumpled red samite coverlet.

Glancing up, she frowned. "By the rood, not more visitors," she groaned. "Am I some mummer's dancer, to be gawked at?"

"Oh, dear," Tibbie said, wringing her hands, "she is quite irritable. We've not got much time."

"Very little," Maisry said as she came forward from a corner of the room carrying a stack of linen toweling. Setting the cloths down, she knelt beside the bed and began to trace gentle circles on Emlyn's rounded, turgid belly. "Easy, my lady," she murmured, "easy."

"Easy this is not," Emlyn gasped. Her cheeks turned a ferocious red, nearly as deep as the coverlet, as she huffed out several breaths of air.

Nicholas knelt beside Maisry and slipped his fingers into Emlyn's. She grasped at his hand, squeezing so hard that his knuckles cracked audibly. "Not much longer, my love," he said quietly, his palm damp next to hers.

"Sod you," Emlyn muttered, opening one eye.

He shot a nervous glance at Maisry, who smiled brightly at him. He knew a wealth of reasons for her smile. Maisry had been delighted, months ago, to learn about Thorne's identity and about his marriage to Emlyn. As for the rest of that smile, Nicholas thought, birthings please women mightily. His own nerves felt taut as catgut.

When summoned at the start of Emlyn's labor before dawn, Maisry had arrived as promptly as possible. Depositing her two sons to play with Christien and Harry, she had hurried to Emlyn's side. Tibbie and Maisry had fallen in with each other like long-lost sisters.

As Nicholas watched knowing glances pass between Tibbie and Maisry now, he suddenly wanted, quite desperately, to flee this roomful of chattering females. He thought enviously of Peter and Guy and Wat, who waited, anxious but comfortable, nursing goblets of ale in the great hall.

Emlyn blew out a long breath. "I am sorry to be rude, Uncle," she said, and then looked at Nicholas in alarm. "Why has Godwin come? Is aught wrong? The babe—"

"The babe is fine and strong," Maisry said. "As are ye."

"Yer husband wants to wed ye again before 'tis born, is all," Tibbie said. "Ye both promised the Lady Julian, and since the excommunication has been lifted, she sent for Godwin, hoping to see ye wed before the babe came. I pray 'tis not too late."

"Wellaway, hurry, if you must," Emlyn moaned.

Cheeks flushed anxiously, Godwin stepped forward and quickly made the sign of the cross over Emlyn and then Nicholas. Drawing a deep, loud breath, Emlyn groaned, a long, guttural sound that sent shivers up Nicholas's spine. When she grabbed his hand, he was amazed by the steely strength in her small fingers.

"Get on with it, Brother," Tibbie hissed. She bustled over

to the side of the bed and slipped her hand under the covers, groping past Emlyn's uplifted knees.

"Tibbie," Emlyn managed to gasp out indignantly, "I am being married!" Glancing up, Nicholas noticed the intense, sudden beauty that bloomed in Emlyn's eyes, blue as a lake lapped with golden light. She crushed his fingers tightly and uttered another breathless moan.

Tibbie, still groping, pursed her lips and nodded sagely. Then she withdrew her hand and wiped her fingers on a cloth.

"Tip of the head," she murmured to Maisry, who nodded and slipped her arms under Emlyn's upper back.

"Push," Maisry said to Emlyn.

"Beloved children," Godwin began.

"Aye, and bless us all," Tibbie added, turning Godwin away from the bed. "She'll have no breath to spare for yer wedding for yet a while, Brother," she said as she drew him to the door. "Tell the Lady Julian that ye made yer attempt. I trow God will smile kind enough on their forest vows for now."

Shutting the door firmly in Godwin's face, Tibbie turned to Nicholas. "Now, my lord," she said, "ye'd better go. Yer looking a mite green. It do lend an odd color to yer eyes."

An hour later, Nicholas sat beside the bed, holding a small, squirming bundle uncertainly in his arms. Once again he looked at the tiny, perfect face of his daughter, and once again raised his eyes to Emlyn's.

She smiled, her face rosy and sheened with sweat, damp golden tendrils trailing along the sides of her face and neck. "Aye," she said softly, "you are a father."

"She is a beauty," he said, his voice reflecting only a part of the deep, complete wonderment he felt. Gently pushing back the silken wrapping, he gazed again at the wisps of pale, fluffed hair that fringed the diminutive head like an angel's halo.

" 'Tis nearly white, her hair," Emlyn said.

"Aye so," Nicholas agreed, covering the little head again. The babe squirmed and curled in his arms, and her slight, warm weight measured the deepest joy he had ever known. "And that should be her name, I think."

"Of course," Emlyn murmured, placing her hand on Nicholas's arm. "Blanche. 'Tis perfect for her." She rubbed his arm thoughtfully. "Whitehawke—"

"Will be pleased enough, I think," he said. "He has softened like butter these months, my lady, under your attentions. I trow, he seems almost human at times." He paused, frowning. "Emlyn, Godwin brought important news."

"Tell me," she urged.

"King John is gone." He glanced at her. "He died of stomach pains, no more than a day or two past, near Lincoln. After losing, they say, most of his royal treasure in the Wellstream estuary, the Wash, near Swineshead Abbey."

"Jesu," she whispered. "Mercy on his soul. Henry is king, then? He is hardly older than Christien."

"Nine years old, I think. He will be crowned in a few days. Whitehawke has declared his support of the boy, as will most of the barons. William Marshal will be asked to regent until the boy is old enough to rule."

Emlyn looked up at Nicholas. Her eyes, bright with tears, glowed with the inner joy of the tiny blessing that lay mewling in Nicholas's arms, and with something more, a glistening hope.

"England, at last, has its chance to begin anew," she said.

"Aye so, my love," he murmured, reaching over to cover her hand with his. The babe kicked against his chest through the soft wrapping, and he smiled. Bending forward slightly, he kissed Emlyn's brow, then drifted his lips toward her mouth.

"As do we all begin anew," he whispered.